LOVE AND THE INCREDIBLY OLD MAN

Love and the Incredibly Old Man

A NOVEL

LEE SIEGEL

THE UNIVERSITY OF CHICAGO PRESS

Chicago and London

LEE SIEGEL is the author of five previous books published by the University of Chicago Press, including *Love in a Dead Language* (1999), and *Who Wrote the Book of Love?* (2005). He is currently professor of religion at the University of Hawaii at Manoa.

The University of Chicago Press, Chicago 60637
The University of Chicago Press, Ltd., London
© 2008 by The University of Chicago
All rights reserved. Published 2008
Printed in the United States of America

17 16 15 14 13 12 11 10 09 08   1 2 3 4 5

ISBN-13: 978-0-226-75705-6 (cloth)
ISBN-10: 0-226-75705-6 (cloth)

Library of Congress Cataloging-in-Publication Data
Siegel, Lee, 1945–
Love and the incredibly old man : a novel / Lee Siegel.
p. cm.
ISBN-13: 978-0-226-75705-6 (cloth : alk. paper)
ISBN-10: 0-226-75705-6 (cloth : alk. paper)
1. Ponce de León, Juan, 1460?–1521—Fiction. I. Title.
PS3569.I377L67 2008
813'.54—dc22
2007043188

Ponce de León wanted his autobiography dedicated to Isabel:

¡Cuán dulces son tus caricias, oh hermana y novia mía!
Un jardín cerrado es mi hermana y novia, un manantial sellado,
una fuente de vida deliciosa.

With those very sentiments, my story is for Elizabeth.

Whenever the name of the first European to set foot on what is now the continental United States of America is mentioned, it is usually as a synonym for man's vanity and folly. Juan Ponce de León is most often remembered as a harebrained old buffoon who was gulled by fanciful myths and legends into a hopeless quest for a so-called Fountain of Youth. Although the actual deeds and accomplishments of the Spanish explorer are shrouded in the mists of history, we will try in this book, so much as it is possible, to separate fiction from truth.

LEO GAVIOTA, *The True Story of Juan Ponce de León and the Fountain of Youth*

Contents

Preface

2005

AN INTRODUCTION TO JUAN PONCE DE LEÓN

The Fountain of Life in the Garden of Eden truly existed as a real material fountain, and from that Fountain a real river flowed out of Paradise. We should be persuaded to believe that all that is narrated in this book actually happened. But the facts do also have significant figurative meanings.

SAINT AUGUSTINE, *De genisi ad litteram*
(On the Literal Interpretation of Genesis)

21 June 2005

Dear Mr. Siegel,

I introduce myself here with no expectation that you will believe me, but with some hope that you might be inclined to trust in my sincerity. Incredible as it may seem, I am, in fact, none other than Juan Ponce de León, the Spanish explorer who, at the age of forty-eight, on an Easter Sunday in 1513, discovered the land I christened Pascua de Florida. While duly acknowledging that achievement, historical accounts have ridiculed me for a credulity which, they imagine, encouraged a vain quest for the legendary Fountain of Youth. The fact is, however, that I did, much to my own astonishment, actually unearth a very real artesian wellspring, the miraculous waters of which did indeed, until very recently, have the power to render living beings essentially immune to illness and resistant to the process of aging.

Subsequent to a series of dramatic events that led people to believe that Juan Ponce de León died in Cuba in 1521 and now rests in peace in Puerto Rico, I have, for almost five hundred years, continued to live incognito, perennially healthy and rather consistently happy, at the site of the Fountain of Life in a fertile garden in Eagle Springs, Florida, a place known as Haveelaq to the Zhotee-eloq tribe of Carib Indians who first greeted me here. It is the Gan Eden of the Hebrews and the hortus deliciarum *of the Christian cartographers who had located Paradise rightly in the Indies, but wrongly in the Eastern ones.*

I am, at this time, rather woefully aware that, alas, after all these years, the end is at hand. The Fountain of Life has run dry. One by one, the eagles in the Garden have disappeared, and the once lush vegetation has begun to wither away. I understand and accept that this is in accordance with an intractable law that all things, inanimate and animate alike, the hardest stones as well as the most delicate blossoms, indeed the entire cosmos no less than you and I, Mr. Siegel, must ultimately deteriorate, disintegrate, and evaporate into oblivion.

Sanguine and enthusiastic as I have always tried to be, however, I do hope to last at least long enough to celebrate my five-hundred-and-fortieth birthday on the twenty-second of July of this year. While I have never allowed myself the fantasy that the Fountain would permit me to live forever, I am, I must concede, somewhat disappointed about having to pass away so soon. Five hundred and forty years may sound like a long time to you, but it is not anywhere even near forever. Isn't it irksome that the most obvious platitude, the tritest and most trivial truth that "we all have to go someday," turns out to be the most absolute and profound knowledge, and that all other truths are secondary to, and contingent upon, it?

At this point I find myself hoping to discover some solace and consolation in telling my story and, by so doing, reminding myself that I have, after all, and for the most part, had a very good time for a very long time that only just now seems not nearly long enough. From time to time over the last half millennium, I occasionally imagined that someday I'd be ready and even content to die. Once in a while I'd suppose that death might, at some point, become a tenable alternative to life. But, in fact, the longer I have lived, the more I have longed to live longer and longer.

It both touches and amuses me to know that there are people who declare, and perhaps even imagine it to be true, that it would somehow be a burden to live forever and that death is some sort of deliverance. They make believe that mortality provides an opportunity for redemption and even access to some sort of eternity. I suspect that such farfetched fancies help some people accept an essentially unacceptable reality. All of us, although few will own up to it, even to ourselves, want to be deceived in matters of death no less than in matters of love. But deep down don't we all know that to die, whether from mishap, violence, disease, or old age, is a pity? And love, contrary to what so many have rhapsodized, only makes death all the more lamentable. I can assure you from my own experience that to stay young and live long is good, very good, and the younger and longer the better. That is, I suppose, why death is so annoying.

Again, I do not imagine that you will be inclined to believe me. But that, at least for the time being, doesn't really matter. Now that I am aware that I am soon to die, I feel compelled to tell my story and record it for others, not merely for the very few who might be sufficiently gullible to believe it, but also for the more skeptical readers who, mistaking it for fiction, might be engaged and entertained by my life. It is, I realize, ironically more for the latter group than for the former that I am going to tell the truth, since anyone who would actually believe it, true as it truly is, would have to be insane. And, in my experience, there is little gratification in telling things to the insane — they only ever hear themselves. There is even less satisfaction in listening to the things that lunatics have to say — they only ever talk to themselves. I would rather that people presume that I am telling a tale than that I am crazy.

There have, of course, been at least moderately sane people who have, understandably but not rationally, believed far more unbelievable books than the one I aim to compose, preposterous tomes like the Torah, Gospels, and Koran, not to mention all the cockamamie scriptures of the Orient. Is it not substantially more mad to imagine that there could be some sort of life after death, as those religious texts propose, than it is to believe, as my autobiography shall testify, that life might be extended for a very, very long time before death?

Because few can be expected to believe that my book is nonfiction, it must, I realize all too well, seem to be a novel in order to be published and read. And so it will, of course, have to be artfully written. Thus I am contacting you, Mr. Siegel, for I am, alas, not much of a writer myself. After the completion of my last logbook in 1513, I did not write anything beyond the occasionally necessary love letter or business contract until the eighteenth century, when I composed several plays, including two about and starring myself, for the stage. These were, however, written in Spanish, largely plagiarized, and not, I must admit, of a very high literary quality. Although I have been speaking English for some two hundred years, ever since the period when British rule here made a familiarity with that language an asset, it is not my mother tongue. I do not, in all modesty, suppose that I can do justice to myself in your language.

Not only am I not much of a writer, I have never been much of reader either. Curiosity, however, has compelled me to study all that has been written about Juan Ponce de León as recommended to me by Miss Lilian Bell of the Eagle Springs branch of the Santa Almeja County Public Library. It was Miss Bell who gave me your name, Mr. Siegel. Over the years, she has dedicated herself to acquiring for her library's folklore of Florida collection, among other things, all volumes written about Juan Ponce de León, fiction and nonfiction, juvenile and adult, alike.

Miss Bell informed me that you had written two books in which I am mentioned. Both were purchased by the library, and one of them has been checked out on more than one occasion. Your literary success, Mr. Siegel, seems to have been significant enough to allow me to surmise that you are in a position to get another book published, and yet not so substantial in terms of either fame or fortune that you, upon reading this letter, will not be tempted by the proposal that you collaborate with me on my memoirs. I shall make it well worth your while. In addition to a ten-thousand-dollar cash retainer for coming to Florida to work with me (plus reasonable expenses, of course), I am prepared to pay you one dollar per word for the finished manuscript. And, in order to motivate you to find a publisher for the work, you shall receive twenty percent of the royalties. That I am enclosing half of your retainer herewith should convince you of my sincerity. Consider this letter contractual.

Although I do not, as I have reiterated, believe that you will believe the stories I'm going to tell you, I do hope that you might allow yourself to believe that I believe them, or, at the very least, to write them down as though you do. It will be your job, as my ghostwriter, to edit my reminiscences into a text that is sufficiently entertaining to be published, sold, and read. It will be your responsibility, as a professional author, to make the hero of the book, Juan Ponce de León (b. 1465, Lebrija, Andalucia—d. 2005, Eagle Springs, Florida), convincingly real and as likable as I have always tried to be. I especially want our female readers to find me attractive. You will, of course, also be in charge of grammar, spelling, and punctuation, as well as of the preparation and submission of the final typescript for posthumous publication.

Having read the passages in your books alluding to me, I have faith in you, Mr. Siegel. Although I was a bit disappointed that you didn't have more to say about me, it was encouraging to discover someone who imagined (albeit without the conviction of imagining that imagination might have been a medium for a revelation of a truth) that Juan Ponce de León might have actually discovered the Fountain of Youth and that he might still be alive. Little did you know that what you had invented was, in fact, a reality.

Since I do not have much time left, I am eager for you to get here as soon as possible. To this end I enclose herein a ticket for a flight leaving Honolulu for Jacksonville on the fourth of July. I hope that this gives you enough time for whatever you might need to do before we begin our work. It will not be difficult for you to get from Jacksonville to Eagle Springs by rental car. Signs along the highway will lead you to the Zodiac Motel where it will be convenient for you to reside while you collaborate with me. From there it will be easy to get directions and find your way here, to the Garden of Eden. I plan to see you on the morning of the sixth of July.

Yours very truly,

Juan Ponce de León

This is, I swear, and have ample documentation to substantiate it, absolutely true. I really did receive the above outlandish letter in June 2005. It was handwritten in a barely legible small scrawl and ornately signed. The signature (fig. 1) is, I was soon to discover, almost identical to that of a Juan Ponce de León on a 1513 petition to the Spanish Crown for a title to conquer, colonize, and Christianize lands sighted off the west coast of Florida (fig. 2, as preserved in the Archivo General de Indias in Seville, Spain, and as reproduced in Leo Gaviota's *The True Story of Juan Ponce de León and the Fountain of Youth*).

Fig. 1

Fig. 2

The letter had been folded around five of what appeared to be genuine one thousand-dollar bills, each engraved with the face of Grover Cleveland. Also enclosed was an Avis rental car voucher and a ticket for a confirmed business-class seat on an American Airlines flight from Honolulu to Jacksonville, via Denver, on July 4 (with a return on July 22). Affixed to the envelope, which had been addressed to my university office, were three twenty-two-cent commemorative stamps, each bearing the portrait of Juan Ponce de León.

It was hard to believe.

While there was, according to the long-distance information operator, no listing in Eagle Springs for either a Ponce de León (whether under *P, D,* or *L*) or a Garden of Eden (under either *G* or *E*), there was a number for the Zodiac Motel. And the man who answered the phone there assured me both that I did have a prepaid reservation for a room at the Zodiac and that the Garden of Eden really did exist: "But it closed down to the public a couple of months ago."

I wouldn't have taken the letter seriously, and I certainly wouldn't have gone to Florida, if not for the cash. Yes, I confess, I did it mostly for the money. Not only was another five grand supposedly waiting for me there, there was also that promised dollar per word for the finished manuscript. I was confident that if, in fact, the character who wrote the letter really did want me to help him write the story of Ponce de León, I could come up with at least a hundred thousand words, about two hundred and fifty pages. This freelance summer job would bring in a lot more money than I earn in a year as a professor or that I have ever been paid for anything I've written.

Assuming as I did that the proposed book, given the absurdity of its premise, would never get published, I was hardly tempted to fantasize about royalties. But maybe, I reflected, heading east at thirty-five thousand feet above the Pacific Ocean, I could write a true story, a journalistic profile of "The Man Who Thought He Was Ponce de León." The *New Yorker* might give me a few thousand for it, I imagined, at least if it were amusing enough in a *New Yorker* sort of way. While being rollickingly hilarious, I promised myself, it would also have something or other serious to say about the ways in which human beings struggle to come to terms with old age and the inevitability of death. Comic but poignant, silly but wise. If not the *New*

Yorker, Esquire or *Vanity Fair* might bite. And if not them, I told myself as my plane began its descent into the Jacksonville International Airport, maybe I could convince an editor at *Modern Maturity* to shell out a couple hundred bucks for it.

But it wasn't only the money that tempted me. The figure of Ponce de León had long been of some interest to me literarily. It was true, as noted in his letter, that I had written two books in which I referred to Ponce de León (*Love and Other Games of Chance: A Novelty* [New York: Viking Press (2003), 379–386], and *Who Wrote the Book of Love?* [Chicago: University of Chicago Press (2005), 57–71]). And, ironically, one of the very first things I ever wrote was about him. That was over fifty years ago when, in the fourth grade, I was constrained to learn about "Great Explorers of the New World." Assigned to do a notebook on the Spanish conquistador who discovered Florida, I plagiarized my biography from the *World Book Encyclopedia*. It amused me to think that I'd be rewriting that school project after all these years.

Something else in the letter startled me—the man's mention of his birthday on July 22. While I am aware that the mathematical probability is greater than 50 percent that in a group of only twenty-three people at least two will have the same birthday, I was, nevertheless, so intrigued by the happenstance that my own birthday falls on that very same day that, despite a more rational impulse to dismiss the coincidence as mere coincidence, I could not help but sense a kind of significance in it. It was almost as if it established, whether I liked it or not, some sort of magical connection between the writer of the letter and me.

The timing of the invitation was also convenient. It was summer vacation and I wasn't making any progress on a novel I had been doggedly trying to write for several years. Not only that, the woman with whom I had lived for seven years had left me a month earlier. I was at a loss and lonely, and, in my case, loneliness always fosters restlessness.

And so, believe it or not, I went to Eagle Springs, Florida, checked into the Zodiac Motel, and then, after a long deep sleep, on the morning of July 6, I asked Mr. Wiseman, the motel's owner and manager, for directions to Ponce de León's Garden of Eden. I was given more information than I asked for: "Ponce de León! *Oi!* The guy is *meshugeh* if there ever was *meshugeh*. You think you know what *meshugeh* is? I'll tell you what *meshugeh* is—it's some shmuck who for more years than anyone can remember gets dressed up like a Spanish explorer and tells people that the Garden of Eden isn't somewhere over in Israel like it's supposed to be, but that it's right here in Florida. Not only that, he pretends that he's got the Fountain of Youth there and that, thanks to it, he's over five hundred years old. That's *meshugeh*. The Fountain of Youth! *Oi! Oi!* I'll tell you what the Fountain of Youth is—it's a *kaneh*."

"What," I had to ask, "is a *kaneh*?"

"Siegel! Are you a Jew or what?"

I confessed that, yes, I was Jewish.

"You call yourself a Jew and you don't know from *kaneh*? A *kaseer*, a *gluystiyah*, a *cristiyah*—we've got more words for it in Yiddish than the Eskimos have for snow. It's an enema, Siegel—yeah, a warm enema every night before you go to bed. I'm telling you, that's how to stay young. That's the only real fountain of youth. At least that's what the Talmud says."

In order to escape a very loquacious and overly familiar Mr. Wiseman, I insisted that I was late for my appointment with Ponce de León.

All along the roads that took me from the Zodiac Motel to the Garden of Eden that sultry Florida summer morning, there were, among expanses of cypress and cabbage palm, bright clusters of white and pink oleander, orange and purple bougainvillea, and the crimson blaze of flame tree blossoms. I saw a sign: "Ponce de Leon's Fountain of Youth, Garden of Eden, and Museum of Florida History. 3 Miles Ahead. Children and Senior Citizens free."

The man who claimed to have unearthed the legendary Fountain of Youth was waiting for me in the empty parking lot in front of the main gate to his Garden of Eden ludicrously dressed for the occasion in a conquistador costume: over a pale blue doublet, there was a high-collared padded plum houppelande, its funneled sleeves ballooned at the shoulders and scalloped at the cuffs; through the slashes in the dark blue puffed breeches, a satin lining that matched the color of his doublet had been decoratively pulled. The soft black leather of his gloves matched that of his silver-buckled knee boots. The crowning touch was a conquistador helmet dramatically festooned with crimson plumage. The uniform blackness of his beard suggested that it had been dyed. Only the dark Ray-Ban sunglasses and cigar were anachronistic. The costume made it difficult to guess his age. The sunglasses kept a distance between us. Given the heat and humidity of the Florida summer, the costume must have been uncomfortable.

"I was expecting someone much younger." Grandly saluting me with an antique Iberian short sword, he spoke in a noticeably rasping voice.

"And I was expecting someone far older," I joked, playing along with the performance. "It's a pleasure, no less than it is an honor, to make the acquaintance of the illustrious Juan Ponce de León."

Returning his sword to its filigreed scabbard with a theatrical flourish, he coughed. "Come along, Mr. Siegel. You must be eager to see the Fountain." Mr. De Leon seemed anxious and in an unnecessary hurry. His nervousness, indeed his strangeness, made me uncomfortable. I was not looking forward to this. But I didn't feel I had any choice but to follow him as he led the way through the gate into a garden that seemed strangely bleak in contrast to the landscape leading up to the estate. There were, so far as I could see, no flowers in the Garden of Eden. There were dead leaves along the path on which we walked, and those that remained on the trees, bushes, and shrubs looked parched. The seemingly unnatural wilting of the vegetation suggested some sort of botanical blight.

Stopping abruptly, and turning to face me, Mr. De Leon asked if I was satisfied with what he was paying me: "Tell me the truth. Let us be honest with one another. If you need more money to do a good job, you must say so. Money doesn't matter so much to me now, not so long as I am assured that, when I am dead, Isabel will have enough to live in comfort and at least modest luxury for the rest of her life. What's important to me now, as I explained in my letter, is that you write my story, and that you do it well enough for people to want to read it and, in doing so, find some pleasure in it. You must do your very best, Mr. Siegel, better than you did on those other books you wrote. You've got to write this as though you really care, as if you believe it, or at least as though you almost believe it. Can you do that?"

I said I would try. What else could I say?

The tour of the grounds continued: "I do hope you realize, Mr. Siegel, that you are in the actual Garden of Eden. Yes, it's true—the Paradise of Genesis. Although, as you shall learn, there are many mistakes, if not outright lies, in the first book of Moses, there is some truth in it as well. The biblical story of the Garden of Eden had, until I came here, always seemed to me a poetic allegory written in the past tense to describe a future paradise into which credulous Jews and Christians fantasized they might be admitted after death or after the coming, first or second, of a messiah. No reasonable person, I reasoned, would ever believe in the actual existence of waters that could prevent disease or arrest aging. Just as you naturally don't believe in the Fountain now, neither did I for the first forty-eight years of my life. Actually, to be perfectly honest with you, I have from time to time over the years been a little uneasy about my belief in such a nonsensical notion. But, alas, Mr. Siegel, I have no choice but to believe in it, since I have, after all, been alive for five hundred and forty years. What could be more convincing than that?"

We came to a clearing in the withering shrubbery where there was a circular, white granite basin about fifteen feet in diameter and about five feet deep. "That's it!" he exclaimed, "the Fountain of Life." I would have imagined that Mr. De Leon would have constructed something much more ornate and spectacular as the featured item in his theme park.

"You'll need to describe it in such a way that my readers can, in envisioning it, feel the mystery of it, the miraculousness. Bring the Fountain to life, Mr. Siegel."

I didn't know what, if I stuck to the truth, I would be able to write about it, except to note that it was rather dirty, and that, in the center of its empty tank there was a cracked column supporting four spigots, "one," I was informed, "for each of the four rivers that flowed out of Eden." And atop the column there was a tarnished bronze statue of a Spanish conquistador.

"Over the centuries," my new employer commented, "I have used a variety of statuary to disguise the Fountain which, when I first discovered it, was but a bubbling artesian spring and pond with no adornment. This particular statue of me has ornamented the Fountain since 1915 when I first opened the Garden of Eden and Museum of Florida History to the public."

Mr. De Leon invited me to interrupt him if I had any questions. "You are, Mr. Siegel, perhaps wondering, 'Where is the Tree of Knowledge with its forbidden fruit?' That was perhaps the most frequently asked question by visitors to the Garden over the years. I'd explain to them that, contrary to Moses's version of the story of creation, it was forbidden to eat any of the fruit of any tree in the Garden just as it was forbidden to pick any of the flowers. Since none of the plants in the Garden, being nourished by the waters of the Fountain of Life, were subject to aging or pestilence, none had the need nor, therefore, the capacity, to reproduce. All of the fruit in the Garden was seedless, all of the flowers without pollen. Once picked, the fruit and flowers would not be replenished. They would be gone forever. That was the terrible knowledge—the knowledge of gone-forever-ness—that the first inhabitants of the Garden were to gain when they ate the fruit from the trees of Paradise. Do you understand, Mr. Siegel?"

"Yes," I said out of politeness.

"Do you have any questions?"

"No," I dissembled.

He coughed to clear his throat and continued: "In any case, you'll learn everything you need to know about the Garden of Eden and the Fountain of Life in the coming days. This is just an introduction. Come along. Let's go to the house."

The impressively grand whitewashed Spanish colonial plateresque building that turned out to be Mr. De Leon's Museum of Florida History had been built, I was informed, of tabby, limestone, and coquina as a mission in the sixteenth century.

We entered a cobbled courtyard and I was directed to seat myself in one of two cane chairs beside a weather-warped wooden table in the shade of an arched loggia. Dark, dry vines barely adhered to its stone pillars. Walking away from me to the open doorway into the house, Mr. De Leon called out, "Isabel, mi redactor esta aqui."

A stunningly pretty young woman appeared with a silver tray. She could not have been much older than twenty. Her immaculate white cotton dress was sleeveless, but her arms were covered by a grass-green shawl upon which bright blue and violet embroidered flowers were in full bloom. There were no cosmetics to enhance the resonant darkness of her alert eyes or the alluring ruddiness of her full lips. A lock of her black hair that had missed being tied into the bun at the nape of her neck played casually across her pale forehead, and a curl lay poised by each delicate ear, the lobes of which were adorned with glistening red gems. Setting the tray on the table, then standing behind my host, she remained silent and was not introduced. I noticed that her feet were bare.

On the tray there were two tumblers and a crystal pitcher of a dark refreshment in which floated ice cubes and slices of lime. "Rum," Mr. De Leon exclaimed with a cough, "I invented it." As if that had been a stage cue, the girl filled his glass and then mine. Also on the tray there was an antique cedar cigar humidor, a box of wooden matches, a ceramic bowl of popcorn, and a white envelope.

"Isabel," he said, "¿Me puedes traer mi morfina por favor?"

After a moment of silence, during which he intently watched the girl walk back to the house, he handed me the envelope. It contained five one-thousand-dollar bills, the balance of my advance. It was hard to believe.

Opening the humidor, he casually claimed to have invented cigars: "Yes, I was the first person to distill rum and the first to roll tobacco in a tobacco leaf. You smoke, I hope, Mr. Siegel. Have one. I buy this brand not so much because they are particularly good, but because they're named after me— Las Bacueñas' Ponce de León Puerto Rican Maduros. I like that. It assures me that there is some justice in the world. There are, as I am sure you know, those who insist that smoking is bad for you. But I've been smoking for almost five hundred years and, until very recently, I've been in perfect health. Smoking, I learned long ago from the natives of the Indies, is a salubrious act and a holy one as well." Mr. De Leon was, I was somewhat startled to notice, inhaling the cigar smoke.

The girl returned with a small silver pillbox. After my host had washed down a tablet with an exuberant gulp of punch, she refilled his glass and returned to the house. He took another sip, pushed the bowl of popcorn toward me, coughed, and resumed: "Let's get down to business, Mr. Siegel. We have a lot to do, and not much time. I will expect you here each morning, about an hour or so after sunrise. And we'll work until sundown. You will listen, Mr. Siegel, to what I tell you each day, taking notes if you must, and then, each evening, I want you to write up a draft of whatever story I have told you that day. The next morning, I'll go over what you have written, making comments to help you rewrite, correct, edit, polish, and whatever else it is that you writers do to come up with a finished book. I am, as I explained in my letter to you, no writer. Otherwise I would not have had to hire you. It's my responsibility to give you a true account of my life, and it is your job to transform that into something literary, to fashion fine characters out of the people I tell you about, to give my life style, structure, and a plot, to spice it up with felicitous and evocative similes, metaphors, and other figures of speech. Your task is to write, mine is to remember. To remember . . ."

With another gulp of rum punch he swallowed another pill, puffed on his cigar, coughed, and told me to help myself to the popcorn. And then, suddenly standing, he grandly announced the theme of the book: "Love. Yes, love. Love and time, love and age, love and death. Love true and false, glorious and foolish, tragic and comic. Yes, I'd like my autobiography to be a love story. It is not that I am so arrogant as to presume to be privy to any particular wisdom about that fantastic sentiment or its terrific powers any more now than I did when I fell in love for the first time some five hundred and twenty-five years ago in Andalucia. No, after all these years I still do not have any control over love or what it does to me, transporting me to the most joyous heights, plunging me into the most dismal depths, and dropping me willy-nilly and dumbfounded at all places in between. But how does one write about it? Being, or having been, in love seems to be an impediment to writing about it, since the true lover always feels that his feelings cannot be put into words. That, once again, is why I have hired you, so that you can do justice in the book to love and to the women with whom I have been in love, that you will make adorable heroines of them, and that with poetic diction you will make vivid the joy of the transport of *cardar*ring them."

He stopped, sighed, and nodded. "*Cardar*—that's the verb I'd use if I were composing my story in my mother tongue, the Andalucian Ladino dialect of my childhood. I would write *cardar*—a loving, passionate and tender verb—literally: to card, curry, comb, and brush, to groom, clean, set aright, adorn, and restore, to coddle, soothe, please, serve, adore, to explore, enrapture, and beautify, not to mention to make love to and fuck—yes, all those things all at once. You must try to find some English equivalent, Mr. Siegel. If you do, I'll pay you double for the word—two dollars each time you write it. And, I can assure you, it will be used often in my book."

Mr. De Leon's long-windedness and overblown grandiloquence might have irritated me if not for the five thousand dollars in the envelope in my hand. As I watched him down another glass of rum punch, I could not but be impressed by how well he held his liquor, not to mention his morphine. No sooner was the pitcher empty than, as though by some clairvoyance, the barefoot girl silently returned with a fresh one, only to immediately leave us alone again.

Topping up our glasses, he enthusiastically started up again, quite apparently enjoying the part he was playing. "I began my life as an actor," he began. "'Love,' according to lines I first recited in a command performance of *El Amor y el viejo* for Their Majesties Fernando and Ysabel five hundred and thirty-three years ago, and yet remember as if it were yesterday, 'keeps the young man young, and makes the old man lose his age.' The old Castilian is sweet on the tongue: 'El amor mançebo mantiene mucho en mançebez, e al viejo faz perder mucho la vejez.'" He coughed, inhaled cigar smoke, and coughed again. "If that were true, that love keeps us young—and, believe you me, it is not—I wouldn't have needed the waters from the Fountain of Life to be alive today. I have been in love so many times during the past five hundred and forty years that I can hardly remember all the women who have meant the world to me. Have you ever attempted to do it, Mr. Siegel, to remember all the girls and women you've *cardar*red, each one of them, all of the nakedness you've gazed upon, all of the flesh you've touched and kissed and tasted, the hair you've smelled, the sighs and laughter you've heard?"

He didn't pause to hear my answer. "I've been trying to do just that in preparation for our work together, Mr. Siegel. Of course the first one, no less than the last, is easy. I close my eyes and see her, the girl at Casa Susona, number one. Then there's Celestina, my young bride, number two, Queen Ysabel, *tres,* Filomena, *quatro,* then the Taino girl, *cinco,* and then, right after her, there is, I am certain, someone missing. It vexes me that I can't, for the life of me, remember her name, face, or figure, the color of her skin, eyes, or hair, not her nationality, not what language she spoke, nothing about her except that she was there. Number six is, I'm very sad to say, lost forever. Continuing to count across the centuries, among the scores of well-recollected women, wholly resurrected in memory, I see just parts of others, floating like jetsam from the wreckage of love on an unfathomable sea of time. Some are vaguely recalled only by a face, a neck, by arms or legs, hips or thighs, by an ear, or even just a fingertip. I remember a mole next to the nipple on a girl's right breast. There was a matching one on her cheek. I remember women's lips parting into smiles, others forming the blossom of a kiss, another mouth spraying water, and another breathing out smoke. I remember a certain woman's eyes, sparkling aquamarine, and can still hear her whispering my name. I see the pearl buttons of a crimson tunic, a tiara of green parrot feathers, a woman's drinking gourd and smoking pipe, a wine glass broken and the white linen around it reddened with the blood of the virgin grape. I remember cornucopia-shaped earrings of black glass, candlelight flickering on a thigh, and I hear cries of 'por Dios, por Dios' over the echoes of a Ladino song: 'Del amor yo non savía.' I see a tortoise-shell comb with a single strand of golden hair tangled in its teeth, the large coral beads of a rosary, a crucifix and dagger, and the illegible handwriting of a love letter." He stopped, sighed, shook his head, relit his cigar, and then continued more slowly: "I'll tell you all that I can remember about these women, Mr. Siegel. There is among them one with whom, I am certain, I was madly in love and quite intimate for some time, but about whom I remember nothing except her gravestone in St. Augustine's Huguenot cemetery. Above the roses that I place there from time to time in my attempt at amorous recollection, I see words engraved in marble: 'In Loving Memory. Rest in Peace. Anna Maria Ulm. 1785–1806.' I know nothing about Anna Maria except her name, that she died when she was only twenty-one, and that I loved her."

He paused to pour another drink, cough, and push the bowl of popcorn closer to me. And then he promised that he would do his very best to remember everything he could about his life as accurately as possible so that I could write a true story. "The truth is what we're after. And we have no choice but to rely on memory for that truth. But, alas, in that dependence we must keep in mind that Mnemosyne, the goddess of memory, bondmaiden of Venus Aphrodite and mother of the Muses, was known by the ancients to be a liar."

Again he paused. "And without the sustenance of the waters of the Fountain, memory fails me more and more each day. We don't have much time. Are you ready to begin your work, Mr. Siegel?"

Although uneasy about what I was getting myself into, I slipped the envelope into the breast pocket of my jacket, and claimed that, "yes," I was.

"I must tell you, Mr. Siegel, that I'm worried about something," Mr. De

Leon divulged. "I am concerned that there might be, especially among the female readers of the chronicle of my love affairs, some who will consider me a cruel lover and not forgive me for breaking so many hearts over the years. I will rely on your literary acumen and rhetorical skills to convince them that, because of the Fountain, I had no choice but to end each liaison, and that I, no less than any of the women, suffered great sorrow each time I had to part with one of them. Let's make it a point to note that I always ended my affairs as lovingly as possible. It's your job, Mr. Siegel, to make the hero of my autobiography a wonderful lover, the kind of man that any woman would love to *cardar* and be *cardar*red by. Do you think you can do that?"

Again I said I'd do my best.

"Good," he exclaimed with a smile of satisfaction. "Then we'll get started on chapter one tomorrow morning. It's the story of my childhood, boyhood, and youth in Spain." Abruptly he stood, closed his eyes, and whispered, "Tomorrow."

As I got into my car, he drew his sword from its scabbard to salute me good-bye. And, as I drove off, he, sword aloft, cried out, "¡Vale!"

After lunch in Eagle Springs at the Johnson Family Diner across the street from the town's branch of the Santa Almeja County Public Library, with nothing better to do, I decided to introduce myself to the woman who had given my name to the man who had hired me as his ghostwriter. I asked her about him.

"Oh, I've known him for years," a gleefully grinning little Miss Bell, obviously elderly but quite spry, told me. "He's done so much to keep our history alive with that museum of his." A permed blond wig, cat-eye glasses, and a bright patch of rouge on each cheek made the old librarian appear clownish, but in a sweet sort of way. She spoke of Mr. De Leon with a girlish affection apparent in her voice and smile. "I'm a history buff, you see— Florida history. And, as everyone knows, it all began with Ponce de León. I remember reading about him in grade school, when I was just a little girl in St. Augustine. He looked so dashing in the pictures in our history book, so swashbuckling in that plumed helmet of his, and he had those dreamy eyes and seemed so gentlemanly. And now that I'm older—you probably won't believe it (nobody does) but I'll be turning eighty this month—he's still one of my favorite characters in history. I've read practically everything that's been written about him. And no one, I'm sorry to say, has, in my opinion, really done justice to him yet. You know, it was I who suggested that he hire you to help him write the book."

I thanked her and said that I was flattered.

"Well," she continued with a persistent smile, "to be perfectly honest with you, I had advised him to contact Philip Roth, John Updike, Salmon Rushdie, and Dan Brown. It was so discouraging that not one of them answered his letters. That's when I came up with your name. I'm so pleased that someone is going to help him."

Miss Bell insisted on issuing me a temporary library card so that I could borrow books about the famed conquistador. She recommended Leo Gaviota's *The True Story of Juan Ponce de León and the Fountain of Youth* and Douglas Peck's *Ponce de León and the Discovery of Florida: the Man, the Myth and the Truth*. I also checked out Raoul Pipote's *The Rape of Virgin America* and the *University of Chicago Spanish-English Dictionary*.

1465–1493

WHEREIN PONCE DE LEÓN, AFTER HIS
CHILDHOOD, BOYHOOD, AND YOUTH IN SPAIN,
IS DISPATCHED BY QUEEN YSABEL TO THE
INDIES IN SEARCH OF A FOUNTAIN OF YOUTH

OLD MAN. How swiftly pleasures vanish, and, as we recall them, how sad we become, feeling that times past were so much sweeter than the present.

LOVE, *grinning*. But I've come here to offer you fresh pleasures, new delights to help an old man forget the past and feel young again.

OLD MAN, *shaking his fist*. Do not mock me, rascal! Go away! I am too old and infirm for pleasure. I am too old!

LOVE, *laughing*. Have you never heard, Old Man, the pretty fable of the Fountain of Youth?

OLD MAN. Oh, I've heard a lot of nonsense in my time.

LOVE, *feigning seriousness*. But there can be, and often is, some truth in nonsense.

LEANDRO DE COTA, *Dialogo entre el Amor y el viejo*
(Dialogue between Love and the Old Man)

The gate to the Garden of Eden had been left open. On making my way back to the courtyard where I had been the day before, I was greeted by the young woman Mr. De Leon had addressed as "Isabel." Escorting me to what she called the "Spanish Room" of Ponce de Leon's Museum of Florida History, she asked that I wait there for my host.

I looked at the extraordinary collection of antiquities in the room's several large display cases: gold coins, silver medallions, and copper badges, a curious brass astrolabe with both Latin and Arabic inscriptions, a compass with a diagrammatic sun and moon and decorative stars and planets etched on its tarnished face, some brightly glazed earthenware crockery, crusted glass bottles, green-patinated pewter flasks, a time-tarnished silver flagon, a shiny gold signet ring engraved with Hebrew letters, and numerous manuscripts, incunabula, maps, charts, and diagrams. There was also the small painted portrait of a woman wearing a crown. These sundry objets d'art and documents did seem impressively and authentically ancient.

Hearing Mr. De Leon's cough even before he entered the room, I turned to greet him. His soft brimmed hat was less fancifully plumed than the conquistador's morion had been, and it revealed more of his obviously too-black dyed hair. His plum houppelande had been replaced by a lighter, heliotrope jacket. That he still, even indoors, wore the large Ray-Ban sunglasses, made it impossible to see his eyes. As he was no longer wearing gloves, I could see liver spots on his hands. I reckoned he was about my age—about sixty, maybe a bit older.

Without so much as a "good morning" or "how are you?" he directed me to be seated at a wooden table upon which there were, as on the day before, two glasses, a pitcher, humidor, clay ashtray, a box of wooden matches, and a ceramic bowl of popcorn.

"Are you ready?" Mr. De Leon asked as, standing over me, he handed me sheets of paper on which he had written a chronology of Ponce de León's life in Spain. "You can use this tonight," he continued before I could answer his question, "when you write today's story. It should help you keep the facts straight. Go on, Mr. Siegel, read it. Read it now, before I begin. I'll be back in a few minutes." He left the room and I did as I had been told:

1465   I am born on the 22nd of July in the town of Lebrija. At the ritual circumcision, on the eighth day after my birth, my father, an itinerant actor and lion tamer, names me Samson ben Aryeh.

1469   My father's troupe is commissioned to perform at the celebration of the marriage of Ysabel, the queen of Castile, to Fernando, the king of Aragon, and, for the first of many times in my life, I am transported by what the poets call *amor a primera vista.*

1472   We stage another spectacle for Ysabel, this time to celebrate both the baptism of one of her children and a victory in battle against the Moors. I fall even more deeply in love at second sight.

1473   My half brother, Setho ben Aryeh, comes to live, travel, and work with us.

1478   I become a Son of the Commandment under the tutelage of Rabbi Solomon ben Maimon de Luna, and Pope Sixtus IV agrees to issue a papal bull establishing an inquisition that gives Ysabel the autonomy to extirpate heresy in Spain.

1479   When my father decides that conversion is advantageous, I am baptized Johannes Pontius by a bishop of the Roman Catholic Church.

1480   With the death of my father, Setho and I take over the management of our troupe. I marry Celestina Guarra, an actress in our little company, and we perform during festivities arranged to welcome the queen to Sevilla.

1482   The Moors lose Alhama to Ysabel's army under the command of Fernando and, after a celebratory dramatic performance, I consummate my love for the queen.

1485   Cristobal Colon comes to Spain, and Celestina's father, Jaime Guarra, after appearing before a tribunal of the Inquisition, is burned at the stake for heresy in Sevilla's Plaza de la Virgen de las Aguas Santas.

1491   Fernando captures Granada for Ysabel, and the queen, by honoring our acting company with the Charter of Melpomene and Thalia, makes us official entertainers to the court.

1492   Ysabel issues the Edict of Expulsion, dictating that, under punishment of death, all Muhammadans, Jews, and other infidels either convert to the Roman Catholic faith or emigrate from Spain. My mother leaves for the Orient, heading east with the Jewish physician Johanan Yarhoni, and, on the same day, Rabbi Solomon ben Maimon de Luna leaves for the Orient, heading west with Cristobal Colon.

1493   Knighting me Don Juan Ponce de León, Ysabel dispatches me to the Indies in search of the legendary Fountain of Youth.

I wondered where (and why) he had come up with this. I had discovered in my reading the night before this meeting that there is little reliably documented information to serve a true historical chronology of the explorer's life in Spain:

Nothing whatsoever is known about Ponce de León prior to 1506 when he petitioned King Ferdinand for permission to conquer the Indians of Borinquen (Puerto Rico), to make Christians of them for God and slaves of them for the Crown. The supposed "fact" that Ponce de León sailed to

America with Columbus in 1493 has been established solely on the basis of the fanciful histories of the Spanish colonial period in the New World by Bartolomé de Las Casas (*Historia general de las Indias*) and Gonzalo Fernandez de Oviedo y Valdes (*Historia general y natural de las Indias*). The truth is that the conquistador's name does not appear on the membership rolls, nor in any of the official logs, for Columbus's second voyage to the Indies. Almost everything we have been asked to believe about Ponce de León is fiction. (Raoul Pipote, *The Rape of Virgin America* [Chicago: The University of Chicago Press, 1965], 22).

The authors of the two biographical texts that Miss Bell had recommended had, however, been willing to take the liberty of inferring an early life of the discoverer of Florida. Neither account bore any resemblance to the life of Ponce de León as delineated in Mr. De Leon's chronology:

Juan Ponce de León was born in 1474 in San Tervas del Campo, Valladolid. . . . It was from his noble Visigothic León family heritage that Juan Ponce de León obtained his character and physique, being red-haired, robust, virile, brave, and aggressive in battle. . . . Ponce de León was trained in hunting and warfare at an early age and actively fought against the Moors when he was only fourteen years old. (Douglas Peck, *Ponce de León and the Discovery of Florida: The Man, the Myth, and the Truth* [St. Paul, MN: Pozo Press, 1993], 2–3)

Ponce was born in León in 1469. He came from a long line of Spanish nobility, but his family had fallen on hard times. When both his parents died, little Ponce was adopted by a Spanish knight and had to work for him as a lowly page, setting the table for his master, tidying up the house, and even cleaning the stables. But young Ponce had dreams of making something of himself someday. As a teenager he studied hard and excelled in both geography and history. He was a good athlete and applied that talent to developing his skills as a soldier. His accomplishments in battles against the Moors earned him the special favor of Queen Isabella. (Leo Gaviota, *The True Story of Juan Ponce de León and the Fountain of Youth*, Hispanics of Achievement Series 13 [Jacksonville, FL: American Scholastic Press, 2000], 12–14)

In none of these biographies is there any suggestion that Ponce de León might have been either a Jew or an actor; none gives 1465 as the date of his birth or mentions Lebrija as his birthplace. Peck maintains that Juan Ponce de León had never searched for a fountain of youth, but had, rather, been after gold. Pipote reports that "after his death, rumors were widely circulated that the explorer had endeavored to find a fountain of life in hopes that its waters might provide him with a cure for sexual impotence."

"Are you done?" Mr. De Leon asked as he returned to the room.

"Yes," I answered, and he asked if I had any questions.

"No," I responded and, slowly pacing in a circle around me, he said, "Good. Or is that good? I'm not sure. We'll see. Note that I was born in Lebrija, the ancient Roman city of Nebrissa. That's significant because the town had always been notorious for the amorousness of its natives. Perhaps it was the wild mushrooms that grew in the woods around it, the pomegranates that flourished there, or maybe it was the waters of its mountain springs. The inhabitants of Nebrissa, according to Roman accounts, celebrated the orgies of Bacchus. Scantily draped in animals skins, they sang and danced drunkenly in wild worship of Priapus, who they called Hortanes. And it remained an orgiastic town in my day, with Priapus canonized as San Hortano, the patron saint of *juglars*."

Mr. De Leon took a cigar from the humidor, bit off the end, and lit it. He poured himself a glass of rum punch, indicating with a hand gesture that I might do the same. "I'll tell you about the people in the chronology," he continued. "And, I'm sure I told you yesterday, I expect you to make appealing characters of them, Mr. Siegel, and to introduce them into a plot that you construct by ordering and organizing the incidents in my life in such a way as to arouse the interest and empathy of my readers. They should begin to care about me as the protagonist and narrator of the story right from the start. It is very important to me that, for the most part, most of the characters in my book are in some way likable, not necessarily good, but at least sympathetic. Thus we'll say as little as possible about such unredeemably unappealing scoundrels as Torquemada the Inquisitor or Cristobal Colon, who was, as we used to say in the Ladino of my childhood, a *gilipollasqueroxo*."

"What," I had to ask, struggling to pronounce it, "is a *gilipollasqueroxo*?"

"Or *gilipoxo* for short," Mr. De Leon, after hesitating long enough to cough, clear his throat, inhale cigar smoke, and take a hardy gulp of punch, answered with a glower. "The slang is not easy to translate. Think of the worst thing you can say about a man in English, write it down, and you can use it every time true history constrains me to refer to Colon."

"Something like motherfucker, or cocksucker perhaps?" I asked to assure him that I would not be puritanical in writing his memoirs.

"No, no," he scoffed dismissively, "something much, much more derogatory than either of those hackneyed invectives."

Mr. De Leon seemed genuinely jealous of Christopher Columbus. "Why," he asked with blatant disgust and emphatic dismay, "is there a Columbus Day celebrated in America but not a Ponce de León Day? It was I, Don Juan Ponce de León, who discovered the land mass that is the continental United States of America. But I am, alas, remembered instead as a dreamy buffoon who searched in vain for a nonexistent fountain of youth, while that idiotic Genoese *gilipoxo* is lionized as the discoverer of America even though he didn't even know where he was. He thought that the Dominican Republic was Japan, Cuba was China, and that India lay just ahead, about where Texas is in fact. Everyone, then and since antiquity, knew that the earth was round, everyone except Colon, who actually imagined it was pear-shaped. So too everyone in their right mind realized that the Orient was far too far away to be reached by sailing west. The happenstance discovery of an unknown land occurred not as the result of any remarkable knowledge or courage on Colon's part, but rather on account of his utter foolishness and obstinacy. To hell with that sniveling *gilipollasqueroxo*. Look at how much time we've lost talking about him already! Please, Mr. Siegel, don't interrupt me again. Questions will only sidetrack me. There will be neither time nor need for questions. I'll tell you everything you need to know. Let's start with my family.

"We were, as you can see from the chronology, actors. My father was the manager of a troupe that included my mother and me, and later my poor brother Setho, a drunkard named Jaime Guarra, his wife, Xonita, their daughter, Celestina, and always a couple of other men, players who rarely lasted very long because they were never real thespians, but rather just out-of-work Jews that my father would recruit somewhere — usually in a synagogue, drinking saloon, or brothel. They'd only stick with us until something better came along. Celestina and I traveled in the pageant cart with our mothers while the men rode mules. We'd set up our stage in town squares. My father had constructed machinery that enabled me to fly as a cherub amidst clouds of cotton wool.

"I think of those days, and they seem like only yesterday. One minute you're a child, and then, all of a sudden, you're five hundred and forty years old! The older you are, the more quickly the years, decades, and generations pass. Call me greedy, but I cannot help but wish that I had just a few more centuries left. The older I get the more I feel that I'm just beginning to live.

"My father always seemed old to me. He was already fifty when I was born, while my mother was not yet twenty. He had been married before — I don't know how many times — and had enjoyed plenty of mistresses. Actors were expected to be philanderers.

"I remember my father on the stage. The memory remains, after all these years, so vivid. 'I'm the strongest man in the world,' he'd announce with comedic bravado. 'I'm Samson!' The outrageously bulky padding in the sleeves and legs of his costume that was supposedly to make him look strong, wasn't really meant to make him look strong at all. No, it was supposed to make him look ridiculous. So too was the overstuffed codpiece that was rigged so that its contents rose and wiggled as he recounted tales of his amorous escapades with Philistine women—the maiden of Timnah, the harlot of Gaza, and the ravishing Delilah. 'Never tell a secret to a woman,' was the moral of his monologue. Love had made a weakling of the strongest man in the world, the mighty judge of Israel who had slain a thousand Philistines with the jawbone of an ass: 'Beware of love,' Samson warned his audience. 'Love is more dangerous than a lion!'

"That was the cue in our *Farsa de Samson y el león* for my mother to release the young lion of Timnah, played by an old lion that my father had won from a drunken Morisco in Barcelona with a trick deck of cards in a game of andaboba. The cards are there, Mr. Siegel, in that case. You can have a look at them later.

"As I was saying," Mr. De Leon continued intently, "the lion would bound out from behind the curtain to dramatically growl, snarl, and shake his mane. And he put on such a convincingly ferocious act that, the moment he appeared on stage, the audience couldn't help but gasp in terror. Even though his teeth had been filed down, and his claws—not to mention his testicles—had been removed, it was frightening when the huge cat, circling Samson, took a swipe at the strong man with his prodigious paw. But Samson laughed defiantly at the beast."

After wrestling the lion to the ground, and pretending to kill him, Samson, so Mr. De Leon explained, posed with one foot on the carcass to deliver an account of his exploits. "It made people laugh to hear the man who had brought down the temple of Dagon talking in the Sayagues dialect like a country bumpkin. And the lion, who was so adept at making audiences shudder with fear, could also make them laugh. They roared with laughter whenever the ferocious beast of Timnah farted. And this he did a lot. His chronic flatulence was a result, no doubt, of his diet. In the wild, he certainly would not have been accustomed to eating things from our table like olives, eggplant, carrots, potato fritters, omelets, stewed hens, and anchovies. But that's what we'd give him to hold him over until the Sabbath when my father would splurge on an entire mutton for him. As soon as he saw my mother kindling the tapers, the lion knew that he was about to enjoy a real meal. Thus the cat learned to love the Sabbath, so much so that my father considered him not only a member of our family but a Jew as well. To solemnize that status, Rabbi Solomon ben Maimon de Luna was solicited to perform the rites of conversion. The learned rabbi explained that 'according to the sages of the Talmud, castration may count for circumcision in the case of a wild animal converting to Judaism.'

"During the ritual immersion of the lion in a *mikva*, Rabbi Solomon bestowed a Jewish name on him with a recitation from the Torah: 'Judah is a lion's whelp.' And then the rabbi instructed Judah the lion in the *mitzvoth* that he thought particularly relevant: 'No longer may you feed on the camel, rock badger, hare, or pig. And if a man or woman lies with you, both of you shall be stoned to death.'

"When my father later decided that we should convert to the faith of the Catholic Church, he asked the bishop of Sevilla to baptize the lion as well. But, because the dogmatic cleric refused to do so, Judah remained Jewish until the end.

"But back to my father. I want my readers to know that he died on stage. It happened right after Samson had slain the lion. Clutching his chest, Samson fell down next to Judah, who was playing dead, and the crowd laughed over what had seemed to be a pratfall. Surprised by the sudden twist in the plot, I laughed too. I waited for my father to rise and recite his monologue about massacring the Philistines. But he just lay there. Dead silent and still. Confused no doubt by the change in the show, the supposedly dead lion lifted his head and looked around, rose, nudged my father with his nose, sniffed his hair, licked his face, and then, getting no response from Samson, he ambled off behind the curtain. That made the audience laugh all the more.

"A few weeks later, Judah died of grief over the loss of his master. Rabbi Solomon performed the funeral rites for the lion, washing his body and wrapping it in a fringed white prayer shawl. Beside the grave in Sevilla's Jewish cemetery, the rabbi recited the *Hashkaba* to proclaim the mercy of the Lord who had given the lion his strength. When the Edict of Expulsion was issued, a mob of Christian acolytes dug up the bones in that burial ground and cast them into the Guadalquivir River. 'It's a bad sign,' my mother whispered, 'as Marranos, we're in great danger.'"

Try as I have, I can't really remember everything my employer said about the fifteenth-century Spanish actress. He went on and on about her. I do, however, recall that he kept reiterating how beautiful she was and that he asked me how many English synonyms for "beautiful" I could come up with. "There are so many beautiful women in my story, at least five of them in this chapter alone—my mother, Queen Ysabel, Celestina, the flower girl of Lebrija, and even, as far as I remember, the playful *putita* at Casa Susona. I'm counting on you, Mr. Siegel, to make all of them, all of the women whom I have loved, beautiful. Yes, make each and every one of them a carnal vessel for beauty itself, a breathtaking, eternal beauty. In each of them, something eternal was transiently manifested and, through love, revealed to me. Such beauty makes the heart tremble with fear and delight, and it forces us to love. I never chose which woman to love. Love has always been a matter of being captivated by that beauty. I had first seen it in my mother and in my queen. And still I see it. It will not leave me alone. Do you know the feeling?"

Although I didn't really understand what he was saying, I assured him that I did. And that, I suppose, reassured him that he had found a writer potentially capable of articulating his particular ideas and sentiments. I, on the other hand, was unsure. My heart wasn't in the job. I had to continually remind myself about the money.

"I first began to appreciate the subtleties and complexities of this beauty," he continued, "as I watched my mother, sitting before the mirror in our pageant cart, transform herself into Eve, Lilith, Delilah, the Virgin, Death, and others. And each and every one of those women, even Death, was beautiful. My mother was the same age as Queen Ysabel, but she could make herself look half her age or twice as old.

"Sometimes she'd tease me, calling me her *berbante*—her little scoundrel. She'd pretend to be angry with me until I'd just begin to cry. And then suddenly she'd laugh, hug me, and playfully cover my face with kisses.

"She was a wonderful actress as I remember. But her greater talent was sewing costumes, making masks, applying cosmetics and face paint, fashioning lamb's wool wigs and beards, and perfecting all manners of disguises and illusions. She made me look very convincingly aged when, as a young man, I began playing the Old Man in *El Amor y el viejo*.

"Although the Edict of Expulsion did not apply to her as a *conversa*, my mother left Spain in fear of its repercussions. She went with a man who had become her lover after the death of my father, an unconverted Jewish physician named Johanan Yarhoni, the author of both the *Mareoth ha-Shetan*, a diagnostic treatise on the colors of urine, and the *Sefer ha-Shemen*, a kabbalistic tractate on the pharmaceutical properties of semen. The last time I heard from her was in a letter that had taken seven months to arrive in Andalucia from India. In it, she beseeched me to leave Spain, insisting that, being a *converso*, I was in grave jeopardy so long as Ysabel had the power of inquisition."

Mr. De Leon paused to pour another glass of punch for himself and to offer one, together with a cigar, to me as well. He asked me to try to clearly establish the character of his half brother in the first chapter of his book because he would become very important later on in the story. "He was my father's son by a farm girl in León. His biblical name, Seth—meaning 'the Substitute'—turns out, as you'll write in the next chapter, to have been prophetic.

"The ranchers who breed bulls attest that these animals get their physical characteristics from their sires and their dispositions from the cows that bear them. The same, according to my father, is true of lions. And it was no less so of my brother and me. We were close in age, and both of us, folks would often remark, looked like younger versions of our father. But, while I had my mother's sanguine and cheerful nature, my brother was brooding. He was as dark-souled as I was lighthearted. My father had taken him in when his mother died of melancholia. Physicians concurred that her despondency, sleeplessness, and aversion to food and light had been caused by an excess of black bile. But Setho attributed the grief to her having been abandoned by so many lovers, our father among them."

Mr. De Leon stopped, sighed, coughed, and then asked if I had ever been married. I told him I had, "twice."

"I've been married five times," he noted rather matter-of-factly with another cough or two, "not so many times really—an average of only one wife per century. The first was Celestina Guarra. We were married in the Church of San Hortano. She was thirteen years old, just two years younger than I. I had known her as long as I could remember. Celestina was, and still is, the youngest girl I've ever *cardar*red, while the oldest is Izhqee-qiqee, the cacica of the Zhotee-eloq, who was at least a thousand years old at the time." That was uttered casually and with a straight face.

"The fact that Celestina was such a talented actress makes me wonder in retrospect if she was merely pretending to be proud when I, her husband, became one of Queen Ysabel's sundry clandestine paramours. She seemed to take a curious pleasure in listening to accounts of my erotic dalliances with *la Católica*, relishing my descriptions of what positions had been assumed, what words whispered, and what vicissitudes of passion had been explored. It was only after her father had been executed for boasting of having been likewise honored by the queen, that Celestina urged me to stop accepting the royal invitations. 'It's not that I am jealous,' she swore with convincing tears in her eyes, 'but I am afraid for your life.' Unbelievable as it is to me now, I actually believed that she was immune to jealousy. And so I did not hesitate to tell her about Filomena. In a sudden fit of furious pique,

Celestina called me a *gilipollasqueroxo*, shouted threats, and pummeled me with her fists. 'That you have made love to the queen is an honor for us," she shouted, "but that you've fucked a cheap flower vendor is a humiliation. Why, when you can *cardar* me any time you want, would you play *fronto* with that *mitja-nena*?' While *mitja-nena* literally means 'half girl,' it's not so easy to translate—it's more demeaning than bitch, slut, whore, trollop, strumpet, hussy, even cunt, or any other of the English words that come to mind. It's rather like the female equivalent of a *gilipollasqueroxo*. And *fronto*—well, it is, as I am sure you can imagine, quite obscene. See what words you can come up with, Mr. Siegel.

"Why did I imagine I could tell Celestina the truth? I might have learned a lesson about being honest with women from a line I had recited as a young boy playing the part of Amor in *El Amor y el viejo: 'La verda a las de vezes muchos en daño echa*. Truth can cause much harm—especially in love.' Although it took a while for me to learn to lie, I did, out of necessity, eventually master the fine art of prevarication. But don't let that revelation cause you, Mr. Siegel, to ever suspect that I'm not being honest with you. Now that death is imminent, truth has taken on new meaning.

"The last time I saw Celestina, on the eve of my departure from Spain, I swore that I would love her, and only her, forever. Just as she took pleasure in believing that, so it pleased me to make her happy. Are you hungry Mr. Siegel? Let's go to the patio. It's time for lunch."

The main course was albóndigas Fernando, meatballs simmered in an almond sauce, a dish that Mr. De Leon alleged had been one of his favorites in Andalucia in the fifteenth century. "Judah the lion was crazy about these meatballs. He could have eaten a thousand of them. I hope that you don't mind pork. It became my family's habit, once we had converted, to eat ham, bacon, and pork as often as possible as proof that we were not reverting to Jewish customs. A converso neighbor of ours in Triana was burned at the stake when his butcher reported to the prior of the Dominican Convent of San Pablo that the man's wife had not purchased any pork for three months."

The meatballs were served with *boniatos de las Indias*—sweet potatoes. "Although I never did provide Queen Ysabel with water from the Fountain of Life," my host explained, "I did at least send sweet potatoes to her. Like syphilis and tobacco, the sweet potato caught on quickly in Spain. Popcorn, on the other hand, took centuries to become popular."

Isabel had served the meal without joining us. After my first glass of punch, I offered to tell Mr. De Leon something about myself, about my background and ideas about writing. "No, Mr. Siegel, there's neither need for that, nor time," he responded. And he meant it. Never during the time I spent with him did my employer show any interest in the facts of my life.

"No, I want to tell you about a play that I performed with Celestina especially for the queen. It was about the Fountain. Leandro de Cota's *Cancion de canciones: Eloga de Shulamita y Solomon*. I played King Solomon. 'The teachings of the wise are the waters of the Fountain of Life,' I recited from the Scriptures, 'that a man may avoid the snares of age and death.' Not a bad opening line. Enter my brother Setho, captain of my Phoenician naval fleet. He announces that he has brought cargo to Jerusalem from the Orient: gold, bedolach and shoham stones, pepper, ginger, and asafetida, apes, peacocks, and an elephant. And then he presents me with a cask containing a magical water from the mountains of India, reputed there to rejuvenate those who drink it. In the next scene, Celestina, the Rose of Sharon, proclaims that I must choose between the water of India and the wine of her kiss. 'If you drink the waters of everlasting youth,' she proclaims, 'you will tire of me and favor younger women.' Choosing her love over my youth, I pour out the water and sing to her, 'Thou art an enclosed garden, my beloved, a fountain concealed, *fuente de huertos, pozo de aquas vivas.*' And then, after she intones the responsa, 'Let my lover come into the garden,' we turn to the audience to sing the refrain together: '*Bebed, amados, y embriagaos.*'"

No sooner had I finished my meatballs, than Mr. De Leon, who had hardly eaten a bite, insisted that we return to the Spanish Room: "I'm getting tired, and I still have to tell you about the two most important characters in the first chapter of my autobiography, Rabbi Solomon ben Maimon de Luna and Ysabel *la Católica*. If not for them, I would have been dead for the past five centuries and no one would ever have heard of Juan Ponce de León, and you, Mr. Siegel, would not be here in Eagle Springs. The rabbi's astrological prognostication, made when I became a Son of the Commandment under his tutelage, had been that I would live for a very, very long time. Little did I know.

"Try, in describing the rabbi, Mr. Siegel, to convey how very old he was. Write of his white beard, yellowed at the edges, his wrinkled, liver-spotted skin, and note that he stooped and shuffled as he walked, and that his lips quivered and his hands trembled as he spoke."

Once again installed in the room where we had spent the morning, Mr. De Leon explained that the bar mitzvah ritual in medieval Spain was quite different from what it is now. "Once you had a little bit of facial hair, your Hebrew teacher gave you a prayer shawl and took you to the synagogue on the morning of the Sabbath to read aloud a passage from the Scroll of

Moses. And then, on that evening, after the havdalah candle had been extinguished and sweet spices had been smelled, it was the custom for the boy to go to a brothel. Rabbi Solomon escorted me to Casa Susona.

"Like Jacob, the old Jew had twelve sons. Two had died, three had converted, and the others had gone to India to establish themselves in the prospering Jewish mercantile communities there. The rabbi's wife had died long before I knew him and so, except for his students, he was alone. Can you picture him, Mr. Siegel? His hoary head, his wizened form? Try to evoke the mystique of old age and loneliness. At the same time, make him slightly comical. Funny old men appeal to readers."

Mr. De Leon recounted that the rabbi had shown up at his house on the very day of the royal proclamation that the Jews of Spain would have to convert to the Roman Catholic faith, leave the kingdom forever, or be burned at the stake. "I hadn't seen him for fourteen years, not since the pope had issued the bull giving Ysabel the power of inquisition. As Marranos we had to be very careful not to let anyone suppose that we might be clandestinely practicing our old customs. Fraternization with Jews was cause for suspicions that inevitably led to investigations by the tribunals. No one was ever declared innocent in those trials.

"'Samson ben Aryeh,' the old man called out, '*Shalom, shalom*, my son. It's Rabbi Solomon.'

"'Call me Juan Ponce,' I had insisted less in anger than in fear. 'No. No, don't call me anything at all. Go away from here, old man, and don't ever return.' But the rabbi persisted in knocking on the door, piteously pleading in Ladino that I open it, pounding and pounding until I finally complied, not, I confess, so much out of cordiality as out of anxiety that the longer he remained on my doorstep making a fuss, the greater the chance that neighbors would take notice of the old Jew and report me to the bailiffs of the Inquisition for investigation. I let him in to persuade him to go away."

Adopting the stooped posture of a very old man with trembling hands, head nodding, the character who claimed to have been an actor in medieval Spain played the part of the aged rabbi, reciting his lines in a quavering voice: "Listen, my son, please. You must help me. No matter how much baptismal water the Gentiles have poured upon you, you are still a child of Israel. And so you must rise up before this gray head, as the Lord has commanded, and honor the face of an old man by listening."

Stepping out of character, Mr. De Leon commented on the script: "What he asked of me was so outlandish I could hardly believe it. But I swear it's true, and I have documentation to prove it. He wanted me to use what he had heard to be my influence as an official court entertainer to arrange passage for him on one of the ships that, under the queen's sponsorship, were going to set sail for India by a westward route on the same day that all Jews had to leave Spain. 'Why on earth would I do such a thing?' I had protested, 'And even if I were foolhardy enough to do so, why would her Highness even consider such a preposterous proposal?'"

Mr. De Leon answered himself in the old man's voice: "You will do so because you know that I have always loved you. And I am confident that the queen will comply, given that she stands to gain something she values more than the gold, jewels, spices, and textiles of the Orient. If she sends me to the Indies, I am prepared to offer her immunity from disease and old age, to provide her with the youth upon which her beauty and power depend. I am certain, and swear it before our Lord, that I have ascertained the exact location of the Fountain of Life, the waters of which bestow perpetual youth. Tell the queen that, if I am sent to the East, I shall act as Her Majesty's agent, shipping barrels of the rejuvenating waters back to her on a regular basis. The contents of those casks, and the location of the Fountain itself, must, of course, remain secret. Her Royal Catholic Highness will surely appreciate the necessity of confidentiality in this matter. Secrecy will serve her purposes, giving her exclusive access to the waters, no less than it will insure my safety."

Once again Mr. De Leon broke character, becoming himself to cough, offer me popcorn, take a gulp from his glass and inhale the smoke of a Ponce de León Maduro. "I thought the old Jew was either insane or lying, fabricating this nonsense about locating a Fountain of Life as a ploy, given the Edict of Jewish Expulsion, to secure safe and free passage to India where he could join his sons and find sanctuary from the Spanish persecutions of the children of Israel. No, I didn't believe him and certainly wouldn't have appealed to Ysabel on his behalf, but, in addition to promising to send me bottles of the miraculous water, he offered me ten thousand maravedis. Actors can always use some extra cash."

Mr. De Leon tried to convince me that Rabbi Solomon had tried to convince him that he was neither a madman nor a liar by showing him documentation of his discovery. "It's all here, in these manuscripts, maps, and charts. They've been on display in this room since I opened the museum to the public in 1915. Look at this one, the *Sefer Mekor-Hayim, The Book of the Fountain of Life*. According to Rabbi Solomon, it was composed as a commentary on Genesis in the third century by Shimon ben Yohai, a *tzaddik* living in seclusion in a cave in Palestine. It is an abstruse text and I would not have been able to understand it if Rabbi Solomon had not elucidated it for me. The story begins with a mist rising up from the earth in Eden and condensing into a pool that becomes a spring that nourishes Paradise and flows out of it to form the river that is called Pishon in the book of Genesis: 'It is the one that winds through the land of Havilah, where there is gold and the gold of that land is excellent.' That river was located, according to Rabbi Solomon, by Flavius Josephus the Jew in his *Antiquities:* 'Pishon, the first river, is by the Greeks called Ganges. And Havilah, the land of gold, is India.'"

Suddenly modulating his voice back into that of the rabbi, Mr. De Leon again trembled as he spoke: "By drinking the waters of the Pishon, Adam and Eve lived for a thousand years after leaving the Garden of Eden. On account of those waters, the *Sefer Mekor-Hayim* reveals, those who abided closest to the Garden retained their youth the longest. As it branched out into other rivers, the Pishon became more and more diluted of its holiness and power. And so Seth, the son of Adam and Eve, settling a little farther away from Eden than his parents, lived not quite so long as they. And his son, Enosh, settling still further to the east, survived not so long as he. And so on and so on. As the descendants of Man and Woman, through the generations of Kenan, Jared, Enoch, Methuselah, Lamech, and Noah, migrated farther and farther from Paradise, their life spans became shorter and shorter. And, after ten generations, we were cut off from Eden by the Deluge which formed the Erythraean Sea." Mr. De Leon shifted back into his own voice to explain that Rabbi Solomon had identified that sea as the "'the Ocean Mar,' what today we call the Atlantic."

He then showed me another manuscript, its Hebrew letters faded on a fragile vellum that had been made, according to Mr. De Leon, from the skins of aborted sheep. "It is the *Testament of Enoch*. So that you can get every word of it, Mr. Siegel, and remain faithful to the revelation, I shall dictate the text slowly, translating it for you. Listen: 'As if in a dream, I, Enoch, a friend of God, sailed westward beyond the Erythraean Sea to Havilah, the land of gold, lush and fragrant with pepper, cinnamon, ginger, and sandalwood. Into the ear of Zotiel, the cherub guarding the Garden of Life, I whispered passwords that God had taught me when I walked with Him, and thus I was allowed to enter and was escorted to a spring from which the cherub invited me to quench my thirst: "This is the Fountain of Life," the angel announced. "He who drinks from it shall not age so long as he drinks. It is here, in this place where heaven touches the earth, that the eagle drinks." There was I joined by Elijah the Prophet, who, riding upon the whirlwinds in his fiery chariot across the sea to Havilah, had been guided to the Fountain by God so that he might sustain his youth with its waters until the time came for him to announce the reign of Messiach.'

"Speaking of which," Mr. De Leon said, "Shouldn't we have more to drink? All this talking has made my throat dry. As a matter of fact, that's exactly what Rabbi Solomon said, right after reading this very book to me, over five hundred years ago in Triana: 'Shouldn't we have a drink? All this talking has made my throat dry.'"

Isabel had brought another pitcher of iced rum punch and a fresh bowl of popcorn. After filling our glasses and drinking his down, Mr. De Leon carefully opened the *Sefer Mekor-Hayim* to show me an illustration of a fountain. In the center of a circular basin there was a pillar that, with its four faucets, looked rather like the one I had seen on the previous day in Mr. De Leon's deteriorating garden. The ancient text, he explained, delineated an elaborate system of magical correspondences: the four spigots represented the four rivers flowing out of Eden, as well as space (the four directions) and time (the four seasons and four watches of the day), the four material properties (hot, cold, wet, dry), the four humors, the four primary elements of alchemy, and "the four mercurial waters — Aqua Benedicta, Aqua Regia, Aqua Celestis, and Aqua Fortis, which are secretly known as Virgin's Milk, Queen's Sweat, Clown's Tears, and Child's Semen. They are none other than the four emanations revealed in Kabbalah. It should be obvious from this why one who drinks the four waters together, before they are separated from one another, would be subject to neither age nor disease."

It was not so obvious to me, but I was getting paid enough to listen and to try, at least, to understand what the man in medieval Spanish dress claimed a rabbi had explained to him five hundred and thirteen years earlier. The gist of it was that these correspondences suggested three ways of possessing the Water of Life, the drinking of which bestowed immunity to aging and sickness: alchemical — to manufacture it in the laboratory; spiritual — to realize it by prayer and meditation in the synagogue; and geographical — to literally locate an actual fountain of life in the real Garden of Eden.

After pouring another glass of punch, drinking it down, lighting a new cigar, and fetching several more manuscripts from the display cases, Mr. De Leon explained each of these three modes of obtaining the Water of Life.

"'In this book, the *Liver de Arte Distillandi* of the alchemist Hieronimus Brunschwygk,' Rabbi Solomon told me, 'we read that, just as each of the four rivers that flow out of Eden contains a portion of the essence of the Water of Life, so each of the four elements contains a measure of the Quinta Essentia, the ethereal substance which is called Elixir, Panacea, or Sam-hayim. It is the liquid form of the Lapis Philosophorum. And as that stone has the power to transform base metals, purifying them into the perfect gold of Havilah, so the Elixir has the power to purify and perfect the human body, making it immune to aging and disease. Just as the perfect gold of Havilah does not tarnish, rust, or disintegrate, so he who drinks the Elixir is not subject to any degenerative reduction of substances. The alembic in the laboratory, *vas mirabile,* is the alchemical equivalent of the Fountain of Life in the Garden, the matrix from which the divine tincture is drawn.'

"'Just as the Fountain issues four rivers out of Eden,' the old Jew explained, turning back to the *Sefer Mekor-Hayim,* 'so the book of Genesis, in which the Fountain is described, issues four books: Exodus is the river Pishon, Leviticus is Gihon, Numbers is Hiddekel, and Deuteronomy is Prath. Thus to read from the Torah on the Sabbath, quenching our thirst in its streams of words, is to drink from the Fountain.' Obviously, Mr. Siegel, reading the Torah does not prevent any individual from aging, but it truly does, Rabbi Solomon insisted, sustain the youth of Israel. In order for an individual to become truly immune to aging and disease, he would, like Enoch and Elijah, need to locate the veritable Fountain of Life in Paradise, the place where the eagle drinks, in Havilah. And Rabbi Solomon seemed to truly believe that he had determined the exact location of that place by studying certain *mappae mundi* in light of the knowledge he had gleaned from these and other manuscripts. Do keep in mind, Mr. Siegel, that, at the time, I did not take the old Jew seriously."

Once again, Mr. De Leon assumed the posture and voice of the old man and played the part: "In *Sefer ha-Rimmon, The Book of the Pomegranate,* Moses de León proclaims that once we have entered Havilah, we may follow the flight of eagles to the Garden where Elijah dwells, young to this day, hiding there just as secret meanings hide in the Torah. Moses de León refers to the place as Nesharmayim, a location identified in the *Epistles to the Praesidium* of Jerome as 'the Watering Spring of Eagles'"

Mr. De Leon reported that the aged rabbi had used what he called "Gematriatic methods of interpretation" to locate the Fountain: "Gan Eden, the name of Paradise itself, provided the information. *Gimmel* and *nun* for Gan gave him fifty-three, and Eden (with *Ayin* as seventy, plus *Dalet* as four, plus *Nun* as fifty) gave him one hundred twenty-four. And, believe it or not, 124° longitude and 53° latitude were the very coordinates that the rabbi had found listed in the *Mu'jam al-Buldan* of Ibn al-Mamhoon for a garden to which the Muhammadan geographer referred as the 'Paradise of the Jews.' And these figures turned out to correspond exactly to the coordinates in the *Claudii Ptolemaei* as the source of the Ganges, a place known to Ptolemy as Fons Aguilarum, the Eagles' Fountain, and to the inhabitants of India as Garudotsapura. It is none other than Moses de León's Nesharmayim. Ptolemy had actually recorded the coordinates as 144° longitude and 18° latitude; but Rabbi Solomon discovered that, by adjusting the Alexandrian geographer's notion of the size of the earth and his designation of a median to the calculations of the Moors, there was a consensus. The rabbi was confident that he knew the exact location of the Fountain of Life."

Mr. De Leon said that he had finally consented to do what Solomon ben Maimon had asked of him both because of the money and also to get rid of him: "I didn't want the rabbi returning to my house and hanging around. And so, at my first opportunity, I presented his proposal in all of the above detail to the queen who was, I was well aware, not happy about the prospects of growing older. She had just turned forty. 'A crazy old Jew came to see me,' I told Her Majesty, 'claiming to know the location of a fountain of perpetual youth in India.' The legend had been very well known ever since the wide circulation of both the letter of Prester John and *The Voiage and Travails* of John Mandeville, and the Fountain was, furthermore, both alluded to in the *Cancion de canciones,* the play that Celestina and I had recently performed for Ysabel, and described in some detail in one of the queen's favorite romances, *Le livre du preux et vaillant Jason et de la belle Médée.* Nevertheless, I was genuinely surprised that Her Royal Highness was so eager to believe that an old rabbi might really be able to locate the legendary Fountain and procure its waters for her. But that was no less absurd than believing Cristobal Colon could sail to the Orient by a westward route. Like all of us, she was prone to believing what she hoped might be true. And so passage was arranged by royal patent for Rabbi Solomon ben Maimon de Luna aboard the Niña, one of the three caravels that would, under the command of *el gilipollasqueroxo,* be setting sail for India on August 3, the ninth day of the Hebrew month of Av, the date that had been designated as the last day on which unconverted Jews could live in Spain. He left his manuscripts and maps with me for safekeeping."

Suddenly Mr. De Leon stood up. He spread his arms histrionically, gesticulating and orating like the actor he claimed to have been: "*¡O alta fuerça de amor!* O Ysabel, *mi Ysabel, mi Isla Bella, mi Emperadora,* Is-a-bell, Jesu-bel, Yezebel, queen of Castile, León, Aragon, Sicily, Granada, Toledo, Valencia, Galicia, Sevilla, Sardinia, Cordoba, Corsica, Murcia, Jaen, the Balearic Islands, and the Canary Islands too. I loved her more than any woman ever."

Coughing, taking a deep breath, and coughing again, he sat down and settled back into a conversational tone: "And now let me tell you about Queen Ysabel. Let's go back several years. Let's write about the very first time I saw Her Serene Majesty. We had been commissioned to perform the *Auto de los Reyes Magos* as part of the festivities for the celebration of her marriage to Fernando in a palace in Valladolid, and my father had cast me, a four-year-old, as the newborn Christ. He trusted the audience to understand that the Holy Infant wouldn't have been able to recite his lines unless he was played by a boy old enough to talk. Our spectacle was one of many diversions in the many intermissions between the meals that were served during a feast that began at noon and did not end till midnight. Those gathered were celebrating the union not only of a man and woman, of a king and queen, but of Aragon and Castile as well. So resplendent was the sovereign woman that, when the stage curtain was pulled back it was as if a heavy bedroom drape had been suddenly opened on the morning of a bright day. If I were trying to write this myself—which I'm not—I might be tempted, trite as it would be, to compare her beauty to the radiance of the sun. I hope you can do better than that, Mr. Siegel.

"My father, who had played Joseph in the spectacle, felt honored when, after our performance, a page, bringing us wine, bread, goat cheese, and cured ham, announced that the queen wished to receive me after the feast. My father insisted that we eat the ham despite the injunction of our religion against it.

"Moved as apparently Her Highness had been by my portrayal of the Only Begotten Son of God, she had commanded that I be presented to her just as I had appeared on the stage, carrying a small wooden cross and wearing only scant white linen swaddling clothes and the halo that my mother had cut out of bark and covered with gold leaf.

"As the door to the royal bridal chamber closed behind me, I realized that I was alone with her. She gestured for me to approach and assume on her lap the position I had taken in the arms of the Madonna during the performance. The queen was wearing an Oriental tunic of crimson satin with long, wide sleeves under an open, gold-embroidered Marian blue robe that was trimmed with shimmering sable. I remember each pearl button of the tunic. One after another they were undone until her right breast was, much to my awe, entirely exposed to me. I dropped my cross. You must do your very best, Mr. Siegel, to come up with original and evocative metaphors to do justice to the exquisite plumpness, warm firmness, and touching beauty of that white breast with its delicate pink nipple. I never understood why Solomon compared his beloved's breast to a young gazelle. What does that mean? Fruit, on the other hand, makes at least some sense—a breast can have something in common with a peach or pomegranate; and a nipple can always be a grape, cherry, or just about any kind of berry. But mammary fruit is stale and even more mundane than heavenly orbs. And everyone's tired of ruby nipples, not to mention even more worn-out rosebuds. The comparison of the Moorish poet Muhammad Ayir ibn Kus-Umak of his beloved's breast to the golden dome atop the minaret of the great mosque of Zabourahstan, is the kind of thing I'd like from you. It makes the breast holy. Fill in the blanks: 'With her hand pressing against my halo, she guided my mouth to the ____ nipple of her ____ breast, as if guiding a ____ to a ____ on a ____.'

"As though to an audience of kings and judges, if not martyrs and angels, *la Católica* spoke grandly about her mission as queen to represent on earth the Blessed Virgin Mary, *del çielo Reyna*. 'Suck,' she ordered, *'mi hijo, mi caro Jesusito,'* and, as I obeyed, she moaned: *'Cuan amoroso, mi hijo, mi salvador, recuerdas en mi seno.'*

"As the only queen in Europe at the time, Ysabel was, I later came to understand, the most powerful woman in the world and, as such, she believed herself to be the earthly embodiment of both the Virgin Mary, Queen of Heaven, and Venus Aphrodite, Queen of Love. Confident that there was a merger of the divine spirits of those females within her as a phenomenal entity, Ysabel proclaimed herself *la Hypostasia Católica*. She imagined that any aging of her corporeal form gravely afflicted both Mary and Venus.

"I didn't see the voluptuous monarch again until I was about seven or eight years old. Carrying a bow, and wearing gossamer wings and a cloud of fluffed cotton over my genitals, I was playing the part of Amor with my father as the Old Man in a New Year's performance of *El Amor y el viejo* for the royal court in Barcelona. Once again after the spectacle, Ysabel requested that I be delivered to her chambers. I don't think she realized I was the same boy who had been the Infant Jesus she had suckled at her wedding celebration. She who had, on that previous occasion, taken the part of the Virgin Mary, this time became Aphrodite Iberiana. This time, with both breasts exposed, whispering *'Cupidus, mei filius delectus,'* she plucked off my cloud, softly stroked, tenderly caressed, and gently kissed the most sensitive parts of my body, naked but for the wings. This time when I sucked on her nipple, warm milk flowed into my mouth for she had recently given birth to *la Loca*. But perhaps, Mr. Siegel, you shouldn't write about this meeting. It's not that I want to conceal the truth, but I'm afraid that our readers, given modern mores, might not appreciate the sweetness of the mutual pleasure derived from such intimacies, quite customary and acceptable at the time, between a grown woman and a young boy.

"The next time I was summoned for an audience with Ysabel was also after a performance of *El Amor y el viejo*. But in this presentation of the spectacle I was the Old Man, a role I had taken on after my father's death. Even though I was only fifteen years old, by the grace of my mother's skill with cosmetics, I looked the part. In my lamb's wool wig and white beard, yellowed at the ends, I appeared as old as Rabbi Solomon ben Maimon de

Luna. My hands and lips trembled like his, and my voice quavered as I recited, 'El amor siempre fabla mentiroso.' My nubile bride was cast in the part that I had previously played. This transformation of Love, from a boy into a girl, made the Old Man's aging so much more poignant. Her coquettishness mocked him.

"We had been booked to stage our allegory as one of the various diversions planned by the burghers of Sevilla to welcome our queen. She was touring Estremadura and Andalucia to introduce a more efficient military police system in those relatively anarchistic provinces. Holding court in the Real Alcázar, and making it her temporary residence, she spent the first days after her arrival watching displays of Castilian chivalry—hidalgos on horseback killed a hundred and one bulls for her. Their testicles were sautéed in olive oil and served in an almond sauce for dinner, after which plays were performed in the Corral de la Monteria.

"Still wearing the costume and makeup of the Old Man, I was presented to the queen at the doorway into the Guarida del León, a room reserved for private audience. Once again, she was the Virgin Mary. Addressing me as *mi viejo caro*, the Queen of Heaven told me that she could restore my youth, redeem me from aging, and deliver me from death by providing me with libation from the Fountain of Life, which, she avowed, was, according to the venerable Saint Augustine, the womb from which the infant Christ had been born for the salvation of mankind. She, who by virtue of a papal bull was the very Church in Spain, revealed the Fountain to me. Whispering, "It is in the garden of my loins," she commanded me to genuflect before her. Raising up the layers of silk and mousseline skirts in front of me, then parting her heavenly lower limbs, she presented the Fountain and invited me to quench my thirst. "Si quis sitit veniat ad me et bibat," she recited, holding my head securely in place between her legs until the climactic gushing of the *Fuente Milagrosa*. Moaning 'Alleluia, ahhh-lleluia, ahhh-lleluiaaaa,' she released me. That my white beard had come off at the Fountain made it appear that the Old Man had truly become young again.

"At this point, it would be appropriate to describe her Fountain. Let's not refer to it with words so scientific as the Latin *vagina* nor so vulgar as your English *cunt*. In Andalucia we called it a *txitxi* or *farranaco* and had an extensive nomenclature for its sundry constituents. The clitoris was a *xufa*, the almond from which sweet *orxata* syrup is pressed for drinking, or *el gatillo*, which was the trigger of the smoothbore harquebus. The passage leading in from the *txitxi* was *el cañon*, the barrel of that burst-shot matchlock gun. You might make a mandorla of it—yes, that radiant vulva-shaped aureole in which the Virgin is enthroned, or the cruet that contains redemptive Eucharistic wine, or the dripping aspergillum by which we are sprinkled with holy water. Be as rhapsodic as you can—be elegiac, if not dithyrambic— over every detail, every wondrous part and intriguing facet, of the royal pudendum. The queen's *txitxi* is in your hands, Mr. Siegel.

"As intimate as I had been with her, I was not invited to actually *cardar* Ysabel until a year or so later when I was Christ once more, taking that part by royal command in a play in which I saved Mary Magdalena, played by Celestina, from the wrath of my brother, Setho, as the nefarious Jewish high priest who had sentenced the girl to be stoned to death as a punishment for fornication. The queen was especially entertained by plays that exposed the villainy of Jews. Having just received word from Fernando in Granada that the Moors had been defeated at Alhama, Ysabel was in especially high spirits. Her hair, like that of *la Magdalena*, hung loose over her shoulders and, when her sky blue silk undergown slipped down onto the brightly glazed, ornately patterned Moorish tiled floor, I beheld the majestic nakedness of the queen, a vision as luminous and beatific as that had by any of the saints of Christendom—it was an epiphany. Again I am relying on you, Mr. Siegel, to evoke the splendor of that nakedness, so diabolically angelic, so virulently nectarous. At this point in the narrative it would be appropriate for you to use poetic metaphors and similes for each part of her body, taking care that they are built upon, and are harmonious with, the metaphors you've used to bring her breasts and *txitxi* to life."

Mr. De Leon divulged that Ysabel would, every few months or so, order the production of a play, a command that was invariably followed by an invitation to meet with her privately after the performance. "I was always worried that if she noticed the mark of the Jewish covenant on my flesh, it might so repulse her that she'd be incited to have me called before a tribunal of her Inquisition. And so I took care that she did not see my penis in any but the erect state. That was, as you might well imagine, not always easy."

Given historical accounts of *la Católica* as a fervently reverent and righteous apostle of Christian morality and propriety, and an almost saintly, devoted wife and mother, I was startled, and somewhat amused as well, by Mr. De Leon's stories of the queen's cupidity. The author of *The True Story of Juan Ponce de León and the Fountain of Youth*, one of the books I had perused the night before, claiming that Ponce de León "greatly admired the pious Queen Isabella as a cultural, political and spiritual leader," had described her:

> She was a model of virtue, piety, devotion, and domestic economy, who mended one doublet for her husband the king as often as seven times.

Queen Isabella exercised great moral influence on the nobility of Spain in adamantly discouraging inordinate luxury, frivolity, and vain pastimes. . . . Doing everything in her power to preserve the purity of the Holy Catholic Faith against the nefarious intrigues of the Jews, who were employing usury to pervert Christians and undermine their society, the Catholic sovereign was responsible both for the establishment of the Holy Office of the Inquisition and for the Edict of Expulsion which successfully made Spain a purely Catholic country, devoid of heresy and apostasy, and free from the impious influence of Jews, Muslims, and those converts to Christianity who secretly maintained their own iniquitous faiths and perfidious practices (p. 45).

When I expressed surprise over his prurient portrait of the reputedly prudish queen, Mr. De Leon explained that her conquests in love remain as unknown to historians as her political triumphs are famous to them "because every one of her many lovers was keenly aware that any insinuation of intimacy with her would result in a trial for heresy before the Inquisition, a mere formality before being taken to the quemadero for public execution by fire. To say that the queen of Spain was unchaste was as blasphemous as to declare the same about the Queen of Heaven. That's what happened to Celestina's father. He was drunk one night in a tavern in Triana, and couldn't restrain himself from boasting that, after a performance of *La Danza general de la muerte,* he had been summonsed to the Guarida del León. And there, he had sworn, *la Católica* had enticed him, still dressed in the costume he had worn to play Satan, into performing devilishly lewd acts with her.

"But do not write that lust motivated her many unions with many men. No, it was all for the sake of maintaining her youth. As I have explained, she believed it was her obligation to do so as the earthly embodiment and representative of the Virgin Mary and the goddess Venus. The eminently learned Jewish court physician, Johanan Yarhoni, had revealed to her certain secret analeptic formulae, antidotes to aging and agents for rejuvenation. Since the primary ingredient in these medicaments was semen, the queen diligently collected that substance directly into her various bodily orifices, as well as into vials to be mixed with other materials for the manufacture of soaps, shampoos, lotions, and collyria. Although the queen was particularly driven to collect the semen of young men like myself, she also had the seed of those she deemed notably powerful. Proudly she showed me vials of the seminal fluid of Pope Sixtus IV and Boabdil, the ruler of Nasrid Granada, not to mention an ejaculatory elixir milked by her own hand from a white bull she kept in her stables in honor of Europa and Zeus.

"As I've already told you, Mr. Siegel, this obsession with youth also made the queen susceptible to believing that Rabbi Solomon might be able to find the Fountain for her. And so she consented to arrange for the old Jew to sail to India on a ship under the command of *el gilipollasqueroxo*. Though she was pleased when Colon returned to Spain a few months later to announce that he had successfully reached and claimed for her some islands off the eastern seaboard of China, she was, at the same time, very disappointed, to say the least, that he was unable to report anything about the old rabbi except that he had, at his own request, been left on an island the natives called Guanahani.

"The queen then resolutely insisted that I, the only person other than herself who was privy to the rabbi's calculations and purposes, go on Colon's second westward voyage. Mine was a secret mission to find the old Jew and, through him, the Fountain. Embracing me forcefully, she whispered in my ear, 'If you can supply me with the rejuvenating waters, I shall, in return, after Fernando is dead, make you my king, Juan Ponce. We'll keep the secret of the Fountain to ourselves, and, remaining young forever, we shall enjoy eternity on earth together. But now, so that you may be given a position of command in the Indies and have the freedom there to conduct private explorations on our behalf, I will make a hidalgo of you. My lawyers will reconstruct your past to establish a noble lineage.'

"When I protested that I was hardly qualified to conduct a foreign expedition, my sovereign ruler silenced me: 'You're an accomplished actor—it should not be too difficult for you to play the part of a conquistador. You were admirably convincing as the Old Man, Solomon, and Jesus Christ.' Ysabel created the character I was to play in the Indies: Don Juan Ponce de León, a chivalrous and valorous hidalgo who had fought bravely in Granada against the Moors, a descendant of *the* Juan Ponce de León, Marqués of Cadiz and nephew of the late Rodrigo Ponce de León, Grand Duke of Zahara—yes, a member of the illustrious Ponce de León family that had done so much to purge Castile of Jews and Mohammedans, the same Ponce de Leóns whose wealth had been amassed through the cultivation of cane and production of sugar in La Mancha. It mattered little to her that I knew nothing about either war or sugar.

"The last time I saw Her Serene Majesty was on the morning of the day I left Spain forever. After kissing Celestina good-bye and promising to return to her soon, I went to the Alcazar, where I had been invited to accompany the queen for matins in her private chapel. Genuflecting before the monumental crucifix above the altar, she whispered: 'Kneel down, Don Juan Ponce de León. Kneel down behind me.'

"After piously making the sign of the cross over her heart, she bowed forward, supporting herself on one hand while using the other to lift her sumptuous skirts and expose her naked buttocks. At this point, Mr. Siegel, in trying to capture this important scene for my book, I would compare those hind parts to two perfect domes of white marble forming an apse above the altar to which you should compare her *txitxi*, not sparing any adjective to make a point of its ineffable sanctity. Her legs could be the chancel buttress, and her pubic down the altar's brocaded baldachin. Such rhetoric will perhaps enforce the subsequent correlation of Christ's passion with our own, a revelation of the affinity between the rapturous pain of the crucifixion and the rapturous pleasure of sex. To sustain the similitude, the chapel's rose window above the altar would, I suppose, have to be the queen's anus. I do realize, however, that some readers might not appreciate the felicity of that metaphor.

"She raised her head to fix her eyes on her crucified Lord. 'Look at him,' she commanded, *'Ecce homo*. And speak as the priest during the Mass: "*Introibo ad altare Dei*. I will go into the altar of God." And then enter ye unto me. *Ad altare mei qui laetificat juventutem meam*. Into my altar, the joy of my youth, come, come all ye faithful.' As I obeyed, she prayed: *'Te sperma Domini, nostri Jesu Christi, custodiat animam et corpum meam in juventutam aeternam. Amen*. By means of thy seed, may our Lord, Jesus Christ, preserve my body and soul to youth everlasting.' She exulted in the devotional liturgy: *'Per omnia saecula saeculorum*. Forever and ever.'

"Together we gazed at the waxen white body of the King of the Jews nailed to the rough-hewn wooden cross, surrounded by a bright polychromatic court of angels, prophets, kings, martyrs, and saints in bas-relief. Crimson lacquer had been used for the blood on his side, palms, and feet. Three nails of rusted iron, a crown fashioned of the thorny stems of rose bushes, a muslin loincloth stained with lamb's blood, and a wig of genuine human hair brought the dead savior to life.

"'*Hosanna*,' the queen intoned over and over during our communion, '*Hosanna* in the highest!'

"Finally I fell away from her, rolled over on the floor and, stretched out like a plaintive penitent, I mumbled, '*Amen, amen*.' But the beatitude of *la Católica* was unrelenting. Kneeling down over me, she sucked the last drops of sacred fluid from my body. '*Corpus tuum quod sumpsi*,' she recited, '*et sperma, quem potavi, adhaereat visceribus meis; et praesta, ut in me non remaneat senectus, quem pura et sancta refecerunt Sacramenta*. May thy body which I have consumed, and thy semen, which I have drunk, cleave to my very innards, granting that no trace of aging be found in me, whom these pure and holy sacramental mysteries have rejuvenated.'

"You might, by the way, Mr. Siegel, mention here that it was not our habit to *cardar* in the posture of animals. But, there in the chapel, that coital position allowed the queen a vision of Christ without the distraction of my face. It was her way of making an appeal to Christ for guidance and protection. 'And so, Don Juan Ponce de León, on this voyage to the Indies, may you be guided by Our Lord to the Fountain of Life and may the secret of its waters be protected by Him. So go now. You must not be late for the ship. Cristobal is an impatient man.' She gave me a small painting of herself and a rosary, strung with large coral beads, that Pope Sixtus IV had presented to her. They are both on display in this room."

Mr. De Leon stood up abruptly to announce that our session was over. "You must return to the Zodiac. You have a lot of work to do this evening. I'll be eager to read what you have written about my life in Spain tomorrow."

Why, I wondered as I drove back to my motel, was this character going to so much effort and expense to create this persona and play the part, especially now that the Garden and museum were closed? Was it possible that, suffering some mental illness, he actually believed that he was the five-hundred-and-forty-year-old Spanish explorer who discovered Florida, and that he was trying to validate this outrageous delusion by paying me to make a book out of it?

The next morning, on returning to the museum with about ten thousand words, I was received by Mr. De Leon in the Caribbean Room. His walloon-collared shirt on that day was rose-colored, and there was a soft leather skullcap on his head, a silver-buckled belt around his waist, and embroidered slippers on his feet. He was still wearing the dark glasses, and that was beginning to annoy me.

He insisted on showing me memorabilia from the period to be covered that day. Among other artifacts there were Taino baskets, Arawak fishing nets, and Carib spears, a conquistador's sword, morion helmet, crossbow, and harquebus, a coral-studded silver instrument of some kind, samples of *guanín,* and what was supposed to be Ponce de León's leather-bound logbook for his 1513 voyage of discovery. There was also an intricately engraved warded lock with a lever tumbler and covered keyhole, made, he claimed, in Nuremburg in the sixteenth century. "That lock, from the front door of my house in Puerto Rico, always reminds me of my second wife, Leonor. Yes, her pudenda was a lock, and one very hard to pick at that. My phallus had to become a key, a skeleton key, if you know what I mean. Feel free to look around," Mr. De Leon said, "while I read the first chapter of my autobiography."

No sooner had he seated himself and begun to read, than he stopped to express dissatisfaction over how I, using the chronology he had given me, had opened the story: "I was born in the Year of our Lord 1465 on the 22nd of July in the town of Lebrija. At the ritual circumcision, on the eighth day after my birth, my father, an itinerant actor and lion tamer, named me Samson ben Aryeh."

Mr. De Leon shook his head in blatant disappointment: "No, no, Mr. Siegel, that's no good at all. I want something more like 'Bereshit bara Elohim et hashamayim ve'et ha'arets.' Now that's a great opening line! Wonderful even as the Gentiles rendered it: 'In principio creavit Deus caelum et terram.' It startles and grabs you: 'En el principio creó Dios los cielos y la tierra.' It's written with such confidence: 'In the beginning God created the heaven and the earth.' Oh, yes, it's a marvelously provocative beginning. Right away, with only seven words, you've got a strong character, the hero of a story in whom you cannot help but be interested. It makes you want to get to know him. Immediately he does something big, really big, and you can't wait to read on to find out how it all turns out. That's what I need for my book—an opening like that. Simple and yet profound. Something that makes people really care about Juan Ponce de León from the very start. The introductory words are no less important in writing a book than they are in approaching a woman. The opening must be seductive. The first words should make the reader, or the woman, want more."

As he continued to read, Mr. De Leon repeatedly stopped to look up at me and further complain. My writing, he grumbled, wasn't at all "thrilling or even just interesting. And it's not very funny either. It sounds like I'm lying, and I don't come across as particularly heroic or attractive. Why is that?"

He was additionally disgruntled that I had not been able to come up with English equivalents for *cardar, gilipollasqueroxo, mitja-nena,* or *fronto.* And he was unimpressed with the adjectival superlatives and nominal metaphors that I had chosen to describe various parts of the queen's body. I had spelled her name Isabella. He insisted that I spell it Ysabel. "She was," he complained, "much more beautiful than you have made her. Neither Celestina nor my mother are anywhere nearly beautiful enough. You have not yet turned the stories I told you yesterday into something wonderful. I'm not paying you to take dictation. I've hired you to write a meaningful and entertaining book, one that will endure long after I am gone. I'm sorry, Mr. Siegel, but you've still got a lot of work to do if you want that dollar per word."

I had ended the chapter: "And so on the 25th of September 1493 I set out for the Indies aboard one of the seventeen ships under the command of Admiral Christopher Columbus." "What," Mr. De Leon asked as he handed the typescript back to me, "is engaging about that? You might, Mr. Siegel, consider something like this: 'As I boarded the caravel, I sincerely believed that, because my journey was undertaken for the sake of love, any suffering I might experience in the Indies would be ennobling and glorious. At the time, in my youth, I fancied that love itself was the Fountain of Life.' The final words of a chapter, no less than one's last words to a woman, are as important as the first."

Given my employer's dissatisfaction with my draft of the first chapter, I had no choice but to scrap what I had given him. And I did not have the time to rewrite it because he was adamantly eager to go on to the second chapter, the narrative of Ponce de León's adventures on the islands that were to become the Dominican Republic and Puerto Rico. For the sake of that story, and before telling it, Mr. De Leon provided me with another chronology:

1493   I sail to Hispaniola, win a Taino slave girl in a game of cards, and discover popcorn

1494   I invent both rum and cigars

1500   I marry Leonor Núñez de Guzmán

1504   Queen Ysabel of Spain dies, and so too does my Taino lover

1505   My son, Pedro Ponce de León, is born and I am appointed adelantado of Higuey

1506   Celestina is burned at the stake by the Inquisition and my brother Setho arrives in Hispaniola

1508   Nicholas de Ovando appoints me adelantado of Borinquen

1512   Due to the machinations of Diego Colon, I am removed from my post as governor of Borinquen, but am granted a royal patent authorizing me to find, explore, and govern the island of Beimini

1513   I discover a land that I christen Pascua de Florida

It took him all day to tell me the story. There was, of course, lots of *card-arring* in it, and lots of beautiful women. "So beautiful!" he would exclaim, "Make that beauty real, Mr. Siegel. Bring their beauty back to life!"

When, on Saturday morning, the ninth of July, I arrived at the Garden of Eden and was received in the Zhotee-eloq Room of Mr. De Leon's museum. I was utterly exhausted from having stayed up all night to work on the chapter that follows. Before reading it, Mr. De Leon asked if I rewritten the first chapter yet. I had to confess that I hadn't had enough time.

"Time," he muttered, "if only we had more time."

Once he had read chapter two, however, he became sufficiently encouraged to congratulate me and, even more significantly, to count out ten thousand eight hundred and thirty-six dollars in cash. I could hardly believe it. The money substantially assuaged my fatigue.

This is not to say that Mr. De Leon did not have certain reservations about the Caribbean chapter: "I'd still like it to be more comical. I'm not convinced that your sense of humor is as acute as my own, Mr. Siegel, and I can't help but be concerned about that. And you have yet to come up with a word for *cardar*. And I don't understand why you insist on referring to Colon as Columbus."

I tried to explain that I had used "Christopher Columbus" because that was what the man who had been credited with the discovery of America was called in English, and that anything else didn't sound right or familiar enough to the American ear. But Mr. De Leon argued that "Colon" was even more apt in English than "Columbus," because "in your language, it designates the portion of the large intestine just beyond the rectum, the filthiest part of the human body. It is, like Admiral Colon himself, usually full of shit."

Acutely conscious of my employer's obsession with powerfully seductive first lines, I had sat at the small desk in my room at the Zodiac Motel the night before, working on that opening, struggling to think of something original, startling, and engaging. I had been on the verge of giving up, and settling for merely trying to figure out how I would convince Mr. De Leon that "I set sail for the Indies in 1493" would do, when, all of a sudden, it came to me. Since Mr. De Leon had informed me in his letter of introduction that he was "not much of a reader," I assumed that he would probably not recognize it. I had been right, and I was relieved when, after reading the following chapter, my employer said: "Now, this is much better. And I especially like the opening."

1493–1513

WHEREIN PONCE DE LEÓN SETTLES IN THE NEW WORLD, BECOMES GOVERNOR OF HIGUEY AND OF BORINQUEN, INVENTS CIGARS AND RUM, AND DISCOVERS POPCORN AND FLORIDA

The Mother of Christ bares her blessed Bosom so that men, in receiving of its ineffable plenitude, might be granted Redemption. The hallowed Breast of the Holy Virgin is the Fountain of Life (*fons vitae*), overflowing with the sweet milk of pure love (*amor purus*). He who parts his lips [in prayer] to drink from it shall be delivered from the afflictions of mortal flesh to relish the abundant life of the ageless Spirit. Taste and prove it (*gustate et videte*)! . . . Give us drink, Our Lady, from thy glorious Breast and, by grace of its mysterious nectar, let us enjoy immortality.

SAINT HORTANES OF LEBRIJA, *Sermon for the Summer Feast of the Lactation of the Virgin*

It was the best of times, it was the worst of times; it was the age of wisdom, it was the age of foolishness; it was the epoch of belief, it was the epoch of incredulity; it was the season of light, it was the season of darkness; it was the spring of hope, it was the winter of despair; we had everything before us, we had nothing before us.

The Worst of Times

At sea, expansive and indifferent, I was gripped by the persistent ache of loneliness, choked with desire, cramped by a fragrant memory of disheveled hair, craving the taste of an earlobe ferreted out by a tongue in those locks, the imperturbable feel of an eager nipple petrifying between lips, a fleshy almond swelling beneath a burrowing finger. A sigh was remembered as an orison, the vision of candlelight flickering on nakedness an epiphany. Lambent thighs welcomed wide, arms enlaced, rump clenched, back and belly arching; the warm sapors and salty savors of sweat, the milky trickle of arousal, and a sudden climactic ooze—oh, the sweet fermenting mash of sex.

The rocking, rising, and falling of the caravel lurching susceptibly on sullen rolling swells of a moody Ocean Mar, prodded loneliness and aggravated regret. I missed the great queen who had dispatched me and the little actress who had asked if I might stay. I missed the pretty girls gathered in the patios of Sevilla, women glancing down from open windows or fanning themselves coquettishly to half hide risqué smiles as they passed in shadowy lanes, girls dancing tipsily in the taverns of Triana at night, working tired in orchards in the morning, lolling lazily in the grassy meadows of Lebrija on sunny afternoons—singing, joking, giggling, winking, blushing, whispering, whistling, stretching, scratching, yawning, dozing, and all the other little things that women do, those sweet nothings that make them so irresistibly lovely and always take my breath away.

Never in all my years have I been able to tolerate being alone. When I say alone, I mean without a woman. And when I say a woman, I mean one who, in some way, loves me, even just a little. Even a woman whose breath or body odor is somewhat sour, even a woman who complains or nags a bit, one who weeps or sulks, even one who is heartless, bitter, or prone to jealousy, is better than no woman at all. And this is especially true if she is pretty.

Among almost a hundred times as many men, there were four women on the Santa Minga. *Fatima was a Moorish dancer. An impoverished but entrepreneurial hidalgo, who had acquired the odalisque as a spoil of battle in the conquest of Granada, was escorting her to India with plans to establish a public house where Oriental noblemen might enjoy a cup of wine, listen to Fatima sing a houri love song, watch her dance a zambra, and then purchase the precious pleasure of an intimate hour with her. The second was a Jewish* conversa *who spoke Arabic as well as the Moor. She had been commissioned as a translator by the captain of our caravel, supposing, as he did, that that Oriental tongue would be understood by the natives of our destination. The captain also had a new bride in tow, a shy girl who, when on deck, was always veiled and ever escorted by the oldest of the quartet, the Marquesa of the Balearic Isles, a widow of illustrious blood who was determined to establish herself in the court of the Great Khan in Cathay and thereby regain the wealth to which she had been accustomed until her son, after the death of the marqués, had banished her from her islands.*

While I never spoke to these women, I went out of my way to watch and eaves-

drop whenever any one or more of them appeared from the women's cabin. And lying on my cot at night, when I thought the sailors around me were asleep, I'd imagine the women coming secretly to my cramped and musty quarters for an amorous assignation, sometimes just one, sometimes one after another, occasionally the captain's wife and the marquesa together, several times the Jewess and Moor, and once all four. In these lusciously indecent reveries of intimacy, the Moor was cool and detached but artful and adept, the marquesa clumsy and inept but tempestuous and flamboyant, the wife of the captain shy and self-conscious at first but, once unveiled, fervent and even ecstatic. And the Jewess was all of the above. Each one of them would whisper that they loved me. And then they'd vanish, as though washed overboard and swept away by an enormous wave suddenly rising out of a restless, petulant, and salacious sea.

By moonlight, on deck, I'd try to look ahead, out across the immense oceanic sprawl, beyond the ghostly dark silhouettes of the other caravels, for signs of land and life, imagining the swarthy girls of the Indies. It had been reported that all of them were beautiful. The voluptuous heathen women of the opulent Orient sparkled with gold ornaments dangling from their ears and noses, silver rings on their dainty fingers and toes, strings of pearls, diamonds, rubies, and emeralds wrapped around their wrists and ankles, draped around their necks, and girdling their robust hips. Those precious gems could be picked up like pebbles on their shores. Trained from childhood in lovemaking's fine arts, Oriental ladies took pleasure in bestowing love. It was further said that, due to the Asiatic diet, their tawny skin smelled spicy and their rosy lips tasted of honey. Standing on the deck of the ship, somewhere in the uncharted Ocean Mar, I already loved so many of them, sight unseen.

When, at long last, we dropped anchor at Navidad, where Admiral Columbus had left forty men from his first voyage to build a settlement, we found that there were neither women nor gems, nor anything that was beautiful. There was not a living soul, but only what was left of sundry corpses—mutilated, eviscerated, and decomposing, lashed together or strewn apart, flame-charred, and maggot-infested. Empty eye sockets of heads impaled on stakes stared at me, and mouths from which tongues had been plucked silently shrieked terrible warnings. Playing the part of a conquistador required that I react to the grisly spectacle with sangfroid and aplomb. There was no sign of Rabbi Solomon ben Maimon de Luna.

Upon returning to Sevilla from his first voyage, Columbus had brashly avowed that the natives of what he thought were islands off the eastern coast of China were so artless, simple, and cowardly that "the whole land could be conquered in a few days with no more than fifty men." Thus the Admiral was, to say the least, perturbed by what the supposedly timorous primitives had done at Navidad. He led the landing party in a solemn vow to the Blessed Virgin to avenge the murders with the execution of one hundred heathens for each martyred Christian.

Columbus had also promised the Crown enough pure gold to finance a crusade by which the Catholic monarchs might conquer Palestine, claim the Holy Sepulcher, and build a great cathedral on the site of the old Temple of the Jews. Just as she hoped I might find the waters by the means of which she could enjoy perpetual youth, so my majestic Ysabel hoped that Columbus might provide the gold by means of which she could become queen of the Holy Land. Each hope enhanced the other.

The little gold ore that was unearthed in the early years in the Indies was, however, mostly poor quality guanín. But undaunted, Columbus, as the newly appointed viceroy of the Indies, instituted a system of forced labor wherein each native was required to gather or mine enough gold every month to fill his Castilian master's helmet. The punishments for not doing so were left to the discretion of individual conquistadors.

Columbus had sent some of these exotic idolaters back to the court of Castile. News had it that one of them, a muscular young Taino, appearing before the queen naked except for the chains around his waist, wrists, and ankles, and the parrot feathers and strings of puffed corn in his hair, had so touched Her Serene Catholic Majesty, that she declared herself Mother of the Indians.

In an expression of love for the innocents of the Indies, Ysabel had declared that they, in return for their labors, should receive instruction in the Catholic faith and be baptized. The compassionate monarch forbade making slaves of any of her new children other than the criminals among them. Thus, in order to maintain an economical workforce, the conquering settlers had no choice but to provoke the rebellions that would make transgressors of them.

Rebel Indians were hunted down with macamastins, a kind of vicious mastiff that had been bred in Aragon for hunting wild pigs. Sometimes on a Sunday after Mass, a fight between a macamastin and an Indian would be arranged as a divertissement to appease the spirits of those nostalgic for the festive spectacles of bull baiting back home.

Many of the Castellanos who had been lured to the Indies by the prospects of the fortunes to be made there missed their homeland with its whitewashed pueblos, marble mansions, triumphal gateways, imposing cathedrals, and the market squares where winsome peasant girls sold pomegranates, figs, olives, and almonds. They missed the fragrance of the orange blossoms of Valencia, the sweetness of the luscious wines of Catalonia, the stunning vistas of the snowy Sierra Nevada, and the lush wetlands of Doñana Jerez; they missed dancing on patios on summer evenings, and drinking wine by a fire in winter. Many of the more sentimental ones missed the romance of Holy War, the thrill of heroic combat with Moors, the glory of slaying an infidel with lance or sword, the elation of seeing blood run, and the exaltation of taking harem women by force. The most pious of all missed the Inquisition—the extravagant spectacle of autos-da-fé in public plazas, the exuberant transport of being swept up in a massive wave, an exhilarated crowd following a procession of chained convicts to the quemadero for execution. They missed the pomp and fervor of it, the curling up to heaven of black smoke against an Iberian sunset, the resplendence of lustral bonfires as night fell, the heady aroma of burning flesh, and, above the stirring choruses of screaming heretics, oratorios proclaiming the majesty of Jesus Christ and the glory of the Blessed Virgin.

Although putting down a rebellion of naked Indians armed with only bows and clubs wasn't so gratifyingly challenging as a martial encounter with armored Moorish troops brandishing scimitars and shouting "Allahu akbar," it would have to do. So too, while the execution of unrepentantly rebellious heathens did less to affirm the almightiness of God than did the burning of heretical Marranos or Mariscos, it at least heralded the sovereignty of Christ in the virgin land.

In order to convince the innocents of the Indies to renounce their zemi — the eagle and serpent, sun and moon, manioc root and tobacco — and to worship in their stead the tormented body of a man, thorn-crowned, blood-splattered, and nailed to a cross, so that they might enjoy eternal life in heaven, the reverend evangelists of the Catholic Church demonstrated the torments of the hell awaiting them if they spurned the redemptive love of Jesus Christ. For his first sermon in the Indies, Fray Dionisio Buil, an apostolic delegate who had sailed aboard the Santa Minga *with me, delivered a homily on the words of Our Lord: "If a man abideth not in me, he shall be cast forth as a branch and wither. And men shall gather them and cast them into the fire, and they shall be burned."*

Just as many Jews and Muhammadans had done back home, most of the Taino and Arawak claimed to accept Christ as their redeemer. It was a reasonable alternative to the harrowing tortures that were the foreplay to execution. But for the caciques it was a matter of honor not to abandon their gods. I witnessed the solemn sacrifice of Cotubanama, a defiant cacique from the islands of Las Once Mil Virgenes. After holding up a crucifix and muttering "In hoc signo vinces," Father Dionisio proclaimed that "those who have chosen not to accept the gift of baptism by the waters of life, are now baptized with the fires of death." He invoked the Blessed Mater Doloroso as twelve conquistadors, costumed in ecclesiastical white mantellettas, *played the parts of the twelve apostles of the Lord. Sedulously they heaped kindling beneath the head of the chieftain hanging upside down from a gibbet in the square of San Juan Bautista.*

Father Dionisio was particularly intent on performing this ritual of penitence for the Caribs who were adamantly averse to accepting the authority of their new sovereigns, either Fernando and Ysabel or Jesus Christ and the Virgin. Shortly after our arrival in Hispaniola, a Carib cacique had visited Father Dionisio professing an interest in the Catholic faith. What he had heard about the Eucharist appealed to the cannibal in him. But when the Indian discovered the actual ingredients for what was supposed to be a feast of human flesh and blood, he laughed at the priest and at all of Christendom as well. The following day, upon the doorstep to his newly founded church, Father Dionisio found a gourd of congealed blood and a leaf upon which there was a piece of raw lean meat.

Reputedly the most vicious of all the Carib tribes were the northern Zhotee-eloq. Everyone was afraid of them. But Father Dionisio dreamed of converting them, of taming, subduing, and showing them that God is love. It was an age of foolishness.

The Best of Times

As much as it was the worst of times for the natives of the Indies because of Spaniards, dogs, and Christ, it was the best of times for me because of alcohol, tobacco, and a Taino girl.

Though I cannot be credited with the actual discovery of potable alcoholic spirits—an honor due to the Muhammadans (whose religious injunctions, ironically, forbid them from imbibing it)—history should have acknowledged Juan Ponce de León as the originator of rum. And although I do not deserve recognition for the discovery of smokable tobacco—a distinction belonging to the Indians (whose religious ordinances required its sacramental enjoyment)—I should at least have been recognized for inventing the cigar, because, while the Indians wrapped dry tobacco in corn husks, it was my idea to roll crushed tobacco in a tobacco leaf.

Because Queen Ysabel had decided that I should masquerade as an aristocratic sugar planter from León, devising that as a guise in which I'd secretly search for the Fountain of Eternal Youth, it seemed in keeping with the part that I, pretending to know a few things about agriculture, took cane cuttings from La Gomera, the fleet's last stop in the Canary Islands before the long westward journey to the Indies. Upon arrival in Hispaniola, I was, by order of Her Serene Majesty, made an encomendero, entitling me to over a hundred acres of land for the cultivation of sugarcane and a repartimiento of some eighty natives to work my fields. The crop flourished so astonishingly during the next few years that I hardly knew what to do with the vast surplus that remained after sending as much of it back to Sevilla as the pilots of the cargo caravels would accept.

I appointed an old cacique named Canouba to manage my workforce, and accepted the fact that, as an enslaved chieftain, he would be constrained by a Taino sense of honor to execrate me as his master. To do otherwise would have been a shameful submission to the oppression of his people by the invidiously vicious newcomers to his island. But despite a formal antipathy to me, Canouba could not help but recognize that we had at least three pleasures in common: smoking tobacco, drinking intoxicating beverages, and cardarring Taino girls. His scorn was more ceremonial than personal.

It amused him that, because I found the smoke of the burning corn husk irritating to my throat, I rolled my tobacco in a tobacco leaf. For him, irritation was a substantial and crucial part of enjoyment. That was true with wine and girls as well: he only really enjoyed drinking if it rendered him too ill to work the next day; and an appreciable part of the delight of sexual dalliance with any one of his five wives, he confided, was in the pain he derived from being subsequently slapped, scratched, and bitten by the other jealous four. It also amused Canouba that I ate the popped kernels of corn that the Taino strung into ornaments.

Whenever he arrived at my home, always on the pretext that it was to report on my fields, he'd immediately remove the shirt and breeches that he had been obligated to wear since his baptism. Maria Taino-Pinzon, my Indian slave and mistress, would bring him charcoal to paint his eyes. Once that was done, and he had adjusted the parrot feathers and strings of popped corn in his hair, Maria would solemnly kiss the cacique's fingers and toes. And then the three of us would smoke Taino tobacco and drink Castilian wine.

One night, once the drinks and drinkers were drunk, I attempted to amuse them with an imitation, and dared them to try to guess who it was that I was mimicking. Adopting a pontifical posture, gesticulating wildly and pitching my voice high, I was all bombast and rage: "In hoc signo vinces." To participate in the mockery and show that they recognized Fray Dionisio Buil, they crossed themselves ingenuously, and Canouba cried out "hallelujah," pronouncing it in a way ("aley hi luey") that means "shit on your face" in Taino. They laughed, sighed, and shook their heads in an ambiguous manner that might have expressed either mirth or sorrow.

It was Canouba's turn: after strutting jauntily around the room, humming happily and grinning foolishly, he picked up an empty wine bottle and, pretending it was full, mimed downing it. And then another bottle, and another. I couldn't imagine who he was supposed to be. When Maria pointed at me, Canouba granted that she had won the round. When Maria took her turn in the game, I thought she was perhaps acting the part of the pretty mulatta bride of the innkeeper in Santo Domingo, or the alcaide's wanton daughter, or any one of the Castellanas who had come to the Indies in search of prosperous husbands, coquettish girls, playfully seductive and shamelessly charming. Canouba laughed, smacked his lips, and slapped his knees in the manner by which the Taino applaud: "La Virgen Santa Maria!"

Some credit for the invention of rum should be given to Canouba. When he arrived at my house with a gourd from which he urged me to drink a frothy amber brew, I assumed it was manioc beer, the traditional Taino intoxicant, and aware that the drink is highly poisonous if not properly concocted, I refused it. But Canouba assured me that the beverage was something new and wonderful—a dulcet refreshment made from the juice of my sugarcane. The fermentation process had, Canouba cheerfully boasted, been started with his own sputum. It had been his idea that, because we had such a large surplus of cane, and because the ships from Sevilla were unable to meet the demands of the growing population of Higuey for Castilian wine, we ought to produce and sell this beverage locally. It was my idea, however, to distill the crude and unstable potion. Following the instructions in one of the books I had brought with me from Spain, Rabbi Solomon's manuscript of Hieronimus Brunschwygk's Liver de Arte Distillandi, *for the construction and use of presses, furnaces, distillation towers, and filtering fountains, and adhering as closely as I could, given the local availability of ingredients, to the recipe for what Brunschwygk had called* aqua vitae, *I concocted the world's first batch of what would someday be known as "rum," a liquor which was, I believed, as much like the miraculous waters of the Fountain of Life as any libation could be. Like those waters, rum, so much more potent and stable than wine, had the capacity to make an old man feel young, a sick man feel well, and a sad man smile. I called it Leche de la Virgen.*

Histories of the conquest of the New World invariably report that Viceroy Nicholas de Ovando made me governor of Higuey first and then of Borinquen in recognition of my military prowess and as a reward for my conquests over the natives of the island. The truth is that I never fought an Indian in my life. In 1505 Ovando had appointed me adelantado of Higuey because he was so fanatically fond of rum and of me for having produced it. Well aware of the potentially ample benefits of being in the good graces of the viceroy of the Indies, I manufactured for him (and certain other influential representatives of the Crown) special reserves, sweetened with molasses and fortified with triply distilled spirits.

Whenever Ovando was drunk—pretty much every time I saw him—he would be sure to beg me to do my imitation of Christopher Columbus. I had mastered the admiral's effeminate lisp and lilting Genoese accent, his imperious strut and ostentatious swagger. And when I'd lampoon his obsequious bow to the Catholic sovereigns ("Oh yes, this whole land could be conquered in a few days with no more than fifty men, for the natives of the Indies are very cowardly"), Ovando, tears running down his flushed cheeks, would laugh so convulsively that he had to clutch his sides as if to keep from bursting open. It was on the occasion of first seeing me do this imitation of the self-important gilipollasqueroxo, *that the inebriated viceroy appointed me governor of Higuey.*

It was a few years later, in 1508, just after I had introduced him to the enchantment of smoking tobacco, that Ovando installed me as governor of Borinquen. He granted my request for ten caballerias *of land on that relatively unexplored and unsettled island (which Canouba had assured me would be excellent for the cultivation of tobacco) so that I might manufacture cigars for him. I called the smokes "bacueñas" after Bacue, the Taino tobacco goddess. I was confident that they had the potential to someday become as profitable as my Leche de la Virgen.*

My own fascination with tobacco had begun the first time I saw Maria Taino-

Pinzon smoking. Reclining naked on our bed, her eyelids slowly closed as she breathed the smoke in, and then, as she breathed out, her eyes opened only slightly. She seemed transported, floating in a beatific tranquility, a heathen state of grace. When smoking tobacco, she believed, you were burning up the earthly body of Bacue and, by taking in her smoky spirit, you infused yourself with her divinity. And then, in exhalation, Bacue's released spirit wafted up, curling into the heavens to merge with the resplendent light which was the spirit of the Cacique of the Sun. Maria would collect the ashes of her tobacco on a fresh tobacco leaf and then, once she had finished smoking, she would rub them on her belly and breasts.

She taught me how to smoke. Pressing her mouth against mine, she blew the spirit of the goddess deep into me, and then, wrapping her arms around me, she squeezed it back out of me. I breathed her smoke as if it were her soul. And when we were finished, she anointed my chest with ash. And then I cardarred *her.*

The Season of Light

In the beginning Maria Taino-Pinzon had let there be light. She had redeemed me from the intractable dark loneliness of a month on the ship and another on land, two months with only dream women, specters of sex and phantasms of love, memories and anticipations. And in that redemption I came to understand the ways in which I was no less a slave than she. Love, I realized, is slavery; all lovers are bonded and indentured.

With the rigged deck of cards my father had used to win Judah the lion from a drunken Morisco, I had won the Taino girl in a game of andaboba from Don Diego Pinzon de Carajo, commander of the troops charged with the conquest of Hispaniola. It's always easy to trick a man who is intelligent and brave, brave enough to be reckless, and so intelligent that he supposes he can't be fooled. First I won his cash—several thousand maravedis. Confident that his luck would have to change, that at some point his invocations of the Virgin Mary would pay off, and that I couldn't continue drawing kings and queens with nearly every deal, he wouldn't quit the game. And so I won his sword, and then his morion, crossbow and harquebus, his killer macamastin, and a coral-studded silver instrument with which he boasted to have molested Indian women when his own instrument of flesh proved too tired for the task. The stakes for the final hand were agreed upon: if Diego Pinzon was the winner, I would return his weapons, helmet, dog, and give him double his money; if he lost, the nubile Taino slave girl would be mine.

Her name had been Guiney until Fray Dionisio Buil formalized her initiation into the Catholic faith by christening her Maria Taino-Pinzon. In addition to a baptismal name, it was the custom for slaves to be given a hyphenated surname to indicate both the converted heathen's tribe and the identity of his or her Castilian master.

Although she was afraid of me at first, I put her at some ease by consenting to let her go about my home as naked as she had been accustomed to being before becoming a slave of Christ, the Crown, and Don Diego Pinzon de Carajo. The girl painted her oval face chalk white. Her slender forearms and calves and her delicate hands and feet were charcoal black. Vermillion glyphs—zigzags, crisscrosses and exclamatory dots—adorned her trunk and thighs. There were concentric scarlet rings around the ebony nipples of her small breasts. Those breasts and her lower belly were most often daubed with tobacco ash. She wore a necklace of puffed corn kernels and a tiara of green parrot feathers. There was hardly a trace of hair on her body, and that on her head was, except for three long braids, cropped short. Her large eyes, all the more dusky for the white pigment on her face, were especially beautiful when their astonishing dark brightness was tempered by tobacco-induced languors.

We tried to teach each other how to speak our respective languages by pointing at things. I said "agua," she said "jiguey"; she said "neemu," I said "arbol"; I said "flores," she said "gueso"; I said "yo," she said "ai"; she said "io," I said "tu." With a hand over my heart, I repeated "yo," then said "te," switched my hand to her heart, and then, moving my other hand back and forth between us, said "Amo. Te amo. Te quiero." As if understanding, she moved her hand back and forth just as I had done, said "Nigo ai io nigo," and laughed. Laugh. Risa. Gibi. With my hands on her cheeks, gazing adoringly into her eyes and smiling, I whispered, "Guapa." Imitating my gesture and tone, she said, "Guino, gui-guino!" and laughed again. "Gibi," I said, and she nodded yes, yes, and laughed: "Gibi-gibi."

In my struggle to understand and speak to her, I recalled something Rabbi Solomon ben Maimon de Luna had said years before when, as a child, I was forced to study Hebrew with him. "Elohim," the old Jew had told his students, "gave language to human beings just so that we could speak of love and, in doing so, come to cultivate it. The first words ever spoken by a man were about a woman. The first human utterance was an expression of love: 'This one is bone of my bones and flesh of my flesh.' But in giving us language so that we could love, the Creator, blessed be He, also gave us the power to lie. The second human utterance was a lie."

In Castellano and in Taino, Maria Taino-Pinzon and I gradually began both to articulate affection and to lie. She said she was happy ("gueji") and I said that I had been sent from the heavens by the Cacique of the Sun to deliver her from Don Diego Pinzon, who, I had learned from her, had captured her brothers and her husband on the islands of Las Once Mil Virgenes and sent them away in chains. Pinzon's dog had killed her father. Offering her sisters as prizes to his fiercest soldiers, the conquistador had kept Maria for himself. Occasionally, she divulged, he would invite his men to enjoy her in his presence. With ardent embraces and sweet lies I tried to make up for Spanish abuses. Maria trusted me, I think partly because, unlike Pinzon and the conquistadors who had raped her, I was circumcised like a Taino man.

Because Maria, despite my behests and much to my disappointment, refused, for some reason that I never understood, to sing for me, I would sometimes sneak into the house and hide so that I might have the pleasure of overhearing a Taino song:

The Zhotee-eloq girl abandons her homeland by canoe,
Leaves behind the gushing wellspring's sacred waters,
Leaves behind the ever-blooming blossoms,
Paddling, paddling, swiftly, swiftly,
Leaves forever the hallowed wellspring,
Panting, panting, breathless, breathless,
Leaves it all to grow old, so old and frail,
In a garden of withered flowers,
In the arms of her aging Taino warrior.
In his embrace the aged Zhotee-eloq woman dies,
Old and frail, dreaming of the sacred waters
And the fragrance of the blossoms of Haveelaq.

Although I kept her as a maid and would often spend a clandestine cardarous *afternoon alone with her in the servants' quarters, I stopped sleeping at her side when, on the very first day of the sixteenth century, Father Dionisio solemnized my marriage to Leonor Núñez de Guzmán, the woman who would become the mother of my son, Pedro. Maria Taino-Pinzon had given birth to a mestiza daughter whom she named "Florida" in Spanish, "Guesoeo" in Taino. Since it was not the custom for a hidalgo to acknowledge the patrimony of Indian children, she sent our daughter to be raised by her grandmother on the islands of Las Once Mil Virgenes.*

Leonor Núñez de Guzmán was the daughter of an aristocrat, Pedro Núñez de Guzmán, a zealous champion of the Catholic faith, who boasted of having exhausted his family fortune in subsidizing campaigns against the Moors. Like many a Castilian gentleman unable to come up with a dowry worthy of his family's name, Don Pedro had sent his daughter, still unmarried at twenty-three, to find a wealthy hidalgo husband in Hispaniola. Most of the women who had ventured to the Indies for that purpose pretended to be chaste in the understanding that virginity was desirable in a fiancée. I soon discovered, however, that these ladies were generally eager to be seduced, and ready to be embraced by any man who was rich and could convince them that he would never compromise their honor by divulging intimacies with them. My experience as an actor made me rather successful with such oaths.

I first saw her on a Sunday afternoon in the shade of her parasol at a garden party at the residence of the royal commissioner, Don Francisco Bobadillo, whom I liked enormously because he had arrested the fanatical Columbus and sent him back to Queen Ysabel in chains. Although a veil concealed her face, I sensed that Leonor was beautiful—I could smell her beauty and hear it in her voice when Bobadillo introduced us. And then, as her delicate white hand slowly raised her lacy black veil, her bright eyes, even more beautiful than I could have imagined, immediately bewitched me. There was also something about her lips that made me feel uncommonly desperate.

When I asked if I might show her the island, my cane fields and distillery, and the home I had built, she coquettishly replied that she would not answer my question until I had answered one of hers: "If you were to get to know me, Don Juan Ponce de León, would you rather discover that I am a virgin or a whore, chaste or wanton, that I have been with no man or with many?"

It was a difficult question to answer honestly. I care for neither virgins nor whores since, for me, to love without fucking (as one must with a virgin) and to fuck without loving (as one must with a whore) are equally and enormously woeful. If Leonor Núñez was a virgin, I reflected, she might, after being deflowered, develop such an appetite for sexual pleasure that she would be curious about other men— younger, more virile ones or even older, more experienced ones—wondering if they might please her more than I. On the other hand, if she was a woman of easy virtue, I might not be able to please her so well as some previous lover had. In either case, dissatisfaction was inevitable, and infidelity likely. What I would have wanted to discover, in all honesty, was that she was a woman of some experience, but not of very good experience, who, after a session in my bed, would be so pleased that she would never want any other man ever again. And so I lied: "Both Maria the Madonna, the Blessed Virgin, and Maria Magdalena, the abject whore, loved our Lord Jesus Christ with all their hearts. Thus I would serve either Maria with devotion." Doña Leonor Núñez de Guzmán appreciated my piety—I fucked her that very night.

When we went to Mass together the following Sunday to celebrate the summer feast of the Lactation of the Virgin, no sooner had Father Dionisio intoned the Dismissal, than she asked if she might visit my estate again "to learn more about fermentation and distillation."

I suspect that bringing Leonor Núñez to my home saddened Maria Taino-Pinzon, but Tainos are trained to hide sorrow from their lovers, no less than Castellanos learn to conceal infidelity from theirs. Although my Indian mistress knew about Doña Leonor, the lady from Sevilla seemed to believe me when I swore that, ever since arriving in Hispaniola seven years earlier, I had been without a woman, "though not without dreams that one, the perfect one, might someday come." The gentlemanly prevarication was agreeable to her: "That," she observed, "would account for the fervor of your embraces."

Because the Catholic lady seemed as startled by the sight of my penis after our first intimacy as the Taino slave girl had been comforted by it on the night I had won her from Diego Pinzon, I tried to reassure Doña Leonor, that I neither was, nor had

I ever been, either a Jew or a Moor: "As I was born on the feast day commemorating the circumcision of Our Lord Jesus Christ and his presentation at the Temple, my devout parents, as is the tradition of the aristocratic families of León, had the sacramental operation performed by a bishop of the Catholic church so that they might make an offering of my foreskin to the Blessed Virgin." Thus convinced that my penis resembled the hallowed Phallus Purus of the Son of God, she would kiss it with the same piety and nearly as much of the regularity with which she kissed the gold crucifix on her rosary.

Had I been younger, I doubt I would have consented to marry her. But I had turned thirty-five and was, although it seems ridiculous to me now at five hundred and forty, feeling the burden of aging. The gray hairs that I was discovering more and more often in the mirror aroused in me an impulse to perpetuate myself by fathering legitimate offspring.

And had I been wiser, I doubt I would have consented to marry her. Leonor Núñez was as hard-hearted as she was beautiful, as headstrong as she was cultivated, as self-righteous and demanding as my native mistress was supple and surrendering. But I imagined that marriage would dulcify the patrician lady from Sevilla. I had intimations of her capacity for tenderness only when I fucked her. If I fucked her roughly and wildly enough—"como el león" as we used to say—with sufficient ferocity and fortitude, afterward, she would sigh softly, whimper, close her eyes, and doze off with a smile on her lips. If, however, I were to make love to her gently or cardar her adoringly, right afterward she'd get out of bed, complain that all I cared about was my own pleasure, that I was drinking too much Leche de la Virgen and smoking too many bacueñas, that I wasn't strict enough with my slaves, that I hadn't yet given her the jewelry that I had promised her.

While I did not ever actually like my wife, I could not, despite myself, help desiring her, obsessively craving to subdue her, to tame her as Samson had the ferocious lion of Timnah, to conquer, convert, and take possession of her, raising my banner over her just as the Crown had done over its newfound virgin lands. This terrible need and pathetic desire was, I suppose, powerful enough to qualify as a certain kind of love. I had imagined that once she took the solemn Catholic vow to be unto me as the Church was unto Christ, she would become adoring. Several years later I hoped that maternity might accomplish what matrimony failed to do.

Although both Maria Pinzon-Taino and Canouba advised me against the marriage, I did not listen to my slaves. Love is as deaf as it is blind.

The Season of Darkness

Death was my mother. "Yo soy la Muerte," she would begin with a beguiling smile on her lips in our version of La Danza general de la muerte: "A la danza mortal *venid los nacidos todos del mundo." While it was conventional for Death to be played by a man, usually one skeletally gaunt with white paint on his face, wrapped in a black cassock and carrying a scythe, my father's idea was that Death should be a beautiful woman, robed in crimson and holding a chalice. He wanted Death to be fascinating. I was on stage, sitting at my mother's feet, as a reminder to the audience that we begin to age as soon as we're born, that the young child has already begun to die. And as that child, it was my part to ask questions:* "¿Qué se fizerieron las damas? *What has become of the ladies? What has become of their robes and scents, their dances, songs, and laughter?* ¿Qué se fizerieron las llamas de los fuegos encendidos de amadores? *And what has become of the flames of the fires lit by their lovers?" Death would then assure me that the dead were dancing still and sweetly singing in the heavens.*

Even now I try to believe it, though I know it isn't so. Now I know that "in the heavens" is only "in our memories." Only there can I still hear my mother singing Death's lies: "Este mundo es el camino para el otro . . ." *And there I hear Maria Taino-Pinzon's tobacco-fragrant voice: "Leaves behind the ever-blooming blossoms, leaves forever the sacred wellspring." I see Ysabel, my serene high sovereign, in the royal court of those heavens, majestically dancing in her gold-embroidered crimson robe so lushly trimmed with sable. Celestina dances too, more a gambol than a dance, playful and a little naughty. I behold a celestial cotillion of a thousand women pirouetting and hear a choir of them singing. But I know it isn't real. The flames of the fires that I, as their lover, once lit have been extinguished forever. The heavens are dark, chill, and silent. There is only memory, ever-fading as it is. The most difficult and woeful part of living for so very long has been having to accept the deaths of women I have loved.*

Ysabel, my queen, and Maria Taino-Pinzon, my slave, died in the same year. In the delirium of the fever that was taking the lives of so many of the few Taino who had survived the other illnesses we had imported to Hispaniola, Maria barely muttered the words, "panting, panting, breathless, breathless," mumbling over and over, "leaves it all, leaves it all," trying, it seemed, to find the melody and muster the energy to sing. Kissing her febrile cheek, I whispered "Nigo ai io nigo," and left. My wife, who was certain to be angry whenever I was late, was waiting for me to take her to Ovando's house, and I cannot endure the anger of women any more than I can suffer their sorrow. Although, unlike the Zhotee-eloq girl of her song, Maria Taino-Pinzon did not die in a lover's arms, Fray Dionisio Buil had, so he later assured me, arrived in time to perform the last rites for her.

When the news reached Hispaniola that the Catholic sovereign had passed away, I tore up the letter that was to have been dispatched to her on the next ship to Sevilla. Regularly during the ten years I had been away, I had sent her avowals that, although there was no sign or word of the old Jew, I was still searching for the waters that would keep her young forever. By questioning the natives of her Indies, giving them gifts and bribes, and using torture only as a last resort, I was, I would falsely assure her, getting closer and closer to the Fountain. Hope encouraged her to believe me. As I gazed at my lies being consumed by the flames of the distilling stove, I remembered the pearl buttons on her Oriental tunic, the fragrance of her breast, the taste of her milk, the feel of her fingertips on my stomach, the warm flow of her fountain, her confident voice ("Quoniam suavis est Amor"), and enchanting whisper ("Per omnia saecula saeculorum"). I loved her more than any woman ever.

My brother Setho, arriving in Borinquen that same year, told me that Celestina had died. "Your wife missed you, my brother—of course she did—missed you terribly. I did too. And naturally, after you had been away for several months, she yearned for the comfort of your embraces. We deliberated whether or not we should observe the custom of the leviratic marriage as ordained in Holy Scripture and practiced by our ancestors in accordance with God's commandments. It was my solemn duty to do so, Celestina argued, more for you than for her or myself. She further assured me that, because I look so much like you, she would, while in my arms, have the pleasure of imagining that you were cardarring her. Through me, she believed, you and she might be at least momentarily reunited. And so, dear brother, because of our love for you, we consummated the covenant, though secretly, of course, given our anxiety that rumors of it might have us arrested for Judaizing.

"When she played the part of Love in El Amor y el viejo, *your beautiful Celestina recited her lines so seductively that it was not surprising that courtiers in the audience would fall in love with her, and try to woo her with gifts, letters, poems, and all sorts of other demonstrations of affection.*

"One of the most ardently persistent of her suitors, a nephew of Torquemada, went so far as to write that if she refused yet another proposal for a tryst with him, he would, he swore in the name of the Madonna de la Misericordia, take his own life. We laughed over the letter, hoping he might be foolish enough to keep his promise.

"He must have been watching the house to know that I was not at home on the Friday night he climbed over the wall, broke through a window, and tried to take Celestina by force. She bit his lip, pulled his ears, scratched, kicked, and pummeled him, spitting at him and cursing him as he fled. That showed him the fire and spunk of the girls of Andalucia.

"She was arrested two days later for witchcraft and heresy, and taken to the Casa de la Penitencia. I supposed I had some power with the Crown since, after you left, your wife and I maintained our good standing as court entertainers under the Charter of Melpomene and Thalia. But, when I appealed to the queen on her behalf, Her

Majesty told me that even she could not intervene, as the trial had been ordered by Torquemada, the Grand Inquisitor himself. His nephew had given testimony that he had gone to her home on a Friday night in order to present her with a rosary blessed by his uncle as token of his admiration of her portrayal of the Virgin in our Llanto por nuestra Señora. *He had claimed that, upon arriving there, he had seen the Marrana in the window, her head covered with a shawl, lighting two white candles as is the custom of Jewish women. He had, furthermore, avowed that he had heard her reciting words in a language that he could not understand.*

"In the agony of fiendish tortures by chain and rope, water and fire, rack and pulley, hoisting and gagging, Celestina must have confessed quickly to crimes she had not committed, because she was executed only a week later in the same quemadero *where her father had been burned at the stake some twenty years before. I did not, of course, join the exultant crowd who gathered to witness the execution, but one of the actors who had worked with us reported that, before the fire was lit, she had begged the executioner to strangle her to death so that she would not have to endure the prolonged agony of the flames. 'The Inquisition,' he said, 'showed their mercy by granting her that last request.'"*

I wept over the story of the death of Celestina, devastated by thoughts of the pain undergone by flesh that I had once been so pleased to soothe. And my brother wept with me.

Setho had come to me because he was afraid to remain in Spain after the death of the queen. "I trusted that she would protect me. I knew that it was only because of her fondness for me as an actor, that I, as the brother-in-law of the heretic Celestina, had not myself been arrested, tried, and executed."

I asked Setho if he had any news of my mother. He didn't. As I had never heard that my beloved mother had died, it was not until I was well over a hundred years old that it occurred to me that surely it must have happened. I wondered if she herself had ever believed her lines about dead women singing and dancing in the heavens. She delivered them as though she did. But she was, of course, an actress.

After my father died, I stopped taking being alive for granted. Ever since then, whenever there is news that a man whom I have known is dead, that report always makes me vividly conscious of being alive: "He is already dead and gone, but I am here and still alive." I disassociate myself from the dead. On the other hand, whenever I hear that a woman whom I have loved has died, I am overwhelmed with a recognition of the hard fact that I am dying, that to be alive is to pass away: "A la danza mortal venid los nacidos todos del mundo . . ." The dead seem to be calling for me to join them, to dance with them. Whenever, over the past five hundred years, I learned that a woman I cardarred has died, I would, in memory of her, abstain from drinking the waters from the Fountain of Life for several days, sometimes even longer. I would allow myself to mourn and to age a little, cherishing the sadness that lends tenderness to love and makes so beautiful its transience.

The Winter of Despair

I shivered with the chill of time, felt the frost of age, and, although I was only forty-seven at the time, supposed it was the winter of my life. I witnessed the years on my wrinkled skin, felt them in the trembling of my hands, heard them in the slight rasp of my voice, tasted them in the staleness of my breath. I had lost a few teeth. I would wake up more and more frequently in the night to urinate and in the mornings my back ached. Reading had become difficult. At times I couldn't remember the names of people I had known for years, and women passing in the streets no longer glanced at me as they had when I was a younger man. Twenty years in the Indies had begun to wear on me. And I was dismayed by how quickly those years had passed. That Diego Colombus, the gilipoxo *son of* el gilipollasqueroxo, *had convinced the Crown to remove me as the adelantado of Borinquen and appoint him in my place disgraced me. But even worse than that public humiliation was a private one: I was becoming impotent.*

My penis taunted and mocked me just as Love had belittled the Old Man in El Amor y el viejo. *Angered whenever I was unable to fulfill what she considered my connubial duty, my wife would deride me, asking, "What kind of man are you?" One night she declared that she wished she had taken the advice of the Marquesa of the Balearic Islands and married a younger suitor, "someone like Don Diego de Guebo."*

I tried to cure myself with memory, imagining, as I lifted up her nightclothes in the dark, that my wife was Her Serene Highness Ysabel of glorious memory, or the nubile Celestina, miraculously resurrected, or even Filomena the flower girl of Lebrija, or the obliging whore at Casa Susona who had once so efficiently aroused such memorable fervor in my loins. I pretended she was Maria Taino-Pinzon who, I was certain, would have been able to heal me with tenderness if not with magic herbs from the Taino pharmacopoeia. I fantasized that she was the pretty mulatta wife of the innkeeper in Santo Domingo, or the coquettish daughter of the jailer of Salvaleón. But no matter how hard I tried to make it otherwise, Leonor Núñez de Guzmán stubbornly remained herself in bed.

Wanting to believe that my progressive malady was her fault and not, like the graying of my hair, aching in my joints, and wrinkling of my skin, a natural and inevitable sign of growing older, I considered what women I might choose to put my virility to the test. I was all too well aware that, because I was married, none of the many women who had come to the Indies to find husbands would be available to me.

My brother had told me that the buxom wife of the pug-nosed Captain Juan Ceron was so starved for pleasure and thrilled by amorous adventure that, whenever her husband went off on one of his frequent naval expeditions, she would seek out lovers quite indiscriminately. Setho had, so he divulged, enjoyed her enormously. Upon hearing one day that Captain Ceron had left Borinquen to lead a campaign against unruly Caribs on the southern islands, I asked Setho if he might introduce me to her. "I'm confident," he said, "that you'll be delighted with her exquisite sexual excesses. Don't bother trying to talk to her before you give her what she craves. She itches to get right down to business. But afterward she'll talk your head off, boasting of all the men she's had and what she's done with them. She told me that former viceroy Christopher Columbus had the smallest penis she had ever seen."

Although I was amused by the news about the Columbus penis, I was disheartened by the story, afraid that if I were to be impotent in her bed, it would become the subject of an anecdote with which she might entertain future lovers.

In my quest to test my potency with someone other than my wife, I finally resorted to going to Casa Fatima in Santo Domingo. Fatima herself no longer practiced the trade, but had, after the death of her Castilian patron, taken over management of the whorehouse. Although I had not spoken to her years before, when we were passengers together on the Santa Minga, *she had become one of my best customers, serving as she did my Leche de la Virgen at La Casa. The place was decorated in the Moorish style, with woven carpets over brightly tiled floors and plush satin cushions for lounging about in the so-called harem room where men selected a girl from a parade of lovelies. Fatima had the same number of whores as Jesus had apostles: a mestiza, two Moriscas, an African, three Tainos, a Maroon, and the rest were Castellanas— one a conquistador's widow and the other three girls who had, due to their well-earned reputations for licentious promiscuity, failed to find husbands in the Indies. After promising that none of them had syphilis, Fatima explained that she would have to inspect me for sores. Submitting to the examination, I took some comfort in the thought that as a Muhammadan she would respect my circumcision.*

The mestiza was the most beautiful. Her lips were sumptuously ruddy, her eyes large and dark, and, when she removed her blue satin robe, I noticed that there was hardly any hair on her body and that her breasts, though small, were perfectly formed. As she helped me undress, I, trying not to proceed too hastily, asked her about herself. She was from the islands of Las Once Mil Virgenes, she explained as she pulled off my right boot, and then, as the left boot slipped free in her hands, she told me her name: "Florida." All of a sudden, I realized who the girl was. Stunned, sickened, and heartbroken, I pushed her away, pulled my boots back on, shook all the money out of my purse onto her bed, and fled from Casa Fatima. I have tried for hundreds of years to forget this incident; but the harder I do so, the more painfully vivid the memory becomes.

I turned to Dr. Chanco, a gentleman more than twenty years my senior who had formerly been a court physician to Fernando. "I myself am perfectly fine and healthy, Doctor," I swore to him, "but my friend and mentor, Viceroy Nicholas de Ovando, has a terrible problem. As he is too embarrassed to visit you himself, I have come in his stead. He is—poor devil—impotent. Since he has done so much for me, I would like to repay him by finding some way for him to regain the vigor that makes my own life so worthwhile."

The physician divulged that, while he himself had never experienced the aforementioned affliction, he had been sent to the Indies by Fernando the king precisely because of it. "Because he believed that, as recorded in the accounts of Megesthanes and Onesikritos, the doctors of the Indies have in their pharmacopoeia many herbs with the power to reinvigorate a feeble phallus, the king sent me here on a secret mission to find those medicaments for him. Because I dared not return to Spain without them, I have remained here all these years. But my own personal opinion in this matter—although it is the judgment of one who has, as I've said, never suffered from the malady in question—is that there is no real cure for impotence. Nor should there be—impotence is a blessing. Thus many of our saints and the good fathers of our Holy Church have prayed for, and been divinely granted, that blessing. Impotence is God's way of allowing a man to devote himself to spiritual pursuits."

Not interested in pious endeavors myself, I wondered if, perhaps, the natives of the Indies might in fact, as King Fernando had believed, have herbs for the cure of my disability. I asked Canouba about it, assuring him that they were not for me, but for my friend, Viceroy Ovando. "True Taino men," he claimed, "never have that problem. Only Spaniards and those Tainos who become Christians have it. Christianity makes men impotent."

I had given up hope. And my hopelessness might have persisted if not for a Zhotee-eloq woman. Her name had been Liqizhotqi before she had, as one of the Indian slaves granted to me in my repartimiento, *been christened Luisa Zhotee-León. Appearing before me one day with tears in her eyes, hands together and genuflecting in the Christian manner, she told me that she had left her homeland as a young girl to marry a Taino and live with him on Hispaniola. When his tribe had been made slaves as a punishment for plotting a rebellion in Higuey, she had stayed by his side and thus come into my service. She asked for mercy and the freedom to return to her homeland in the north. That her husband had died of the same fever that had taken Maria Taino-Pinzon some years earlier moved me. Touching the woman's soft cheek with my fingertips, I consented to her request.*

Not expecting me to be so liberal, she rose and, with a radiant smile, wrapped her arms around my waist in the manner by which many Indians expressed gratitude. And then, as I watched the Zhotee-eloq woman walk away from me, down the lane and out the gate of my estate, I relished the sense of power that she, bowing down before me in supplication, had allowed me in asking me to be kind. I felt stirrings of revival. That part of me that had been so diffident began to rise up, as if trying to salute the woman farewell. Hope began to eclipse despair. Winter whispered promises of spring once more.

The Spring of Hope

Because Diego Columbus had replaced me as governor of Borinquen, I reckoned he would next try to take over my tobacco plantation. He had already claimed half my workers in a redistribution of all repartimiento Indians on the island. Life under Columbus would, I felt, be as unsatisfying economically as my life with Leonor Núñez was ungratifying erotically. And so I filed a petition with the Crown for an asiento *to explore the northern island known to the Indians as Beimini.*

Once the patent was granted, I set out, with an ever restless Juan Ceron as skipper of my caravel, from the port of San German for Aguado with everything and nothing before me. Sailing north by northwest, I came upon what I thought was an island and anchored in eight fathoms of water off its uncharted coast. As it was Easter Sunday and the hills were bright with flowers, I named the land Pascua de Florida. Hopeful that it might be well suited for cane and tobacco cultivation, I was determined to go ashore immediately.

My sailors protested, arguing that among the Taino and the Arawaks, the Zhotee-eloq of these northern islands were reputed to be the most vicious Indians in the New World. They were said to anoint their arrows with poisons so virulent that one scratch would instantaneously paralyze a man. Their marksmanship, fearlessness, and malevolence were legendary. But from what I knew of one Zhotee-eloq, the woman called Liqizhotqi, I trusted in their capacity for tenderness, and would not be dissuaded.

Old Diego Pinzon, boasting that no bow was a match for his harquebus, insisted that he would come with me, as did my captain, the adventurous Juan Ceron. Fray Sebastian de Spina, a newcomer to the Indies who had been assigned to the expedition for evangelical purposes, had convictions that the more savage an Indian was, the more he was in need of instruction in the Catholic faith. "I am not afraid," he said, "for God is always with me." Diego Buil (brother of Father Dionisio) and young Diego de Guebo were also eager to come ashore. When the former conquistador claimed to have once eaten a Carib's liver, the latter added with a laugh: "While I fucked his wife." The two of them rowed us to shore.

"Look!" Father Sebastian exclaimed: "A pelican! Pelicans are symbols of Christ's love."

As sea birds chased the crabs that scurried amidst the myriad brightly colored shells dotting the fine white sand of expansive beach, and as the saline aroma of sea gave way to heady perfumes of jasmine and lavender, we made our way up the beach and into a cypress grove, where I decided we should separate in order to further explore the terrain and determine if it was inhabited.

Father Sebastian and I marched straight ahead, away from the sea, while Ceron and Pinzon ventured off to our left, and the other two Diegos headed to the right. Beyond the cypresses there was a grassy meadow adorned with azalea and circled with gigantic palm trees. "Palms," Father Sebastian announced joyously, "are a symbol of Our Lord's arrival in Jerusalem."

Like throngs of angels over clustered clouds, golden humming birds hovered above sprays of white blossoms. Turkeys, scurrying about in the underbrush, would intermittently raise up their heads to look at us, then duck down and gobble loudly as if reporting our arrival to other, more timid, creatures. Father Sebastian pointed out an eagle circling overhead: "The eagle is the symbol of the resurrection, as we know from the Psalms—'Thy youth is renewed like the eagle's.'"

We had walked for almost an hour through the voluptuous terrain when Father Sebastian asked if we might pause to pray. "Look at these flowers! They seem to be spring lilies, symbols of the Blessed Mother of Our Lord. Let us praise the Holy Virgin, petitioning her to bless this virgin land as we claim it for her Son." He insisted that I genuflect with him, putting my hands together in a gesture of devotion as he recited, "Tú, Virgen, triumphas del triumphante, fuente y juventud perseverante . . ." and then and there he gasped. I turned and saw the arrow in his chest. And then another, and another, and another, and another—five in all, all in the region of the heart. Father Sebastian had died instantaneously, without even a moment in which to appreciate his slaughter as holy martyrdom.

About a dozen of our assailants appeared from behind the foliage, their naked bodies daubed with charcoal and vermillion, their hair adorned with tobacco leaves. They walked slowly toward me with the chilling grace of wildcats closing in on helpless prey. Suddenly they stopped, stood dead still, and silently stared at me.

Remaining on my knees, I removed my helmet and dropped it on the ground in a gesture I hoped they might interpret as one of peaceful surrender. On the chance that they might understand some of the Taino language, I assured them in that tongue that I meant no harm, that I had come ashore only because I had been so enchanted by the beauty of their island: "Guino, gui-guino!" Assuming that they had heard of the atrocities committed by my people on islands to the south, I declared that I was neither a conquistador nor a priest, that I wanted neither their gold nor their souls. "Hie qui ey ninoni—I want nothing. Eiye gueyey—Only to live."

Following behind these Indians, there was one with facial hair—a beard, long, white, and yellowed at the edges. While the others were youthful, muscular, and fit, he, as naked as the rest, appeared aged and frail. His wrinkled skin hung loose on his frame and his hands trembled. After a few terrible moments, during which I was frozen still and choked silent by the fear that I was about to be slaughtered, the old man shuffled toward me, stopped, suddenly smiled, and then spoke in the Ladino language of my childhood: "Samson ben Aryeh, my son, shalom, shalom! *Welcome to the Holy Garden of Gan Eden!"*

THREE

1513

WHEREIN PONCE DE LEÓN HAPPENS UPON THE
GARDEN OF EDEN, DISCOVERS WITHIN IT THE
FOUNTAIN OF LIFE, AND DEVISES A PLOT BY
WHICH TO KEEP IT SECRET

And here I must make protest to your Holiness not to think this conveyed lightly or rashly, for they have spread a rumor throughout all the Court that there is an island some three hundred and twenty-five leagues from Española where is found a fountain of such marvelous virtue that the waters thereof being drunk maketh old men young and sick men fit.

PIETRO MARTIRE D'ANGHIERA, Letter to Pope Leo X

If there be any truth in the rumor of your report, it is a matter of some urgency that this fountain be located by our own trusted delegates and that, in confidence and secrecy, its waters be poisoned, defiled, or in some other manner extirpated. For if mankind were to have recourse to an earthly elixir granting abiding youth and invariable salubrity, there would cease to be a necessity for our Holy Faith. Is it not on account of infirmities, aging, and mortality that men are wont to believe in Christ, Our Lord, and trust in His Church to grant them eternal life?

POPE LEO X, Letter to Pietro Martire d'Anghiera

When Mr. De Leon received me on Saturday morning, he was dressed in fawn taffeta breeches with a matching braided doublet and satin cap, smoking a cigar and still wearing dark glasses. While he read over the Caribbean chapter in the Zhotee-eloq Room of his museum, I inspected the displays of eagle-feather chaplets, strings of bacula, alligator-tooth necklaces, ornamented smoking pipes, snuffing tubes, tobacco grinders, shell gouges, drinking gourds, bows, arrows, arrowheads, quivers, and other such aboriginal artifacts. Once he had finished reading what I had written and paid me for it, he insisted that we go out into his withering garden so that he could tell his story of the discovery of the Fountain of Life while sitting in its presence.

As I followed my employer along the pathway, he reiterated both his disappointment that I hadn't rewritten chapter one yet and, at the same time, his general approbation over what I had been able to accomplish in chapter two. He was so pleased with the opening ("It was the best of times, it was the worst of times") that I considered emending the chapter to close it with "It is a far better thing I do, than I have ever done before; it is a far, far better rest I go to than I have ever known."

"I'm pleased," Mr. De Leon avowed, "with how you've worked in my having invented cigars and rum. The world should, at long last, be made aware of that fact. Above all else, it is rum, cigars, and women that have made my long, long, long life so very pleasurable to live. And thus I am proud of the fact that I came up with the idea for two of those three things. I love to drink rum before *cardar*ring a woman and to smoke a cigar afterward. That experience, beginning with a sip and ending with a puff, no matter how often it is repeated, is always sublime, even glorious, bestowing as it does a feeling of unqualified contentment with the moment. All three—rum, cigars, and women—can, of course, be dangerous; but the danger, at least for me, enhances the pleasure. Smoking is, by the way, far less hazardous to your health now than it was when I first arrived in the Indies. Back then smoking tobacco made you smell like a native, and that was dangerous because of the killer macamastin dogs that had been trained to sniff out and attack the Indians. Yes, Mr. Siegel, I do like what you've written about cigars and rum, but, to be perfectly honest with you, I think you could have made more of the fact that I also invented popcorn. It's true that the Taino and Arawak did heat kernels of corn to make them puff. But popcorn was never a feature of their diet. Rather, as you do mention, they used it decoratively, stringing bracelets, anklets, and necklaces out of it. It was I who discovered that eating popped corn could be enjoyable. Did I neglect to tell you about it yesterday? It happened quite by accident when, in the midst of *cardar*ring, I haphazardly got a mouthful of it, clustered as it was between my Taino lover's breasts, salty and moist. Still now, some five hundred years later, whenever I take a bite of popcorn, I cannot help but remember how my *cardar*ling's skin smelled and tasted, and how beautiful she looked, naked except for the strings of popcorn around her neck. It amused and bewildered Maria Taino-Pinzon that I liked to eat her ornaments. You might add that to the chapter.

"Look at it," Mr. De Leon sighed as we arrived at the dry fountain with dead leaves in its empty basin. "Not so very long ago it bubbled with the miraculous Waters of Life. Even the sound of it was soothing." Directing me to be seated on a wrought iron bench, he took his place on the rim of the marble basin and continued his critique of the previous chapter: "Now then, speaking of Maria—I'm concerned that my readers might disapprove of my behavior with her, and that they might censure me for not acknowledging the mestiza as my daughter. As the hero of the story, I don't want to come across as cold or callous. I loved Maria Taino-Pinzon, loved her more than any woman ever. And I want that to be evident in the chapter. Should it be suggested that I'm sorry, that I regret what I did? Of course, it's easy to be sorry now for things I did and didn't do hundreds of years ago, and it's as tempting to regret that I didn't marry the Taino girl and raise our daughter as it is to regret that I did marry Leonor Núñez de Guzmán and father a son by her. But, no, I don't want my autobiography to be encumbered by regrets, especially not in matters of love. And so, although it isn't completely true, let us write that never in my entire life have I had regrets. Sometimes, I've learned, you have to lie a little in order to convey a larger and more important truth. Don't you agree, Mr. Siegel? Oh, and by the way, I think it would be best if you dropped that business about the girl named Florida at Casa Fatima."

The fatigue that I was feeling from having stayed up all night was exacerbated by Florida's July heat. That I had not been able to fully stifle a yawn on the phrase "larger and more important truth," annoyed Mr. De Leon. "Are you bored by my story, Mr. Siegel?" he asked.

Insisting that, no, I was not bored, but rather just tired from having worked on his book throughout the night, I assured my employer that I was ready to pick the story up from where we had left off the day before with Rabbi Solomon ben Maimon de Luna welcoming Ponce de León to the Garden of Eden.

"Try to capture my utter astonishment," Mr. De Leon began. "The very old man didn't look a day older than he had the last time I had seen him, twenty years earlier in Sevilla. I was especially amazed, as I'm sure you can imagine, because I did not at that time believe in the existence of the Fountain of Life myself."

Mr. De Leon wanted me to make his description of the rabbi comical. "Stark naked except for the paint on his limbs and the tobacco leaves covering his head, he looked very funny indeed. Once my fear of being killed by the Indians had subsided, I couldn't help but laugh. There's something humorous—don't you think?—about the sight of a very old man's penis."

After comically describing the rabbi, I was supposed to recreate the story that the rabbi had told Ponce de León—how he had determined the location of the Garden of Eden, and how he had made his way to what is now Florida. It began with the rabbi's confession that he had lied to Juan Ponce in Spain, that he had known all along that Paradise was not in India to the east, but in a terra incognita to the west. He had been confident that he would find the Fountain of Life by sailing westward with a misguided Columbus.

As on the day when he had told me about Ponce de León's early life in Spain, Mr. De Leon once again modulated his voice and stooped over to play the part of Rabbi Solomon ben Maimon. His hands trembled and his lips quavered as he delivered the old Jew's monologue: "I knew that Colon was deluded. All reasonable men were well aware that China was at least thirty-five hundred parasangs around the globe to the west of Spain, yes, about twelve thousand miles away, three times farther than Colon imagined, and that a voyage there by a westward route would take more than three months, much longer than either supplies or the patience of a crew would last. Based on a study of geographical, astronomical, theological, and kabbalistic manuscripts, I was, however, assured that the earthly Gan Eden, and in it the Fountain of Life, was approximately twelve hundred parasangs from Sevilla, the exact distance to the west as the Himalayan town of Garudotsapura was to the east. I calculated with some certainty that the source of the river Pishon would, furthermore, be situated on the same line of latitude in the west as the source of the river Ganges was in the East. It would be in an uncharted land, a new world, a region of the earth from which we had been cut off ever since the great Flood in the time of Noah. The Garden of Eden was precisely indicated on the *mappa mundi* of the mystical cartographer Moses de León when that map was turned and read upside down. I was, furthermore, certain that the Ocean Mar [here Mr. De Leon broke character for a moment to remind me in an aside that the Ocean Mar was what we now call the Atlantic Ocean] was none other than the Erythraean Sea, described in the *Testament of Enoch* as 'a great sea, with currents swirling in all directions, keeping the descendants of Adam out of Havilah, as if with swords of fire.'

"Are you getting all of this, Mr. Siegel?" Mr. De Leon, becoming himself once more, asked. "It's very important. It explains why it makes perfect sense that this Fountain would be discovered here in Florida. I'm telling you what the rabbi told me as precisely as I remember it. And I want you to write in an arresting manner, like a detective story with clues that intrigue the reader. Listen carefully. Rabbi Solomon told me that he had gone ashore with Colon at a place that the *gilipoxo* imagined to be an island off the eastern coast of China. After claiming the land in the name of the Catholic sovereigns, Colon distributed such trifles as glass beads, buttons, little bells, and spoons to the natives, as well as sewing needles and thimbles to the prettiest of the naked women. He ceremoniously presented their cacique with a purple biretta. In return, the natives offered him kernels of popped corn and dried tobacco leaves. Showing them samples of gold, the ignominious admiral inquired with hand gestures, facial expressions, and suggestive noises, if they so happened to have any such metal on their island. Naked except for his new purple hat and the strings of popped corn around his neck, the cacique, according to Rabbi Solomon's account, delivered an animated oration, pointing, gesticulating and pantomiming to make its essential content understood. Rabbi Solomon, naked as the cacique, acted it out for me. I'll spare you, Mr. Siegel, by not recreating the act myself. But the gist of it was that, while his tribe — at least so the chieftain claimed — possessed no gold, there were islands to the southwest that were rich in the ore. The Taino natives of those islands, being friendly and mild-tempered, would, furthermore, give Colon as much of it as he might ask for. Then pointing northward, the cacique shouted, 'Qorib, Qorib!' With a substantial shift in demeanor, shaking his hands menacingly, he was warning Colon to beware of Qoribs. By biting his own arm and then smacking his lips, he insinuated that they were cannibals. He growled, snarled, gnashed his teeth, rolled his eyes, and jumped up and down: 'Haveelaq. Haveelaq. Zhotee-eloq, Qorib Zhotee-eloq. Lahat lahatqi Zhotee-qorib-iotiq Qorib Karub noko otoo!" Colon's interpreter, a Jesuit fluent in Latin, Greek, Hebrew, Aramaic, and Arabic, translated this as: 'The Zhotee-eloqian heathens of Haveelaq are the most ferociously satanic of all the Sodomitic tribes of Carib savages.'

"So, Mr. Siegel," Mr. De Leon asked, "Do you get it? Do you detect any of the clues in the cacique's warning and understand how Rabbi Solomon deciphered them?"

When I confessed that I didn't think I did, Mr. De Leon explained it in a tone that seemed at once impatient and condescending: "Haveelaq is obviously Havilah, the land identified in the first book of Moses as surrounding the Garden of Eden. The tribe the cacique had referred to as 'Qorib' are what we call the 'Caribs,' the natives of the Caribbean. The Calusa word *qorib* is *kerub* in Hebrew and *querieb* in Spanish, which is to say *cherub* in English via the medieval Latin. The Zhotee-eloq tribe of Carib Indians were obviously cherubim, the descendants of Zotiel—Zhotee-el—the fierce cherub who, according to the *Testament of Enoch*, guarded the eastern gate into Paradise. It makes perfect sense. And so it was clear to Rabbi Solomon that the Garden, and within it the Fountain of Life, would be found in the north, in the area the natives called Haveelaq, and that it would be guarded by Zhotee-eloq Indians. Now do you understand, Mr. Siegel?"

Satisfied by a feigned assurance that I did, Mr. De Leon continued the story. By giving them pieces of Spanish glass, Rabbi Solomon had in time been able to solicit the native fishermen of various tribes to paddle him by canoe northward, from island to island, up through the Bahamas and across to Florida where "he landed on a beach not far from where the Matanza Shopping Center stands today. The old Jew had continued heading north on foot until, a few days later, he encountered a Zhotee-eloq scouting party, the very same guardian warriors who would find me twenty years later. Just as I would have been slain if not for Rabbi Solomon, so he would have been killed by them if not for Elijah the prophet."

Despite my employer's previous insistence that there should be no interruptions, I couldn't restrain myself. "Wait a second," I exclaimed. "Are you asking me to write that Elijah, the prophet in the Bible, was living here in Florida?"

"Yes, that very Elijah, Elijah the Tishbite," Mr. De Leon calmly answered after pausing to light a fresh cigar. "Elijah, the adversary of the acolytes of Baal, the prophet for whom the Jews set out a cup of wine and open their doors on the Passover. Elijah had come here, just as Enoch revealed, riding upon whirlwinds in a chariot of fire, and he had been living here for thousands of years."

"No, Mr. De Leon. I'm sorry," I insisted, "but I don't think it works at all." I tried to explain Coleridge's notion of poetic faith and the willing suspension of disbelief. "Let me be perfectly honest with you—I actually like the premise of your book, and I think that readers will, for the sake of enjoying the story, willingly allow themselves to go along with that premise and pretend, as many readers do while reading, that you, as the narrator, are Ponce de León, that you discovered the Fountain of Youth, and that, through the magical power of its legendary waters, you have been alive for five hundred years."

"Five hundred and forty," he corrected me.

"Whatever," I continued. "The point is that, within the literary reality created by that primary suspension of disbelief and game of make-believe, everything that happens should make sense. By suddenly introducing the prophet Elijah into the story, you risk breaking the spell of fiction, causing your audience to lose interest and dismiss the narrative as too absurdly fantastic. No one really enjoys a story in which anything can happen. I strongly feel that we should leave Elijah out."

Clearly disgruntled by my interruption, Mr. De Leon stood and began to walk around the empty basin of his fountain. Without looking at me, he spoke: "You know, Mr. Siegel, perhaps you're not the right writer for this book. Miss Bell had suggested others, but I chose you because you had already written a few interesting things about me. And now I don't have time to find another ghostwriter."

Stopping in front of me, he looked directly and menacingly at me through the dark lenses of his glasses. "Now, listen, Mr. Siegel, I'm the author of this book. You're just the writer. I'm paying you a lot of money to do that writing, and I expect you to do a professional job. The truth is that Elijah the prophet was living here when Rabbi Solomon arrived. And he was still here when I showed up twenty years later. And I became fairly well acquainted with him over the fifty years during which I lived among the Zhotee-eloq. Those are the facts."

"But it's ridiculous," I said, and was, at the time, suspecting, no less that he, that I wasn't the right writer for this book.

"I understand that it might *sound* ridiculous," my employer snapped impatiently. "That's why—as I keep having to reiterate—I've hired you to ghostwrite my story in such a way that it does not seem ridiculous or, if it must seem so, that the ridiculous, while being ridiculous, is sufficiently engaging to inspire readers to wish it were true, or to imagine that it might at least possibly be true. What you personally do or do not believe, is inconsequential. The fact of the matter is that Elijah had been brought here to this earthly Paradise, so that he could, by the grace of the waters of the Fountain of Life, remain alive until the time came for him to announce the inauguration of the Messianic Age. And, just as described in the second book of Kings, the prophet was—believe me—an irascible man. Rabbi Solomon told me that Elijah had become all the more so after he, the rabbi, had informed him of the state of the world to the east of Eden, beyond the Erythraean Sea. It had distressed, angered, and made quite a curmudgeon of the champion of Yahweh to hear that, because of a false messiah from Nazareth, most people were no longer waiting for the true one, and that those heretics who had—to use your words, Mr. Siegel—'willingly suspended their disbelief' and accepted the false messiah, were, furthermore, tormenting and persecuting the children of Israel. Be sure to put all of that into my book, Mr. Siegel. Elijah was right here, right where I am standing now, in this very spot here by the Fountain, when Rabbi Solomon first introduced me to him. He was a bowlegged man with one crossed eye, a full white beard, long white hair, and a remarkably large nose. And by the way, you might spell Elijah with a *zh* — Elizhah — to convey the Zhotee-eloq pronunciation of it — the *j* sounded like the *s* in *illusion*.

"Now, where was I?" he asked, clearly annoyed and flustered.

"Just as you would have been slain if not for Rabbi Solomon, so he would have been killed by the Indians if not for Elijah the prophet."

"That is correct. I would have been killed by the Zhotee-eloq warriors, as were Fray Sebastian, Captain Ceron, and the three Diegos, if not for Rabbi Solomon; likewise the old Jew would have been slain by them for trespassing on their land if not for Elijah. The prophet had saved the rabbi's life in an initial hope that he might be the messiah Elijah had been expecting for some fifteen centuries."

Since my employer was now standing over me so that he could see the legal pad of paper on which I had been making notes, I wrote in large and legible letters: "Elizhah the Prophet saves rabbi. Rabbi saves Ponce."

Seating himself on the bench next to me, Mr. De Leon described how the area in which we were sitting had looked when he first arrived there in 1513. He spoke of a perennial springtime in an interminably lush Pascua de Florida. "The only birds in the Garden," he commented, "were the eagles. They chased off the other birds, just as the Zhotee-eloq chased off other human beings." He talked about the first time he had seen, heard, touched, smelled, and tasted the supernatural waters of the Fountain of Life: "Gazing into the still pool, fed by the artesian spring, I saw a reflection of an aged face. My skin was wrinkled, my hair and beard gray . . ."

Tired as I was, my eyelids would, from time to time throughout the morning, start to slowly close, and, fearing that I might fall as fast asleep as the three apostles in the Garden of Gethsemane, I struggled as best I could to keep them open. When I almost dozed off, Mr. De Leon, much to his displeasure, had had to nudge me: "Wake up, Mr. Siegel, we still have a lot of ground to cover. Let's have lunch. Hopefully that will revitalize you."

After a light meal, served by Isabel on the patio, my fatigue had become all the greater, and so it was not easy for me to make sense of all that Mr. De Leon told me that afternoon. But the basic story was that Ponce de León had, after being introduced to the prophet Elijah and the cacique and cacica of the Zhotee-eloq, been directed by Rabbi Solomon to return to his ship so that his crew wouldn't come looking for him. There the conquistador reported that Fray Sebastian, Captain Ceron, and the three Diegos had been killed and their brains, hearts, livers, and testicles had been eaten by the Zhotee-eloq, "who are even more ferocious and bloodthirsty in reality than they are by renown." He had made up an elaborate tale to explain how he had barely escaped the fate of his comrades. And then he had had to concoct a plan that would allow him to return to the Garden of Eden alone and unknown.

For the next few months, Juan Ponce de León devoted himself to establishing a reputation for the area that would discourage subsequent exploration. "The waters of this forbidding place are mephitic," he had written in the leather-bound logbook on display in the Caribbean Room, "and the land is overrun with venomous snakes, monstrous alligators, and swarming scorpions. The cannibal natives of the place are the minions of Satan. There is, furthermore, no evidence that there is either gold or any other resource of value in this vile and sinister place. What I rashly named Pascua de Florida should have been christened Muerte de Zarzal."

Sailing south and around the tip of Florida, the Spanish explorer had sought out regions, far away from Haveelaq, that, being rich in gold and inhabited by meeker Indians, were far more attractive for conquest and settlement than lands up the eastern coast.

In order to return to the Garden of Eden, Mr. De Leon explained, Ponce de León had had to disappear: "I told my wife that I was going to Castile to petition the Crown for an asiento to conquer, colonize, and Christianize the lands that I had discovered along the west coast of Florida. I assured Leonor that, although I needed to liquidate some of my properties on Higuey and Borinquen to finance the project, I would leave her more than enough money for her and my son to continue living comfortably in Puerto Rico until my return. I further promised her that, once I was governing the lands granted to me by the king, regions rich beyond belief in the purest gold, she'd be one of the wealthiest women in the Indies. Avarice encouraged her to believe it.

"Next I had to lie to my brother Setho. What I told him was that, having fallen madly in love with a Calusa maiden in Los Martires, I wanted to leave Leonor and spend the rest of my life with the native girl. I claimed I loved her more than any woman ever. It was his sentimentality that encouraged him to believe me, and his conviction that men must stick together when it comes to duping women allowed him to go along with the plot I had devised for my disappearance. Not only did the scheme appeal to the actor and lover in him, there was money in it too. 'On the day of my supposed departure for Spain,' I told Setho, 'you'll become me—Don Juan Ponce de León. It will be easy to pull off since we look so much alike and, in any case, I haven't been seen in Spain for over twenty years. As my substitute you will, as long as you follow my advice, be able to live in abundant luxury in Sevilla. Here's all you have to do. Give a box of bacueñas to King Fernando and show him how to smoke them. Once he's smoked a few, he will, I can assure you, crave more and ever more of them. To that end, you will be able to convince him to grant you the rights for the importation of tobacco. When the nobles of the court hear that the king is smoking, they'll certainly want to try it; and once they do, they too will want more. When merchants hear that courtiers are smoking, they, in turn, will be dying to try it. Soon farmers and peasants, even beggars, all of Spain, then all of Europe, and then the world, will be smoking. There is, dear Setho, I am sure of it, a fortune to be made in tobacco. And that fortune will be yours. Do, by the way, try to remember to send some money back here to Leonor and my son every once in while.'"

And so, according to Mr. De Leon's story, Setho ben Aryeh, disguised as Don Juan Ponce de León, left for Sevilla on the same day that his brother, our hero, disguised as a mercenary sailor, set out for Haveelaq via one Bahamian island after another. "I never saw my wife or brother again," Mr. León said. "And it was not until fifty years later in Puerto Rico that I discovered what happened to the man pretending to be Juan Ponce de León. My brother died my death in Cuba."

Tired as I was, it was a relief to be informed that that was the end of the story, that I could leave, return to the motel, and finally get some sleep.

Mr. Wiseman greeted me at the reception desk with an inane joke about Viagra that began with an old Jewish man in Brooklyn telling his wife that he's taking her to Florida to look for the Fountain of Youth. After politely mustering the semblance of a laugh over a punch line I don't remember, I went to my room hoping for short nap, just enough sleep to enable me to fashion the day's tales into a first-person narrative that would satisfy my employer. I wanted to be paid again.

Lying down on my bed, I skimmed through Raoul Pipote's *The Rape of Virgin America*, and couldn't help but take an interest in his version of the story of the death of Ponce de León:

He [Juan Ponce de León] returned to Spain in order to petition the Crown for a contract setting terms for the settlement of Florida that gave him sole rights to all profits from the slave trade and other hegemonic commercial enterprises there. That accomplished, he returned to the Caribbean. Uprisings of oppressed Native Americans in Los Martires, Las Once Mil Virgenes, and Puerto Rico, however, delayed his return to Florida. After the chiefs charged with instigating those uprisings had been captured, tried, and systematically executed under his command, Ponce de León set out with two caravels for the land he had discovered and now had a license to exploit. Going ashore near Sanibel Island, his party was attacked in defence by the native inhabitants, and he was wounded in the thigh by an arrow. Ponce de León died a month later in Cuba from an infection that had developed in that wound.

Until their decimation in the eighteenth century both by foreign diseases and by forced assimilation into the plantation economy that had been imposed upon them by the Spanish Crown, the Taino of Cuba, Puerto Rico, and Florida held an annual festival to celebrate the death of the conquistador who had, for so many years, profited so enormously from the oppression of indigenous peoples. This celebration allowed the oppressed an opportunity to ritually mock the figure of foreign authority, in this case Juan Ponce de León as impersonated by a Taino trickster-clown during the festivities.

I fell asleep in the midst of reading a very different account of Ponce de León's death in one of the other books I had checked out of the library. And I didn't wake up until morning. This was somewhat upsetting, since I had also hoped, in addition to writing the story of the day, to rewrite the first chapter that night so that I could collect my fee for it as well. I did, at least, make it to the Garden of Eden on time.

Isabel opened the museum door for me and escorted me back to the Zhotee-eloq Room where, once again, she asked me to wait for my employer. As she arranged the humidor, matches, ashtray, bowl of popcorn, glasses, and pitcher of punch on the table at which I was to be seated, I took the opportunity to ask questions.

"What's his real name?"

"Juan Ponce de León."

"Where's he really from?"

"Spain."

"Okay, okay. But why's he going to all this trouble, bothering to get dressed up in a costume every day just for me? I mean, I'm quite willing to work on the book without all of that. In fact, I might be able to do a better job if he'd be straight with me. What's the real story here? Why doesn't he just tell me the truth?"

"But he is telling you the truth," Isabel answered nonchalantly, and left the room before I could ask another question.

A few minutes later, Mr. De Leon arrived in yet another sixteenth-century costume. He was even more upset than I imagined he would be to hear that

I had nothing new for him to read. "Am I not paying you enough?" he asked. I apologized and tried to assure him that, now that I had slept, I'd be able to get some writing done. "I'll do yesterday's chapter tonight, as well as to-day's, and I'll try to go back over the Spanish chapter as well. I'll be caught up by tomorrow."

Without acknowledging either my apology or my promise, Mr. De Leon demanded that we get to work on Ponce de León's fifty years among the Zhotee-eloq Indians. "I do not have a chronology for you today, Mr. Siegel, because, of course, chronological time did not exist in Haveelaq. Without time, reality is, as I am sure you can imagine, quite different from the reality in which you and my readers live."

His description of the vanished Zhotee-eloq that morning had an al-most ethnographic tone. "I want my book to be educational," he had said, "as well as entertaining."

After pouring us each a glass of punch, lighting a Ponce de León Puerto Rican Maduro, and pushing the bowl of popcorn toward me, he began. "With a few exceptions, all of the more-than-a-thousand-year-old Zhotee-eloq natives appeared to be in their mid-twenties. And they remained so. They were muscular, slender, and graceful. While their complexions were some-what lighter than is typical of the natives of Florida and the Caribbean, their eyes were darker, their hair thicker, and their lips fuller. The women were the most beautiful I have ever seen in my very long life. Their manner was demure, their thighs firm, breasts full, cheeks dimpled, and their smiles were bright enough to illuminate the Garden at night.

"The Zhotee-eloq were at once both vicious and gentle. Trespassers on the land surrounding their Garden were slain with poison-tipped arrows instantly and dispassionately, without the slightest reflection or remorse, and the intruders' bodies were ceremoniously offered to the ravening alli-gators of the Pizho-on, the river known as the Pishon in Hebrew and now as the Matanza. On the other hand, no Zhotee-eloq was ever harsh, impolite, or indifferent with another. They would tenderly touch and stroke each other even in passing, just as a greeting, and nothing asked of another was ever denied.

"We lived in open circular dwellings roofed with tightly woven vines overlain with palm fronds and supported by cane poles. Each woman of the tribe was in charge of one of these homes, constructed for her by the men, and into which any of the men might be invited to sleep on mats wo-ven by a women's *qo-teeo* of mat makers. A *qo-teeo* was something like a guild or club. Other *qo-teeo*s included manioc pounders, honey gatherers, poison harvesters, pipe fashioners, body painters, bow and arrow makers, spies, and Tobacco cutters. Be sure to capitalize the *T* in Tobacco, Mr. Siegel, because Tobacco was one of the principle deities of the Zhotee-eloq.

"We painted our bodies black, red, and white with charcoal, cinnabar, and calcite, and our hair was festooned with Tobacco leaves. The women hung necklaces of bacula around their necks, what they called *zhizhee*, which is to say, raccoon penis bones. The men's necklaces were strung with alligator teeth. In addition to Tobacco leaves, the cacique, cacica, and Elizhah adorned their hair with eagle feathers, which were also used to ornament the Tree of Life.

"Our diet consisted of cassava bread, roasted batata or sweet potatoes, squash, and sea grapes. These products, like our Tobacco, were cultivated on the other side of the Pizho-on and harvested in abundance by the men of the agricultural *zho-teeo*, which was the men's equivalent of a *qo-teeo*. Other *zho-teeo* included hut builders, gold gatherers, gourd cleaners, Fire (with a capital *F*, please) keepers, Tobacco keepers, feather trimmers, and guardians. The Zhotee-eloq were rather disinterested in food. It took a few years for me to overcome my hunger for meat and craving for spices. All oral gratification in Haveelaq was derived from smoking Tobacco, drinking water from the Fountain, and licking and sucking on another's mouth or genitals. *Shoqizha*, the Zhotee-eloq word for 'delicious,' was reserved for exclamations of delight taken in those activities alone.

"Rabbi Solomon explained to me that the breath of life that, according to the Torah, God breathed into the nostrils of the primal man was Tobacco smoke, which in Zhotee-eloq was called *ruaqhee*, pronounced *ruach* in Hebrew. To inhale Tobacco smoke was for them to be inspired and most completely alive. Lovers blew it into one another, back and forth from mouth to mouth. The Tobacco plant was considered female, Fire male, and Tobacco smoke was thus understood to be the pleasurable byproduct of the union of that male and female. Each member of the tribe had a collection of smoking pipes—one for the morning, a different one for the evening, another to share with lovers, another for friends, and others as well. They were made by the pipe maker's *qo-teeo* and decorated with ore provided by the gold gatherer's *zho-teeo*."

Mr. De Leon paused both to fill our glasses and to show me seven of these small gold-encrusted pipes on display in the room. "I switched from smoking these pipes back to cigars only after the Spanish soldiers had exterminated the Zhotee-eloq."

Ignoring my attempt to interrupt him in order to ask about that extermination, Mr. De Leon continued his description of the tribe. "The cacique and cacica were responsible for upholding social traditions. While the cacique was the groom of the Fountain of Life, Tobacco, and the phoneme *Zh*, the cacica was the bride of the Tree of Life, Fire, and *Qe*. Their sexual union, as ritually performed on the nights of both the full and new moon, was understood as a ceremonial reaffirmation of the connection between the Tree and Fountain, as well as between Tobacco and Fire, and *Qe* and *Zh*.

"I do hope you're getting all of this, Mr. Siegel. This information is crucial if you are to do an acceptable job at establishing the setting in which I lived during my fifty years with the Zhotee-eloq. Do help yourself to the popcorn. And have a cigar if you wish.

"Because death in Haveelaq was only ever accidental, the result of things like alligator attacks or falls from trees, we did not bathe in the rivers, but only in pools fed by the Fountain; nor did we climb tall trees, walk along high precipices, or play any rough physical games. There were, however, archery competitions for both the men and the women, and we had a game called *eezho-ozhoo*, that was much like hide-and-seek except that only the men hid, and when found by a woman, you were obligated to smoke with her and *ozhoo-qeezh*. That was the Zhotee-eloq word for *cardar*, a verb that is, in fact, even more semantically rich and phonologically luscious than *cardar*. *Ozhoo-qeezh* was restrictively conjugated only in the present tense and always in the dual: '*ee-ozhoo-qeezh* (we two *ozhoo-qeezh*),' '*t'ozhoo-qeezh-ee* (you two *ozhoo-qeezh*),' or '*lo-ozhoo-qeezh-la* (those two *ozhoo-qeezh*).' There were no imperative, conditional, preterite, future, perfect, imperfect, nor any other tense forms. And it could take neither a direct nor an indirect object.

"In addition to playing games of *eezho-ozhoo*, we found amusement in whistling contests and competitions in which teams demonstrated their mastery of Tobacco smoking skills and styles. It was a Zhotee-eloq custom to make music by strumming bows and blowing on Tobacco pipes, and we often entertained ourselves with recitations of strings of syllables without meaning, as well as with imitations of animal sounds and movements."

De Leon explained that the Zhotee-eloq picked neither the fruit nor the flowers within the Garden proper, but only those growing on the other side of the Pizho-on. Although the vegetation in the Garden, being nourished by the Fountain, was perennially in bloom, the plants bore neither seeded fruit nor flowers with pollen. "Similarly," he elaborated, "just as the waters of the Fountain sustained and enhanced the sexual potency and vigor of men, as well as the sexual receptiveness and sensitivities of women, at the same time, in both men and women, it caused sterility and the extinction of any desire to produce offspring. The Zhotee-eloq women did not ovulate or menstruate and the men, though they ejaculated, rather eruptively and plentifully at that, produced no sperm. It makes sense, don't you think so,

Mr. Siegel? The life of a species, or some group within a species, is preserved by means of sexual reproduction. Individuals grow old and die, but, by leaving progeny behind, they contribute to the sustenance of the life and youthfulness of the collective group. For members of a group who neither age nor die, there is, of course, no need for reproduction."

Much to Mr. De Leon's chagrin, I interrupted to point out that, if there really were a Fountain of Life, following his line of reasoning, there would no longer be a need for sex at all. After once again reminding me not to interrupt him, my employer dismissed my objection with a declaration that, while sex was not needed as a means of reproduction, it was needed to bestow the great pleasure ("even greater than the pleasure derived from smoking Tobacco") that inspires people to want to stay young and live on.

"Okay," I conceded, but explained that we ought to try to make our description of the Indians consistent with the basic premise of the story: "Perhaps it would be interesting to say that, because they had no need or wish to reproduce, their sexual endeavors rarely involved genital contact and that the gender (or, for that matter, even the species) of their sexual partners was irrelevant. I'd also like to suggest that we might say that, because they did not grow old, they had no need, inclination, or impulse to love."

Blatantly aggravated by my ideas, Mr. De Leon demanded that I, "please," just listen. "What you think would be interesting to write about the Zhotee-eloq is of no consequence. What is important is to tell the truth about them, and that is what I am trying to do. And, in any case, why, Mr. Siegel, would you say that, because they did not grow old, the Zhotee-eloq would have no need, inclination, or impulse to love? On the contrary, because they did not grow old, their capacity both to love and appreciate being loved was far greater than that of those subject to illness and aging. When one of them said to another, 'I'll love you forever,' it meant substantially more than it does for people who are subject to sickness and aging.

"I want to talk about religion now," Mr. De Leon announced. "Although I have, at various times in my life, been obliged by circumstance to be both a Jew and a Christian, and I was even a Catholic priest for a few years as you'll soon learn, I have never been a pious man. The idea of God has never made much sense to me. And it's hard for me to understand why so many people believe in one or more of them. However, given the existence of the Fountain, and the fact that, because of it, I've been alive for over half a millennium, I cannot help but believe in something, some sort of power responsible for the creation of the phenomenal world, all of the first things, animate and inanimate alike, including the Garden of Eden and the Fountain of Life. But, taking into account the nature of this world and what goes on in it, it seems only obvious that, after generating the universe, that power was spent, or perhaps, like a dispassionate god, it abandoned what it had created, taking no interest in it or control over it, and most certainly not offering any revelations or any salvation to the creatures descended from those who were spawned here, right here in the Garden of Eden, at the beginning of time."

That was a preface to his explanation of the Zhotee-eloq cosmogony. After chanting a hymn in the language of that tribe, Mr. De Leon translated: "In the beginning a mist rose up in Haveelaq. In the beginning the mist condensed into our Fountain. In the beginning the Fountain turned the dust of the world into mud. In the beginning the Tree grew out of the mud. In the beginning the Tree bore the uterine fruit from which all moving and breathing things were born." Noting that the Tree was called "*Etzhayeem,* The Tree of Life," and adding that Spanish soldiers had cut it down, he then admitted he had always thought that the Zhotee-eloq mythology, though not without charm, was as frivolous as that of any religion. Like so many peoples, they had had a deluge story which, I was told, explained the creation of the eastern ocean as a barrier to keep away the people, who, because they were never satisfied with what they had, would be sure to pick the fruit and flowers of Haveelaq, and, in their insatiable thirst for immortality, drink up all its waters.

"The Zhotee-eloq worshiped the Tree and Fountain of Life, as well as Fire and Tobacco, and other minor fetishistic deities, including the eagle, scorpion, alligator, and sweet potato. Elizhah, so Rabbi Solomon informed me, had tried to convince them that there was a transcendent being, one God (Eloq) who was ultimately responsible for their existence as well as for that of the Garden, Fountain, Tree, Fire, Tobacco, and all the syllables of their language. Eloq was visible in the flight of eagles and the swimming of alligators; Eloq could be felt in the *ozhoo-qeezhing* of a lover and the sting of a scorpion; Eloq could be heard in the crackling of Fire and the bubbling of the Fountain; Eloq could, furthermore, be tasted in the waters of the Fountain and in the smoke of Tobacco. The Zhotee-eloq were amused by the prophet's simplicity.

"The Zhotee-eloq had no eschatology, or any sort of doctrine of salvation. While there were no seasonal rites (since spring was perpetual), there were ritual performances by the cacique and cacica at each new and full moon. These affirmed the proposition that, just as the moon was rejuvenated each month by the waters of a heavenly Fountain, so we were rejuvenated at the same rate by the earthly source of those supernal waters. That makes sense. Don't you think so, Mr. Siegel?"

While there was, according to Mr. De Leon's account of the tribe, no occasion for birth, puberty, or marriage rites, there was a solemn funerary ritual during which the body of the deceased was fed to the eagles in the Garden. "Death was rare and as such it was taken very seriously in Haveelaq, much more seriously than it is by us. Can you imagine how unbearably sad it must be to lose someone you have loved for hundreds, even thousands, of years? Someone you never expected to lose? Death was always accidental. And therefore always shocking. During the funeral rites for a deceased member of the tribe, the names of the all of the Zhotee-eloq who had ever died were recited as the survivors circumambulated the Tree of Life. And afterward the entire tribe would go without drinking water from the Fountain or smoking Tobacco until the next new moon.

"When the Spanish troops slaughtered the Zhotee-eloq, and chopped down the Tree of Life," Mr. De Leon sadly noted, "I was not there to perform the customary obsequies for them. I had no way to honor them. I want to do it now, finally after all these years, with your help, by writing this book, yes, by telling their story and recounting their names so that they might at last be known and remembered. Being remembered is, after all, our only possible deliverance from oblivion. Don't you agree, Mr. Siegel?"

It was time for lunch.

After we had eaten a rather bland vegetarian stew of roasted sweet potatoes and squash, served by Isabel in memory of the lost tribe of Indians, we returned to the room in which they were honored so that there I could be told about the fifty years that Juan Ponce de León had lived among them.

That life sounded rather tedious to me, so regimented and regulated, and certainly not very exciting. Nothing much seemed to ever happen between the dramatic beginning and the dramatic ending. "I'm afraid," I confessed, "that the chapter could be boring."

"Boring?" Mr. De Leon said, mocking my tone of voice. "There is, I can assure you, nothing boring about perfect and perpetual contentment. I suspect, Mr. Siegel, that you are imagining that to live for thousands of years could be boring in an effort to justify the relative brevity of your own life."

Driving back to the Zodiac in the early evening, and stopping in Eagle Springs only to pick up something for dinner, I thought about what and how I would try to write about those fifty years in a way that didn't make them sound quite as monotonous as they had to me. I guessed that it would probably please Mr. De Leon if I began the chapter with the words *"In the beginning."*

FOUR

1514–1564

WHEREIN PONCE DE LEÓN BECOMES A ZHOTEE-ELOQ INDIAN, LIVES AS ONE OF THEM IN PARADISE, AND ATTEMPTS TO SAVE THEM FROM EXTERMINATION

Until we instructed the Indios of Florida in our Holy Faith, they were so simple and ignorant as to fancy that fire and water, certain animals and birds, and even dry leaves, the smoke of which they breathe into their lungs, were divinities worthy of reverential worship by means of licentious song and lewd dance. They put credence, furthermore, in such profane nonsense as a magical wellspring of waters which they believed could effect such miracles as only the Creator of Heaven and Earth, and his Only Begotten Son, Our Lord Jesus Christ, might perform. But once shown the light of Holy Scriptures, they were wont to behold that light and by its radiance see the truth. We have the testimony of one Fray Juan Arquero regarding a tribe known as Joti Iloque [*sic*]. No sooner had our goodly priest told these hitherto hostile cannibals of the Passion of our Lord and instructed them in the doctrines of our Church, than they disavowed their savage manners and beseeched him to perform for them the sacrament of baptism that they might find salvation. . . . This tribe is now extinct.

FRAY FRANCISCO FALLOFOSA, *Noticias sacras de la Nueva España* (Reports on Religion in New Spain)

In the beginning there was no time. There was awareness of rhythmic fluctuations of solar and lunar light and darkness, but no sense of when, no feeling that days, weeks, months, or years followed one after the other, farther and farther away from a particular and irretrievable beginning, and closer and closer to an ultimate and inevitable end. Daily life in Haveelaq was eternal life, lived perpetually in the beginning. Time began only with the apprehension that it might end.

My fifty years in Paradise are remembered as a single day into which eighteen-thousand days and nights are compressed. On the eve of that day, just as the sun had set, Rabbi Solomon escorted me to the hut of Izhqee-qiqee, the cacica, sister and consort of the cacique, bride of the Tree and Fire, and the human manifestation of Tobacco, the Water, and Zh. He had told me exactly what to do, when, where, and how—everything but why. And he had taught me my first word of Zhotee-eloq: shoqizha: *"Say it, Samson ben Aryeh, my son," the rabbi instructed. "Say it when the cacica gives you a sip of the Water, and again when she breathes Tobacco smoke into your mouth. It means 'delicious.'" It was the last time he called me Samson ben Aryeh. During the initiation, I was given the name Tatuzh-utat, which means "Old Man."*

The cacica was no less a majestic queen than Ysabel, nor any less an exemplar of her faith. She was beautiful in the same way la Católica was. Theirs was the beguiling splendor of power, the fascinating beauty of a serpent or a panther. Her crotch, buttocks, nipples, and cheeks were stained crimson, her teeth black, and her arms from the elbows to the finger tips painted bright white. She wore a necklace of raccoon bacula and a wig of amber Tobacco leaves on which white circles had been drawn.

After silently undressing me and then feeding my garments to her bridegroom, Fire, Izhqee-qiqee led me to the Fountain for ablution. Meticulously she washed every part of my body with strong hands and sure fingers, cleansing me, it seemed, of time and all the sundry sicknesses that afflicted those who lived outside Haveelaq. She whispered the name "Tatuzh-utat." Then she painted my body—black my torso and limbs, white my face, and red my genitals, lips, and hands. Leading me back to the Tree, she directed me to circumambulate it three times while she intoned my new name, each time louder and louder, until several dozen of the tribe appeared, among them Rabbi Solomon, the prophet Elizhah, and a man who, by his eagle feathers, I recognized as the cacique. Each one of them pronounced my name and Zhotee-eloq words I guessed to be welcoming and congratulatory.

I was embarrassed to be naked and painted. And that embarrassment, I must confess, never completely disappeared during my fifty years with the Zhotee-eloq. But I was so pleased to harbor hopes that it might be true that I would no longer be subject to age or illness, that I endured the embarrassment of having a brightly red-painted penis.

"It's not over," Rabbi Solomon coached in Ladino: "Stay with her, Tatuzh-utat. Walk behind her wherever she goes." I followed her through the Garden, the bowers, pathways, clearings, coves, and grottos, under roosts of eagles and past beds of flow-

ers, this way and that, learning the topography of Paradise, until we arrived back at the Fountain spring where, once again, we were alone.

A drinking gourd, decorated with painted lines, zigzags, and circles—black, white, and red like those on my body—had been placed on an elevated mound by the edge of the pool where I had been washed. Holding it in both hands, the cacica sipped ceremoniously before passing it to me and gesturing for me to drink, drink more, drink all of it. "Shoqizha," I said, and the gourd became mine.

Next Izhqee-qiqee led me back to her hut and bade me enter and be seated on a mat while she prepared a gold pipe. She lit it from the brazier of the Fire that had consumed my clothes, puffed on it, and then, sitting next to me, put her mouth against mine to blow smoke into me just as Maria Taino-Pinzon had once done. "Shoqizha," I said. And then she gestured for me to suck smoke from the pipe myself and blow it into her. Easing me onto my back, she straddled me and whispered words that, even though I didn't understand them, aroused me. We exchanged breath, sigh, touch, clutch, squeeze, and ozhoo-qeezh. And when it was over, "Shoqizha" I said, and she motioned for me to leave.

That was the only time I was ever intimate with the cacica. No one except the cacique was permitted to ozhoo-qeezh with the cacica except under ritual circumstances. She was expected to devote herself entirely to her four consorts: the cacique (by uniting with him and painting his body); Fire (by keeping his brazier ever fed with dried Tobacco stalks); the Tree (by decorating his branches with eagle feathers); and Qe (by repeating that sound during union with the cacique, while tending the Fire, and while caring for the Tree). It was her duty, furthermore, to protect the Tree from female strangler figs, ravenous air plants, the persistently issuing roots of which would wrap around the trunk of their host. Embracing that god and growing to encase him, they would finally, if unchecked, suck the sap and life from him. While the cacica murmured Qe during ozhoo-qeezion with the cacique, he chanted Zh, just as he did while clearing any debris which might happen to fall into his elemental consort, the Fountain. And he did the same when, in that Fountain's principal pool, he washed the leaves of Tobacco, his botanical consort, for distribution to the tribe. In the ritual union of the cacica and cacique, the Water of Life became manifest as the fluid of her detumescence just as the Tree of Life was embodied in his erect phallus.

The cacique ratified my transformation and initiation by giving me a Tobacco pouch, a bow, and five arrows. And thus began the perpetual day. . . .

Liqizhotqi was always near me when my eyes opened. We drank the waters of the Fountain at dawn, she from my gourd, I from hers. And then, after bathing in a Fountain pool, we went to smoke with members of her sororal qo-teeo and their lovers. Tenderly we touched and stroked each member of the group. Hers was the qo-teeo of Spies, and, because of her years in the southern islands among the Zhozhote-buqo—the "Bearded Scorpions"—she was responsible for reporting specifically on them. Perhaps they were called Zhozhote-buqo *because their armor resembled the segmented exoskeletons of scorpions. Or perhaps it was simply because they were known to be venomous.*

Our second pipe of the day was smoked with my zho-teeo, *men responsible for the drying and trimming of Tobacco leaves. And then we'd go back to Liqizhotqi's but to* ozhoo-qeezh. *And then we smoked again.*

After lunch I joined the members of my zho-teeo, *first to trim Tobacco, then for archery practice, and then I went to find Liqizbotqi so that we might bathe again, splashing each other in the pool fed by our wellspring, then* ozhoo-qeezh *once more, and smoke again.*

I wasn't conscious of it in the beginning, but I had loved Liqizbotqi ever since watching her walk away from my estate in Puerto Rico. Her sadness on that day, and the way in which it gave way to joy, had allowed me to imagine that I had the power to repair the sorrows of women. Prospects of such reparation have always aroused me to love.

Although she was at least a thousand years my senior, she — with her coruscant eyes, swollen lower lip, and round dimpled cheeks — appeared, by grace of the Fountain, much younger than I. But, because she had been away from the Garden for almost ten years, Liqizbotqi looked older than the other women in Paradise, and, so it seemed, was not so attractive as they to the men. Perhaps it was not because I had been kind to her years before, but only because she had no other consort when I arrived in Haveelaq, that she was so eager to offer me Tobacco from her pipe and Water from her gourd. Since at first I spoke no Zbotee-eloq, I told her in Taino that she was beautiful, "guino," and also that I loved her, "Nigo ai io nigo." She taught me how to make that declaration in Zbotee-eloq: "A-a-zhozho qiqe-a-a."

As a Zbotee-eloq, I could drink from the Fountain as I pleased and ozhoo-qeezh *any woman who offered me Tobacco from her pipe. While I took wholehearted advantage of the first right, the only woman I ever really wanted to be with was Liqizbotqi. I loved her more than any woman ever. "Really wanted," however, is, of course, different from "desired." And I could not help but so desire others among the beautiful women of Haveelaq that, on occasion, what I desired compromised what I really wanted. In any case, by Zbotee-eloq custom it would have been impolite to ever turn down a woman's offer of her pipe.*

In the late afternoon there were games of eezho-ozhoo *in which I, along with the other men, would hide in the lush foliage of our Garden. Because we were, according to the rules of the game, obliged to smoke and* ozhoo-qeezh *with whichever woman found us, I'd cheat by telling Liqizbotqi in advance where I'd be. That she could not run straight to me without causing others to suspect our ploy meant that other women sometimes found me first. By bathing in the Fountain's pools, however, Liqizbotqi believed we washed away the touch of other lovers. . . .*

The women of Liqizhotqi's qo-teeo *teased her. Her possessive tendencies with regard to me were an ill effect, they said, of having aged in the southern islands with a Taino husband and Scorpion master. They urged her to offer her pipe to other, more youthful-looking, men.*

Before dinner it was my habit to visit Rabbi Solomon and his three consorts, then to pay my respects to Elizhah the prophet, and then to make the customary offering of freshly cut lustral Tobacco to the cacique.

In the evening, after a communal meal near the Fire, there were whistling contests and competitions in which teams demonstrated their mastery of Tobacco-smoking skills and styles. We made music by strumming bows and blowing on Tobacco pipes, and entertained one another with recitations of strings of syllables without meaning, as well as with imitations of animal sounds and movements. Liqizhotqi and I performed a parody of Scorpion lovers which amused the gathering enormously. The Zhotee-eloq never laughed; rather they gave expression to mirthful delight by smiling while making a gurgling sound and vigorously slapping their knees.

The women waited until late at night to choose a man to enter their hut for the last pipe of the day. Liqizhotqi was sure to invite me. All night I held her in my arms, dozing off, waking up again, gently meandering in and out of sleep and sweet dreams indistinguishable from sweet wakefulness, drifting for the fifty years of exquisite monotony that seem, as I recall them, no more than a single night and day. . . .

The end of the long perpetual day began one morning, just after dawn, with the sighting of the sails of Scorpion galleons and caravels. They were semaphores of the end. On that new day, time began in Haveelaq.

And then, each day, more and more often, there were more and more ships passing offshore. Soon the Spies and Guardians of Paradise were reporting landings both up and down the coast. The boats were delivering Zhozhote-buqos *armed with crossbows and harquebuses, priests armed with crosiers and crucifixes, as well as horses and macamastin killer dogs. They had come for conquest. Subsequent vessels brought mules, pigs, chickens, women, and both African and Indian slaves. It augured settlement. The Scorpions were closing in on us. "Yes," Rabbi Solomon muttered, "the end is at hand."*

The Spies gave testimony that the Scorpions had banished the gods of the Timucua, Surruque, Calusa, Tequesta, Mocama, Taino, and Orista, forbidden their dances, forced them to cut their hair, cover their breasts and loins, and labor in their fields, mines, and houses. They had given them diseases and taken their gold. Liqizhotqi returned from a scouting mission to report that, only a two-day journey away, where the river Pizho-on flows into the sea, a settlement was growing. "There are already far too many of them for us to frighten off or kill, and more arrive each day. A fort is being built out of stones around an old Timucuan longhouse. They are beginning to venture inland. What is to be done?"

Later, on the night she had made that report, we were lying still together on her mat. I thought she had fallen asleep. Still and silent, with her head resting on my chest, and my arm wrapped in somnolent embrace around her, I was dozing off when I felt the tears on my breast.

While it was not customary for either Rabbi Solomon or me, being former Zhozhote-buqo, *to be invited to council meetings, we were summoned by the cacique to the hut of the cacica to give any information or advice that might answer that question— "What is to be done?" Flight was, of course, not an option, since migrating further inland to a more safely remote location would, of course, mean leaving the Fountain. We would, we knew, soon begin to die.*

The cacica had courageously proposed that she go to the Scorpion settlement, seduce their pale cacique, and then, with him in her embrace, slit his throat.

"You're more likely to taken as his slave than as his lover," Rabbi Solomon woefully warned. "And even if you killed him, another would immediately be appointed to take his place, and his first executive imperative would be revenge." Tears slowly welled up in the old Jew's eyes, and then suddenly trickled down through the wrinkles of his cheeks into the white beard, yellowed at the edges. His hands and lips trembled more than ever. "The Christians will destroy us. That's their nature." He turned to Elizbah. "Our only hope is that Messiach will deliver us, that finally you will be called to announce him. When will that be? When will he come?"

Except for the sound of the bubbling waters of the Fountain spring, there was a gloomy silence as everyone waited for Elizbah's words. The prophet closed his eyes and put his hands over his face.

For days I had been thinking about our predicament, trying to reason like a Spaniard again. I couldn't restrain myself from speaking out. "I have an idea, a plan. It might not help, but I think it's worth a try. It's better than waiting for them to take the Garden and enslave or kill us. Listen. Please, listen to me. I'll go to their settlement disguised as a priest of their Church, I'll attempt to negotiate an asiento designating our land a Christian estate under my ecclesiastical auspices, and then I'll solicit sanction and aid from them to build a walled mission here, a protected sanctuary consisting of a church, monastery, convent, and vineyards. The Fountain will be enclosed so that only you and I—yes, you, the brothers and sisters of the Holy Order of San Hortano, and I, the founder of that order—shall have access to its waters."

That my plan would constrain the Zhotee-eloq to pretend to be Christians was almost as vexatious to the council as it was to Rabbi Solomon. But, for want of any better stratagem, they consented to let me try to save them from the Scorpion hordes.

For the first time in our fifty-year love affair, Liqizhotqi, who had, I reckoned, always considered me affectionate, now imagined, I supposed, that I was intelligent and even a little bit brave as well. Although she did not actually say so, I could hear the appraisal in her murmured sighs and moans, feel it in the ardently flexing sinews of her arms and legs, and taste it in her desperately succulent kisses after the council meeting during which I had made my proposal.

I was confident that I could play the part of a priest at least as convincingly as I had once played Christ and Solomon, both Love and the Old Man, the angel Gabriel and Lucifer, not to mention Don Juan Ponce de León. My imitation of Fray Dionisio Buil had, as I recalled, always impressed Canouba, Maria Taino-Pinzon, and Viceroy Nicholas de Ovando. I had mastered the nuances of a priest's demeanor, all the sanctimonious mannerisms and bombastic figures of speech.

Padre Sebastian's bloodstained cassock, which had been kept in the hut of the cacique for the past fifty years, was my costume. I'd explain the five arrow holes in it to the Spaniards by telling them that, as a priest of the Order of San Hortano, it was customary for me to wear a vestment punctured in five places, "to remind us of the five wounds in the flesh of Our Lord," and stained with paschal wine, "to remind us of Christ's blood, spilled for our redemption." While I was pleased enough with the costume, I was disgruntled to have to shave my beard and tonsure my scalp with a chert scraping knife. But a real actor, my father had taught me, is willing to endure any hardship for the sake of a convincing performance.

In composing my monologue, I left ample room for improvisation and theological digression. I rehearsed my lines with Rabbi Solomon and the prophet Elizhah as they escorted me out of the Garden and to the border of Haveelaq:

"I am Fray Juan Arquero, founder of the Order of San Hortano, and humble servant of our Crown and Church, of our Lord Jesus Christ and his Blessed Mother, the Ever Virgin Santa Maria. I was dispatched to this place some years ago by His Holiness, our Holy Father, Bishop of Rome, Vicar of Jesus Christ, Successor of St. Peter, Prince of all the Apostles, to secretly conduct for him a search for a legendary Fountain, the waters of which were rumored to arrest aging and provide immunity to disease. Having traversed this land, north and south, all along the coast and far inland as well, I am assured that no such Fountain exists or has ever existed, save in the body of the Blessed Virgin herself who, as the Psalms divulge, is 'the Fountain of Life in whose light we shall see the Light.' The fable of an earthly Fountain of Life is but the hopelessly hopeful fantasy of credulous souls and craven spirits, who, for lack of faith in the resurrection as offered to us by our Lord Jesus Christ, and attainable only through the intercession of the Holy Virgin, are afraid of death. My quest for that Fountain, taking me to so many places in this New World, found its culmination in a land the heathens call Haveelaq, some six leagues to the northwest, the homeland of the Zhotee-eloq. Their longstanding and widespread reputation, among Christians and Indians alike, as ferocious cannibals, has kept them isolated from the other inhabitants of Pascua de Florida. And, indeed, when I happened upon them, they were intent on taking my life and devouring my flesh, and surely would have done so had I not been able to speak their variant vernacular of

Caribo-Timucuan. I had studied all of the languages and dialects of Las Floridas so that I might, in the performance of my duty to the Supreme Pontiff of our Holy Church, question sundry native tribes about the mythic Fountain. 'I invite you to kill me and feast upon my flesh,' I announced to the archers encircling me with drawn bows, and I did indeed expect at that moment that it might be God's will that I become a martyr of our Holy Faith. 'And,' I continued calmly, 'I will rejoice in my death, confident as I am that in being slain I shall find the peace and glory of life everlasting in the world to come.' I believe that those words, articulated as they were with the self-assurance that our Faith has provided me, particularly impressed the heathens for, as I spoke, they slowly relaxed the strings of their bows. 'But before you kill me, allow me to offer you a precious gift. That you may appreciate its value, permit me to tell you a story.'

"Unnotching the arrows from their bowstrings and returning them to their quivers, the savages seated themselves on the ground around me. Everyone, everywhere in the world, wants to hear a good story. And so I told them of the Nativity of our Lord, the Adoration of the Shepherds, the coming of the Magi, the Flight into Egypt. They seemed particularly entertained by the Massacre of the Innocents. There I stopped, explaining that my throat was dry. In the words of Our Lord upon the cross, I said, 'I thirst.' And then, so that they might hear the continuation of the marvelous tale, they insisted on taking me to their village where I could drink water and eat cassava bread. After I had done so, all of the tribe, the women as well as the men, gathered to hear of the Baptism of Our Lord and of his Temptation. They listened in awe as I recited the Sermon on the Mount in their tongue. I recounted the parables of the Good Samaritan and the Prodigal Son, and told them how our Lord had turned water into wine at Cana. I described his other miracles to them as well—the loaves and fishes, the healing at the pool of Bethesda, the raising of Lazarus from the dead, and his walking upon the waters. And then, repeating that I would accept my death at their hands with gratitude and serenity once I had finished the story, I asked if they might first allow me some hours of prayer, meditation, and sleep. They readily agreed to this. In the morning, our Sabbath, I related all the details of Christ's Passion, from his entry into Jerusalem up to his Crucifixion on Golgotha. And there I stopped. I kneeled down before them and prayed in silence. 'Please, please,' they cried, 'tell us more. Tell us what happened to Jesus Christ.' And so I spoke to them of death and resurrection, of the Appearances and Ascension, and of the World Beyond: 'And, once you slay me, it is to that world that I, through his Love, shall go, body and soul resurrected to enjoy everlasting bliss in the richly flowered Garden of Paradise.'"

"How, they asked, might they too gain admission into that wonderful Garden? I answered and they were pleased. And then, as I baptized them, one by one, I witnessed their transformation from vicious savages into gentle folk, pure in heart, meek and mild as little children.

"At that very moment the Blessed Virgin in Glory suddenly appeared in the sky above us, surrounded by a radiance, and supported on the heads of cherubs. Our Lady spoke to the sound of heavenly harps: 'In memory of this triumph of truth and love, on behalf of my Son, I command thee, Fray Juan Arquero, to build for these simple souls, my newly beloved children, a walled mission and protected sanctuary consisting of a church, monastery, convent, school, and vineyards.' And then there was a great miracle: the sky turned golden, the earth seemed to tremble, and hanging from the branch of a barren tree there was a rosary of large coral beads.

"And thus, my revered Adelantado, I come, as a servant of God, in hopes that you may be inclined to help me fulfill the mandate of the Virgin Santa Maria and the will of her son, Our Lord, Jesus Christ."

After Elizbah had confessed that the soliloquy was so craftily composed and eloquently delivered that I almost had him believing the story, Rabbi Solomon suggested that I add something about the land of Haveelaq being entirely lacking in gold or any other resource which might be of any value to the Christians. I took his advice.

The theater in which I performed my spectacle was the library of the luxuriously furnished manor of Pedro Menendez de Avila, adelantado of Florida and comendador of Santa Cruz de la Zarsa. Under the authority of Philip II, he had founded the settlement he christened San Augustin de Florida.

My audience included the adelantado himself, his wife, Doña Maria de Solis, the alcalde, Geronimo Ovando (who was introduced as none other than the grandson of my old patron Viceroy Nicholas de Ovando), several elderly aldermen and their nubile brides, an unpleasantly gaunt bailiff and chief of police, two liveried Taino slaves, and one African servant. Because of his presumed familiarity with ecclesiastical rhetoric and evangelical doctrine, the attendance of Fray Francisco Fallofosa, a soft-spoken Jesuit with a flagrant facial twitch, worried me a bit.

Menendez had strong, rather taurine, features. His hair was cropped short and his full black beard made a striking contrast to the soft white lace of the ruffled collar on which it rested. In order not to be distracted during the delivery of my monologue, I tried not to look at all that was visible of Señora Menendez's full and powdered bosom above the embroidered bodice of her purple satin gown. She was, I surmised, in her late twenties, just a bit older than the Zhotee-eloq women appeared to be. Until I saw her, I had not thought about the fact that I had not, in some fifty years, touched a non-Indian woman, let alone one who was less than a thousand years old. The sight of her skin aroused memories of the nakedness of pale bodies, the feel of silken hair, the sound of impassioned Castilian whispers, the smell of Andalucian orange water on a lover's fair neck, and the taste of Valencian muscat on her cherry lips. And so I tried to keep my eyes on her husband as I recited my lines.

While I had begun the performance seated on a divan, I stood to recount my initial encounter with the Zhotee-eloq, and then, in acting out the story, I fell to my knees dramatically before them when I spoke of falling to my knees even more dramatically before the Indians. I rose, turned, paced, stopping momentarily near each member of my audience in turn as I told them what I had told the Indians about the life of Christ. Standing at the window so that the light coming through it would cast me in silhouette, with my arms spread before me and hands wide open, I said, "And thus, my revered Adelantado, I come, as a servant of God, in hopes that you may be inclined to help me fulfill the mandate of the Virgin and the will of her son, Jesus Christ, Our Lord and Savior."

Rising from his ornately carved and plushly upholstered chair, Menendez approached me, took my hand in his, and spoke. "Holy father, you are to be congratulated on your evangelical accomplishments and adulated for your part in a wondrous miracle. It would be an honor for me to assist in any way I possibly can to see that the will of the Blessed Virgin be done in Florida as it is in heaven. I shall provide permits and revenues as well as slave labor for the construction and maintenance of the mission compound." I presented the rosary of coral beads, the rosary that Queen Ysabel had given to me, to Señora Menendez, who believed it to be the string of prayer beads that had been miraculously manifested by the Virgin.

It seemed inappropriate if not unjust that the audience applauded the adelantado rather than me, but, being sufficiently pleased over the apparent success of my theatrical recital, I did not bother too much over what, in different circumstances, might have irked the thespian in me. Menendez vowed to work out the details soon. "But now let us adjourn to the dining room for a repast."

At a table grandly set with fine linens, delicate porcelain ware, and silver cutlery, we enjoyed albóndigas Fernando, boniatos de las Indias, and a salad of almonds, oranges, and watercress. Bananas and marzipan were served for desert. And with all of it, from the first course to the last, there was Riojan wine. Not having had any meat or alcohol for fifty years, it was difficult for me to restrain myself from gobbling the meatballs and gulping the wine in an unpriestly manner as Señora Menendez, sitting across the table from me, expressed her admiration for the courage and equanimity with which I had faced death at the hands of the former cannibals. After duly informing her that it was not courage but faith in Our Lord Jesus Christ that had rendered me so staunchly unafraid of death, I couldn't help but add, "and your meatballs are delicious, as are your sweet potatoes and bananas. Not to mention this nectarous wine. In our Holy Scripture, as I am sure you are well aware, the maid of Shulam, who is none other than Our Holy Church, compares to wine the kisses of her beloved, who is, of course, none other than our Lord. The kisses, she proclaims, are even sweeter than wine. Permit me, as one who has chosen a life of celibacy to better serve our Holy Church and Blessed Virgin, to invert the inspired metaphor and say that your wine is even more luscious than any kiss I might be able to imagine, save that of the Virgin, of course." I could divine by the sparkle in her eyes, flutter of their lashes, blush of her pale cheeks, and sudden flapping of her fan, that the lady genuinely appreciated compliments.

After the meal we returned to the library where Menendez served a postprandial snifter of what he called rumbullion. *When, at the first sip, I realized that it was none other than my own Leche de la Virgin, it was difficult for me to restrain from boasting that I had invented the liquor. My resolve was further challenged when offered a bacueña, which the adelantado called a* cigaro, *noting that they were becoming "all the rage in Spain. Philip II himself smokes no fewer than ten a day." Lighting mine for me as well as those for the alcalde, the bailiff, each of the two aldermen, and himself, then pausing for a sip of his rumbullion, he sat down next to me and reiterated his commitment to my cause. "Let us convene tomorrow," he said and turned to the aldermen to request that they bring other members of the cabildo, St. Augustine's town council, to that meeting which was to be held in Menendez's offices in the Castillo de San Marcos. He asked the Jesuit to bring certain clergymen, and the bailiff to prepare a roster of "black African and red Indian slaves who might be leased from their masters to build the Blessed Virgin's mission."*

As I was offered a room at the Menendez manor in which to sleep that evening, I had the opportunity, in the middle of the night, to sneak downstairs and back into the library to quaff my enormous thirst for more Leche de la Virgen. Since I had neglected to bring any tobacco with me from Haveelaq, I swiped a few bacueñas as well.

When I arrived in the dining room for breakfast, Señora Menendez was just leaving. "I'm afraid, Father," my charming hostess said, "that your scheduled meeting with the adelantado and his council will have to be postponed, for my husband was called away from St. Augustine at dawn. Report was received last night that the French fleet was caught in a storm near Fort Caroline, that their ships were wrecked, and that, as a result of that providential mishap, their forces are camped on beaches to the north. Commander Menendez has assembled our army and set out overland to engage those stranded Gallic Protestants in battle. They will likely take captive those prudent or frightened enough to surrender, and do whatever else needs to be done to insure that the French heretics do not hinder Spanish rule and the establishment of the Catholic faith in Florida. But you are, Father, welcome to stay in our home until his return. If you do consent to wait for him here, I can assure you that you will find ample diversion in our library. We have a respectable collection of theological literature."

Grateful for the open invitation to the room where the rum and cigars were kept, I went straight there for a bottle of that wonderful libation and a handful of smokes. These I took with me into the garden, where, sitting on a bench by a small ornamental fountain crowned with a quaint statue of the god Amor, I thought about what I might ask Adelantado Menendez to provide for my Holy Sanctuary. Confident that I had some degree of control over the Christian governor, I scripted the next act of my miracle play.

Later that afternoon when Señora Menendez sent her Taino slave girl to bring me from the garden to the library, I thought it premature for news of her husband's return to St. Augustine. I expressed hopes for receiving such news soon.

"I share those hopes, Father," reported the handsome lady. She was standing before me in a periwinkle day gown and a brightly flowered mantona daintily trimmed with Sevillian silk fringe. She offered me neither a glass of rum nor a cigar, nor did she even ask me to be seated. "Yes, I do," she continued with an air of urgency as she fingered the rosary I had given her. "For in my beloved husband's absence I find myself struggling with all my might to restrain myself from committing in action a sin which I cannot help but commit in thought. That is why I have summoned you, Father, so that you can relieve me of the burden of an onerous confrontation between conscience and womanhood. Will you hear my confession?"

Of course, in order to maintain the credibility of my pose as a priest, I had to consent. Genuflecting before me, she made the sign of the cross over her heart and recited, "Forgive me Father, for I have sinned. I confess to almighty God, and to you, that I have sinned through my own fault. I have sinned in my thoughts, in my desires, in my hopes, and even in my dreams just last night. I beseech the Blessed Santa Maria, Ever Virgin, all the angels and saints, and you, Father, to pray for me to our Lord Jesus Christ who suffered and died for our transgressions. Hear me, Father. Before you I now accuse myself of the mortal sin of lust. Forgive me, Father, and pray for me, for I sin right now even as I speak. Yes, I sin at this very moment, gripped as I am in the powerful clutches of an overwhelming compulsion to—oh, dare I say it? Yes, yes, I must confess for the sake of deliverance! I must. I confess to an overwhelming desire to lift up your cassock and, yes, expose your sex. Yes, your sex! Yes, yes, expose it to my curious eyes, then to my eager fingers, and then to my open lips and the tremulous tongue of a mouth that is wickedly ravenous for the divine lusciousness of your chaste manhood."

Noticing the effect of this sacramental peccavi as it became apparent beneath Fray Sebastian de Spina's old cassock, Señora Menendez, still on her knees, raised up the ecclesiastic vestment and moaned, "Te quiero."

I couldn't finish the chapter without talking with Mr. De Leon more about this scene. It was, most likely, merely because it was late in the day and almost time for me to leave, that, when he got to the climax of the story, Mr. De Leon had described Ponce de León's sexual escapade with the wife of the adelantado of Florida so laconically: "She fellated me. And then I *card-ar*red her. This is an important passage, Mr. Siegel—readers always appreciate a good sex scene—don't they? One that's well written. Sex, if things are handled nicely, is always engaging."

So the next morning, after another long night of strenuous struggle with writing, seating myself across from my employer in the Mission Room, I handed over the chapter, forewarning my employer that it wasn't quite finished. "I'm just not sure what you want out of the sex scene with Señora Menendez," I explained: "It might be described in so many different ways: pornographically, romantically, lyrically, philosophically, psychologically, comedically, even clinically—so many ways. How do you want it done?"

"Can't sex be all of those things at once?" Mr. De Leon, wearing his usual dark glasses and a long black cassock that had five holes in the chest, asked. "All of those and more? Just as in life. I can vividly remember *cardar*ring Señora Menendez four hundred and forty years ago as if it were yesterday, and it was, I can assure you, dirty, romantic, wonderful, frightening, sweet, steamy, beautiful, bestial, sublime, funny, wild, befuddling, tender, rough, and so many other things that *cardar*ring should be. You must make it, in its marvelous ineffability, all of those things."

"The problem," I persisted, "is that real life as experienced in the phenomenal world is, and must be, very different from life as it can be represented in writing and experienced in reading. I need to know what you'd like that particular sexual experience to intimate literarily about sexuality more generally and perhaps about love as well. And what does it tell us about the two characters engaged in it? Unlike in real life, everything in a book should ideally be qualified by some sort of style and conveyed in respect to rhetorical narrative conventions. Everything should have some significance, should serve some aesthetic end. Each scene should develop the plot, build the characters, or elaborate a theme. So, tell me Mr. De Leon, what do you want out of this episode?"

"You're the writer," Mr. De Leon said just as he had said, and would continue to say, so many times during our daily meetings. "What do you recommend?"

"I'm sorry, but no—I'm only the ghostwriter. I personally would never have considered writing a novel about Ponce de León. It's your idea, for better or for worse. You're the author. It is, as you yourself so often say, your book. And to do my job, I need to know what *you* want."

After pausing to cough, light a Ponce de León Maduro, and inhale a few puffs, Mr. De Leon asked what I would do with the sex scene if, on my own, I ever decided to try to write "a book about Ponce de León or, for that matter, one about Lee Siegel."

"Well, I always find sex a challenge," I confessed. "Not doing it, I mean, but writing about it. It's as hard to write about sex as it is to write about death, tough to write about it well, because it's so easy to write about it poorly. Lots can be written about sex or death that is true, and lots that's interesting, but very few things can be written about either one that are both interesting *and* true. What's so vivid, profound, real, and all-consuming when you're making love to someone, or even just remembering it, or imagining it in anticipation, runs the risk, despite all attempts at verisimilitude, of becoming trite or hackneyed, corny, bathetic, mawkish, schmaltzy, vulgar, or just plain silly on the page. It's the same with death. It's difficult to convey in words the sorrow one feels over the loss of a loved one. When it comes to sex, it's best, I think, not to be too explicit, but rather to suggest, to understate, writing just enough so that readers are prompted to remember sexual experiences of their own. The writing should blur the boundaries between their own erotic reveries and our verbal reconstruction of Ponce de León's sexual sensations. But, to be more specific and answer your question more directly, if this were, in fact, my book, if it were being written by Lee Siegel rather than Juan Ponce de León, I'd probably skip the fellatio. While, on the one hand, blowjobs can be quite effective in pornography . . ."

"Just as they can be in life," Mr. De Leon interjected, coughed, and abruptly terminated the discussion with an adamant complaint that we were wasting valuable time. Pushing the customary bowl of popcorn, box of cigars, and pitcher of iced rum punch toward me, he began to read what I had of this chapter. And then, when he got to the end, where a kneeling Señora Menendez was raising up his cassock, moaning, "Te quiero," and about to fellate him, he announced that, even though it wasn't quite done, he would, in order to encourage me to finish the chapter, pay me for the six thousand twenty-five words I had written.

After counting out the cash for me, Mr. De Leon made a few comments on my work: "I'm generally satisfied with both chapter two and with what you have of this chapter so far—but do please bring the final sex scene to me tomorrow. Also, as you go over the chapter, do try to make both Liqizhotqi and Señora Menendez more beautiful. On a positive note, I like the opening line, and am encouraged by the fact that I have not noticed too many misspellings or grammatical errors. But please, Mr. Siegel, do try to finish this chapter as soon as possible and to do something with chapters one and three. But now, let's get to work on chapter five. We don't have much time. As Rabbi Solomon once said, 'The end is at hand.'"

That evening, before attempting to write chapter five, Mr. De Leon's account of the Mission of San Hortano, I had tried to complete the current one. Starting with Señora Menendez, still on her knees and moaning "Te quiero," I experimented with different styles, sensibilities, conventions, and intentions.

In all three of my attempted pornographic dramatizations of Ponce de León's sexual encounter with the wife of the governor of Florida, fellatio was described in lurid detail (a tumid shaft, succulent glans, slithering tongue, and nibbling lips) and Señora Menendez repeatedly groaned, barked, sighed, whimpered, mumbled, and screamed the verb "fuck" (both in the second-person singular imperative and in the infinitive proceeded by the desiderative "I want," both with and without a direct object). In one of these pornographic renditions, the Taino slave girl, as rendered with "robust sweat-wet breasts" (not to mention "acorn nipples") and sexual froth oozing down "the tawny insides of her lithe thighs," participated in the sexual frolic. Like her mistress, she too reiterated ecstatic cravings with the verb "fuck," or rather "qweryika," a word that I made up while claiming that it was, according to Ponce de León, the closest Taino equivalent to "fuck," "but far more illicit and bawdy than your overused English 'fuck.'"

I had, I realized, gotten carried away. All three pornographic versions of the episode (each of them containing the word "throbbing") were, as one might well imagine, too tawdry to show to my employer or even to merit inclusion here. In any case, I deleted them, and can't remember any one of them well enough to reproduce it faithfully even if I cared to do so. After a futile attempt to describe fellatio lyrically (by turning Ponce de León's penis into a clarion flute upon which Señora Menendez played a melodious baroque fantasia), I became more philosophical about oral sex, invoking the blowjob thematically in an affirmation of elective affinities between infantile orality and postpubescent genital sexuality. I wanted fellatio to exemplify the intrinsic affiliation between the primary instinctual drive for individual self-preservation as manifest in the mouth (as thirst and hunger) and the subsequent instinctual drive for the preservation of the species as manifest in the genitals (as the male impulse to discharge sexual fluids). Psycho-philosophical discourse degenerated, however, back into pornography when, in an effort to make classical psychoanalytic concepts graphic, it seemed reasonable (at three in the morning) for the woman with a phallus in her mouth ("sucking upon it with all the engrossment and oceanic feelings of an infant at the breast") to suddenly insert fruit into her vagina. Where, I wondered, did I come up with that? Words were getting out of control. All of my blowjobs turned out to be tasteless. I had not even begun to write the story I had been told that day about Ponce de León's escapades as a Catholic priest. "No more fellatio tonight," I told myself and started over from the beginning of the ending:

Señora Menendez, still on her knees, raised up my ecclesiastical vestment and moaned: "Te quiero." And then, surrendering to her beauty no less than to her lust, longing to kiss the lips that had issued so delicious a confession, I fell to my knees, gazed into her smoldering eyes, wrapped my arms around her delicate waist, and whispered, "And I want you as well."

Aware that in succumbing too readily to her irresistible seduction, I'd risk compromising my priestly guise, I assured Señora Menendez that, according to the admittedly controversial homilies of San Hortano of Lebrija, should we proceed with what nature was so urgently bidding us to do, and that neither my monastic vows nor her matrimonial ones would be compromised, and no sin committed, on the following conditions: that, during the union for which we mutually and so pressingly longed, she not wear her wedding ring nor I my cross; that she not think of her husband nor I of my church; and that she not make any loud noises nor I spill my seed inside her. "It is perilous, according to San Hortano, to restrain desires that, if they go unfulfilled, perpetuate themselves and lead to even more sinful thoughts and iniquitous longings. Did not our Lord, in the Garden of Gethsemane, cry out, 'If it is not possible for this cup to be taken away unless I drink it, so be it'?"

"Oh, father," the adelantado's wife sighed, as she fell backward on the softly carpeted floor, lifted up the lush layers of her gown, and separated her legs in invitation. "You don't understand. I want to sin. I'm dying to sin. For only in the feeling that I am mortally sinning am I capable of experiencing any of the rapturous sensations of which I am deprived in the bed of a lawfully wedded pious husband. The more egregious, heinous, and lewd the iniquity, the more powerful, convulsive, and eruptive is my bliss. I want you, Father. Make a whore of me — a fornicatrix! Allow me the ecstatic and glorious transport of vice in your embrace, the splendid, unbridled thrill of corruption as you penetrate, debauch, and deprave me."

As the legs opened wider, the knees were bent so that the soles of the supplicant's dainty satin shoes were flat on the wool carpet. Making the sign of the cross over her loins, I recited, "If it is not possible for this cup to be taken away unless I drink it, so be it. Thy will be done."

And after it was over, I stood up to give Señora Menendez penance to pray and to perform the charitable deed of urging her husband to invest as much money as possible in the building of a mission for the Zhotee-eloq Indians in Haveelaq. It was the will of the Blessed Virgin Santa Maria. Then making the sign of the cross over her perspiring brow, I solemnly uttered my lines: "I absolve you of your sins in the name of the Father, the Son, the Holy Spirit, and the Blessed Santa Maria Soccorso. Ave Maria, gratia plena, Dominus tecum. Amen." It was a far better thing I did than I had ever done before.

The next day, Mr. De Leon was grievously disappointed to learn that, having worked so long on the above description of Ponce de León's sexual encounter with the wife of the adelantado of Spanish Florida, I had not been able to produce chapter five for him. Reading over the only words I had been able to write, he complained, "Even though I would have liked much more graphic description between 'thy will be done' and 'after it was over,' it will have to do because we're running out time, and there's so much more to be done. You've only written about a hundred years. We've got four hundred and forty to go."

When I reported the five-hundred-and-nineteen word count on the above passage so that I could be paid for it, Mr. De Leon shook his head disapprovingly: "To be perfectly honest with you, Mr. Siegel, there are, in my opinion, too many adjectives. Too often you use two, three, or even four or more words when one would suffice. Here for example, listen: 'The more egregious, heinous, and lewd the iniquity, the more powerful, convulsive, and eruptive is my bliss.' Et cetera, et cetera. 'Allow me the ecstatic and glorious transport of vice in your embrace, the splendid, unbridled thrill of corruption as you penetrate, debauch and deprave me.' Don't you think it would more effective, not to mention economical, to more succinctly write, 'The more lewd the iniquity, the more powerful the bliss. Allow me the ecstasy of vice as you corrupt me'? Or, rather than 'corrupt,' use 'penetrate,' or 'debauch,' or 'deprave'—but just one of them, not all three. Your prolix gives me the suspicion that you're putting in superfluous words just because of our dollar-per-word agreement." Counting the words he wanted expunged, he deducted twenty-two dollars from what he owed me for the passage. It wasn't a criticism of my writing I hadn't heard before.

My employer also did not conceal his substantial disapproval of what he considered my lack of productivity. "You still haven't finished chapter four, Mr. Siegel. It should end with Menendez announcing the slaughter of the Zhotee-eloq. Why haven't you written that yet? And another thing, what happened to the blowjob?"

Given all I had to do, I wasn't able to deliver my revision of the final page of this chapter for a couple more days, not until we were almost up to the nineteenth century. In the same spirit in which he had edited the first draft of the sex scene with Señora Menendez, Mr. De Leon expunged eighteen adjectives, seven nouns, three adverbs, and a verb (at a cost to me of another twenty-nine dollars) from my final draft. As edited by him, that five-hundred-and-seven-word end of chapter four read as follows:

At the sound of the hooves of the horses drawing the carriage into the courtyard, Señora Menendez rose up from the floor, straightened her gown, wiped her lips and chin with a aristocratically monogrammed Aragonese handkerchief, and picked up her rosary and painted fan from the mahogany desk upon which the Holy Scriptures prominently lay open next to a majolica vase of fragrantly fresh red roses.

The manner, at once affectionate and polite, in which she welcomed her husband, was testimony to her gentility, and that she was consulting with a priest assured the adelantado of her piety as well.

"Your presence is propitious, Father," the adelantado, in a soiled military commander's uniform, said as he unbuckled his scabbard belt, "for I have something of great importance to report to you. I am proud to announce that, as I had hoped, we found the French on the beaches near Fort Caroline. Not only had the troops been despoiled by the tempest which wrecked their ships, but a substantial number of them, having ventured inland, had been slaughtered by Indians. In this state of devastation, the commander of these troops, none other than the detestable Lutheran heretic Jean Ribaut, had no option but surrender. For the glory of our Crown and Holy Church in Florida, I ordered them—several hundred of them—executed. Before issuing that command, however, I questioned Ribaut personally. Given your description, Father, of the mildness and temerity of your Zhotee-eloq Indians, I was, to say the least, surprised to learn from him that it was none other than those natives who had killed so many of his troops. I could only conclude, again based on your testimony, that, in baptizing these savages and giving them instruction in the doctrines our Holy Catholic Faith, you had warned them of the evil ways of our Protestant competitors for the conquest and rule of the New World. Yes, I assumed that the Zhotee-eloq had acted as our allies. And so that I might congratulate and reward them for that allegiance, I sent a party of twenty men to bring their delegates for an audience with me at Fort Caroline."

The adelantado paused to remove his regimental jacket and offer me a cigar and snifter of rum before continuing his story. "I am sorry to have to report, Father, that only three of my emissaries were able to escape from the clutches of your Indians with their lives. And by their account, the Zhotee-eloq are veritable devils in the flesh. New Spain must be ruled with determination. Don't you agree, Father? Surely you do. Justice must be meted out swiftly and conclusively. And so, that night, my troops, almost five hundred of us, well armed and armored in expectation of what we had thought would be a fierce battle with the French, attacked Haveelaq. I am obliged to inform you, Father, that every one of your Zhotee-eloq Indians has been executed."

FIVE

1565–1647

WHEREIN PONCE DE LEÓN BECOMES A PRIEST
OF THE CATHOLIC CHURCH, VISITS HIS TOMB
IN PUERTO RICO, AND ESTABLISHES FLORIDA'S
MISSION OF SAN HORTANO

You are an enclosed garden, my sister, my bride, a fountain sealed,
A garden that puts forth pomegranates with all choice fruits;
You are a garden fountain, a well of water flowing fresh from Lebanon.

SHIR HA-SHIRIM (Song of Songs)

The Fountain is thus said by the Zaddikim to be the generative organ (*ra-cham*) of Shekhinah, Bride of the Holy One, His Indwelling, Divine Presence, Heavenly Queen and Earthly Garden; and the waters flowing therefrom are the emissions of the ecstasy of Her coupling (*zivvug*) with the Creator, blessed be He forever and ever. It is a thirst for these waters that draws the infant to the mother's breast, incites the young man to seek a wife, and makes the old man long for the vigor of his youth.

SHIMON BEN YOHAI, *Sefer Mekor-Hayim*
(Book of the Fountain of Life: A Midrash on the Song of Songs)

The Enclosed Garden is none other than our Holy Church wherein the Fountain is the Immaculate Heart of the Virgin, and its fresh flowing wa-

ters are naught else but Love. By Love alone can we be truly cleansed. Only
Love will quench the real thirst.

SAINT TERESA OF AVILA, *Meditaciones sobre los Cantares* (Meditations
on the Canticles)

"The opening must be seductive," Mr. De Leon had insisted. "First words
should make the reader, or the woman, want more." In an effort to satisfy
my employer, I had drafted opening line after opening line, trying to come
up with something "seductive" to get us from the ending of chapter four,
"every one of the Zhotee-eloq Indians has been executed," to the beginning
of chapter five, the adelantado's explanation of that tragic event. Nothing seemed to work. I became so desperate that I actually typed "Stately,
plump Pedro Menendez came from the stairhead, bearing a bowl of lather
on which a mirror and razor lay crossed." Promptly deleting that, and then
musing that what was good enough for Kafka ought to be good enough
for Mr. De Leon, I wrote, "As Ponce de León awoke one morning from a
troubled dream, he found himself changed in his bed into some monstrous
kind of book." No. That didn't work either.

I realized that I was wasting too much of the time for which I was so
pressed. I decided to go on, without a beginning, to the second paragraph,
to write Menendez's speech, and, once the chapter was done, I'd try again
to come up with an opening to replace this one.

*"I presume, Reverend Father, that you'll be much relieved to hear that at least no
children were slain. They must have run off. To where, however, I do not know, for
there was not a single one of them in the village when we attacked. Nor were there
any elderly savages, save two pale old men with long white beards—medicine men
or sorcerers I suppose. Other than that pair of rascals, there were only warriors,
the women among them no less fierce than the men. But they were helpless against
us. We far outnumbered them and, by attacking the village in the dead of night,
we had surprise on our side. Having warhorses and killer macamastin dogs, not to
mention firearms, crossbows, and padded leather armor, cinched our victory over
the insurgent heathens. They must have undergone some sort of satanic apostasy
in your absence, Father, for we found no evidence whatsoever of any practice or es-
pousal of our Holy Faith among them. Thus we did not feel obliged to provide them
with Christian burial. Rather we dragged their bodies to the river, wherein they were
greeted most enthusiastically by alligators.*

*"I understand, Father, that this must be very distressing to you given your as-
sumption that you had effectively Christianized these heathens. Do be assured that*

I, perhaps no less than you, pray to Our Lord that we might accomplish the pacification of the natives of Nueva España by means of the Gospel. But where the Word fails, the sword must prevail. As both a devout Christian in the service of our Holy Roman Church and a diligent military commander in fealty to our glorious Spanish Crown, I had, as I am sure you can appreciate, no choice but to make an example of the Indians of Haveelaq. Again and again unfortunate events have demonstrated that the Indian merely pretends to accept our Faith, solely out of greed for the gifts he might obtain by doing so or out of fear of the punishments he might suffer for not doing so. Only too often have we, trusting in the sincerity of their sham professions of the true Faith, let down our guard. Thus were the Jesuits slaughtered in Chesapeake last month, as were the Franciscans in Apalachee the month before, by the very Indians to whom they had most charitably given the precious sacramental gift of baptism.

"Perhaps you will suppose, Father, that, since your Zhotee-eloq are dead, there is no reason to proceed with the construction of the mission. But that is not, I can assure you, my supposition. No, I remain as dedicated as ever to making the will of the Holy Virgin manifest on earth. And as She has asked that a mission be built in Haveelaq, so it shall be done. As a man of my word, I shall, as I have staunchly vowed, use the power and authority vested in me as adelantado of Florida to provide the revenues, materials, and slave labor necessary to demonstrate our unswerving devotion to Santa Maria Amabilis. Inasmuch as I suspect that the children and elderly Zhotee-eloq who fled from their village will eventually find their way home, I would suggest that, in addition to the proposed church, monastery, convent, and vineyards, we also build a school and hospital. I shall, furthermore, provide you with new Indians to take the place of those whom you trusted to be obedient members of your proposed congregation at the mission. We are, at the moment, holding many—far too many—insubordinate Tainos, Arawaks, Caribs, and Timucuans in our overcrowded garrisons. Freedom from prison shall be offered to those among them who will make their home for a minimum of five years in Our Lady's mission, taking catechism and subsequent baptism there under your authority and at your discretion. Naturally we shall make it quite clear that any one of them who might be so rash as to accept this offer only to then take flight from the mission shall be hunted down with macamastins and duly executed.

"I know, Father, that you must be well aware that while I do, as adelantado, have the capacity to release funds, supplies, and slaves for Our Lady's project, final authorization for it rests with the cardinal of Nueva España, who is currently in residence in San Juan Bautista de Puerto Rico. I shall arrange for you an audience with His Holiness there. As it will take several days to prepare the portfolio of letters and documents necessary for that meeting, I invite you to stay here as a guest in my home until your departure. I know that would please Señora Menendez, for she

is, in her devotion to the Blessed Virgin, very enthusiastic about your evangelical endeavors. My wife, I can assure you, Father, is a zealous woman."

On each of the five mornings before my departure for Puerto Rico, I was summoned to the library of the manor by Señora Menendez the moment she heard the sound of the hooves of the horse that took her husband to St. Augustine's Castillo de San Marcos. So eager was she to have her confessions heard, that each time I arrived she was already on her knees. Adelantado Menendez's wife was, as he had testified, a zealous woman.

Each time, after the rite had been performed, I would stand up, lower my cassock, make the sign of the cross over her succulent lips and flocculent mound of Venus, absolve her of her sins in the name of the Father, the Son, the Holy Spirit, and the Blessed Virgin, and then give her a new penance to affirm that absolution. Each of those penances required her to persuade her husband to do more for the mission that was so dear to the Immaculate Heart.

Of course I knew, as I listened to the atrocious story of the slaughter of the Zhotee-eloq innocents, that it was true; but I struggled not to feel the anguish of fully accepting the reality of the massacre. It wasn't until I was on the bulk headed for Puerto Rico that I suddenly had to gag myself with the sheets of my cot to prevent other passengers from hearing the wails of misery that were erupting from within me over the stark realization that all of my friends—everyone I had loved for so many years—were dead. Every single one. Dead. Forever.

One by one, I saw them pass before me in the darkness as if to say good-bye. I whispered their names to assure them I remembered:

Liqizhotqi—O my Liqizhotqi!—Izhqee-qiqee our cacica, Elizhah and your twelve beautiful consorts (Qizhoo-po, Poqitozh, Qiterzho, Moqo, Bizhoq, Bizhoq-ooqo, Bizhoq-ezhu, Bizhoq-qizho, Potoqo-oo, Rizhozho-qi, Niqee-ezhu, Zhoo-ooqo) and Zhoo-eeqi, Zhoto-lelo, Voviqiqi, Eetoqi-oidi, Ooroqoqo, Dizhopo-ti, O-iqi-to, Pi-poqito, Pipoqito-ooqo, Lozho-qiqa, Lozho-ooqo, Lozho-ezhu, Agaqiqo-zhi-ii, Mo-qozhizho, Butamiqi, Butamiqu-ezhu, Utamiqi, Tamqiqi, Tamzbizhi, Tamzho-zhi, Tamzbozhi-ooqo, Azhoo-oqi, Azhoo-izhu, Qitozhi, Qitozhi-qizho, Qitozhoo, Qitozhoo-ezhu, Qitozhi-eeqi, Loqizhiqi, Lazhiqizho, Miqizhotqi, Oozhoqee-qiqee, Iqizhoo-to, Zhoqipozhee, Ooqiterzho, Poqoqi, Mizhoq, Mizhoq-ooqo, Mizhoq-ezhu, Mizhoq-qizho, Lotozho-oo, Riqozho-qi, Tiqee-ezhu, Oozhoo-ooqo, Oozha-eeqi, Oozhomo-qilo, Totiqiqi, Aotozhi-oidi, Airoqozho, Pizhoqo-tito, A-aqi-to, Bibaq-ito, Nipozhoto-ooqo, Lalizho-zhiqa, Lalizho-ooqo, Lalizho-ezhu, Iqazhiqo-zhi-ii, Loqozhizho, Itutamiqi, Itutamiqu-ezhu, Itapamiqi, Olamqiqi, Natoozhi-zhi, Notamzhizho, Aqamzbozhi-oozho, Izhotoo-oqi, Izhotoo-izhu, Lizhitozhi, Tiqiozhi-qizho, Tipitozhoo, Piqizhoo-ezhu, Noqitozhi-eeqi, Liqiqozhiqi, Qilaq-iqizho, Tizhoqee-zhiqee, Atizhoo-qo, Oozotupozhee, Oqiperzho-oo, Qoqoqi-zhi,

Nizhoq, Nizhoq-qizho, Atizhoq-ooqo, Atizhoq-ezhu, Atizhoq-qizho, Alopozho-oo, Aqiqozho-qi, Bibiqee-ezhu, Izhoo-iqo, Izha-aqi, Azhoqo-qili, Ulotizhiqi, Ituzhi-oiqi, Anitoqozho-oo, Itizhoqo-itito, I-iqi-to, Nibazhito, Mitozhoqo-ooqo, Datizho-zhiqo, Dadizho-ooqo, Dadizho-ezhu, Oqazhizho-zhi-ii, Omozhizho, Imumamiqi, Inunatiqu-ezho, Atipatiqi, Udalqiqi, Upatoozhizhi, Botazhizho, Booqamzhoqi-oozho, Oozhati-oqi, Ozhoqoto-izhu, Rizhidozhi, Riqiozhi-qizho, Rititozhoo, Bizhizhoo-ezhu, Motiqito-eeqi, Piqiqoqozhiqi, Poqitaqiqizho, Rozhiqee-zhoqee, Qamizhoo-qo, A-zhoomed-ozhee, Iqitezho-oo, Qiqiqo-zho, No-zhiqi, Nozhiqi-qizho, Oqizhoq-ooqo, Oqizhoq-ezhu, Oqozhiqo-qizho, Aqotozhi-oo, Azhizhiqo-qi, Diqiqee-ezhu, Diqizhoo-iqo, Oozha-aqito, Oozhoqi-qili, Olodizhiqo, A-Opuzhi-oqiqi, Abotoqozhi-oo, Anozhoqi-itito, A-aqo-toqi, Pipazhiti-aqato, Pobazhoqi-iqo, Zhapizho-zhiqi, Ru-oqoo, Ru-ozhi, Taqidizho-ooqi, Naqizho-ezhoqi, Opapazho-zhi-piqi, Poqizhizho, Itutatiqo, Iputamiqu-ezhi, Matinatiqo, Adapaq-iqi, Latadoqizhi, Nipaqizho, Qoqamzhoqi-oozho, Qozhati-oqi, Qazhoqoto-azhu, Qizhitozhi, Qipozhi-qizho, Zhitozhoo-eqi, Zhizhipo-ezhu, Zhomiqito-eeqi, Zhaq-iqozhiqi, Pozhozhiqiqizho, Zhoqizho, Tozhito-zhiqi, Ozhipito-iqo, Zhoozhoo-ezhu, Zhiqizhiqi, Laqiqizhoti, Zhoqee-zhiqee, Atizhozho, Tupozhi, Pazhoqoqi-zhizho, Qizhotizh-ezhi, Zhopozhiqo, Zhoqibiqa-aqi, Zhoqoqi, Lotizhiqi, Tuzhoqa, Ipoqo-zho, Mizhoqi-nito, Mizhoqi-ezhu, Mizhoqi-ooqo, Mizhoqi-eeqi, Obizhilo-mimo, Obizhilo-lelo, Obizhilo-ezhu, Zhoqodati-zho, Zhoqodati-eqi-piqi, Niqezho, Qo-qilelo, Dizhoqa-zhizho, Omozhizhu, Niqiozh-ezhu, Ritiqozhoo, Tiqizhoo-ezho, Poqibozhi-eeqo, Miqiqzbozhi, Qimapiqizhi, Zhizhoqee-Thiqee, Amizhoo-qi, Oozotupo, Otoqizho-oo, Qaqiqo-zhi, Pinizhoq, Pizhoq-qinoo, Mami-ezhu, Nuniquti-oozho, Papiqili-qiqi, Patozhita-oqi, Zhizho-oozho, Oozhati-qo, Tizhi-tozhi, Didiqirozhiqi, Riditozhi, Zhomotiqito-eeqi, and, of course, Rabbi Solomon ben Maimon de Luna.

REQUIESANT IN PACEM.

A year later, once the construction of the mission was completed on the grounds where the Zhotee-eloq had lived for more than a thousand years, I declared the day on which they had been slaughtered the Feast Day of San Hortano. And on that day, each year I light a memorial pipe of tobacco in their honor and, just as they had done for those among them who had by some mishap died, I recite each of their names aloud again. As grief over their deaths receded with the years, it became more and more important to me that memory of them did not.

Upon arrival in San Juan for my meeting with the cardinal, I chose an inn for its fine name without being put off by its rather tawdry front: Posada Ponce de León. The rough settlement in which I had lived as adelantado of Borinquen had, during my fifty years of absence, become the stately city of San Juan Bautista de Puerto Rico with a colonial presidio and formidable garrisons, a monumental cathedral as well as quaint parish churches, a royal treasury and mercantile warehouses, rollicking brothels and a popular theater, comfortable inns and raucous liquor shops, stores offering merchandise from all over Europe and the New World, even one vending spices from the real Indies. In the horse-and-carriage-crowded streets of San Juan, merchants, soldiers, sailors, priests, farmers, moneylenders, hawkers, buskers, barbers, prostitutes—Spaniards, Portuguese, Dutch, Negroes, Indians, and Maroons—strolled, jostled, and rode, chatted, joked, argued, and cursed.

After dispatching the posada's liveried Negro steward to deliver the portfolio that Menendez had prepared for the cardinal, I went to purchase nonecclesiastical clothing so that I might, as I waited to hear from His Holiness, try to have some of the sort of fun I had not enjoyed for some fifty years. I needed distraction from the misery I was feeling over the loss of the Zhotee-eloq.

Assuming from my cassock that I was a priest, the haberdasher, as a gesture of devotion to the Church, gave me a discount on the clothes I claimed to be purchasing as a gift for my brother, "a fellow about my size." He assured me that my brother would cut a dashing figure in a periwinkle silk shirt worn under a decoratively stitched, purple linen waistcoat, and in sea-blue taffeta Zaraguelles breeches adorned with silver cords, a Catalonian cape, black velvet cap, and silver-buckled boots.

Changing into that swanky outfit, I was thrilled, after so many years of nakedness, to be in real clothes again. I went straightaway to a liquor shop, chosen like my lodgings for its name: Bodega Reina Ysabel. Not only was the barmaid pretty, she was frolicsome, poured rum charitably, laughed with abandon, and sang delectable songs for the amusement of her rowdy clientele:

Limpiale el rostro, y la mano
siente al Amor que se esconde
tras las rosas, que el tiempo
va violando sus colores.

My applause and praise so pleased her that, despite the bustle in her bar, she readily allowed herself to be engaged in playful conversation. "There's something about sad songs," she announced, "particularly if they are melodious, that makes me very happy."

Since at that time it was generally only priests and actors who were clean shaven, I claimed to be an actor. It gave me a certain satisfaction that this lie was actually the truth. That true lie prompted her to confide that she hoped to become an actress so that she might someday sing in a legitimate theater rather than a liquor shop. That, in turn, inspired me to elaborate my story: "I'm currently performing in a little theater in Florida, playing the part of a priest in a comedy of my own composition entitled La fuente de juventud. *I'm visiting San Juan in hopes of raising funds to produce it on a grander scale in this more civilized city. There is, by the way, a barmaid in the play, a singing barmaid in fact."*

After closing the bodega that night, the intrepid girl came to my room at the Posada Ponce de León. Greeting her dressed in my cassock, I explained that I was wearing it in case she might wish to rehearse the scene from my play wherein the priest meets the barmaid. I gave her her lines: "I must confess, O Reverend Father, that if you were not a priest, I could—though I should be ashamed to declare it—love you." And then I recited, "O fair maiden, I too have a confession to make. I am not, alas, a priest, but have merely disguised myself as one. If my true identity were to be known, dire indeed would be the consequences."

"And then what happens?" the barmaid asked expectantly.

"They embrace," I said, paused, and then posed the question: "Shall we rehearse?"

Right after I had dramatically cardarred her, she sat up in bed and asked at what point in the play she would be singing and "What song shall I sing?"

"Sing 'Limpiale el rostro.' Yes, sing it now. It's the finale of act one."

The next morning as I was waiting for the cardinal in the cathedral's Capilla of the Incarnation, inspecting the display of reliquaries, monstrances, and ornate chalices, I happened to notice the inscription carved in the marble of one of several tombs wherein were inhumed various illustrious Spanish conquerors of the New World:

JUAN PONCE DE LEÓN

1469–1521

Man of noble lineage from León, courageous soldier in Granada, diligent colonist in the New World, loving father and husband, pious champion of the Catholic Faith, gallant conqueror and just governor of Puerto Rico, valiant discoverer of Florida. He surrendered his Soul to God and his Body to the Earth in Havana

REQUIESCAT IN PACE

While it was understandable that they had the year of my death wrong, it irked me that they were four years off on my birth. Naturally intrigued by the sight of my own tomb, I was rereading my epitaph when I felt the soft touch of a hand on my shoulder. I turned to see the man who, by his scarlet mantelletta, matching biretta, and sapphire signet ring, I recognized as the cardinal.

"Juan Ponce de León," he said, and, "Yes," I answered to the name I had not heard in over fifty years.

"Yes," the cardinal commented, "I knew him. Not well, and only at the very end of his life. That was some forty years ago. As a young priest recently sent to the diocese of Cuba, I was flattered to be offered the opportunity to perform the sacrament of last rites for such a famous man. He was so delirious at the time that, as I prayed

for his soul, he just kept moaning over and over, 'I don't want to die, I don't want to die.' Hardly what you'd expect from the noble, courageous, and pious conquistador as epitomized on his tombstone. But come along to the rectory now, Father Juan, we have much to discuss. Let us allow old Juan Ponce de León to rest in peace."

"What was he doing in Cuba?" I wanted to know.

"Have you not heard the story? He had been wounded in the thigh by a heathen's arrow in Florida and was taken to Havana for treatment of what soon became a festering infection. But I really don't know very much about him. If, for any reason, you are really interested in him, you could talk to his son, Pedro Ponce de León. He lives in the residence his father built here when he was adelantado."

The cardinal was an elderly man, probably in his eighties, only twenty years or so younger than I. Because his lips quavered and his hands trembled as he spoke, he reminded me of Rabbi Solomon ben Maimon—a clean-shaven, Roman Catholic version of the old Sephardic Jew. He congratulated me for having catechized and baptized the recently slaughtered Zhotee-eloq Indians. "At least," he commented on a positive note, "they died as Christians. Now, as your endeavors may give even more Indians that opportunity, I am prepared, as the representative here in Nueva España of His Holiness, the Bishop of Rome, to endorse your proposal to establish a mission in Florida. But I do have one small favor to ask of you before granting you the Church's approbation. You see, I have in residence here a Discalced Carmelite nun by the name of Maria Fuentes. It would be greatly appreciated if you would be so good as to take her back to Florida with you and confine her in your mission convent which, being far more isolated than any of our convents here, will better serve her very particular spiritual needs. Sending her with you will, furthermore, relieve me of my apprehensions about her possible influence on the nuns of Puerto Rico."

The cardinal then told me a story that, given my impatience to visit my son, seemed all too long and drawn out: "Not very long ago in Sevilla, a young nun of the same Carmelite order was tried before a tribunal of the Inquisition and then publicly executed, burned at the stake, that punishment having been decreed upon her confession that Our Lord Jesus Christ had revealed his love for her in a holy vision in which He communed with her, 'face to face,' she declared, 'eye to eye, mouth to mouth, and all other parts of our bodies as well.' Yes, she claimed to have had carnal knowledge of our Lord, and was adamantly unrepentant about making so blasphemous an allegation. 'O llamas de amor,' she is said to have cried out as her flesh began to burn in the Plaza Santa Madre de Dios, 'O flames of love—consume me, consume me now. As I burn, my Lord, with your love, for your love, soothing is the pain of your fire, joyous the anguish of this passion.' The preceptress of this abject girl's order, a venerable prioress by the name of Teresa of Avila, wrote to me of the affair. Sor Teresa felt personally responsible for the execution of her student. She was full of remorse, believing that her written accounts of her own visions and transver-

berations might have exerted an all-too-powerful influence on the fragile-souled novice nun. Maria Fuentes had begun to manifest the same symptoms of erotic madness as those which had affected the executed sister of the order. Fearing that she too would be called before a tribunal of the Inquisition, Teresa was anxious to get the girl out of Spain, and so asked if I might give her refuge here. As I was not inclined to turn down the request of such an erudite exemplar of Catholic piety as Sor Teresa, Maria Fuentes has been here, in the Convento de la Magdalena, for the past several months. In a letter sent with the girl, Teresa felt it appropriate to confide in me that young Maria, ignorant as she is of the true nature of the monthly curse of Eve that afflicts all healthy young women, inevitably has her fits of hysteria during that period. The maiden attributes the bleeding and pain, not uncommon, I have been told, at the onset of the menstrual event, to being pierced by a golden spear. Each month the vision is the same: our Lord Jesus Christ thrusts the spear with which he himself was wounded on the cross into her womb, pulls it almost out, pushes it deeper back in, in and out, over and over again, increasing the girl's pain until, at the nadir of her rapture, that excruciation turns into beatific pleasure. Her cries of anguish fade into sobs of bliss. She fancies that the menstrual discharge on her sheets is hymenal blood, and that each month her virginity is renewed so that she can surrender to Christ as a virgin once more. In addition to vows of purity, chastity, and obedience, Teresa had judiciously insisted that Sister Maria take vows of silence and enclosure so as to insure that she not speak to anyone of her visions. But during her ecstasies, she cannot help but speak, professing aloud her love to our Lord. The other girls in the cloister hear her ravings. And that, as you can well imagine, poses significant danger. Deprived of the experience of carnal union with men, our sisters could become susceptible. Ecstasy is contagious. And so, Father Juan, I do hope you will agree to take Maria Fuentes to Florida. When not in rapture, she is, I can assure you, an obedient soul who will do your mending and washing, clean your chambers, and assiduously perform whatever other menial tasks you might demand of her."

I wanted to ask whether or not the girl was pretty, but realized that such a question coming from a priest might seem out of character. For the sake of assuring his authorization to build the Mission of San Hortano for the Holy Virgin in Florida, I promised to return for the young nun in the morning. I kissed the cardinal's sapphire signet ring and left for the home where I had lived so many years before.

Anxiously approaching the old coquina house, I was amazed by the towering cypress trees. I remembered the delicate saplings I had planted just before leaving Puerto Rico. Because Leonor disliked cypresses, I told her I was planting spruce trees. "Cypress trees are gloomy," she had said about the trees on my estate in Higuey. "They're bad luck." I wondered how many years it had taken her to realize I had lied.

As I walked through the gate, I remembered walking out of it years before. I had *turned to look back. My young son, alone on the doorstep, was waving good-bye. And I remembered that he was crying.*

He opened the door. "Yes, Father, what do you want?"

It pleased me to realize that, being dressed as a priest, I could call the gray-haired old man "my son." "I want to talk to you about your father, my son. May I come in?"

Although Pedro Ponce de León seemed far more frail than I, his face, I imagined, looked quite as mine might have looked had I not shaved my graying beard. He had my eyes.

"What do you want to know about him?" my son asked impatiently, without inviting me into my house. An answer came to me on the spur of the moment: "It is not actually I who is interested in your father, my son. It is rather our Holy Father in Rome and his college of cardinals. They've sent me to gather information in support of a popular movement to canonize your father. San Juan Ponce de León! In his conviction that your heroic father deserves veneration as a saint for his martyrdom in Florida, His Holiness seeks substantiation of some of the sundry miracles that have been attributed to him."

"Miracles?" my son asked in a scoffing tone, still not inviting me in. "What kind of miracles?"

"A very old man who had been under your father's command on his second voyage to Florida has given testimony that when your valiant father was struck in the thigh by the Indian arrow that ultimately caused his tragic death, his wound flowed not with blood, but, miraculously, with wine."

"That's ridiculous," my son grumbled, and I recalled what my father had said about lions and other animals inheriting their looks from their sires and their dispositions from their mothers.

"There are, my son, other miracles reported about your noble and gallant father. May I come in so that we might talk about the great Juan Ponce de León?"

"There's not much to talk about. I have very few memories of him. Nothing very pleasant. And certainly nothing about miracles. I do remember how angry my mother was with him because he had tried to teach me — a seven-year-old boy — to smoke cigars. And I remember how upset my mother was when he left us to go back to Spain. It took him almost seven years to return and, by that time, my poor mother had passed away. Although he did, at that time, provide me with a stipend, never did I feel that I was the beneficiary of genuine paternal affection. He doted far more on his second wife than on his only son. I don't have any more information for you. Please go now, Father. I don't mean to be rude, but I'm tired and I'm not feeling very well. And I'm busy. Good-bye."

I wouldn't let him close the door. I wanted to know if my son's life had been a good one, pleasant and rewarding, if he had been married, and if I had any grandchildren. "His Holiness insists that I also find out about you, my son."

"Am I being considered for sainthood as well?" Pedro asked, sneering and exaggerating the sarcasm in his voice to further convey his annoyance. "Listen, Father. It's time for you to go. This whole thing is nonsense. My father was a greedy and egotistical old man. I can assure you that your candidate for canonization was far more interested in finding gold for himself in Florida than in spreading the Gospel for your Lord there. And if his blood seemed like wine to anyone, it was not because of a miracle, but because he was a drunkard. Juan Ponce de León was not a religious man. And, for that matter, neither am I. So, do please go away."

"And I'm not a religious man either," I blurted out.

"What are you talking about? You're a priest!" my son exclaimed.

"No, my son, I'm not!" I protested.

"Then what, in God's name, are you doing here, dressed up like one, and telling me that the pope wants to make a saint of my father."

Because my son looked so old and seemed so feeble, I wanted to take him in my arms, hold and comfort him, tell him I loved him, and that I had thought of him so many times over the last fifty years, always hoping that all was well with him. I couldn't restrain myself from telling him the truth. "No, I am not a priest, my son. I am your father. I am Juan Ponce de León."

"What are you talking about?"

"The truth, my son, is that, much to my own astonishment, I found the Garden of Eden in Florida and discovered within it the legendary Fountain of Youth. By the grace of its miraculous waters I am essentially immune to illness and do not age. I want to take you with me to Paradise where we will share the waters and live together, father and son, for centuries to come. Come with me, my son."

"Is this some sort of prank that someone's put you up to, or are you simply a raving lunatic?"

"This is no joke, and I am not mad. I love you, my boy."

"Go away!" my elderly son angrily shouted as he slammed shut and bolted the door to my home.

I was so heartbroken by the encounter that even the clement embraces of the singing barmaid of San Juan could not comfort or console me. Before she'd come to my room at the Posada Ponce de León that evening, she had insisted that I take her to the Teatro Cristobal Colon to see Ignacio Fregona's Dio, amor, y mujer. *Later that night, as I caressed her breasts in preparation for our intimacy, she asked for my professional opinion of the drama. "There was too much* Dio *in it," I told her as my hand roamed down across her belly, "and not enough* amor." *And that, I found myself having to explain, might have contributed to my lack of sexual ardor that night.*

The cardinal handed over his nun in the morning. Because of her vow of silence, she did not respond to my greeting, and because of her vow of enclosure, a veil prevented me from seeing her face. I installed the girl in the women's cabin of our schooner, and didn't see her again until our arrival in St. Augustine. I took her with me straight to the Menendez manor and, although Señora Menendez offered to lodge the girl in her own bedroom, I insisted that the nun's vow of poverty precluded the enjoyment of such luxury and that a space in the stable would better suit her, "and there she will have the joy of contemplating the manger in which Our Lord was born." My nun's asceticism gave the Menendezes a sense of the kind of place the Mission of San Hortano would be.

Not having made confession for some ten days, Señora Menendez was eager to do so. In performing that sacrament, I was unnerved to affirm that, having been deprived of the waters of the Fountain of Life for nearly a fortnight, I was impotent. La minga floja! I wanted to return to Haveelaq immediately. Inspecting my head in a mirror, I discovered new gray hairs. I was afraid of catching a disease. I needed to drink the holy water of Paradise as soon as possible. Belying the shame I felt over the flaccidity of my phallus, I told Señora Menendez what Dr. Chanco had once said to me: "Many of our saints and the good fathers of our Holy Church have prayed for, and been divinely granted, this blessing. Impotence is God's way of encouraging a man to devote himself to spiritual pursuits. It is time for me to dedicate myself, body and soul, to the building of the Mission of San Hortano for the Blessed Virgin, Alma Redemptoris Mater, Regina Caeli.*"*

"Ave Maria," Señora Menendez repeated three times, and then piously declared "Once the Queen of Heaven's wishes have been met, I pray that you will once again deign to serve sinners like me in need of earthly absolution." I vowed that I would.

Thanks to the generosity of Adelantado Menendez, there were plenty of black African and red Indian slaves to demolish the circular wattled Indian huts in Haveelaq, and to build, with tabby, limestone, and coquina, the church, monastery, convent, and residence that I had designed for the compound of the Catholic mission. I transformed the bubbling artesian spring of Haveelaq into a marble fountain. A statue of the Virgin, donated by Señora Menendez, gazed up into the heavens from its place atop the four-spigotted column in the center of the Fountain's basin.

I realized that I needed to have water from the outside brought to my estate and into the mission. Otherwise my Indians wouldn't age, my vines wouldn't yield grapes, my hens wouldn't lay eggs, and my lambs would never become sheep. That would lead to suspicions and eventually to the discovery of the truth. Everyone in the world would hear about it. Greedy for perpetual youth—afraid of disease, old age, and death—they would invade Paradise and exhaust the waters from the Fountain of Life. It would be the end. And so, on receiving word from the adelantado that my request for resources to dig a channel to divert water from the Matanza River into reservoirs in Haveelaq had been denied, I left immediately for St. Augustine.

"Your mission is draining Florida's treasury," the adelantado insisted. "You'll have to make do with the water already at your disposal." Despite my solemn invoca-

tions to, and evocations of, the Blessed Virgin, I was unable to change Menendez's mind. I left the Castillo de San Marcos and went straight to his home, where, confident in the potency of the waters I had been drinking since last seeing her, I informed Señora Menendez that her prayers had been answered: "Through the intercession of the Our Lady of Mercy, her son, Our Lord, Jesus Christ, has, in gratitude for all you have done for the Mission, directed me here to hear your confession and bless you once more."

Although I do not consider myself in any way prudish or puritanical—and I certainly do not usually allow myself to judge the sexual proclivities of others—I was genuinely shocked by Señora Menendez's subsequent confession. Holding the rosary I had given her as she genuflected before me, she closed her eyes, made the sign of the cross, and then spoke with a voice that quavered perhaps from fear of divine retribution, perhaps from sexual arousal, or more probably from a bit of both. "Forgive me Father, for I have sinned. I confess to almighty God, and to you, Father, that I have sinned through my own fault. I have sinned in my thoughts, in my desires, and in my actions. I beseech the Blessed Virgin, all the angels and saints, and you Father, to pray for me to Our Lord Jesus Christ. Hear me, Father. In your absence, I have sinned and, without recourse to the sacrament of confession, have had to seek penance on my own. Longing for you so that I could sin and be forgiven was itself, I know, a mortal sin. I sought absolution in the only way I could—with this rosary, saying 'Ave Maria' as I rolled each precious holy bead between my fingers. As I did so I thought of the homilies of San Domingo: 'The rosary we touch is but the outward symbol of the true rosary which is within us.' O Father, I had such strong thoughts of you, yearning with all my heart for relief from the pounding of pent-up lust, that I could not help myself. O what an egregious transgression! This rosary that became manifest by a miracle in the wilderness of Florida, each coral bead of which was blessed by you, became the true rosary of which San Domingo spoke. It was within me. With all three groupings of the beads—the Sorrowful, the Joyful, and the Glorious—well inside of me, the Christ of this crucifix, hanging over the portal into my womb, promised forgiveness. Clutching Him between my fingers, I tugged and, as the beads passed out of me, as if being born from me, so excruciating was the pleasure that I could not help but moan, 'Ave Maria,' with each and every one of them."

Given the extravagance of what she considered her sins, and her unwavering faith in the ablutionary powers of her husband's money, I felt I could ask for almost anything. As penance for having masturbated with a rosary, she did everything in her considerable power over her husband to persuade him to dig a channel that would bring water from the Matanza into Haveelaq.

And so, by grace of the complementary depravity and piety of Señora Menendez, additional slaves were leased to construct the canal which supplied a reservoir on my estate with ordinary run-of-the-mill water. Any time I wanted anything for the mission, I merely made a visit to the Menendez manor in St. Augustine. By the power of the sacrament of confession, the church's tower was equipped with a sonorous bell, and the cellar in my residence was stocked with Riojan wine.

Señora Menendez's religiosity knew no bounds. During a subsequent confessional session, she beseeched me to strip her naked ("just as the Roman centurions stripped our Lord"), to bind her with the ecclesiastical cincture that belted my cassock ("just as Jesus Christ was bound"), and to flog her ("just as our Savior was scourged"). Although I found such sexual behavior beyond the usual boundaries of my own amorous repertoire, I complied with her wishes, forgave her her trespasses, and announced her penances. The absolution for the pleasure that the adelantado's wife's had derived from being tied up and whipped in imitation of Christ required a charitable donation of several of the Spanish Baroque paintings that hung on the walls of the Menendez manor.

Construction of the mission had been sufficiently completed after nine months of work to allow for the arrival of my congregation of renegade Indian neophytes. The men were transported directly from the garrisons to the mission. Though having contracted, in exchange for freedom from prison, to dedicate themselves for a minimum of five years to catechistic study and eventual baptism, they proved to have no interest whatsoever in the Catholic faith. This suited me very well, sparing me as it did of the burden of such tedious clerical activities as teaching the Scriptures, delivering sermons, and celebrating the Mass.

Along with the men, I was sent women and children, the latter being mostly orphans of Indians who had been executed for rebellions against both Spanish rule and Roman Catholic authority. The women were either the widows of those Indians or the wives of milder heathens who had been taken as slaves in punishment for a variety of misdemeanors.

My Indians were content. The food at the mission was much better than in the garrison. Albóndigas Fernando, the recipe for which I had been given by Señora Menendez, were especially popular. And labor at the mission wasn't particularly demanding, except during the grape harvest. In any case, the Indians were motivated to do that work, since they were assured they could have as much of the wine we produced as they could drink. My flock seemed to enjoy getting drunk. I permitted them to play the ball games that other missionaries in Florida had forbidden, and I put no restrictions on singing and dancing. Although the convent and monastery had been designed to house the men and women separately (with the children in the women's quarters), I encouraged my wards to sleep anywhere and next to any one they wished. I was so permissive that a few of them, believing as they did that I really was a priest, actually began to take a bit of a fancy to the Catholic faith.

The only time my Indians seemed disgruntled was when, on the occasion of a visit by the adelantado, his wife, or any representative of the Crown or Church, I insisted that they sober up and pretend to be Christians by putting on the clothes that Señora Menendez had provided for them — brown sackcloth habits for the men, and white cotton smocks for the women. They were further requested, during such visits, to try to maintain serious expressions on their faces and to occasionally put their hands together as though in prayer to recite: "Padre nuestro, perdonanos como nosotros perdonamos a nuestros deudores."

That the Mission of San Hortano was not open to the public gave the impression that it was a sanctuary for acolytes who had chosen to renounce the world in order to devote themselves wholeheartedly to meditation and prayer. This gave our institution a prestige that, in turn, inspired people who believed that charity is a fundamental Christian virtue to donate money and goods. Religion was making me rich.

Despite the easy life in the mission, my Indians tended to leave after their five contracted years. They did so in hopes of finding a new life with members of their own tribes farther inland and away from the settlements of the despotic Spaniards. This was fortunate for me, because otherwise they might have noticed that I wasn't aging. By order of the alcaide of St. Augustine, they were inevitably replaced by newly manumitted slaves, freed prisoners, and fresh widows and orphans.

Seven years or so after the founding of the Mission of San Hortano, Adelantado Pedro Menendez was called back to Spain to assemble a fleet to reinforce Spanish forces in Flanders. When I went to the fort in St. Augustine to bid him farewell, I couldn't resist the temptation of then calling on Señora Menendez so that she might make a last confession. . . .

I was sorry to see her go, not only because her penances provided me with anything I wanted for the mission, but also because I took great pleasure in forgiving her for her sins. In a way, I loved her. A little bit at least. One should not, I have come to realize after many, many years, always require that love be such a big deal.

But the great love during my life as a priest was for my nun — Sor Maria Fuentes de la Sueña. She was always barefoot and clad in a simple white floor-length habit with a matching white wimple and veil. The first time that veil was raised in my presence, I saw the perfectly beautiful face that so many artists for so many centuries have attempted to render in Annunciation portraits of the Virgin. That ineffable, shimmering beauty evades capture by chisel, brush, or pen. It vanishes the very moment that marble, paint, or words force it to be still.

So austere was the young nun's spiritual practice, and so strictly did she maintain her vows, that she drank only water and ate only bread, consenting on Sundays, however, to mix wine into her water and to dip her bread in honey in recognition of the joy of the day of the resurrection of her beloved Lord, Jesus Christ. I was eventually able to persuade her to eat cherries on feast days by showing her that the Christ child was holding a cherry in his hand in one of the paintings that Señora Menendez had donated to the mission.

Just as the cardinal had warned me in Puerto Rico, the girl would begin to suffer raptures at the onset of her monthly period. In the beginning, before the construction of the mission had begun, I had housed Maria Fuentes in the cacica's hut while I took residence in the cacique's. These were far enough apart that I had hardly heard the screams and moans that were symptomatic of her mystical transports. But I heard them all too well once my residence was complete. I had moved her into a room in it, a cell with windowless whitewashed walls adorned with a crucifix and furnished only with a cot and a table for a water pitcher, cup, candlestick, and missal.

In the middle of the night I was awakened by the terrifying cries of anguish. Any decent person would have rushed to her side. Naked and writhing in pain on her cot as a girl might on the Inquisitor's rack, she sobbed, "¡Por Dios, por Dios!" I sat next to her, struggling to restrain her flailing limbs. Once her arms and legs finally relaxed and her shrieks had become modulated into dolorous moans, I dipped a cloth in her water pitcher to wipe her febrile brow and cheeks. When her eyes closed, I assumed the spiritual seizure had passed. But then, all of a sudden, the girl sat up, threw her arms around me, and covered my face with kisses while ripping at the back of my cassock, and trying to pull me on top of her.

It took all my strength to resist and restrain her, and all of my patience to remain with her until the rapture was over. It was several hours before she fell into deep sleep. I softly stroked her cooled cheeks with my fingertips.

The next month, when it happened again, I clamped her wrists together with one hand, and used my other hand to press her down against the cot. "God, oh my God, why do you forsake me," she cried out. "Why do you refuse me? Am I so unworthy of your love? Am I so wicked and impure? Why must you deny me? If you will not give me your love, then let me die. Yes, kill me, yes, kill me, yes, yes, for to die by your hand gives greater joy than to live without being caressed by it."

It was only out of pity for the poor girl that I, unable to deny her the theophany, finally surrendered. I embraced Maria Fuentes, not because I desired any pleasure, but only to soothe her, to ease her pain and allow her the joy of intimate communion with the Word made Flesh. When, each month, I made love to her, it was, in the words of the apostle Paul, "not I, but Christ in me."

In keeping her vow of silence, Maria did not speak to me. She did, however, while in my arms, speak to her Lord: "Oh my beloved, thou art both within me and around me, showing me the perfection of love, the oneness of what I, in my ignorance and confusion, sometimes imagine to be two separate beings." How could I have denied her such bliss? Any truly compassionate and charitable man would have done the same.

The girl I had been required to bring with me from Puerto Rico had been about eighteen years old at the time. It wasn't until some fifteen years later, when she was about the same age as was her Lord when he was crucified, that my love for her became so overwhelmingly strong that, against my better judgment, I began to fill the pitcher in her cell with water from the Fountain of Life. I wanted her to stay young and healthy forever, so that I might love her endlessly. I loved her more than any woman ever.

The problem was, I soon discovered, that, once nourished by that holy water, Maria Fuentes ceased menstruating. And because she did not suffer that periodic pain, she ceased having her rapturous visions. Deprived of her monthly union with Christ, Maria Fuentes went into such a depression that she refused to mix wine into her water, dip her bread in honey, or eat the cherries that I brought to her cell.

While I wanted to stop giving her the waters of the Fountain of Life, at the same time, I felt that that would be, in a sense, to kill her—I would be subjecting her to disease and aging once more. I did not know what to do, and cannot know what I would have finally done if she herself had not solved the dilemma.

I was startled to say the least when, for the first time in her years in my residence, she appeared at the doorway to my room. And for the first time in fifteen years she spoke to me—not to Christ, not to Christ in me, but to me, Fray Juan Arquero. "I have, Father, prayed and meditated long and with all my heart, trying to divine why I have been abandoned, why Our Lord no longer finds me worthy of communion with Him. And although I am ignorant, I believe that now I understand why my Beloved no longer comes to me and what it is He wants of me. The first commandment is that we love God with all out heart and soul, and this I have done every day of my life. And in so doing, I am afraid that, in my greed for his Love, I have ignored the second commandment that my Beloved gave us during the week of his Passion: 'Love one another,' He instructed. 'Love them as I have loved you.' It is, I am certain, my Lord's will that I obey that commandment now. And so, Father, I am here to ask your permission to return to Puerto Rico so that I can ask there permission of our cardinal to return to Spain to ask my teacher, Sor Teresa, for permission to care for the sick and the aged. My Beloved is asking me to serve others as I have served him—with Love."

If any other woman I have ever loved had ever asked for permission to leave me, I might not have given it so readily. But I loved Sister Maria Fuentes so purely and chastely that I could not have denied her anything. I cannot say that about any other woman, not that any of them ever wanted to be loved in any way chastely.

I was lonely without her, desperately lonely, and in my case loneliness always fosters restlessness. Well aware as I was that amorous fraternization with any of the pretty Indian girls living in the mission would be likely to cause trouble in the community, I was hesitant to pursue any of my interests in them. I was, after all, a priest. And so, disguising myself as an actor visiting Florida from Spain, I began to make forays out into the world, leaving the mission for a few days at a time, sometimes longer, but, for fear of a relapse of impotence, never for more than ten days or so. I did this even though I knew that I aged during the times I went without water from the Fountain.

I would have liked some of the love affairs which I enjoyed on these forays to have lasted. But that would have meant giving up my guise as priest, which would have then put me in jeopardy of losing the mission, which would have meant relinquishing the Fountain, which would have been to begin to die again. When, during some of these love affairs, a woman I'd begun to care for was lying naked in bed with me, her head resting on my chest, dozing off in a languor precipitated by amorous exercise, I would sometimes imagine, especially if she were very pretty, that I could love her with all my heart, and that she would love me with all of hers, and that we could be happy together, happier than either of us had ever been or even imagined being, happy together for the rest of our lives. But then, inevitably, it would occur to me how brief that happy life would be without the Fountain. Not to mention that I'd probably become impotent again. And that realization would make me ease her head off my chest, gently slide my arm out from under her, get out of bed, quietly dress, and leave. I did, however, always remember to kiss her good-bye. I'd do so softly and gently on the forehead so as not to awaken her.

I had these adventures, on and off, for seventy years, always making sure not to return to the same town or village too soon. That was not so difficult to do, as more and more new settlements were springing up all over northeastern Florida — places like Fort Caroline, Piconata, Goshen, and Cuscowilla. One day, I remember, I was making my way to a liquor shop in Paynestown in hopes of drinking some rum with one of the fun-loving sort of girls who frequent such establishments, when an old woman, walking toward me in the gloomy black costume of widows, stopped, stared, and then suddenly lunged forward to grab my arm. "Juan," she exclaimed, "Juan Baco! Is it you? I can't believe my eyes!" Snow-white hair showed through the black lace of her mantilla. The little clump of hair sprouting from the mole on her cheek was white as well and, as she spoke, I could see that all but a few of her teeth were missing. Her strangely azure eyes, however, were as bright and alert as any young girl's. "Yes, yes it's you. Tell me it's you! Juan Baco, the actor from Lebrija. Hardly a day in the last fifty years has gone by that I haven't thought of you. When I woke in your room at the inn and discovered you had gone, I was heartbroken. I was bereft. I didn't know what to do. You left without even saying good-bye."

Although I vaguely remembered calling myself "Baco" on a foray to Paynestown many years before, I resolutely informed the old woman that I had no idea what she was talking about. I introduced myself to her as "Pedro Ponce from Puerto Rico."

She fell silent and seemed confused. "Oh, of course not. No, of course you're not Juan Baco," she finally sighed. "He'd be an old, old man by now, wouldn't he? Older than me. He's probably dead by now. Oh, I am sorry. So sorry."

So genuine did her sadness seem that, not having anything other to do than look for the companionship of a woman a lot younger than she, I took her arm in mine and offered to walk with her. "Yes, please do walk me home," she muttered. "I live alone. My sons, my husband, they're all gone."

She was so stooped over that I could barely see her face. While walking with me, she kept apologizing and attributing her mistake to old age. "It's not good, getting old," she muttered. "You get confused." As we continued our walk, she began mumbling the name to herself— "Juan Baco, Juan Baco"—over and over.

Declining an invitation for something to eat and drink, I said good-bye on her doorstep. Looking at her face as I did so, I suddenly remembered those bright and strangely azure eyes and that mole. And it reminded me of another mole, the same size, on her right breast, right next to the rosy aureole of her nipple. I remembered the feel of the papillae well enough to count them.

"Good-bye, Señorita Espinosa," I said leaning over to softly kiss her on the forehead. "Good-bye, Juana." And she did not, at least at that moment, remember that she had not told me her name that afternoon.

It was during that visit to Paynestown that a war broke out between the Christian and non-Christian Indians. It was the year of the Apalachee Rebellion and "the black vomit"—the first epidemic of yellow fever in the area. When it swept through my mission and the Indians began to die the horrible death it caused, those not afflicted ran away even if their five years were not up. I gave a little water from the Fountain of Life to those who were sick. Although I knew that, while it prevented disease, it could not cure it, I thought it might help a little. It didn't. In a matter of months, I was the sole resident of the Mission of San Hortano. With both Menendez and the cardinal long gone, I could do what I wanted with the property. And so I put it up for sale. It was purchased by a wealthy tobacco merchant from Valladolid whom I named Don Juan Gaviota de León. Being a rich business man would, I reckoned, be more entertaining than being a priest.

While telling me this story in the Mission Room, Mr. De Leon had stopped at various places in the narrative to show me things he considered relevant to it. There was a portrait of Father Juan Arquero, signed "Adele Carter '89." Mr. De Leon, though still in dark glasses, was wearing a black cassock with five holes in it that was identical to the one in the painting. There were religious objects and accouterments on display, "all of them donated to the mission by the pious Señora Menendez": a censer, cruet, Eucharistic chalice, pyx and paten, and a marble statue of the Virgin. "She stood atop the pillar in the Fountain. The design of the Fountain itself, as I constructed it over the Zhotee-eloq well and pool, was based upon the diagram in the manuscript I showed you, the *Sefer Mekor-Hayim*."

I inspected a collection of ecclesiastical vestments, including a white linen amice and an embroidered purple chasuble with a matching silk stole and maniple. "Handle it with care," Mr. De Leon said, as he handed me a frayed linen wimple which, he claimed, had once covered "the beautiful neck, cheeks, and shaven scalp of Santa Maria Fuentes. Never could I have imagined that a bald woman could be so beautiful." I was shown the clothes that he said Ponce de León had bought in Puerto Rico to wear when, while pretending to be a priest, he pretended to be an actor—the periwinkle shirt, purple waistcoat, taffeta breeches, indigo cape, and black velvet cap. Most impressive was his collection of Spanish Baroque paintings, including one of the Annunciation, another in which the Christ Child was holding a cherry, and another in which the Virgin Mary, enthroned upon cloud, was expressing milk from her right breast into the mouth of a kneeling saint, identified by Mr. De Leon as San Hortano de Lebrija.

He had, on that day, given me the list of the names of the slaughtered Zhotee-eloq Indians, "so that I wouldn't forget a single one of them." I had suggested that he consider not including them, noting that some readers might not have the patience to get through a long list of what seemed to be nonsense syllables. "That's their problem," Mr. De Leon snapped with annoyance. "The inclusion of the names is very significant. Each and every one of them must be remembered. Their names must be published."

Since I hadn't had time to write this chapter, number five, on the night after hearing the story for it, Mr. De Leon, much to his chagrin, was not able to read it until two days later, on Wednesday, July 13, when we met in the museum's Judaica Room. Although my employer was, at that time, somewhat discouraged that I didn't have an opening line for this chapter, he did, nevertheless, pay me for what I had written.

"Nine thousand and ninety-nine words," I reported, "if you count the list of two hundred and thirty-three names of the Zhotee-eloq Indians which you wrote out for me."

"Yes, of course, I'll pay you for them," he insisted. "They're the most important words in the chapter."

Pushing the bowl of popcorn and pitcher of rum punch toward me, Mr. De Leon coughed a few times to clear his throat and then voiced a few reservations about the chapter. "I'm not sure about your rendition of my relations with Señora Menendez. You've written about her in a way that makes her seem somewhat perverted. It's true that her sexual curiosities, indulgences, tastes, and compulsions were imaginative and admittedly eccentric; but she was, in fact, no more or less perverted than any of us."

Although he had mixed feelings about the rosary scene, Mr. De Leon decided to leave it in, but he demanded that I cut a frank and luridly graphic description of Father Juan's last meeting with Señora Menendez. It had come right after "Going to the fort in St. Augustine to bid [Adelantado Menendez] farewell, I couldn't resist the temptation of then calling on Señora Menendez so that she might make a last confession."

"Even though she really did insist that we do that," Mr. De Leon explained, "and even though you did an adequate job of describing it, I don't want to include it. It comes across as too lewd on the page, and indecent, even though at the time we were actually so engaged, it seemed, for all of the new pleasure it afforded us, quite wonderful, sweet, and even rather innocent."

The scene was, in fact, very kinky, and well beyond the wildest sexual fantasy I have ever had, or even heard or read, let alone written, about. And so, at the request of my employer, it has been expunged. Cutting out the two hundred and thirty-three words of that pornographic description from the chapter was, however, at least financially compensated for by my employer's willingness to pay me for each of the Zhotee-eloq names that he himself had written down for me.

"I wish," Mr. De Leon said, "for the sake of making the chapter more complete, that I had had more time to tell you about more of the love affairs I enjoyed in those years after Maria Fuentes left the mission. Yes, I wish had had the time to tell you how Eliza Coneto put her virginity up as the stakes in a game of andaboba with me, and to tell you all about Angela Gallante, the plump little laundress with bright red hair in Cuscowilla, about the giggling widow with the foul-mouthed hundred-and-twenty-year-old parrot in Apalachee, and about how I cured the bailiff's pretty daughter of hiccoughs in Ocala. Oh, if only we had more time."

Mr. De Leon suddenly hesitated, looked down, and seemed to be considering his words. He coughed a few times, looked around, and then spoke in a lowered voice: "Listen, Mr. Siegel, I have a confession to make. I didn't exactly tell you the truth on Monday about my nun's first rapture in my home. On that occasion I didn't actually resist Maria Fuentes with *all* my strength. In fact, I didn't resist her at all. I admit it—I gave in to her. Yes, I made love to her during that first fit. But I didn't tell you that yesterday, and I don't want you to write it because it might give my readers the mistaken impression that my own sexual desire was being satisfied, when the truth is that I made love to her, as you have correctly recorded here, 'out of pity for the poor girl.' Yes, I made love to her only because I did not have the strength to deny her the joy of the holiest of holy communions. But leave it as you have it here. I wouldn't want anyone to imagine that I ever took advantage of a girl I so dearly loved. You notice that I say *made love* and not *cardar* for what I did. *Cardar* would imply mutuality in aim and pleasure. No, I *made love* to her—more *for* her than *to* her. Yes, I made love, formed and fashioned it for her, made palpable for her the joy of the love referred to in the proclamation that 'God is Love.' For Maria Fuentes that was really true—her God was Love. For me it's always been the other way around."

1647–1763

WHEREIN PONCE DE LEÓN BECOMES A
WEALTHY MERCHANT, PURCHASES THE LAND
OF THE MISSION OF SAN HORTANO FOR THE
CULTIVATION OF TOBACCO, BECOMES HIS OWN
SON, AND THEN HIS GRANDSON

Tobacco, rare, divine, glorious and most excellent tobacco, goeth far beyond all other panaceas, potable gold, and philosophers' stones. That the
natives of the Indies did not suffer the diseases which have so long afflicted
us is due testimony to the sovereignty of this sacramental herb as a remedy
to infirmities, illnesses and other griefs. Thus many Christians both in the
New World and now here in our own land have already and eagerly adopted
the salubrious habit and, having done so, are quick to avouch that in the
sublime state precipitated by sucking in the delectable smoke of tobacco's
burning leaves, they feel most youthful, hale, and content with life.

   KORO MALAJETXEBERRI, *Las marzvillosas e encriebles virtudes de tabaco*
   (The Marvels and Unbelievable Virtues of Tobacco)

Let me tell you a story about love and death.

While Mr. De Leon approved of that opening line for chapter six, he was
very discouraged that it was all that I had written of the one hundred and
sixteen-year-long account of Ponce de León's phenomenal success as three
tobacco merchants: Don Juan Gaviota de León, his son Pedro Gaviota de
León, and Pedro's son, named Juan II after his grandfather. Not only had

there been love and death in the tale, there was also tobacco and money, a beautiful woman and dastardly villain, and an intrigue and murder as well. "If you handle the material skillfully, Mr. Siegel," Mr. De Leon had said, "the chapter will be a real page-turner, the kind of story that will keep my readers on the edge of their seats."

He had told the story on Tuesday, but, because I had stayed up all that night writing about the Mission of San Hortano, I was, on Wednesday morning, able to deliver, along with chapter five, no more of chapter six than that ten-dollar first line.

Mr. De Leon was getting way ahead me, already telling a story about Ponce de León dedicating a synagogue, and I still had to write chapters one, three, and six, not to mention "a seductive opening" for chapter five and a description of a blowjob for chapter four. And I was exhausted.

After a long day of tales about Jews in British Florida, I was so fatigued that I returned to the Zodiac without stopping to pick up anything for dinner. Without the energy to so much as undress or even take off my shoes, I lay down on the bed and don't remember anything until the pounding on my door.

"Siegel, are you in there?" Mr. Wiseman was shouting. "Are you there? Come on, Siegel. There's someone here to see you. A girl! Are you in there? You're not dead, are you? I hate it when I find dead people in my motel." It was almost noon.

Isabel was waiting for me in the lobby. "He's upset that you didn't show up this morning. Very upset. He doesn't believe you'll be able to finish the book in time. It must be done before you leave. You only have a week left." It was the first time I had seen her wearing lipstick or shoes—a cherry red gloss on her lips and on her feet aquamarine espadrilles that matched the color of the silk band on her broad-brimmed straw hat. Large sunglasses were a glamorous touch.

I asked her to inform Mr. De Leon that I couldn't come that day, that I needed time to catch up with him. "Tell him I'll be there early tomorrow morning. Tell him I'll have the story of love, death, and tobacco for him then, as well as the story of the Jews, and that I'll try to have chapters one and three, and the first line of five as well."

"He'll be furious if you don't come today," the young woman insisted. "He's become very irritable these past few days. Surely you've noticed. You have to excuse him. He's very old, as you know, and he's also quite ill. He's getting weaker and weaker by the day, drinking and smoking more and more, taking more and more morphine, and now he's begun to rely on the cocaine to remain alert enough to work on the book."

"Cocaine?"

"Yes, I mix it into the rum punch," she said as matter-of-factly as if she had been talking about Sweet'N Low.

No wonder, I realized, that after the days of drinking lots of that punch, I had twice been able to stay up all night writing. No wonder I had, after being so stimulated, also become so exhausted. No wonder my lips and gums had felt a little numb. And no wonder I had become enthusiastic about the book at times.

In her disappointment that I would not be going back to the Garden of Eden that day, Isabel, agreeing to convey my promises to Mr. De Leon, reiterated her prediction that he would be furious.

"That's what I call a girl, Siegel, a real *yingeh tsatskeh* if you know what I mean," Mr. Wiseman commented from behind his desk as soon as she was gone. "*Oi, oi,* if only I was young again, what I wouldn't do to schtup a tomato like that!"

He insisted on telling me an old joke about an old Jew who, going into the confessional in a church, tells the priest that he's having sex with an eighteen-year-old girl. "That is indeed a mortal sin," the priest says, and then, discerning from the old man's Yiddish accent that he's Jewish, asks, "But why are you telling me? I'm a Catholic priest." Mr. Wiseman guffawed heartily as he exaggerated his own Yiddish accent to deliver the punch line: "Vat d'ya mean? I'm tellin' everybody!"

As he didn't get quite the laugh out of me that he had hoped for, Mr. Wiseman felt it necessary to inform me that a sense humor has the power to keep a person young: "Or feeling young at least. Take it from me—the more you laugh, the younger you feel. You should try to laugh more. By the way, Siegel, do you mind if I ask you a personal question? Tell me if it's none of my business, but what, I've been wondering, are you doing here? We don't normally get people for more than a day or two, since there's nothing to see in Eagle Springs, especially not now since the Garden of Eden went bust. So what are you doing? And what's with you and that Ponce de León shmuck?"

When I explained that I had been hired by Mr. De Leon to help him write a book about Juan Ponce de León and the Fountain of Youth, Mr. Wiseman became enthusiastic. "You're a writer! A writer! Have you ever heard of Ernest Hemingway?"

Upon being informed that, yes, I had heard of Hemingway, Mr. Wiseman claimed the author had stayed in room number six of what fifty years earlier had been the "brand new Zodiac Motor Inn. My wife, Pearl, God bless her, named it the Zodiac because it has twelve rooms—you know, like the signs of the Zodiac. Why didn't you tell me you're a writer? I would have reserved Hemingway's room for you. That's where you should be. Yeah, in room number six. It'll be good for your writing. We can move you today."

When I tried to assure Mr. Wiseman that room number three was quite adequate, he countered, "The Hemingway room has a bigger desk, and books in it, and there's even a pencil sharpener attached to the back of the closet door. It's perfect for a writer."

For the sake of the larger desk, I packed my bag to make the move. As we entered my new room, Mr. Wiseman pointed out four books on a high table in the corner. "That's the complete works of Hemingway. Well, they used to be complete. One of our guests lifted a few of them. Pearl loved Hemingway, you know. Yeah, she read everything the guy ever wrote. Every word. And look, you've also got a copy of *Gone with the Wind* that someone left here last month. Now that's what I call a book. They just don't write them like that any more. And, of course, you've got a Gideon Bible just like the one in your old room. They don't write them like that anymore either. To be honest with you, I'd like to get rid of it, because it's got those goyish chapters in it. But I don't get that many Jews here and so, I figure, what the hell!"

Since I didn't have to spend the day with Mr. De Leon, and believing as I did Mr. Wiseman's assertion that there was nothing to see in Eagle Springs, I decided that, before getting down to work on all the writing I had to do, it might be interesting to see St. Augustine. In retrospect, I realize that I was just procrastinating. I asked Mr. Wiseman for directions.

"Look, Siegel, once you get there, you've got to go the Flagler Wax Museum. Hemingway's there. Yeah, he's typing on his old typewriter just like he used to do here in this very room fifty years ago, right there at that table in the corner. Their Hemingway, I can tell you, looks just like the real thing. They've got everybody at Flagler's museum: Elvis Presley, Christopher Columbus, George W. Bush, Grover Cleveland, Michael Jackson, and, of course, Ponce de León. If you're going to write a book about him, you ought to at least see what the shmuck looked like."

Before driving on to St. Augustine, I stopped off at the Santa Almeja County Library to ask Miss Bell for suggestions as to what I should read to learn about Spanish and British rule in Florida, about Jews and tobacco in the state's history, and about the Zhotee-eloq Indians.

"Juan is an expert on those Native Americans, you know," the cheerful librarian informed me. "Nothing has been written about them yet. But Juan can tell you all you'd ever want to know about them, and more. By the way, how's he doing? I've been worried about him ever since he closed down the park. Is he feeling alright? And how's your work with him going?"

"Fine," I assured her. "But I'm not sure why he thinks it's so important to play the part, to dress up like Ponce de León every day."

Miss Bell laughed. "He's been doing that for years. It's what he does. It's who he is. It pleases him and it has pleased visitors to the park for as long as I can remember. What's wrong with that?"

I left the library with several books on the history of Florida, including *The Sunshine State from Prehistoric Times to the Present* ("with a new preface 'On the Future' by Governor Jeb Bush"); a study of Franciscan, Jesuit, and Dominican missionaries in Florida called *The Calumet and the Cross;* Gerald Vizenor's *The Heirs of Columbus;* and *Keeping Peace in Paradise*, a biography of Adelantado Pedro Menendez de Avila. Miss Bell had enthusiastically praised the latter: "It's written like a novel. The author, Eagle Springs' very own Wilfred Grant III, used the techniques and conventions of fiction to bring the facts of history to life. It's just as entertaining as it is informative. I would think that's the kind of book you could write about Ponce de León."

It took over an hour to drive to St. Augustine, and, by the time I got there, I was ready for a drink. I found a tavern overlooking the Matanza and chose it, despite its rather tacky exterior, for the sake of its name: Ponce's Place. It wasn't the only establishment in St. Augustine paying tribute to the Spanish conquistador: I had noticed a Ponce de Leon Bowling Alley and Video Arcade on Menendez Street, a Ponce de Leon Miniature Golf Course on Grant, a Ponce de Leon Health and Fitness Center on Flagler Avenue, and a Ponce de Leon Retirement Home on Columbus Boulevard.

Sitting at the bar in Ponce's Place, drinking a Cuba libre, I mulled over the story Mr. De Leon had told for chapter six. It had started out rather slowly and without particular reference to either love or death. There had been an elaborate explanation of how the Mission of San Hortano had been turned into the Gaviota Tobacco Plantation and Cigar Manufactury, how the buildings in the compound had been transformed into a fermentation hall, sweating barn, and storehouse, and how the marble Virgin atop the pillar in the center of the Fountain had been replaced by a bronze lion.

And then there had been a detailed and rather technical lecture on the germination, harvesting, drying, curing, and fermentation of tobacco. Mr. De Leon had shown me a display of the knives, strippers, shapers, gauges, molds, rollers, and vices that had been used to make cigars in the hall that had previously been the San Hortano Mission church. Also in the Tobacco Room was a portrait of Don Juan Gaviota de León I, signed, like the paint-

ing of the priest in the Mission Room, "Adele Carter, '89." And Mr. De Leon
had dressed for the day in an outfit not unlike the one worn by the tobacco
magnate in the portrait.

Mr. De Leon had explained that it had been obligatory for him to let each
of his workers go after five years or so, and to hire new ones, as a precaution
against any of them noticing that he was not aging. "And, at about the same
rate, and for the same reason, I'd have to terminate my love affairs."

That's when we got to love and death. "Because of the Fountain," Mr.
De Leon had said, "I would, whenever I was *cardar*ring a woman, become
acutely aware that she was, at that very moment, in my arms, dying, and
that I was not. That awareness spiked the pleasure of love with a measure
of melancholy." He had then repeated something he had said on the day
we had first met, that because of the Fountain, because of the secrecy it
required, he had had no choice but to terminate each liaison. "But I, no less
than any of the women, suffered the great sorrow of love when having to
say good-bye. Do try, Mr. Siegel, to make it clear that I always ended my
affairs as lovingly as possible."

Juan Gaviota de León had been in some sort of love with some forty
women in the first fifty years that the Gaviota Tobacco Plantation and
Cigar Manufactury had been in operation. Finally wearied by affair after
affair, seduction after seduction, good-bye after good-bye, Juan Gaviota
de León, now masquerading as his son, Pedro Gaviota de León, decided
to settle down and devote himself to a single woman. He married Justa
Respalona two hundred years to the year after he had wed Leonor Núñez
de Guzmán. "She was young, only twenty-one years old, and very pretty—
make her very pretty, Mr. Siegel—and best of all, she was attracted to older
men. Having been in my fifties for a couple hundred years made me quite
adept at picking them out. In a room of young women, I can intuitively
spot which among them are attracted to older men. Thus I don't waste any
time trying to seduce girls who prefer men closer to their own age."

Installed at the bar in Ponce's Place, I thought about that as I watched
the Flagler College girls drinking beer, telling stories, giggling, hoping, I
presumed, to meet some boys or men. The girls caused me to think about
what I had written in the first person at the end of chapter five about Ponce
de León's romantic forays and the casual love affairs he had enjoyed hundreds of years before: "When, during some of these love affairs, a woman
was lying naked in bed with me, her head resting on my breast, dozing off
in a languor precipitated by amorous exercise, I would sometimes imagine,
especially if she were very pretty, that I could love her with all my heart,
and that she would love me with all of hers, and that we could be happy

together, happier than either of us had ever been or even imagined being, happy together for the rest of our lives."

Ordering another Cuba libre, I made some notes on Mr. De Leon's account of Ponce de León's third marriage. "Well aware that, by grace of the Fountain, I was sterile," he had said, "I wouldn't have married Justa if she had wanted children. 'My cousin, Ruffina, was so beautiful until she started having babies,' she had told me. 'She's my age. But now, after only two children, she looks ten times older than I do. And her breasts are saggy too.'"

There had been a long list of Justa Respalona's qualities, among them, "She took to *cardar*ring like a duck to water. Of course, I'll expect you, Mr. Siegel, to come up with a better simile than that, something more original like 'an alligator to swamp water,' or 'an eagle to the vastness of the sky.'"

Mr. De Leon had spoken ill of Ponce de León's mother-in-law. "She opposed the marriage, and tried to convince her daughter that I was too old for her. Figuring that she thought we were about the same age, I suspected the widow had her eyes on me for herself."

Without giving me any of the specifics which might be entered as evidence of the professed marital bliss, Mr. De Leon had insisted, "Write about how happy we were, Mr. Siegel. I loved Justa more than any woman ever. And she loved me more than any man. We were very happy together and the cigar business was booming."

He had explained that it had taken her almost ten years to notice that he wasn't aging, that when she turned thirty he still looked like a man of fifty. Vanity allowed her to believe that his love for her kept him looking as young as ever. After another ten years, however, the forty-year-old Justa Respalona Gaviota de León thought something strange was going on. It didn't concern her so much that he didn't seem to be getting older as it dismayed her to realize how, compared to him, she was aging so quickly. When Ponce de León's third wife turned fifty, she knew that there was definitely something unnatural about her husband.

After attending a theatrical performance with her mother in St. Augustine of Antonio Mira de Naboroso's *El viejo y el demonio,* in which the hero sells his soul to the devil in return for perpetual youth so that he can seduce young women, a frightened Justa had bluntly asked her husband, "Have you made a pact with Satan? Tell me the truth."

"And I did tell her the truth," Mr. De Leon said, slowly shaking his head with apparent regret, adding that he again wished he had heeded the lines he had recited as a young boy playing the part of Amor in *El Amor y el viejo:* "La verdat a las de vezes muchos en daño echa": truth can cause much harm—especially in love. No, I shouldn't have told her the truth. But I was only two hundred and thirty-five years old at the time. Perhaps I'd know better now, now that I'm older.

"It would have turned out better if I had let her imagine that I had made a bargain with the devil. Of course, before telling her about the Fountain, I made her solemnly swear never to reveal the secret of the Fountain to anyone." Señora Gaviota would not have believed the preposterous story of the Fountain of Eternal Youth, had she not had living proof of it in the person of her husband.

"At first we were very happy, so happy—write about how happy we were," Mr. De Leon had insisted again. Happily they had bathed together in the Fountain, splashing one another with its magical waters. Drinking that water, Mr. De Leon had divulged, "aroused her more than any of the aphrodisiacs in the Seminole pharmacopoeia. The realization that she was not aging made her feel as though she was getting younger. Her amorous performances became as playful and exuberant as they had been when I first married her. We *cardar*red every day, sometimes more than once, and afterward, lying next to me in bed, sharing a cigar, she loved hearing my stories of the olden days, stories she listened to as if for the first time despite how many times I had told them to her already. I talked about being an actor in Spain and the adelantado of Higuey and Borinquen, about my life among the Zhotee-eloq Indians and the Mission of San Hortano. I didn't tell her about all the women, however, as I didn't want to make her jealous. One day, right after a good *cardar*ring, Justa sat up in bed with a great smile on her face to announce that she was going to bring her eighty-three-year-old mother from St. Augustine to live with us, 'so that we can nourish her with the waters. So that she doesn't have to die.' When I refused, reminding Justa of her vow never to reveal the secret of the Fountain to anyone under any circumstance, it caused a rift between us."

And one rift had led to another. One morning, as they were bathing together in the pool, Señora Respalona-Gaviota had submerged herself and, as she often did, she held her breath to stay underwater as long as possible. Suddenly she had jumped up, sprayed him with water from her mouth, and screamed, "Damn you! Why didn't you tell me about this thirty years ago? How could you do this to me? If only you had loved me more, you would have told me the truth long ago. I'd still be twenty-one years old. I wouldn't have these wrinkles." Lifting up her naked breasts, she had complained that, if only he had loved her more, "they'd still be perky."

Justa's fiery anger had slowly cooled into a smoldering sadness. In time, the marriage might have become at least a little happy again if only her mother hadn't died. On the day she left the plantation to attend the funeral in St. Augustine, she had had stern and sobering words with her husband. "You killed her. Yes, you killed my mother. If only you had let me bring her here, she'd still be alive. You're a murderer! My mother tried to persuade me not to marry you. And now you've killed her! Why didn't I listen to her?"

Although Justa seemed to have calmed down after returning from the funeral, she was hardly either the very happy young girl Ponce de León had married or the relatively happy fifty-year-old woman with whom he had first shared the waters of the Fountain of Life. She'd often go out for an entire day, where to, she never said. Several times she needed to spend a few days in St. Augustine to work out the details of her mother's will with lawyers there. "No longer did she take pleasure in hearing my stories," Mr. De Leon had sadly recalled, "they made her yawn. Speaking of which, why are you yawning, Mr. Siegel? Are you too growing tired of my stories?"

"No," I had insisted with an apology and the excuse that I was tired from having stayed up the entire night before, writing. He had then poured a glass of rum punch for me and continued the story, which turned rather melodramatic with the introduction of a handsome young villain named Diego Cabeza de Cabra. I considered it my duty as a ghostwriter to comment that I didn't think that all of the nasty characters in the book should be named Diego—"Diego Pinzon, Diego Buil, Diego de Guebo, Diego Columbus, and now Diego Cabeza de Cabra. Maybe we should call him Pablo, Miguel, Alphonso, or Garcia, or something ironic like Jesus, Jesus de Cabra."

"But the truth of the matter," Mr. De Leon had objected, "is that his name was Diego. Let us not compromise historical fact by changing any of the names of anyone in my book even if it's to protect the innocent. This Diego, no less a scoundrel than the others, showed up uninvited at my home claiming he had met my wife at her mother's funeral and that she had suggested that I might have some managerial work for him in the tobacco business. I sensed that something funny was going on."

While I knew that Mr. De Leon was not, by his own admission, much of a reader, the whole episode sounded like it had been lifted straight out of a romantic novel: an embittered Señora Justa Gaviota and a nefarious Diego Cabeza de Cabra were, as our hero suspected, having an illicit love affair. A comely mulatta named Beata, recruited as a spy from the team of girls who rolled Gaviota cigars, confirmed it for Pedro Gaviota de León, and informed him that there was good reason to believe that the lovers were plotting to get him out of their way. Beata further divulged that, in following the scheming Diego in the aftermath of one of his trysts with the Señora, she had discovered that he had another lover, a young barmaid in

St. Augustine. I was supposed to make it clear that Justa had told Diego about the Fountain, that Diego had told his nubile mistress about it, and that Diego and Justa were planning to kill Pedro. And then, of course, once that was done, Diego and his callow sweetheart would dispose of Justa.

"And so I did it," Mr. De Leon had said. "I did what had to be done. But let's go now. It's time for lunch."

"Did what?" I had to ask.

"Isn't it obvious?" he asked back. "I don't think we need to go into details. I'm sure readers will be quite able to use their own imaginations. They might recall that, after fifty years as a Zhotee-eloq, I would have become adept at archery. The important thing is that you write everything I have told you in such a way that readers will forgive me for doing whatever it is that they will imagine I did. You can't live for five hundred and forty years without doing a few things you regret and even a few things that are truly evil. I regret telling Justa the truth, just as I regret doing what I believed I had to do as a consequence. But—remember?—I don't want regrets in my book. You might note, however, that doing what I did do in the eighteenth century didn't seem quite so wicked then as it does now, in retrospect. Morality has a way of changing over the years. But enough about that. Isabel has lunch ready for us."

After a meal of merluza Católica with a salad of oranges, watercress, and goat cheese, we had returned to the Tobacco Room, where Mr. De Leon showed me *El Insular de Florida*, a Spanish weekly newsletter, consisting of six six-by-ten pages of folded paper that had been printed in St. Augustine in July 1735. Removing it from a display case, Mr. De Leon had handled the brittle pages with considerable care as he translated for me:

> Tobacco lord Don Pedro Gaviota de León and his wife of many years, Justa Respalona-Gaviota de León, died last week after being attacked by alligators while boating on the Matanza River. Whilst the remains of their mutilated bodies are too meager for burial, a funeral service will be duly conducted in their memory on Sunday in the Church of Santa Maria de la Misericordia. Don Pedro's son and heir, Don Juan Gaviota de León II, is expected to arrive from Cadiz to take over management of the Gaviota Tobacco Plantation and Cigar Manufactury in the Santa Almeja Prefecture.

Mr. De Leon added that the disappearance of Diego Cabeza de Cabra and his young mistress had gone unnoticed. He sighed. "I would have liked to have gone to the funeral to pay my respects to my wife and to see who showed up to pay their respects to me, but I feared that I might be recognized. Except for the fact that my hair was very black while my father's was gray, and that I had only a mustache and goatee while he had a full beard, I was the spitting image of the older man. Even though I had no friends, being reclusive as I was then, I supposed a few of my workers might have come to the cemetery. Beata would certainly have been there, since she had been having a love affair with me, the man she believed had been eaten by alligators. Like all of my plantation workers, she was dismissed from her job per the posted instructions of Juan Gaviota de León II."

With the old newspaper still in hand, Mr. De Leon remarked that the year 1735 was a significant one for his book. "A plot should have a beginning, middle and end. Isn't that so? And here we are, right in the middle—1735 is halfway between 1465 and 2005."

Before driving back to the Zodiac from St. Augustine to write chapters six and seven, I stopped at the Flagler Wax Museum to see Ponce de León. He looked much younger than Mr. De Leon. He was also taller, his nose was larger, and, of course, he was not wearing dark glasses. No less than Elvis, Hemingway, and Grover Cleveland, with whom he shared a room, he needed a good dusting.

Back at my desk in the Hemingway room, hoping to catch up with Mr. De Leon, I started on chapter seven, the story of the Jews. Once that was done, I planned to work on the chapter about the tobacco merchant and Justa Respalona. At least, I consoled myself, I already had an opening line that met with my employer's approval.

I tried to come up with a comparable one to start chapter seven. "Just as my father had considered it advantageous to become a Gentile in 1478, so I considered it expedient to become a Jew again in 1763"—no; "I became a Jew again when Florida became British"—no; "I loved Shulamit Morteira more than any woman ever"—no; "In the beginning"—no; "Call me Samson"—no; "Stately, plump"—no, no, no.

Given my success with plagiarizing a beginning from *A Tale of Two Cities,* I decided to look at the opening words of the four Hemingway books that had come with room number six of the Zodiac in hopes of finding something worth stealing: "He lay flat on the brown, pine-needled floor of the forest" (*For Whom the Bell Tolls*)—no; "Robert Cohn was once middleweight boxing champion of Princeton" (*The Sun Also Rises*)—no; "In the late summer of that year we lived in a house in a village that looked across the river" (*Farewell to Arms*)—no; "He was an old man who fished alone in a skiff in the Gulf Stream" (*Old Man and the Sea*)—no. The last of these books had been inscribed: "For Pearl Wiseman, with gratitude for your hospitality, Earnest Hemingway, July 8, 1955." That Ernest was misspelled suggested forgery.

I was just about to look at the first page of *Gone with the Wind* when Mr. Wiseman knocked on my door. Insisting that he had something that would help me with my work, he came in and handed me a plastic sandwich bag containing what turned out to be an old argyle sock. "It's Hemingway's. Yeah, Siegel, believe it or not, it's one of Ernest Hemingway's socks. My wife, Pearl, God bless her, found it right here in this very room under the bed when she was cleaning up after he checked out. She wanted to write to him, to notify him that we had found it, and that we'd be happy to return it. 'What, Pearl, are you *meshugeneh*?' I say, 'Just throw it away like all the other *bobkes* and *drek* people leave behind.' But she says, 'Manny, you're the one who's *meshugeneh*. If we don't send it back to him, we should at least keep it. This sock will be worth a fortune someday. Believe me.' So I believed her. And a couple years ago, after Pearl's passing, I decided to sell it. I took it to Lickley's, an antique store in St. Augustine, to see what I could get for it. But Lickley tells me that in order to get anything at all, I needed to have some proof that it's the real thing. 'Manny,' he says to me, 'your wife should have gotten a letter from Hemingway documenting that this sock was really his.' And then the putz says, 'Manny, if you can find a photo of Hemingway wearing only one sock, one that matches this one, then maybe we can talk.' So, you see, Siegel, the problem is that nobody believes me. But it's true. *Gloib mir!* I swear it's true. Do you believe me, Siegel?"

Figuring that so long as I was playing along with one old man claiming to be the Spanish conquistador who discovered Florida, I might as well go along with another one alleging to have one of Hemingway's socks, "Sure, Mr. Wiseman," I said, "I believe you."

"Of course you do, Siegel. Jews don't lie to each other. We stick together—don't we? That's why I'm going to do you a favor. I'm going to sell you the sock. No kidding, I figure that as a writer you can get a lot more out of it than I can. Lickley said that if I had that letter from Hemingway, he'd give me a grand for it. But I don't need the letter because you believe me. Right? And because I like you, Siegel, and because you're a Jew, I'm going to give you a deal on it. The sock's yours for only five hundred bucks. It's a steal."

Insisting that I needed to get back to work, I declined Mr. Wiseman's offer, adding that, although I believed him, I was neither a collector of literary memorabilia nor very much of a Hemingway fan.

"What do you mean, you're not a Hemingway fan? He won the Nobel Prize, didn't he? And besides, look at the sock. This is a genuine Pilgrim brand diamond-pattern sock knit out of the best quality yarn. Not only that, it's seamless and it's got an elastic ribbed top and a reinforced heel and toe. And it's in very good condition, almost like new. Pearl always said that Hemingway was probably wearing it when he wrote *The Old Man and the Sea*. Now that's what I call a great book. Don't you wish you could write a book like that? I'll tell you what Siegel—you can have the sock for four hundred, and I'll throw in that autographed copy of *The Old Man and the Sea*."

In order to get rid of him, I promised Mr. Wiseman that I would discuss the sock further with him after I had finished my work. "I've got a lot of writing to do before morning."

"Okay, Siegel, but I'm telling you, you've got to buy the sock," Mr. Wiseman muttered, and then, just as I was about the close the door behind him, he turned to me and said it: "Jews must stick together. We're not just a religion—we're a family."

And I had my opening line to chapter seven.

SEVEN

1763–1783

WHEREIN PONCE DE LEÓN BECOMES A JEW
AND DEDICATES FLORIDA'S FIRST SYNAGOGUE
FOR CONGREGATION BETH MEKOR-HAYIM

May the children of the Stock of Abraham, provided that they do not become a public charge or nuisance, come to dwell and flourish in East Florida and enjoy here all the opportunities granted other inhabitants of our glorious Empire save the right to the ownership of slaves. By the grace and goodness of His Royal Majesty, King George III, Jew and Christian alike shall sit in safety under his own vine and freely drink each from his own wellspring. May God grant prosperity to the Jew in the Colony of Florida.

JAMES GRANT, "Address to the Hebrews"

"Jews must stick together. We're not just a religion—we're a family," Rabbi Ma-nasseh Morteira said on the day he disembarked the caravel from Curaçao. He would utter the same words again, twenty years later, as he boarded a transport vessel for Charleston. He made the proclamation on the occasion of my wedding to his daughter, just as he did at her funeral. He exclaimed it when things seemed hopeful for Jews in Florida, just as he sighed it when prospects were grim.

I had returned, a prodigal son, to the family of Israel with the inauguration of British Rule in Florida. Just as my father had considered it advantageous to become a Gentile in 1478, so I considered it expedient to become a Jew again in 1763, the year Governor James Grant renamed Haveelaq "Eagle Springs," and summoned me to his office in Fort St. Augustine to discuss the operations of the Gaviota Tobacco

Plantation and Cigar Manufactury. And I remained a Jew for the same number of years that children of Israel wandered in the wildness.

"*British firms have found Virginia and the Carolinas most salutary and convenient for the development of a colonial tobacco industry,*" explained the gouty, hippopotamic statesman, his pale eggyolk-yellow skin seeming all the more wan and jaundiced in contrast to his russet wig and red satin uniform. "*It is, therefore, my mandate to impede any such production of that tawny, noxious weed here in Florida as may compete with British interests to the north. While it is the benevolently ordained policy of our Crown to entitle you, Señor Gaviota—though you be an Iberian—to maintain ownership of your legally acquired properties and chattel, it is my official imperative to discourage your current agricultural endeavors. I, furthermore, personally abjure that vile vixen, Lady Nicotiana, who, like all whores, offers but transient euphoriae for which one dearly pays with perpetual dependence, depravity, and disease. Have you, Señor Gaviota, considered the cultivation of sweet* Citrus sinensis? *You Spaniards seem to have a way with oranges.*"

Despite legal indemnity, I feared that, as a Spanish Catholic tobacco farmer and merchant in what had become Protestant British Florida, it was quite possible that I'd lose my plantation and with it my Fountain, and with that, my life. Fulsomely assuring the governor of my enmity for both the Spanish Crown and Roman pope, I profusely professed loyalty to His Majesty King George III and allegiance to the esteemed governor himself. That Grant had issued a proclamation inviting the Jews of the Spanish colonies in the Caribbean to immigrate to Florida gave me the occasion to tell someone something true about myself: "*Although I have been known here as Juan Gaviota de León II, my real name is Samson ben Aryeh.*" *I further convinced him that I had converted to the Catholic faith only to avoid the persecutions and abuses which Jews had been made to suffer under Hispanic rule in the New World.* "*But while I was a Catholic in outward appearance, I have ever and always remained a Hebrew in my heart. And as such, I am perpetually grateful to the Parliament of Britain for passing the Jewish Naturalization Act.*"

"*Oh,*" the governor exclaimed, "*how terribly auspicious this is!*"

In an effort to populate his uncultivated provinces, Grant had promoted, throughout the New World and Europe, the reputation of Florida as an "*Earthly Paradise.*" *Free land,* "*as fair, fertile, and fruitful as the Garden of Eden,*" *was offered to any white gentleman who had sufficient resources to import labor for the development of the agricultural economy of British East Florida. Because Jews were not, however, according to the proclamation, permitted to own slaves or have indentured servants, they were hindered from becoming farmers. But Grant believed in their potential to abet economic development as clerks, accountants, bankers, brokers, and fiscal advisors.* "*The Jews are a shrewd and cunning race,*" *he proclaimed.* "*Stiffnecked as the Scriptures attest them to be, they have a way with lucre. There's a boatload of them arriving from Curaçao in the next few weeks—eighteen Israelites together with I don't know how many wives, children, and animals. It would be an amply appreciated service to the Empire, Mr. Aryeh, Judaist that you so expediently confess to be, if you would join me in welcoming them to St. Augustine. They will surely trust you, as one of their penurious tribe, when, on my behalf, you assure them that the British have taken to heart the words of Jesus Christ: 'Forgive them, for they know not what they do.' I do truly wish the wandering Jew to imagine a new Israel in East Florida situated as it so providentially is on the same latitude as Palestine. I personally bear no grudge against the Hebrews for the torment and crucifixion of Jesus Christ. I have, sir, let bygones be bygones."*

My consent to be of diplomatic service to Governor Grant was rewarded by an immediate appointment as "Factotal Satrap of Jewistic Affairs" so that I might act as a liaison officer between Florida's imminently arriving immigrants and the British Crown. *"You will serve your people by informing me of their needs, which I will hasten to satisfy as best I can, and, at the same time, you will be in a position to alert me, if needs be, to any subversive intentions which might happen to brew among them."*

Comparing Florida to Egypt and himself to Pharaoh, the governor took to calling me his Joseph. *"I have a proposal which I trust you will find amply amenable, since its implementation will benefit your Semites no less than it will satisfy my British colonial interests. I am prepared, on behalf of His Majesty George III—God save the King!—to support the establishment of a temple for the Children of Abraham that they might worship according to their ancient habits and curious customs. The problem is, as you must surely understand and appreciate, that British statutes in East Florida currently restrict newly arriving immigrants of the Hebrew persuasion from acquiring land. Ah, that's where you come in, my Joseph. The solution to the problem is obvious, is it not? Your properties shall be a land of Goshen for your brethren, a promised land fragrant with orange blossoms. Not only will this avail the Judean in Florida, it will also curb the competition that the Gaviota Tobacco Plantation presently poses to British tobacco firms in Virginia and the Carolinas."*

And thus the cigar factory that had once been the church of San Hortano became the synagogue of Congregation Beth Mekor-Hayim. My tobacco fermentation hall was transformed into a kosher slaughterhouse, and my Fountain into a mikveh. Tobacco was uprooted for the planting of orange trees. I cooperated with Grant, convinced as I was that, had I refused the governor's proposal, my land would have been taken away from me anyway by subterfuge if not by force. Governor Grant could be as ruthless as any pharaoh. He boasted of his handling of the Seminoles of East Florida: *"A less benevolent administrator would have subdued the recalcitrant red man in battle. But I, by simply burning the forests in which he hunted, secured his surrender without spilling a single drop of heathen blood. In this way, I have made Florida a peaceful land, ripe and ready for Christian settlement."* He was also proud *of a husbandry program he had instituted on his own lands for the breeding of Negro slaves. The plan was to utilize the same scientific methods that had been developed in Suffolk to cultivate draft horses that were, he said, "as docile and obedient as they are hardworking and strong. And the whip reaffirms what breeding potentiates."*

Although James Grant could be tyrannical with men, he was, I soon discovered, dominated by women. While cocksure in his administrative office in Fort St. Augustine, he was henpecked in his home.

At this point in the draft of this chapter that I was to present to Mr. De Leon on Friday, July 15, there was my written rendition of what my employer had told me about the Grant women. In the same room in which Father Juan Arquero had, on so many occasions, heard the confessions of the zealous Señora Menendez, Samson ben Aryeh had been introduced to the five women of the household: Governor Grant's mother and sister, his wife, and two daughters. I was satisfied with the image I had come up with to evoke them: "Squeezed in together on a single divan, the billowing folds and layered bunches of their sumptuous shimmering satin and velveteen dresses—indigo, purple, blue, all lace-trimmed—overlapped, imbricated, and intermeshed so that they seemed to merge into a single sprawling, throbbing creature with five mouths, its ten arms the undulant tentacles of a sort of human anemone." Sustaining the metaphor, I had turned the governor into a clown fish swimming symbiotically amidst the tentacles, at once protected by the creature and luring prey for it. Having been apprized, in rather lurid detail, of the occasional interactions that Samson ben Aryeh had illicitly enjoyed with Grant's women during the governor's tenure as an administrator in British East Florida, I had done my best to use words to conjure up the escapades in a way I thought would satisfy my employer. Contrary to my expectations, however, Mr. De Leon told me to expunge the fifteen hundred words that came at this point in the narrative.

"It takes up too much space," he had insisted once he had read the chapter, "and it delays getting to the Jews. And, besides, Mr. Siegel, don't you think that its vulgarity detracts from the more lofty tone of my love story? It might mislead my readers into imagining that I did not love Shulamit Morteira with all my heart. Omit the Grant women and get to the Jews' arrival in St. Augustine. Yes, cut right to 'I had first seen her among the daughters of Jerusalem.' I like that line. Perhaps it should open the chapter. It's more seductive than your 'Jews must stick together.'"

I had first seen her among the daughters of Jerusalem who, behind their men, solemnly descended the gangplank of the frigate that had brought them to Florida.

Shulamit Morteira was as handsome as her namesake: as resplendently dark as the tents of Kedar and curtains of Solomon, a rose of Sharon, a lily of the valleys, as exquisite as Jerusalem, fair as the moon, clear as the sun, and as breathtaking as any army with banners. Shimmering like the fish pools in Heshbon by the gate of Bathrabbim, her eyes were doves at play under locks as fragrant as a garden of pomegranates.

Though I hadn't spoken Ladino in almost three hundred years, my mother tongue returned to my mouth just—so it seemed—that I might enchant her: "Te quere conocer, Morena. Dime si tienes amante. Te lo baré defender" (I'd like to get to know you, Dark Beauty. Tell me if you have a sweetheart. And if you do, I'll chase him off).

When she told me to go away ("Presto aléxate de mi"), and called me "berbante" (scoundrel) I, pretending not to hear it, told her that she was beautiful. "That must be why men are always bothering me," she said with a smile. "Go away, berbante, or you'll be the one who's chased off."

No matter what she said, it was sweet to hear. The voice—its tone, timbre, rhythm, and pitch—was my mother's. Whenever my mother had called me her little berbante *it had been an affectionate tease inevitably followed by a hug, a laugh, and kisses all over my face. After my mother's death, her voice, I believed as if it could be so, had remained in the world, silently waiting for a throat, a mouth, a tongue, and lips warm enough to do it justice. Finally the voice had found its refuge in Shulamit Morteira.*

No sooner had she told me to go away, than I knew she would want to be close to me. I believed we would drink wine together from a single cup, and then slowly, slowly undress for one another so that the blessed light of ceremonial candles might flicker on a hallowed nakedness. Her navel would be a round goblet of liquor, her belly a heap of wheat set about with lilies, her breasts clusters of grapes, and her lips, threaded with scarlet, would drip with the milk of love and honey of delight.

Lovers cannot help but be tempted by the illusion of destiny. As foolish as any inamorato, I imagined that, because I had been born several hundred years before Shulamit Morteira, fate had been constrained to defy natural law for the sake of love. In love everything always seems to lead up to now. Fate had made it necessary for me to find the Fountain of Life just so that I could live long enough to hear her say, "Presto aléxate de mi, berbante."

Governor Grant, standing in his open Suffolk-horse-drawn carriage on the dock, had been waving for me to join him in ceremoniously greeting the Jews. "Mr. Aryeh, allow me the honor of presenting none other than Rabbi Manasseh Morteira, the esteemed high priest of these Jews. And Rabbi Morteira, let me introduce you to Mr. Samson ben Aryeh, Factotal Satrap of Jewistic Affairs in British East Florida, a man of your own race and creed, to be trusted as such, a Jew if there ever was one, proving himself so by his eleemosynary offer to transform his tobacco plantation into a veritable Hebrew haven complete with synagogue, cemetery, and what have you for your Jewish conveniences."

Cradled like an infant in Rabbi Morteira's arms, there was a cedar box inscribed with Hebrew letters and containing the Torah—"Etz Hayim," he called it, the "Tree of Life." I supposed that he was testing to find out if I really was a Jew when he used the language of those scrolls to ask if he could trust the governor. Remembering the teachings of Rabbi Solomon ben Maimon de Luna, I answered in the language in which the Creator revealed his will to his prophets that we should trust only the God of our fathers ("Hinay El yeshuati, evtach ve-lo efchad"), and added that the Gentile governor was a ben szona. "Governor Grant," I then announced in my newly acquired, but ever improving, English, "serves King George III as justly and magnanimously as the stalwart Haman served the mighty King Ahasuerus." Grant, flattered by the insult, grinned grandly, and the rabbi smiled too.

When the Jews moved into accommodations that had once housed the flock of Indian acolytes at the Mission of San Hortano, Shulamit Morteira chose to sleep in a room with her parents. She was appointed to light the candles in celebration of their first Sabbath in Florida. Shedding tears of joy, her father led the blessing over the sweet wine, her mother that over the warm bread, and then, after a dinner of codfish stew in the hall, once a church, soon to be a synagogue, Ze'ev Mizrahi (who would be the congregation's cantor—a tall young man with a thick black beard and forearms as hairy as Esau's) chanted z'miros in an exuberant Hebrew: "Shavua tov, shavua tov, shavua tov. . ."

Dancing as he sang, Mizrahi kicked one leg high and then the other even higher, spinning, jumping, clapping his hands over his head, and the men jubilantly tapped their knuckles on the table in time as the women, their hair covered with scarves, hummed along with eyes fixed on the virile dancer. "When you're drunk," he sang, "you think you're a rich man, no matter how poor you are. When you're drunk, you feel young, no matter your age. When you're drunk, you imagine all the women love you . . ."

When the jugs of wine that the Jews had brought with them from Curaçao were empty, I brought rum and cigars from my cellar. My new family took such marvelously shameless pleasure in the strong drink that I couldn't restrain myself from announcing that Juan Ponce de León, the man who had discovered Florida long ago, in the Jewish year 5273, had invented the distilled liquor. "He was a Marrano from Lebrija, in Andalucia. Outwardly a converso, but a child of Israel in his heart. Yes, we gave rum to the world! Hosanna to the Jews! "

When Mizrahi stopped dancing so that he could catch up with the other drinkers, everyone begged Shulamit to sing. The more she resisted, "No, no," the louder they *shouted, "Yes, yes." She was, I observed, the sort of woman who, by nature, cannot refuse giving pleasure to men:*

Del amor yo non savía.
Tu mi embizatis a mí,
De el Dio lo topes mancevo,
Por lo que hizitis con mi.

I passed around cigars to the men, but asked that they not be lighted until I had recited a blessing: "'Baruch ata Adonai, Elehenu melech-ha-olam boray tobako. *Blessed art Thou, O Lord, our God, who gave us tobacco.' Ponce de León also invented cigars! Oh, how much the world owes us, God's chosen people!"*

Drunk as I was, utterly swept up and carried away by their enthusiasm and delight, I was thrilled to be a Jew again. I blurted it out: "Oh, my brothers and sisters, let me tell you a secret! We are in the Garden of Gan-Eden. Yes, it's true. The Creator, if not fate or mazel, *has brought you to the Earthly Paradise." They laughed and Ze'ev Mizrahi, downing another cup of rum, broke into a song about paradise on earth and the coming of the Messiah. Shulamit joined in for the refrain:*

Bendita sea la casa esta
Donde guardamos su fiesta
Con alegría y permanencia.

Just after midnight, as the celebrants began to retire to their rooms for sleep, I took Rabbi Morteira aside. "Come outside with me. I must talk to you. It's very important."

We teetered into the garden, where I seated him next to me on a bench near the Fountain. Kissing his hands as had been the respectful custom of Jews in the Spain of my childhood, I asked for permission to marry his daughter. "I want no dowry from you. Only your blessing."

The drunken rabbi laughed at my proposal. "But you know nothing about her."

"I know that her father is a pious man, learned in Torah and Talmud. I know that she is very beautiful, that her glance enchants me, and that her voice takes my breath away. And I know that I shall love her more than any woman ever."

"You're drunk," the rabbi, even more inebriated than I, noted.

"Yes, drunk with love for your daughter, drunk and crazy, yes, madly in love with her. Have I not provided you with a place to live? Am I not giving you a synagogue? Have I not given you rum and cigars? And all I want in return is your daughter."

"I must warn you," the rabbi continued gravely with a hand on my knee, "you

would not be her first man." Despite reiterated insistence that I didn't care about her past with others, but only about her future with me, the old rabbi insisted on informing me that Shulamit had been married at the age of fifteen to the young son of an old Jewish sugar merchant in Jodenwyk. "He ran off to Flanders with a gentile pechugana. *That was over ten years ago. There may have been other men since then. You know how women are."*

"*I don't care if there have been a thousand men!" I countered.*

"*That's what you say now!" He laughed, looked stern, and then asked my age.*

"*Fifty," I answered.*

"*Like me!" the rabbi mumbled. "We're old, Samson ben Aryeh. Face it—you're an old man. She's only half your age."*

"*Was not King David much older than we are when he married the nubile keeper of the vineyards after whom your daughter is named? Did not an aged Moses de León wed a young Rebecca, the poetess of Granada?"*

Confident that I was close, that I was tiring him out and wearing him down, I played my cards as in a game of andaboba. "Does not the first mitzvah in our Torah demand that we be fertile and multiply? If you will offer your barren daughter to me, I will give you grandsons in return, as many as Jacob gave Isaac." That did the trick. "Let it be, Samson ben Aryeh, my son," the rabbi muttered as he rested his head in my lap and, with my hand on his shoulder, he began to snore as only an old drunkard can. The sound of it could have brought down the walls of Jericho.

The betrothal made and the marriage contract written out in Aramaic on parchment, Rabbi Morteira, quite a bit more sober than on the night he had agreed to give his daughter to me, insisted that I wait to consummate the marriage. Under normal conditions, he explained, citing the Talmud, it would have been a full year before she could come to my bed. "But, no less an authority on intimate matters than the physician and kabbalist Johanan Yarhoni, recognizing that there are exceptions for widows and men of advanced age, opines that in the case of such unusual unions, the period between the betrothal and the wedding may be as brief as forty days, forty being an auspicious number for our people: the Great Flood lasted forty days; the infant spends forty weeks in his mother's womb; and the Israelites wandered in the desert for forty years. Forty days should, furthermore, give us time to prepare our synagogue. Let the celebration of the covenant of marriage take place on the day we dedicate the synagogue and celebrate our covenant with Hashem, blessed be He." I hoped that forty days would be enough time for Shulamit Morteira to get used to the idea of marrying me, a stranger, and, from her point of view no less than her father's, I supposed, an old man.

While the cigar factory was converted into a synagogue complete with an ark, bimah, and a barrier to separate the men from the women during services, the Fountain of Life became an enclosed mikveh. The statue of the lion that had re-

placed that of the Virgin in the center of the Fountain's basin was supplanted by a seven-branched bronze menorah on the day the rabbi blessed it. "The mikveh, in which we keep the commandment of immersion, is the Fountain of Life of Gan-Eden." Little did he know that he was speaking the truth. Thenceforth I had to drink from it secretly.

On the day of the wedding, Shulamit's father, two uncles, and Ze'ev Mizrahi brought a new bed and a mattress with fresh sheets and blankets to my residence. They placed the head of the bed facing east toward Jerusalem, and Rabbi Morteira sprinkled rose water on the bedding. They made racy jokes and took turns slapping me on the back, laughing, and calling me "old man." Rabbi Morteira said that, as Jews, we were a family and must stick together. Ze'ev Mizrahi wished me good luck.

Shulamit was immersed in the Fountain of Life. Behind the wooden barriers that had been erected around it, I could hear the women laughing and singing Ladino love songs as they dunked her again and again, washing her for me, purifying her just as she would cleanse herself again and again each month, seven days after each menstruation.

Beneath the wedding canopy Rabbi Morteira spoke to God: "O make these lovers greatly to rejoice even as of old Thou did gladden Man and Woman in the Garden of Eden. For them did Thou create joy and gladness, mirth and exultation, pleasure and delight, companionship and love." He could not hold back the tears as he pronounced those words and, handing the first cup of wine to me, he instructed me to turn to my bride to say, "As the lily among thorns, so is my beloved among the daughters." I passed the cup to her and she recited, "Stay me with flagons and comfort me with apples, for I am faint with love. Set me as a seal upon thine heart, as a seal upon thine arm: for love is strong as death, jealousy as cruel as the grave, and the coals thereof are the coals of a fire which has the most vehement of flames. Many waters cannot quench love, neither can floods drown it. If a man would give all the substance of his house for love, it would utterly be disdained."

Once I had placed the ring on her finger, she could say, "I sit beneath his shadow in delight, and his fruit is sweet to my taste. He brings me into the banqueting house, and his banner over me is love. His left hand is under my head and his right arm embraces me."

At this point in the narrative, Mr. De Leon had suddenly stopped to insist that we go outside and onto a patio I had not seen before. It was, he said, the place where the wedding ceremony had taken place. "I stood here, right here, and she was next to me. The guests formed a circle around us. Can you picture it, Mr. Siegel? The walls are covered with drapes. Try to hear the vows and songs. Imagine it all taking place right here. See how beautiful my bride is! Imagine the joy. Imagine it so that you can describe it faithfully."

And then Mr. De Leon took me to an adjacent plot of land that he said had been Florida's first Jewish cemetery. There were several weather-worn gravestones inscribed with barely legible Hebrew letters. "Here, right here," he muttered sadly. "We buried her here, facing Jerusalem. Imagine it. Now imagine the sorrow that is to come. Imagine it so that you will be able to describe it faithfully."

Upon returning to the Judaica Room, before picking up the story, my employer showed me a silver charm that he said Shulamit Morteira had kept under her pillow at night to protect them both from the Evil Eye. It was on display with a bronze menorah, a silver yod and circumcision knife, some prayer shawls, a kiddish cup, and a few shards of glass. "These are what remain of the wine glass from our wedding," he said, picking up the story from where he had left off.

The wine glass was broken, the white cloth around it reddened with the blood of the virgin grape, and Ze'ev Mizrahi, the robust father of six sons though he was not yet thirty years old, sang the epithalamium:

Come surrender now thy honeyed lips to me,
Come yield to me the confections of thy heart,
Come let thy womb be as a field to be sown,
Come, beloved, and surrender to the one who loves thee.

People were still drinking and singing when Shulamit's mother escorted the bride to her new bedroom. "At this point in a normal wedding," Rabbi Morteira told me, "your father would explain to you that, as Johanan Yarhoni himself expounded, a woman's passion is greater than that of a man. He would describe to you the woman's secret part—the inscrutable racham, *what Kabbalah calls 'the fig of Canaan.' He would counsel you as to what you must do to give your bride the pleasure to which she has, according to our laws, an inviolable right. But, I suppose a man of your age, Samson ben Aryeh, has had some experience with women already and that you are perhaps already somewhat familiar with the fig in question. Let us hope familiar enough to please your bride. A woman who is unsatisfied in her bed is as untrustworthy as Potiphar's Zuleika. Why don't you go to her now?"*

We drank wine together from a single cup and slowly—so slowly—undressed for one another so that the blessed light of seven candles might hallow nakedness. And yes, yes, her navel truly was a round goblet of liquor, her belly a heap of wheat set about with lilies, her breasts clusters of grapes, and her lips, threaded with scarlet, dripped with milk and honey. Selah!

It was the first time I had seen her hair, so dark black in contrast to the bright white of fresh wedding sheets. Her right hand hid the fig of Canaan from my gaze as she spoke. "In keeping with her duty to prepare me for your arrival, Samson ben Aryeh, my mother told me that when a man and woman who have just celebrated the holy covenant of marriage are united on their wedding night and take pleasure, the groom's delight is that of the Creator, and the woman's bliss is nothing but the ecstasy of Shekhinah, Hashem's Bride and Presence. In embracing one another, mother insisted, we must strive with all our might to give one another pleasure and, at the same time, allow ourselves to believe that our enjoyment is holy. We may call it ours, she said, but the pleasure does not belong to us—God and Shekhinah have allowed us to participate in their divine rapture as a wedding gift and a blessing upon our life together. It's a sweet idea. Don't you think so?"

"Very sweet," I answered, as I moved her hand aside to look at the soft, dark down, to touch it, smell it, and be transported by the fragrance. Her hand settled on my neck, and she sighed.

I could hear the distant voices of the revelers still celebrating our union with merry, drunken wedding songs: "Come, surrender, come my beloved, and surrender now."

Her head rested on my breast. "God's pleasure was perfect," I whispered. "The Creator, I can assure you, is a very happy God tonight. And now He'd like to have the subsequent enjoyment of smoking the tobacco He created."

As I rose from the bed to get a cigar, Shulamit sat up to say that, although the Shekhinah had experienced great pleasure, she yearned for even more. "Do you think God might give her that?"

"He ought to be able to do so," I assured her. "Was He not able to create the entire world in only six days? Just give Him a little while to smoke His cigar. And while He does so, He wants to look at you." The beauty of Shulamit's face was the radiance of the Shekhinah, a sacred splendor. God would have been overwhelmed by it.

In the morning Rabbi Morteira brought a large flounder. His wife put it in a dish on the floor of our bedroom and decorated it with flowers. Guests who had had the exuberance to stay up all night drinking and singing pushed into the room to watch the new bride step back and forth over the fish three times. That, her mother had assured her, would make her fecund. "B'siman tov," the crowd shouted and Rabbi Morteira invited them to share bollitos de Susona *with us. "Something to eat to help us drink more, something to drink to help us sing more, something to sing to help us enjoy more, something to enjoy to help us live more, to live more so that we can eat and drink and sing and enjoy more."*

Weakened by love, and as tempted as Solomon to choose the Shulamite over eternity, I considered abstaining from drinking the waters of the Fountain of Life in order to regenerate the seed which would allow me to keep my promise to Rabbi Morteira that I would provide him with grandsons. It was a sweet idea, a noble intention, but the cold and bitter prospect of aging and of impotence ultimately prevented me from going through with it. It would have been to give up love for the sake of love, life for the sake of life.

Rabbi Morteira prayed three times a day—at dawn, at sunset, and in the night. Believing, I believe, that to cardar *three times a day was a way for her, as a Jewish wife, to fulfill the obligation for thrice-daily worship, Shulamit would awaken me each morning with kisses that proclaimed the glory of God, and never let me sleep without the touch that revealed the potency of God, and in the afternoons she'd find me, take me by the hand, lead me to our room, unbutton my shirt, unbuckle my belt, unbalance my heart, unleash my desires, and unveil the bounty of God. Three times a day our heads faced Jerusalem. To me she was that holy city, her hair its gardens, her breasts the temple domes, her loins the tabernacle, her womb the ark of our own covenant. "And with this battering ram," she playfully whispered as she ardently caressed me, "open up my gates, break down the ramparts. Storm the sepulcher. Set me ablaze with the torch of ferocious love. Conquer me. And raise your banner over me."*

In the clutches of love, believing in the divinity of my bride, I would hear the orisons of Sinai in her sighs, taste the wine of Jericho on her tongue, smell the vineyards of En-Gedi in her lustrous black hair, feel the fires of Horeb in her skin, and then, suddenly, the walls of Jerusalem would crumble and inhume me. I'd try to unearth words from the rubble that might convey how much I loved her.

I was grateful to have found Shulamit when I did. Had I been born later and met her when I was younger, I might not have appreciated her perfections to the degree that they deserved to be esteemed. Life was sweet.

There was an orange tree in my garden, sustained for tens of thousands of years by the waters of the Fountain of Life. The oranges on that tree, like all of the fruit in Eden, were, of course, seedless. I discovered that, with cuttings from that original tree, we could raise orchards of orange trees bearing seedless fruit. I sent a basket of these to Governor Grant and he was so impressed by the miraculous fruit that he granted Congregation Beth Mekor-Hayim a world export license for seedless oranges. We prospered beyond all expectations. And in 1779 I invested in bonds newly issued by the Bank of the United States of America in Philadelphia. Everything was good. Everyone was healthy, happy, and very rich. But among Jews, well-being, prosperity, and contentment often incite anxiety. "That's when trouble happens," Rabbi Morteira warned, "whenever we get too rich." During the celebration of the Passover that year, he repeated his warning. "We mix bitter herbs with sweet haroset," he proclaimed, "to remind us in times of joy and prosperity such as these of the sorrows and torments that have been and are sure to be ours again. When you hear people saying 'poor Jew,' you should be pleased. When you hear the words 'rich Jew,' be prepared to run for your lives."

Each menstruation, a painful affirmation that, despite our constant, ardent efforts, she still had not become pregnant, distressed Shulamit. Her father had told her that, according to Johanan Yarhoni, not to procreate was the equivalent of committing murder. The onset of her period troubled me as well, demanding as it did that she leave me and not return to our bed for at least a week, and not until after she had been immersed in the Fountain of Life.

"I don't have to leave you, Samson ben Aryeh," Shulamit told me on the morning of her third Passover in Florida, "not this month, not next month, not for months to come." The sweet joy, that I was supposed to feel because she was at long last with child, was mixed with, and overwhelmed by, the bitter herbs of the knowledge that she had been unfaithful to me. By asking if she was confident that I was the father of her child, I knew that I was asking her to lie.

"Of course, Samson ben Aryeh, my beloved husband, of course," she swore to God almighty, laughed, and swore again. "Who else? After two years of trying—oh, the delight of our dedication to the task!—it has, by the grace and mercy of the Creator, finally happened. Hashem has granted you a child just as he did for the aged Abraham. Prayers have been answered."

I believed that she was lying to me only because she loved me so much that she wanted to spare me a truth that might suggest otherwise. And because I loved her, I lied too by swearing that I believed her. "We made lies our refuge," as the Prophet Isaiah sang, "and under falsehood were concealed tears."

There was an angel in my dreams, telling me the same lies he had told Joseph in Nazareth. As old Joseph forgave young Mary, I pardoned my Jewess. Jealousy, as cruel as the grave, made me all the more perversely impassioned. The vehement flames of its coals set me ablaze. Pulling back the sheets that covered her nakedness, forcing open the legs, ravening over her flesh, biting her stomach, pulling her hair, scratching her thighs, squeezing her wrists, smothering her, clinging, sweating, and gagging in pain and pleasure, I burst into tears. Even the waters of the Fountain of Life could not quench love. In miserable rapture and exalted devastation, I adored my wife despite the lies, hers and mine.

The women tended to Shulamit for three days, doing everything they could to arrest the bleeding. Then there were the chills, the fever, the thrashing, the delirium, then the crying out, the gasping for breath, and the unearthly rattle. And then the stillness, silence, and an eerie calm.

"Min ha-Shamayim te-nuchamu," Rabbi Morteira, his arm around my shoulders in a vain attempt to comfort himself as much as me, whispered as we watched the other men fill the grave. "May heaven comfort you, Samson ben Aryeh, my son. At least we have the child."

The mother had died too soon to hear the naming of her baby, "Simcha ben Samson," to hear the cry as he was circumcised, and to hear her father, unable to restrain his tears, try to give thanks to a savage God for the infant. She died too soon—but so, I suppose, does everyone, everyone but Juan Ponce de León.

Right after her death, I wished I had told her the truth about the Fountain of Life. But it didn't take long for me to convince myself that, had she known that she could chose between possibly dying in childbirth and living on as my barren beloved, she would have chosen death.

Because Ze'ev Mizrahi's wife, Benvenida, had herself just given birth—a girl named Penina—she had milk enough to nurse Simcha. With the infants—Penina on the left, Simcha on the right—cradled in her arms, the mother closed her eyes. The massive pale breasts, engorged with milk and swollen with love, were laid bare as an offering. As the large, dark Sephardic nipples, glistening wet, were devoured, the plush white cushions of flesh throbbed and blushed as they gushed under urgent sucking and the squeeze of little hands.

"So like his mother," Ze'ev whispered, standing next to me with his arm around my shoulder, as we gazed at the infants drinking at the twin fountains of life. "May her spirit abide among us, and may her memory be ever a blessing as she rests in peace." He suggested that Simcha remain with his family so that it would be convenient for Benvenida to feed him. A year later, Ze'ev persuaded me to leave the child with him longer. "We can care for him as he should be cared for."

Ze'ev would throw Simcha up into the air, catch him, blow on his pudgy cheeks to make a funny flatulent sound, and dance round and round with him in his arms, laughing as he did so.

Although I assumed that Ze'ev was the father of my son, I couldn't be angry with him. I understood that, had the situation been reversed, if Shulamit had been his wife, I would have done everything in my power to do what he had done. And I would not have felt guilty about it.

After Shula's death, I started visiting a neighbor, Betsy Pilot, the wife of the commander of the British Thirty-first Infantry Regiment. I'd go to her home whenever her husband was on maneuvers in West Florida. "I do love Lieutenant-General Pilot, I really do," she'd always insist as, lying back on the bed, she'd raise up her legs so that I might pull off her undergarments. It pleased Betsy to believe that she was comforting me in my time of grief over the loss of my wife. "If there's anything she did—you know, with her mouth or fingers or any other part of her body—that you particularly miss and would like to enjoy once more, do not hesitate to ask, Mr. Aryeh. Did she have a favorite position? The Lieutenant-General, bless his soul, especially delights in taking me from behind. He may be conservative in the barracks, but he's a rascal in the bedroom. Oh, what a lucky woman I am to have found a man like Commander Pilot out here in the colonies! If I were to die, I would hope that some good woman would, in my stead, be so kind as to offer him her posterior in memory of me." That Betsy so adored her husband, helped me believe that Shulamit had loved me even when she was in the arms of Ze'ev Mizrahi.

At the ceremonial first cutting of Simcha's hair on his third birthday, Ze'ev lifted the boy up to seat him on my lap. "Kiss your papa, Simcha. Go ahead, don't be afraid. Kiss him and say, 'I love you.'" The boy did as he was told. Ze'ev had a way with children.

Ze'ev suffered his heart attack while dancing on the Sabbath. Rabbi Morteira made much of that at the funeral, as if death on the holy day was somehow more redemptive than on any other day of the week. Simcha let me hold him in my arms as he wept, pushing his face into my jacket so that he did not have to watch the lowering of the body of the cantor of Congregation Beth Mekor-Hayim, wrapped in a prayer shawl, into the grave next to his mother's.

A few years later Rabbi Morteira made a great fuss over the preparations for his grandson's initiation as a bar mitzvah. "After the celebration, Samson ben Aryeh, my son, you may wish to take your son aside for a talk. According to Johanan Yarhoni, once a boy has read from Torah before the congregation, he is ready to learn from his father about intimate relations between a man and woman. It is your responsibility as a father to inform him that is forbidden for him to do as Onan did and spill his seed upon the ground, that it is an abomination to let his seed pass either through the fires of Molech or into a menstruant's fountain of blood. You must tell him that he is forbidden to uncover the nakedness of any member of his family, and that he must not lie with another man's wife, nor have sexual relations with a man, an animal, a bird, a reptile, or a fish."

Despite Rabbi Morteira's counsel, I did not consider it necessary to tell Simcha not to fuck a chicken, an alligator, or a flounder. Instead of merely telling him what he should not do with his penis, I supposed that I might offer him some education as to what he could do with it. To that end, I planned to escort him to the Setting Sun Saloon in St. Augustine just as Rabbi Solomon ben Maimon de Luna, hundreds of years previously, had taken me to Casa Susona in Sevilla on the occasion of my becoming a bar mitzvah. That had made me particularly happy to be a Jew.

Of the eight girls who worked at the Setting Sun, I had one called Mary in mind for Simcha. Not only was she the youngest, but she also had a soft spot for Jews. The first time I met her, noticing that I was circumcised, she had exclaimed with substantial glee, "You must be a Jew! I love Jews! Some people say they're stingy, but I can assure you, they're not. They always give me extra money that I don't have to report to the Mother. Always. And I love how you people yell out, 'Oh God, God, oh my God, God,' as you drip your honey. With you folks, I reckon, that means a lot."

Since the only Jews in East Florida at the time lived on my estate, I was naturally interested in knowing which ones in particular had done business with her. "Well only one, actually, a sweet old man, and generous as they come. A little strange, though. He told me that he's a rabbit."

"Do you mean rabbi? *Rabbi Manasseh Morteira?"*

"Yes, yes—that's his name. He comes often and always brings me gifts. Always

oranges and pastries, sometimes flowers and candies, sometimes wine or even rum. He's such a sweet old man."

"I've got a sweet young one for you," I told her as I pulled my breeches back on. "Rabbi Morteira's grandson. He's my son. Well, sort of my son. He's just a kid, and I don't think he's ever been with a girl, and I'm not sure he's even ready. But I want you to teach him how to please a woman, how to kiss and touch her, and what to say to her."

Just as during the bar mitzvah ceremony grandfather would hand the Torah to father who would in turn hand it down to son, so Mary would, according to my plan, be passed across the three generations of Jewish men. Just as Simcha would, in the synagogue, remove the mantle in which the Torah was clothed, so would he, in the brothel, remove the robe that covered the nakedness of the girl. Her legs would spread apart just as the poles of the Torah scrolls would be opened wide so that the holy word of God might be revealed. The Torah and the whore would, thus, work together to make a man of Simcha ben Samson.

When I told Simcha about Mary, and about what she had in store for him, he was appalled, and cursed me, shouting that he was ashamed to be my son, and that not only was I a bad father, but a bad Jew as well. Angrily he added that being my son made it difficult for him to keep the fifth commandment which God had given to Moses on Mt. Sinai.

When, three years after becoming a bar mitzvah, Simcha announced his decision to celebrate the covenant of marriage with Penina Mizrahi, I supposed it was appropriate for me, given the injunctions in the Torah against incest, to inform him that Penina was his half sister. He refused to believe me. "You're a scoundrel, a drunkard, and a philanderer. Above all else, a liar! You're jealous because Ze'ev was a good man, an honest man, and he never would have broken the seventh commandment given to Moses. Nor would my mother ever have been unfaithful to her husband, no matter what a reprobate he was. You're jealous because I loved Ze'ev as a better father to me than you ever were. You never really cared about me. You're telling these lies because you never wanted to be my father. You always hated Ze'ev."

And so Simcha ben Samson stood next to Penina Mizrahi under the wedding canopy as Rabbi Manasseh Morteira invoked his God: "O make these lovers greatly to rejoice even as of old Thou did gladden Man and Woman in the Garden of Eden. For them did Thou create joy and gladness, mirth and exultation, pleasure and delight, companionship and love. To them you gave a fountain." When Penina gave birth to a son a year later, Rabbi Morteira congratulated me on becoming a grandfather. "What greater blessing, what greater joy," he asked, "can a man have in his old age?"

"Jews must stick together. We're not just a religion—we're a family," Rabbi Manasseh Morteira, cradling the Torah in his arms, told me for the very last time as

he boarded the boat for Charleston, where there was a thriving Jewish settlement. "I'm sorry you're not coming with us. I shall think of you, Samson ben Aryeh, my son, always with affection." The rabbi had decided that the Jews should leave Florida on the basis of rumors, rampant after the success of the American Revolution, that the British were going to cede Florida back to the Spanish.

"You know," the old Jew remarked, "It's truly a wonder—but you don't look a day older than you did twenty years ago, when I met you for the first time, right here on this very dock."

"It's the rum," I told him, "rum and cigars. That's what keeps me young."

"What should I do with my synagogue?" I wondered as I watched the frigate sail out of St. Augustine harbor. "How shall I maintain the Garden of Eden and protect my Fountain?" I asked myself as I rode alone in the public carriage back to Eagle Springs. Standing in front of the mirror that afternoon, as I prepared to shave my beard and brush black dye into my gray hair so that I would look as young as I had when I first saw Shulamit Morteira, I pondered it. "What role shall I play in the next act of this drama?"

Satisfied with this chapter, Mr. De Leon paid me for its seven thousand, seven hundred, seventy-seven words. I was disappointed that he had insisted so adamantly that I expunge the description of Samson ben Aryeh's dalliances with the Grant women, not only because of the extra fifteen hundred dollars I would have earned for it, but also because it had taken me several hours to write, and because I thought it was actually rather amusing. I really didn't want to delete it. And so, despite Mr. De Leon's objections, here it is:

Upon receiving a note, signed "Lady Grant," that expressed a wish to visit my estate for a private meeting regarding a certain confidential matter, I assumed it was from the governor's wife and was, thus, quite surprised when his rotund and aged mother turned up. She got right down to business: "I hope that you might be so cordial as to permit me, Mr. Aryeh my good man, to ask you a somewhat personal and delicate question. Ever since being introduced to you as a gentleman of the Hebrew persuasion, I have—let me be frank with you—been pondering your private member, wondering whether or not it is, as I am told it would be in keeping with the ancient practices of your race, circumscribed."

"Circumcised," I answered. "Yes, circumcision is a Jewish custom."

"Oh, lovely!" the old lady exclaimed. "Just as I had hoped! For you see, never in my long life on this earth have I had the privilege, if not the honor, of beholding in the flesh an example of that modification of the appendage under discussion. Of course, I have read about such religiously mutilated organs in Holy Writ, but have

yet, I'm sorry to confess, to come face to face with one. I can assure you, good sir, that my motives in wanting to see one are in no way prurient and in every way aesthetic. Please, my dear man, let me explain lest you get the wrong impression of what sort of woman I am. After my beloved husband, Lord Grant—may his soul rest in peace—departed this world for a better one, I took up painting as a distraction from grief. At first I tried as best I could to honor my late husband and preserve his memory by devoting myself to drawing his portrait. In every attempt to capture his face, however, I failed miserably. The nose was either too large or too small, the eyes too far apart or too close together, the lips too fat or too thin. The man who had been so noble of visage in life looked an utter cretin on canvas. Terribly frustrated, as I am sure you can imagine, I took to trying to render another part of his body, a part, in fact, which I remembered rather vividly, that organ which he had so gainfully and earnestly employed to deposit the seed in my field that would someday grow into none other than your governor, my son, the Honorable James Grant. I discovered, much to my pride and satisfaction, that I had a knack and natural talent for rendering the membrum virile. *It was neither too small, nor too large, neither too fat, nor too thin—it was, in all modesty—a perfect likeness, all the more so due to my use of chiaroscuro! Excuse me, but would you mind terribly, sir, if I permit myself to use the term* penis? *I do so, I can assure you, not in any vulgar manner as some demimondaine or depraved bawd might, but rather in anatomical reference as artists and physicians do. Whenever* penis *comes out of my mouth, you should hear it as a scientific Latin term—*penis naturalis. *One might suppose that* penes, *since they're basically cylindrical and there's no need for perspective, are easy to capture; but that, I can assure you is not the case—the vessels, wrinkles, and hair can pose quite a challenge to the artist. With charcoal, gouache, tempera, and oils I did my best to bring Lord Grant's* penis *to life. In depicting it life-size, larger than life, and in miniature as well, in profile and head on, up close and from a distance, I devoted all of my energies, talents, and sensibilities to capturing the very soul of Lord Grant's* penis—*may it rest in peace. After having completed some hundred portraits of that particular* penis *, I realized that it would be valuable for the development of my artistic skills to try my hand at other* penes. *I copied all of the illustrious* penes *immortalized in an edition of engravings of European masterpieces—such immortal* penes *as that of Praxiteles' Hermes and the smaller but more divine one of Christ in Hans Holbein's* Madonna and Child. *Though some have said that Christ was a Jew, his* penis *was, I can assure you, in no way circumscribed. It so reminded me of the governor's when he was a baby that, based on my memories of his infancy, I took to sketching it as well. Doing copies of copies and relying on penile memories were not, I felt after a while, doing justice to my talents. I needed real* penes, *as I am sure you can understand, to pose for me. Because our slaves, being slaves, were constrained to do whatever I told them to do, it was convenient* *for me to have them model for me. Painting Negro* penes, *as you can well imagine, required a significant change in my palate. I used a good deal more sienna, ochre, and, of course, brown and black than I had on Lord Grant's, his penis being rather pink, very much the hue of the nose in Hyacinthe Rigaud's celebrated portrait of Louis XIV. Do you know Rigaud's work? A French influence on Lord Grant's penis cannot be denied. At any rate, Mr. Aryeh, my aspiration, as I enlarge my oeuvre, is to depict a wide range and assortment of* penes, penes *of every color, shape, size, and quality, capturing their many different traits, attributes, attitudes, demeanors, moods, postures, eccentricities, and what have you. One cannot help but think of the words of Virgil, 'Quot homines tot penes.' Did he not also say, 'Si quaeris penis amoenam, circumspice?' Naturally the prospect of painting a* penis *that has been ritually mutilated according to Judaic law is an exciting one—a* penis *just like Abraham's, Moses's, Judas's, and Shylock's. And so, Mr. Aryeh, I'll get to the point and reason for my visit. If you would be so gracious as to allow your* penis *to pose for me, I shall repay you in any way I can. Be assured that I have enormous influence over the governor—he's really rather a mummy's mollycoddle. I am in a position to speak with him on your behalf and to your benefit no less than to your detriment."*

As I unlaced my breeches, Lady Grant asked that I not to mention her visit to the governor. "He does not approve of what he deems my 'naughty hobby.'"

While her son may not have appreciated her artistic endeavors, the other women of the Grant household apparently did. First his sister, then his wife, and then his two daughters together, called on me, all of them informing me that they had seen and admired Lady Grant's portrait.

The governor's widowed sister, Phoebe Grant-Granville, confessed to having inherited a fascination with penises from her mother: "I love to look at them, to pet and play with them, to twist them all about, lift them up and down, and bat them about, to tie pretty ribbons around their necks or hang little bells from them. I give them special little pet names and talk to them."

Calling mine "Jewie," Mrs. Grant-Granville invited me to bring it to visit her private cottage on the Grant estate. "Wouldn't little Jewie like to come and have a bit of fun with Phoebe?" I always sensed that the woman resented it that I, like some overprotective chaperone, had to come along with my penis on those visits. "How's my little Jewie?" she'd ask. "Has Mr. Aryeh been taking good care of you? I hope he's made certain that you've had plenty of rest and lots to eat and drink. Shall we play a little game now? Hide-and-seek, mumblety-peg, tug-of-war, bump-the-bunny, or blind man's bluff?" My penis, I discovered, liked bump-the-bunny best.

Madness seemed to run in the family. Grant's daughters—Calliope (age eighteen) and Thalia (fifteen)—were as crazy as his mother and sister. They too, having seen their grandmother's portrait, made appointments with my penis. "As unbelievable as it may seem to you, Mr. Aryeh, Thalia still hasn't ever seen one in per-

son," Calliope announced with the tone and composure of one well acquainted with men's private parts, "and since you, as we understand from the testimony of both our grandmother and our aunt, are a gentleman who is not averse to displaying his King Henry to members of the fairer sex, I do hope you will be so kind as to educate my innocent sister by showing her what it looks like and how it works."

"Now I know how it works," Thalia subsequently commented as Calliope, tugging at the laces of her corset, helped her dress, "but I'm afraid I still don't understand why it works."

Their mother, upon learning from Calliope what I had taught Thalia, called upon me to warn me to keep my penis away from her children. The tenor of her reprimand and caveat was so stern that I was quite surprised when, while sustaining the reproachful tone, Mrs. Grant added, "If you must have a Grant woman, let it be me so that my daughters might be spared your brutish advances. Just as Demeter offered to lay with Pluto in order to protect her daughter, the fair Persephone, from being raped again by the King of Hell, so I, moved by maternal love and duty, am prepared and determined to make that same noble carnal sacrifice for my beloved Thalia's sake. So take me! What, O Death, are you waiting for? Take me now! Take me to the Underworld."

EIGHT

1784–1821

WHEREIN PONCE DE LEÓN OPENS FLORIDA'S
FIRST THEATER AND RETURNS TO THE STAGE
TO PLAY, AMONG OTHERS, CHRIST, COLUMBUS,
HAMLET, AN OLD MAN, AND HIMSELF

ANGELIO. You have read the contract? You understand the terms? And you agree to them?

DON JUAN. Ay, Angelio. No longer do I age. No more am I susceptible to illness. And the lovely maiden Leonor shall lie in my bed embracing me. And after her, the innocent Lisarda. And her fair maid, Beatriz. And the little shepherdess, Florina. And countless other nubile beauties for years to come. And never shall I be too old to enjoy them. Never too frail to please them. Yes, Angelio, I have signed the contract.

ANGELIO. Then your soul is mine!

DON JUAN. A small price to pay for eternal youth! What is a soul, alas, if it is trapped in a body that is old, decrepit, and infirm?

ANGELIO Ha! Ha! My slave! Now you shall behold my true appearance! (*Angelio steps onto a revolving stage machine, which takes him out of sight and replaces him with a figure of the devil. Sky rockets are fired.*) Ha! Ha! Haha!

DON JUAN. Ha! Ha! Haha!—yourself. Why should I care who you are? Bring on the women, dear Satan! Your slave is ready to enjoy himself!

ANTONIO MIRA DE NABOROSO, *El viejo y el demonio*
(The Old Man and the Devil)

"Call me Ponce," Mr. De Leon declared with a flourish of his Iberian short sword as I entered the Theater Room of his museum on that muggy Friday morning with a printout of the story of Samson ben Aryeh, Shulamit Morteira, and the Jews of Florida. "Juan Ponce de León! That's how I introduced myself once Britain had surrendered the Floridas back to Spain by signing the Treaty of Paris. Florida and I were Spanish once more. I had been so named, I'd say, by my allegiant father, Diego Ponce de León, after his renowned forebear, the illustrious Spanish conquistador who discovered Florida two and a half centuries ago, yes, the gallant hidalgo and heroic champion of the Spanish Crown and Roman Church, whose glorious name lives on not only in me but in the hearts of all men who dream exalted dreams. Don Juan Ponce de León! Yes I know, Mr. Siegel, it sounds a bit highfalutin' now, but flamboyance was fashionable in the eighteenth century."

He was dressed in the same outlandish outfit he had been wearing on the first day I met him outside the Garden of Eden. He explained that, except for the sunglasses, it was the costume he had worn in a play he alleged to have written, produced, and starred in to celebrate the inauguration of the second period of Spanish rule in Florida: *Algunas hazañas estupendas de las muchas de Don Juan Ponce de León*. "The message of the play was that, while we as individuals may grow old and die, Spain, nourished by the fresh waters that flow in the rivers and streams of her colonies, shall remain young and vital forever. *Viva las Floridas españolas!* The spectacle affirmed and celebrated Spain's inalienable right to everlasting sovereignty in Florida. This was sensationally dramatized in a climactic scene in which I planted the Spanish colors in Florida ground. Reverential Indians, after saluting both the flag and me, merrily sang, 'Con las armas resplandecientes los caballeros españols vienen del cieolo volando.' The scene so deeply moved Don Vizente Manuel de Zespedes, the new adelantado of Spanish East Florida, that he shed a tear or two. He considered himself an aficionado of theater."

Mr. De Leon looked tired, more gaunt than usual; his voice was weaker and more raspy, and he coughed more than ever. After he had taken the time to read chapter seven, expunging the section on the Grant women and then paying for what remained, he asked about chapters one, three, and six, and I renewed my vows to have them for him soon.

Swallowing several morphine tablets with a gulp of cocainized rum punch, then lighting a Ponce de León Maduro, inhaling deeply, coughing a few times, and clearing his throat, Mr. De Leon said that he hoped I was rested as we had a lot of work to do: "Today's story is a long one."

To make a long story short, Juan Ponce de León had, during the thirty-seven years to be covered in this chapter, both produced eighteen theatrical plays ("an average of only almost one every two years") and had love affairs with thirty-six women, "an average of only almost one a year, my romance with Tamara Xanagrande being the longest, lasting no less than five years, and that with Alicia Olisbo being the shortest, lasting no more than five minutes. But that is not to say that the intensity and sincerity of my passion for Alicia did not, in its own way, match that of my love for Tamara. In regard to these two affairs, in thinking about the brevity of the one and the length of the other, write something about love and time, about the ways in which love transcends time, defies it, or doesn't, about the ways in which time and love are enemies or allies, or both at once. I'm hoping, Mr. Siegel, that you have both the philosophical and discursive wherewithal to come up with some profound things for me to say about the interdependence of love and time. It is, after all, an important theme in my book. As well as being moving and amusing, my autobiography should have a philosophical dimension to it—dare I say, a profundity? If I were writing in the Andalucian Ladino of my youth, I could easily say quite a few very profound things about love and time. I would quote from the maxims of Johanan Yarhoni. But it's difficult to convey the profundity, wisdom, and wit of his insights in modern English. The semantic range of your vocabulary, Mr. Siegel, is relatively limited. So, for example, one of his most cherished aphorisms about love and time will probably mean very little to you: "The broken heart of the monarch butterfly in springtime is forgotten by the gypsy moth in winter no matter how sweetly the sparrows sing to the lions." Mr. De Leon repeated the line with theatrical grandiloquence in Ladino, and then noted matter-of-factly: "That brought a tear to my father's eye every time he recited it, which, I can assure you, was often. Things were, in general, more profound five hundred years ago than they are today. The modern ear is not very well attuned to words of wisdom."

Mr. De Leon devoted the morning to telling me about his dramaturgical enterprises. He claimed to have founded Florida's first professional theater by transforming the building that had previously been a church, a cigar factory, and a synagogue, into Eagle Springs' Teatro Ponce de León. The same building would, in 1915, become Ponce de Leon's Museum of Florida History.

He began by presenting me with an alphabetical list of twelve of the eighteen plays which he had produced and in which he performed. "Eighteen dramas, an average of approximately one every two years: the run of Antonio Mira de Naboroso's *El viejo y el demonio* being the longest, lasting no less than five years, while Shakespeare's *El príncipe desgraciado de Dinamarca* had the shortest run—one night. What was profound in English in

Elizabethan England had become nonsensical by the time it reached Spanish Florida in translation a few hundred years later. When I, as Hamlet, posed the question, 'Ser o no ser, ese es uno dilema muy confuso,' the audience snickered. They knew very well that 'to be' is unquestionably better than 'not to be.'

"At the time the Teatro Ponce de León offered the only entertainment in northeastern Florida beyond those diversions proffered by the saloons, dance halls, and brothels. Theater proved almost as profitable to me as Catholicism, Judaism, tobacco, and seedless oranges had previously been."

In each of the display cases in the Theater Room there were playbills, scripts, sundry props, arrayed parts of costumes, masks, cosmetics, and other such things as one would expect in a gallery devoted to theater history. "Most of my costumes and props," Mr. De Leon mentioned, "were later stolen by Seminole Indians." There were twelve of these displays, one for each of the plays on the alphabetically ordered list that Mr. De Leon had written out for me:

Algunas hazañas estupendas de las muchas de Don Juan Ponce de León [Some of the Many Stupendous Exploits of Don Juan Ponce de León], by Juan Ponce de León in memory of his ancestor

Amor, tabaco y mujer [Love, Tobacco, and Woman], by Setho Ponce de León in honor of his brother

Amor y el viejo [Love and the Old Man], by Leandro de Cota

La brevedad desagradable de la vida [The Annoying Brevity of Life], by Setho Ponce de León in honor of his brother

Farsa de Colon zurramato [The Farce of Columbus the Dumbass], by Don Joel Nacupe

La fénix de Florida [The Phoenix of Florida], by Vizente Manuel de Zespedes

La fuente de juventud [The Fountain of Youth], by Juan Ponce de León in honor of Vizente Manuel de Zespedes

Los milagros chistosos de sexo [The Amusing Miracles of Sex], by Tamara Xanagrande

El principe desgraciado de Dinamarca [Hamlet], by William Shakespeare

La puta virtuosa de Samaria [The Virtuous Samaritan Whore], by Juan "El Pedo" Conen

El robo de Sabina [The Rape of Sabina], anonymous

El viejo y el demonio [The Old Man and the Devil], by Antonio Mira de Naboroso

Also on exhibit in a corner of the Theater Room was a half-life-size bronze statue of *la Católica:* "When the Spanish returned, I replaced the menorah decorating the Fountain with Her Majesty so that finally Ysabel could be bathed in the waters of the Fountain of which she had dreamed."

As I was guided from one display case to another, Mr. De Leon commented on the plays. "I can, I suppose, after all these years, confess that, while I, pretending to be Setho Ponce de León, took credit for the composition of this one, *Amor, tabaco y mujer,* I did, in fact, plagiarize it from *Dios, amor y mujer,* a play by a forgotten hack, Ignacio Fregona, that I had seen many years before with that singing barmaid in Puerto Rico. The changes I made, though minor, turned a didactic religious melodrama into a burlesque satirical comedy—the line between the genres, I discovered, is a fine one. Much of *La brevedad desagradable de la vida* was also, I admit, stolen from Fregona. While Mr. Shakespeare's *El príncipe desgraciado de Dinamarca* was the least successful of these plays (despite my translation, clever plot changes, and energetic performance as the stuttering and limping prince), it was, in my opinion, substantially more entertaining than Governor Zespedes' hackneyed and bathetic semi-autobiographical and entirely self-aggrandizing *La fénix de Florida.* As a connoisseur of theater, the adelantado imagined he could write for the stage. He had all of the arrogance but none of the talent it takes to write something good. The governor was also responsible for *El robo de Sabina,* and, given Zespedes' authority in Spanish East Florida, it was expedient to consent to stage it. Although I don't think it apt to include much discussion of his plays in my book, I'll take a moment to tell you about *El robo de Sabina,* Mr. Siegel, just to give you some sense of Zespedes' dramatic sensibilities.

"General Nathaniel Greene, a depraved bachelor who had been in command of the American army in the South during the Revolution, was visiting East Florida. Well aware that the Americans had their eyes on the colony, Zespedes wanted to ingratiate himself to the general (if not to have something on him that might be of diplomatic value for blackmail in the future). To that end, he requested that I produce a play of his own composition for Greene and his entourage of American military officers. Although Zespedes did conceive of its characters, plot, and theme, to say that he had 'written' *El robo de Sabina* would be misleading. It was supposed to be a realistic reenactment of a true story about the rape of a Christian woman by a Seminole Indian here in Eagle Springs in 1785. Sabina's only lines were 'Help! Help!' shouted in English at the beginning of the performance so that it would be understood by the intended audience of Americans. She was then immediately gagged and bound which, of course, prevented her from uttering another word on stage. And all the Indian ever said was, 'Yes, yes, red man lik'um white woman.' These words were grunted over and over while he had sex with Sabina in as many positions as the particular actor of that evening could manage. That was the whole play. All I did was supply the stage with a set that was supposed to represent Sabina's cabin, the ropes with which she was bound, and the costume and headdress for the Indian. Zespedes also asked that I cast the actress to play Sabina. I hired Mary Jack, the girl from the Setting Sun Saloon (the name of which had been changed with the transfer of rule to El Quilombo, which it remained until Andrew Jackson renamed it the Watering Hole). A different actor played the Indian for each performance. 'Actor' may not be the right word, since the part was taken by volunteers from Zespedes' cabinet and, on several nights, by Zespedes himself. His acting was as bad as his writing. But, as I've said, I don't want to write about any of this in my book. Perhaps I was being puritanical, even prudish, at the time, but, I confess, I didn't approve of it. I must, however, also confess that I didn't condemn it either. After all it entertained the audience enormously, and Mary Jack, flattered to be chosen to play the female lead, was genuinely thrilled with the success of her theatrical debut. It pleased me to please Mary. 'I got a standing ovation after every performance, and sometimes during it,' she boasted. 'And bouquets of roses, not to mention a proposal of marriage from an American colonel. I love acting! I want to quit El Quilombo and work for you. If you let me join your company, I'll love you forever.' And so Mary went on to play the part of Lisarda in *El viejo y el demonio*, Antonia in *La brevedad desagradable de la vida*, and Ophelia in *El principe desgraciado de Dinamarca*. In her opinion, however, those plays did not allow her to show her talent in the way that *El robo de Sabina* had. 'Zespedes,' she maintained, 'is a genius. Unlike most playwrights, he gets right to the part everyone, deep down, really wants to see.'

"Just as I had felt that I had little choice but to produce *El robo de Sabina* and *La fénix de Florida*, so too I felt constrained to stage *Los milagros chistosos de sexo* as conceived by Tamara Xanagrande. She had more power over me than Zespedes had over Florida. I was bewitched by her lips. Before meeting me, Tamara had never seen a play or even read a book. I had to help her write the lines since, despite the fact that she could speak Spanish, English, French, Romani, and Zemblan, the Canary Island girl was illiterate. Even with my assistance, her play was puerile, vulgar, bathetic, and completely unintelligible. But love goaded me to overlook the quality of Tamara's literary accomplishments. Why audiences did the same, I do not know."

I asked about the two plays that were supposedly written by my employer about Ponce de León—*Algunas hazañas estupendas de las muchas de Don Juan Ponce de León* and *La fuente de juventud.* "Why, since you've already written the story of Ponce de León and the Fountain of Youth, do you need me?"

"Well, for one thing, the plays only covered my life up until 1513. They were in Spanish rhymed couplets, and were not, in all honesty, completely true. I never hesitated, at that time, to sacrifice truth for the sake of entertainment. Your job, Mr. Siegel, is to tell the truth and make it entertaining.

"Come over here, Mr. Siegel. Look here, look at this furry codpiece and the huge floppy brimmed velvet admiral's hat that I wore in *Farsa de Colon zurramato.* I was the author of the satirical farce, but, because there were so many people at the time who greatly admired *el gilipollasqueroxo,* I thought it better to attribute it to a fictitious Don Joel Nacupe (an anagram of 'Juan Ponce de León'). I also authored the *La puta virtuosa de Samaria,* based on the story of the Samaritan woman in the Gospels of John. For that I used another anagrammatic nom de plume (Juan "El Pedo" Conen) to avoid the risk of falling out of the good graces of the Most Reverend Francisco X. Capullo, Bishop of the Spanish Floridas. I feared that, if offended by my play, he might use his influence as Zespedes's confessor to close my theater.

"'Every one who drinks the water from your well, Señora, will be thirsty again,' a handsome Jesus, leading up to a dramatic climax, said to the beautiful woman of Samaria. 'But those who drink from my Fountain shall enjoy eternal life.' And then the Samaritan damsel fellated the Lord. As I said, flamboyance was fashionable in those days. Of course, it was all very tasteful and subtly done. The audience couldn't actually see what she was doing because Jesus was concealed from the waist down by the well. She could, one might have supposed, have been merely genuflecting before the Messiah. The audience was left to infer what was going on from the beatific expression on Christ's face. However he understood the scene, His Excellency Bishop Capullo so enjoyed the production that he came backstage to congratulate both me and Tamara. The scene was her idea and she played the part of the Samaritan woman with me starring as Christ, a part I hadn't played since I was a child in Spain. She wasn't a very talented actress, but, I can assure you, she was gifted when it came to fellatio. Speaking of which, whatever happened to the fellatio scene in chapter four?"

I promised I was working on it.

"Good," Mr. De Leon said firmly and continued: "The exceptional oral skills of both Señora Menendez and Tamara Xanagrande should be recognized, if not immortalized, in my autobiography. Tamara relished oral sex, drooling over it, both as its bestower and its beneficiary. I want you to describe her lips, Mr. Siegel, as so delicious, so vividly scrumptious, that it will make our readers thirst like Christ on the cross. And make the description ambiguous in such a way that readers will not be quite sure whether the lips in question—swollen, flush, warm-blooded, palpitant, deliquescent, balmy, rosy, marshy, effusive, eager, and what-have-you—are buccal or vaginal, or both. Make the two orifices leading into the sumptuous body of Tamara Xanagrande indistinguishable from one another on the page. Or rather pages—yes, devote as many pages to those flamboyant lips as your command of poetic language can generate. Of course it must be admitted that, in life, the teeth above and beard below made it impossible to confuse the two unless you were very, very drunk."

Leaning against the display case containing Christ's wig and beard, I couldn't restrain myself from interrupting. More than a few of glasses of cocainized rum punch had made me edgy. "Excuse me, Mr. De Leon, but don't you think that in a book, the premise of which is that its narrator has been alive for five hundred and forty years, we might write a few things about history, about political events, about a few things more serious than Tamara Xanagrande's labia? Surely the author of this book should have something to say about imperialism, colonialism, slavery, genocide, and the oppression of indigenous cultures. In all of the chapters so far, your only real concern has been with Ponce de León's sex life. As I've already tried to explain, the detailed descriptions of women and sex should serve some larger vision, some philosophical idea, aesthetic end, perhaps even some truth. The hero of the narrative should learn something from his affairs and gain some insight into the mysteries of love. So far, the protagonist of our book hasn't changed at all in his relationships with the women in his life. All he does is move on to new identities, and from one lover to another. Frankly, I think we need some character development."

I know, as I think back over my impatient and somewhat fractious outburst, that I was, especially given the fact that I was being so generously paid, out of line, and I quite understand why my employer became angry. Placing his hands on the display case dedicated to *La puta virtuosa de Samaria,* Mr. De Leon leaned across it and toward me, exhaled cigar smoke in my direction, coughed, coughed again, and then spoke sternly. "Do not interrupt me again, Mr. Siegel. How many times do I have to tell you that? And how many times do I have to ask you, 'How many times do I have to tell you that?' How many times do I have to remind you, furthermore, that this is not *our* book, Mr. Siegel—this is *my* book. And in *my* book, there should be little concern with the history or politics that you consider so significant. While I recall practically nothing about Zespedes' political activities in Florida, I distinctly remember his daughter's nipples. Señora Menendez fellating me is more important than Adelantado Menendez capturing Fort Caroline. Furthermore, it is a fact that, in all these years, after having been in love so many times, I have not learned anything from my affairs. Nothing. I want my readers to understand that age does not, despite what anyone may propose in a vain effort to take the sting out of senescence, help one understand love or control it. Although the pleasures of love may be transient, the pain of love never eases up, never, no matter how sweetly the sparrows sing to the lions.

"Furthermore, Mr. Siegel, it is true, as you say, that in all these years I have hardly changed in my relationships with women. What's wrong with that? Why would I want to change? Women have always loved me just as I am. And, as far as my readers expecting something 'more serious than Tamara Xanagrande's labia,' I can assure you, Mr. Siegel, that, in the five and a half centuries that I have been alive, I have come across very few things in this world more serious and significant, more dazzling and flamboyant, more breathtaking and bewitching, than those lips. Do them justice, Mr. Siegel.

"And now, let me continue without further interruption," Mr. De Leon muttered, clearing his throat to continue his paean to Tamara Xanagrande's lips. After eulogizing the smell and taste of them, the feel of them on various parts of his body, he finally said that it was time to move on to other parts of other women. "Yes, I must leave time today for Polly Iffley's fingers, Dominga Zespedes' nipples, and Mrs. Florence Basolon's buttocks. I loved those buttocks more than any buttocks ever. My first encounter with them was not a visual one. Florence hardly knew me at the time, but was a playful girl and bold enough to swagger over and take a seat on my lap, laughing as she did so, and talking about I don't remember what. The feel of those buttocks on my thigh, through her skirts and my trousers, intimated the marvelous." The first time he had seen them, I was excitedly told, he had counted the freckles on them, "seven of them, the same as the number of stars in the Pleiades, and similarly arranged on those heavenly haunches." After further description of their appearance, and an account of how they felt, the softness of the skin and firmness of the flesh, Mr. De Leon said that, although he had a lot more to say about those buttocks, it was time for lunch, "and besides, I'm getting ahead of myself. I did not become acquainted with that particular posterior until the Civil War."

Because it had started to rain, Isabel served the meal in a room in the main house adjoining the museum. I know it will seem that I am making it up, but, unbelievable as it may be, I swear it is absolutely true: lunch that day was rump roast—yes, *colita de cuadril asada*, rump roast with tomatoes, onions, garlic, and spices.

"On the very seat upon which you are sitting, Mr. Siegel, Mrs. Basolon's buttocks once found rest," Mr. De Leon mentioned as I took my first taste of the meat. "And it was here, in this dining room, that I first met Diego Cabeza de Cabra and realized at once, the moment I looked into his eyes, that Justa Respalona was not a faithful wife. He too sat just where you are sitting, Mr. Siegel."

Hardly eating, but heartily drinking rum punch, Mr. De Leon went on to explain that, at the end of the eighteenth century, Juan Ponce de León had again changed identities to conceal the fact that he wasn't growing older. "As Setho Ponce de León, my look-alike, but much younger, brother from Spain, I took over management of the Teatro Ponce de León from myself and dedicated several productions to myself, the supposedly deceased founder of the theater."

Mr. De Leon suddenly asked an odd question: "Does this ever happen to you, Mr. Siegel? Sometimes upon waking up in the morning, I think about it. I realize who I am and where I am, and I can hardly believe it. I wake up amazed to be me, Juan Ponce de León. Does that ever happen to you, Mr. Siegel? Do you ever wake up amazed to be you?"

"I woke up this morning amazed to be in Florida," I answered. "It's hard to believe I'm really doing this."

"Bollitos de Susona," Mr. De Leon announced, pointing to the little dessert dumplings that Isabel brought to the table as soon as I had finished my rump roast. "I wanted you to taste them, Mr. Siegel, because they were served here, in this very room, in celebration of the marriage of Shulamit Morteira and Samson ben Aryeh. You should add a description of them to chapter seven. Note that they're supposed to look like testicles. They're a symbol of fertility. That's why they were traditionally served at Jewish weddings. We had a game, a contest between the men to see who could eat the greatest number of them. I know Ze'ev Mizrahi could have eaten lots more than I at my wedding party. He had a big appetite. It was polite of him to let the groom win."

Mr. De Leon stopped Isabel from taking our empty dessert bowls away. "Before you leave us, would you be so sweet as to recite Antonia's soliloquy from *La brevedad desagradable de la vida* for Mr. Siegel?"

"Los minutos que royendo están los años," the young woman began, only to be interrupted by Mr. De Leon. "En inglés, por favor."

Closing her dark eyes and clasping her hands together, she composed herself to begin again. "The minutes that gnaw away at our years . . ." As her eyes opened, slight tears formed in them as they focused on Mr. De Leon. Flowing with syllables, her lips formed a fountain of words: "the hungry minutes seem to refuse to forgive us as they gather together into the hours that wear away our days . . ." As she delivered the lament, I thought to myself that if I could capture the beauty of her mouth in writing, I'd have a description of Tamara Xanagrande's lips that would amply satisfy my employer.

After lunch, once we had returned to the Theater Room, an impatient Mr. De Leon handed me another list, a handwritten, alphabetically ordered list of twenty-six women's names, nine of them already familiar to me from previous stories. "The inclusion of these names in my book, like the names of the deceased Zhotee-eloq, is very important. I want some trace of each and every one of them, some hint that they were once alive, loved and loving, to remain behind. I don't want them to disappear with me. Their names must be published.

"It is because of insomnia that I particularly remember the names of these women. Insomnia is, according to the *Kez Kol Basar,* Johanan Yarhoni's medical treatise on love, one of the most perilous of amorous passion's many symptoms. It is a symptom that, if untreated, soon becomes an ailment. So Yarhoni prescribed a kabbalistic remedy wherein the sleepless lover was to think of the holy letters of the Hebrew alphabet in their order, and, for each of those twenty-two letters, to whisper the name of a Jewish forebear in Tanak, our Bible, whose name begins with that letter. Starting with *alef,* I would think of Abishag, the young girl from Shunam who lay with David in his old age; then, with *beth,* there was the beautiful Bathsheba, who had been David's adulterous lover and then wife. I made my way all the way to the end, to *tav* for Tamar. But I could never decide whether it was Tamar the daughter of David, Tamar the daughter of Absalom, or Tamar the wife of Onan, who disguised herself as a harlot to seduce her father-in-law. And thoughts of Tamar, whichever one of them came to mind, led me by force to my Tamar—Tamara Xanagrande. I'd picture her lips, my heart would start pounding, and I'd sit up in bed more wide awake than I had been when invoking the Shunamite. Blaming it on the Bible that Yarhoni's treatment didn't work for me, I decided to adapt his prescription to my own experiences, to use Roman letters rather than Hebrew, and women from my own life rather than all those daughters, maidens, wives, widows, queens, and whores of the Bible. So I'd start with *A* for Acabara— Geronima Acabara—the sexually immoderate sister of the bandit Juan 'El Desalmado' Acabara and a bandit herself, love's *desperada.* I'd make my way toward *Z* for Zespedes—Dominga Zespedes—the governor's daughter, a languid lover with intriguingly inverted nipples, passively lying on her back, eyes closed, and a sly smile on her lips most of the time, her flaccid arms and legs wide apart, taking love serenely in; and, when it was over and done, she'd always be sure to politely say, 'Muchas gracias, Señor Ponce.'

"At the top of the list, Senorita Acabara was, on the other hand, a wild one. Her unbound hair, black, thick, and long, would whisk about above me, whipping my face. Her hands clutched my shoulders, the nails digging in, her hips rocking, swaying, pitching back and forth as if Geronima was breaking a bucking horse. And when she was actually on her horse, a spirited Andalucian stallion, loping, prancing, and caracoling, it was as if she were astride a lover, so at one did woman and animal seem to become under the strong and sure grip of the rider's knees, and the controlling action of reins, crop, and spurs.

"If I made it all the way from Acabara to Zespedes without falling asleep, at the end of the list, Filomena Frescachona, the flower girl of Lebrija, would inevitably appear to me. 'Why have you forgotten me? Who is this Maria Fuentes who seems to have usurped my place in your heart? Do you no longer love me?'

"As I went through the alphabet, whispering each woman's name, I'd breathe in on the surname, out on the first name. With each of the names there'd be an image, or a few words, a thought and feeling, a memory that would adumbrate a story and resurrect flesh. Oh, if only I had time to tell you the details of each and every one of those stories, and bring to life all the women who helped put me to sleep." Just as he had commented on the plays on the list that Ponce de León had produced, so he did the same with the women I had not heard about on his list of lovers:

Acabara, Geronima

Burbuja, Bonita ["The ever-anxious wife of Commandante Bernardo Burbuja, always threatening something—to tell her husband or the police, to kill herself or me, or to run away to Cuba. And funnily enough, she did run away to Cuba. Why, I am not certain. But I suspect that it had something to do with love. I was afraid of her. But the fear caused a desire, that desire more fear, and that fear still greater desire. Some years later, during the Civil War, she was replaced on the list by another wife, another *B*—Florence Basolon. *B* as in the buttocks I've told you about."]

Cachonda, Pompeia ["She was a co-worker of Mary Jack at El Quilombo— Mary, the prostitute I had in mind for the initiation of Shulamit's son

into the mysteries of love, Mary who played Sabina in *El robo*. Once
Mary had joined the Teatro Ponce de León, she persuaded me to hire
Pompeia. Prostitutes make fine actresses, she argued, well-versed as
they are in pleasing men by playing the parts of women pleased."]

Doudounne, Odile ["A touring singer and dancer who performed with
her own little orchestra of French dandies for one night only at the
Almeja Bailanda in St. Augustine. Her billing claimed that she had
danced privately for King Louis XVI on the eve of his execution. She
used the same bright crimson gloss on both her nipples and her lips,
and she wore cornucopia-shaped earrings of black glass. She lost one
in my bed, and by the time I had found it, she had left Florida for the
north. On the last of the three nights she spent with me I whispered in
her ear, 'I shall love you for as long as you live.' I still have the earring."]

Espinosa, Juana ["You remember, Mr. Siegel—the young girl with the
azure eyes, the mole on her cheek, and an identical one on her right
breast—yes, the old woman in Paynestown."]

Fuentes, Sister Maria ["You did all right by my saintly nun, Mr. Siegel. As
good as could be expected, I suppose, by one who had never seen her,
or ever been touched by her."]

Guarra, Celestina ["I'm still waiting to see how my young Castilian bride
turns out. Yes, I'm eager to read what you write about her in chapter
one."]

Horca, Avis ["Poor thing. And one of those poor things who survives
just by being so. An orphaned street girl from Barbados, handsome
enough to maintain herself by taking on lovers. Avis said she loved
me, and perhaps it was so. We never know for sure, do we? I forgot
to talk about her when I was telling you about my adventures in the
1600s. I should have told you about her for chapter five. But we don't
have time to go back. Poor Avis. I rented the car for you from Avis, Mr.
Siegel, in memory of her."]

Iffley, Polly ["The red-haired daughter of an American diplomat. She
didn't think sexual intercourse was sexual unless it involved vaginal
penetration and so, to preserve her virginity as a treasure to be offered
to a future husband, she used either her hand or mouth to please men,
among them both Juan Ponce de León and, a year or so later, Setho
Ponce de León. There was something touching about her. And while
a slew of men may have asked for her hand, no man, as far as I know,
ever asked for it in marriage. She told me that she had heard about a
miraculous Fountain in India. 'Its waters,' she said as if she believed it,
'restore the virginity of any girl who bathes in them. If only I had ac-

cess to that Fountain!' She probably wouldn't be included on this list if I could think of any other women in my life whose surname began with an *I*."]

Jack, Mary ["You know—the sweet little whore turned thespian."]

Kitzler, Esther ["The wife of an Austrian diplomat who was attractive not because of her looks which, in any case, I hardly remember, but because of her smell. The unforgettable, overpowering scent of her hair, her skin, her breath, made it impossible to resist her. I had my first sniff of her at a dinner party at the Zespedes' home, the same manor that had been occupied by governors Menendez and Grant. Now it houses the ridiculous Ripley's Believe It or Not! Museum. One whiff of Esther and I ached to plunge my nose into the civetous down of her armpits and her lower belly in hopes of satisfying the olfactory hunger she aroused in me. It was not some perfume, but a natural ambergris, a carnal fragrance, an aromatic oestrual musk. In the carriage back to my home from the inn where we'd rendezvous on occasional afternoons, I'd smell my hands to resavor the enchantment of it. Mona Keegle, an actress in my company who played the part of *la Católica* in *Algunas hazañas estupendas de las muchas de Don Juan Ponce de León,* might have had a chance to be my *K* if she had not been such a drunkard. She was as violently harsh and angry with the world when she had been drinking as she was sweetly supple and tender with me when she sobered up, always swearing never to drink another drop."]

Liqizhotqi

Morteira, Shulamit ["Doña Maria de Solis Menendez keeps trying to barge in here and take over the *M* position. But how can she compete with the Jewess who became my bride? There's another *M* as well, a girl named Masilla, Yolanda Masilla. She also tries to push in here, just as she forced her way into my office at the theater in hopes of persuading me to give her a part in one of my plays, assuming that merely by stripping naked for me she would have the opportunity to act on stage. Her assumption was correct. She played Beatriz in *El viejo y el demonio* and an Indian maiden in *La fuente de juventud, Farsa de Colon zurramato, Amor, tabaco y mujer,* and *Algunas hazañas estupendas de las muchas de Don Juan Ponce de León.* If not for Shulamit Morteira and Señora Menendez, Yolanda Masilla might have been on this list."]

Nightingale, Eve ["I'd rather not talk about her. It's not a nice story. A tale of anguish might detract from a book about pleasure."]

Olisbo, Alicia ["Doña Alicia was extraordinarily beautiful but famously faithful to her husband, Don Julio Olisbo, the Spanish Crown's tax assessor for East Florida, and one of those dull men who boast that they do not cheat on their wives. She was, perhaps, even in love with him. But that, of course, did not prevent me from desiring her. If this pact with Satan business as portrayed in Naboroso's *El viejo y el demonio* were possible, and if I had been given an opportunity to become the devil's slave, to give away my soul in exchange for no more than an opportunity to see Alicia naked, I would have signed the contract in a second. In a moment of such mad love, I asked myself, 'What is the value of perpetual youth, if I cannot behold the nakedness of the beautiful Doña Alicia Olisbo before I die?' I know, Mr. Siegel, that I have often used the word 'beautiful' to describe many of the women in my life, and beautiful they were — I can assure you that I've not uttered it lightly or loosely. But Alicia was not beautiful like other mortally beautiful women, but rather divinely beautiful as men have imagined Venus Aphrodite and the Holy Virgin Mary. I was never introduced to her, never conversed with her, but, around the turn of the century, I would sometimes see her at her husband's side during government ceremonies and church functions in St. Augustine. I would always wonder what she might look like without her clothes. I would try to imagine it. On several occasions she had accompanied her husband to openings at the Teatro Ponce de León. I finally met Don Julio at the card table during a gentleman's evening at the home of Zespedes' successor, the old bachelor Juan Nepomucono de Quesada. It had been noted that Olisbo considered himself an accomplished player. In order to encourage his self-esteem as a gambler, and reinforce his opinion of me as a beginner, at first I lost as much as I convincingly could. He was unaware of the particular qualities of the antique Spanish deck that I asked him to shuffle in preparation for our private game of andaboba. It enabled me to win from him in one evening promissory notes for more money than he had collected in taxes in East Florida that year. Despair drove him to accept my proposition: 'Let's play one more hand, Don Julio, my friend. Only one, and if you win, I shall return all your money. I shall also return all your money if I win. But if I win, you must do me a little favor. You will need merely to admit me to your residence on some evening of your choosing, late at night after everyone has gone to bed. And then you will take me to your wife's bedroom and, while she sleeps, you will uncover her, lifting her nightgown to expose her to me. I only want to see her naked. That's all. You will be present at all times, holding a candle which you will promptly extinguish should she begin to awaken. Nothing more than that, and

no one will know of this other than you and me.' I feared that, had I
asked for more, the devoted husband and righteous Christian might
have turned me down. His trembling hand made the candlelight
flicker on her flesh. I gazed in awe at the naked shoulder blades, back,
buttocks, legs, and the soles of her delicate feet. The vision of Alicia
Olisbo was beatitude and mystery, a glorious transfiguration in which
the outer mirrored the inner as flesh became the medium for the manifestation of a transcendent, numinous, and perfect beauty. And then,
as if by divine grace, something more wonderful than anything I had
hoped for happened—she rolled over and I beheld the neck, breasts,
belly, pubis, thighs, knees, shins, and toenails. There was no difference
between spirit and flesh, between a beautiful woman and beauty itself.
Beauty itself was naked, aglow, infinite, and eternal. Don't worry,
Mr. Siegel, I don't expect you to be able to completely capture such
ineffable beauty in words. That beauty made it difficult for me, as I
tried to fall asleep, to pull myself away and go on to Betsy Pilot."]

Pilot, Betsy ["Whenever I got to P, I'd wonder, 'Whatever happened to
Betsy Pilot?' And wondering about her would lead to thoughts of
Shulamit Morteira, which took me back to M, where Señora Menendez and Yolanda Masilla were still lurking in the darkness. I'd try
to turn away and sneak past Eve Nightingale and Alicia Olisbo and
back to P. But no sooner had I breathed 'Pilot' in and 'Betsy' out, than
I'd remember Shulamit again among the daughters of Jerusalem, 'as
handsome as her namesake, as resplendently dark as the tents of Kedar and curtains of Solomon.' And then, once again, I'd try to make a
break and return to P. 'Pilot , Betsy, Pilot, Betsy, Pilot,' I'd say to myself,
exhaling, inhaling, exhaling, over and over, and sometimes, if I didn't
think about Shulamit, I might almost doze off."]

Q. ["No Q. That always troubled me, so much so that, after almost falling
asleep over Betsy Pilot, I'd suddenly be wide awake again, wishing that
I had tried to seduce Ursula Quinn when I had the chance during my
days as a tobacco farmer. She wasn't very pretty, and not very amiable,
but at least her name began with Q. Sometimes I'd let Doña Quentina
Urraca-Apretada take the spot even though it seemed like cheating,
since it was only her first name that began with the letter in question. I
didn't have a real Q until Ariana Quigley. That wasn't until 1822."]

Respalona, Justa

Sabana ["Sabrina, Sandrina, or Sardina—something like that. I can't
recall her first name, but I do remember that it started with an S. And
I remember that she was learning over the basin, washing the white

linen sheets her mother had sent from Flanders. They were intended for her wedding night, but the girl was too impatient. 'I think of every night I spend with a man as a wedding night,' she happily confessed. When I came up behind her to lift her skirt, it was as if she didn't notice. There was no resistance and not a word. She just kept scrubbing. I reached around her waist to undo the bow that secured her undergarments and they slipped down around her ankles. I caressed and massaged her buttocks, and, still without acknowledging me, she continued to wash the sheets, cheerfully dunking, rubbing, twisting, sluicing, squeezing out the soapy froth and bubbly foam. Her legs were wide enough apart to afford me access to the warm cove in the downy dale between and below gently rounded knolls. Harder and harder her hands squeezed the wet cloth, not faltering for even a moment as I entered that cove. As I moved in and out of her, she continued washing, and the dripping water became cleaner and cleaner, clearer and clearer. Finally exhausted, I had to lie down on the unmade bed, and from there I watched her hang her sheets up to dry in the bright sunlight that poured in through the open window. 'I love clean sheets more than anything in the world,' she said with pride. 'Cleanliness is next to godliness. That's what my mother says.' I wish I could remember her first name. Maybe it was Selena. Something like that. I'll let you know if I think of it."]

Taino-Pinzon Maria

Ulm, Anna Maria ["I told you about her gravestone in St Augustine. Do you recall it? I wish with all my heart that I could remember her."]

Vincilagnia, Lizabeta ["She was a widow. While she wore black and a veil to announce her husband's passing, it was not so much in mourning as it was a notification that she was free. I remember lines I recited in *El viejo y el demonio*. '¿Qual era major fuego,' I, the hero, asked, '*el de la buida, el de la casada, o de la hija moca?* In which burns the greatest fire—in the widow, the wife, or the young daughter?' And the devil answered: 'In *la buida*, the widow.' Wives are dangerous because, in weak moments or in fits of anger or jealousy, they're apt to tell their husbands what you've done. Virgins you seduce are likely to think you ought to marry them. Widows, women like Lizabeta Vincilagnia and Phoebe Grant-Granville, however, are consistently rambunctious in bed, hearty in love, and intent on having a good time. Divorced women are often just as good as widows if they're not too bitter; but there weren't so many of them in Florida in the eighteenth century. It's a funny thing—when, three weeks after her husband's funeral, in the darkness of my bedroom, I had the opportunity to take Lizabeta Vincilagnia into my arms, I couldn't help imagining that it was long ago in Spain and I was with Ysabel again. I pretended to have brought her waters from the Fountain of Life as I had once promised to do. Lizabeta's sighs and sweat, her fingernails on my back, her belly against mine, her tongue in my mouth, all belonged to the queen. The queen of Spain was young, resuscitated, and rejuvenated by love, sex, and memory. While Lizabeta's face was quite unlike *la Católica*'s, their breasts were, at least in memory and darkness, hard to tell apart. When you finally come up with the metaphors to evoke the queen's breasts, Mr. Siegel, you can feel free to use them for Lizabeta's as well. Thinking of Lizabeta's breasts at *V* tempted me to jump over *W* and *X* to Ysabel's at *Y*. But for the sake of beating the insomnia, and because I loved both Sally Whitewater and Tamara Xanagrande, I'd try to stay on track."]

Whitewater, Sally ["A Seminole midwife who tried to teach me Micco-sukee, starting me off with the words for "love" (*lhaamin*), and "fuck" (*iififi*), and a word—*impapmi*—that, like *cardar* and *ozhoo-qeezh*, en-compasses the meanings of *iififi* and *lhaamin* and yet goes far beyond them. When a man and woman *impapmi* they cannot distinguish who is feeling what—his pleasure is her pleasure is his pleasure is hers, on and on in an infinite circle, concentrated in a simultaneous detumes-cence during which their sighs, as they fall asleep and into a mutual dream, merge into a single sigh which, according Seminole lore, calls the rains. It's what the sun and moon do during a full eclipse, Sally imagined, and what heaven and earth did in the beginning to create the Seminole people. You can't helping loving a woman who believes things like that. Because she had syphilis, it was hard for her to find men with whom to *impapmi*. But trusting the powers of the waters of my Fountain, I was not afraid to love her."]

Xanagrande, Tamara ["The lips should say it all. She fell in love with me when she saw me play Juan Ponce de León in *La fuente de juventud*. There's something about a conquistador helmet that arouses women. While men often ridiculed the character for the credulity which encouraged his quest for the legendary Fountain of Youth, women seemed to find such innocence appealing. 'You not need be afraid to love me,' were the first words I heard from the marvelous lips of Tamara Xanagrande: 'I shall open my arms to embrace you, but I will never close them around you. While I would love you, I would never

try to possess you. And I ask only for what I myself am able to give.' We
put those words in her play, *Los milagros chistosos de sexo.*"]

Ysabel *la Católica* ["How I would love to see her again, to tell her that she
had been right about the Fountain, to embrace her once again, and
to tell her all that has happened since I said good-bye to her over five
hundred years ago."]

Zespedes, Dominga ["I think we've already said enough about her
today."]

"Sometimes," Mr. De Leon explained, "if I was still wide awake after going through the entire alphabet more than twice, I'd play around with the
list, rearranging the order in which the twenty-six women appeared to me.
I would make it chronological, starting with Celestina Guarra and ending
with Eve Nightingale; or I'd go from the youngest (Celestina again) to the
oldest (Liqizhotqi), or the chubbiest (Polly Iffley) to the thinnest (Maria
Fuentes), the tallest (Pompeia Cachonda) to the shortest (Mary Jack). The
list that took me from the saddest (Eve Nightingale) to the most cheerful was difficult because Susanna Sabana, Betsy Pilot, and Celestina all vied
for the final spot. And I found it impossible, despite repeated to attempts,
to arrange the women based on either how much they loved me or how
much I loved them. One of the dangers of these alternate lists was that, on
occasion Leonor Núñez de Guzmán would show up uninvited. Another
problem was Anna Maria Ulm, since all I could remember about her was
her name and the dates on her tombstone. I'd wonder if perhaps she might
have actually been the most happy or the most sad, or if she perhaps loved
me more than any of the others.

"There are other women who would have been on my list if only I could
have remembered their names, women I saw perhaps just once, one passing
in a carriage as I walked down Calle Doña Maria Menendez, and another
seated in a box near the stage during a performance of *La brevedad desagradable de la vida.* I looked directly at her as I recited my lines. *'No me tienes que
dar porque te quiera'* — 'You don't have to give me anything to make me love
you.' As she covered her mouth with a black lace veil, her wide eyes suggested that feelings were mutual.

"I remember another woman whose name I do not know and yet whose
face I can see as clearly as that of any on the list. Out of politeness to Bishop
Capullo, who had hired my actresses, Mary and Pompeia, to appear in a
pageant for a celebration of the Immaculate Conception, I had gone to the
Church of the Magdalena. I noticed the stunning woman seated on one

of the benches on the other side of the church, next to a gentleman, pre-
sumably her husband, beneath a painting of the head of John the Baptist on a silver platter. Their dress suggested both wealth and breeding.
Wondering who they might be, I watched them, engaged as they were in
watching the pageant. Her eyes drifted away from Mary. They scanned the
room until, suddenly, they met mine. And just as suddenly, she looked away,
and did not look back at me again. But in that fleeting meeting of the eyes,
there was a perfect complicity. In that instant she was unfaithful to her husband, for in that moment she surrendered herself, willingly or not, to me.
She knew that she had, accidentally or not, by chance or fate, tampered
with my heart. Although we both knew that nothing would ever come of
it, it was as if it had already happened. We knew one another completely
while not knowing one another at all. And that night, while *cardar*ring Tamara Xanagrande, I thought about the woman in the church, and believed
that, at that very moment, her husband was *cardar*ring her, and that, in the
same way that our glances met, she was thinking of me. In that moment we
consummated our love. That's true love, the ache and transport that drives
you crazy and makes you sane, that makes you want to live forever and die
at once."

Suddenly Mr. De Leon stood up: "I'm sorry Mr. Siegel. That's enough for
today. We have to stop now. I'm not feeling very well. I must excuse myself.
Please wait here. Isabel will come to see you out."

Being allowed to leave the Garden of Eden early, I had time to drive to
St. Augustine to buy an ink cartridge for the portable printer I had bought
for this project. I took the opportunity to visit Ripley's Believe It or Not!
Museum in order to see the building that, according to Mr. De Leon, had
once been the residence of Menendez, Grant, and then Zespedes. Not
very amazed by such "Amazing, Bizarre and Unbelievable Wonders," as the
Taino fertility fetishes, Ubangi lip plates, Amazonian shrunken heads, a
two-headed pig in formaldehyde, a matchstick replica of a Spanish gal-
leon, "The World's Largest Manatee Made out of Beer Cans," or even "The
World's Largest Hair Ball," I went for dinner at La Polla Borracha.

The meal was so ungratifying, that, before driving back to the Zodiac for
the night, I stopped at a convenience store to stock up on some packaged
food, and, while I was at it, to get a bottle of rum, a six-pack of Coke, some
limes, a big bag of ice, and a Styrofoam cooler. I couldn't resist the mineral
water "bottled," according to its label, "in Florida, land of the Fountain of
Youth."

As the clerk rang up my purchases, I couldn't help but notice, and then
stare at, the rear end of a young woman who was bending over to read

the cover of a magazine on the magazine stand by the door. "There it is," I mused, "Florence Basolon's fabulous buttocks, the glorious posterior that I must capture in words. And perhaps Dominga Zespedes' nipples are to be discovered under her tee-shirt."

Loaded down with my supplies, I couldn't manage the door. Noticing my predicament, the young woman with Florence Basolon's behind stood up to help me. Smiling with lips as pretty as Tamara Xanagrande's must have been, she asked if she might help me carry the packages out to my car. As she did so, she said I looked familiar. "Weren't you at Ponce's Place yesterday? Yes, that was you sitting at the bar. I remember." After we had loaded the packages into the back seat of my car, she seemed to want to linger. She asked if I was just visiting Florida, then where I was from, then what I was doing there and how long I was going to stay. When I explained what had brought me to the state, she told me that she had visited the museum years before, on a field trip when she was a Brownie, and that she remembered the old man who dressed up like Ponce de León to show people around the park.

As she continued talking, telling me about other field trips she had gone on as a Brownie, I recollected what Mr. De Leon had said about Justa Respalona: "She was young, only twenty-one years old, and very pretty, and best of all, she was attracted to older men. Having been in my fifties for a couple hundred years made me quite adept at picking them out. In a room of young women, I can intuitively spot which among them are attracted to older men."

I figured, much to my amazement, excitement, and delight, that I had one. Why, after all, unless she was attracted to older men, would she have remembered me being at the bar? Why, unless she was flirting with me, would she have walked me to my car? And why, unless she was trying to suggest that we had something in common, was she telling me that she was taking a creative writing course at Flagler College?

But why, if she was so attracted to me, was she then so adamant in turning down my invitation to go to Ponce's Place, "or somewhere nicer if you've got one to suggest," for a drink? Why, if she was flirting with me, was she suddenly so eager to get away from me?

"Good-bye, sir," she said firmly. "I really gotta go now. My boyfriend's waiting for me."

"Thanks for helping me carry my stuff to the car" was all I could come up with in an effort to conceal the embarrassment I was feeling over my admittedly prurient assumptions.

"Oh, it was my pleasure. Really. It's because you kinda remind me of my dad up in Michigan. He's a widower, and about your age, and he has to do all of his shopping by himself too. I know he wishes I was there to help him."

"How long has he been a widower?" I asked, feigning interest in Dad and even some sympathy.

"Ever since Mom died," she answered as she turned and walked away, giving me my last view of what might have been Florence Basolon's buttocks in blue jeans.

I drove back to the Zodiac, where Mr. Wiseman, despite the hour, was eagerly awaiting me. "We need to talk, Siegel. I've been thinking about it, and I've decided that I'm willing to sell you the genuine Hemingway sock for only three hundred bucks. What a bargain! It's a steal. And for three hundred I'll throw in not one but all four of the Hemingway books. How can you turn down a deal like that?"

"You don't seem understand Mr. Wiseman," I tried to explain. "I don't want the sock. I wouldn't want it even if there was another one to match it. And even if you offered to give me the pair of them for free, and throw in not only the Hemingway books, but *Gone with the Wind* and the Bible as well, I wouldn't take them. I don't need any socks, or any books for that matter."

Woefully he shook his head. "I don't understand you, Siegel. What kind of writer wouldn't want Hemingway's sock? And besides, aren't Jews supposed to stick together?"

"Please, Mr. Wiseman," I insisted, "I have a lot of work to do."

In preparation to write chapter eight, covering Ponce de León's life, loves, and theatrical endeavors from 1784 to 1821, I read over the two alphabetical lists I had been given, and made some notes based on what I could remember of Mr. De Leon's commentary on those lists. Other than knowing that Tamara Xanagrande's lips were supposed to play a major role in the chapter, I didn't know how to begin. In hopes of finding some material for a setting for the narrative, I looked through the history books that I had checked out of the Santa Almeja County Library. Listed in the index to *The Sunshine State from Prehistoric Times to the Present* there were entries for Ponce de León, Juan; Fountain of Youth, legend of; tobacco, cultivation of; Missions; Native Americans (with subentries for the Arawak, Calusa, Carib, Seminole, Taino, and Timucua, but nothing for the Zhotee-eloq). I also found pages for Grant, James; Menendez, Pedro; and Zespedes, Vizente Manuel de; but nothing on Gaviota de León, Juan. I started to read about those characters in Mr. De Leon's story. Turning to the pages listed for Zespedes, I was interested to read that "in 1789 a theatrical manager from Spain was appointed by Governor Vincent Zespedes to stage a re-enactment of the coronation of Charles IV as the King of Spain. The spectacle was attended by many dignitaries, including the distinguished American General, Nathaniel Greene, who had commanded the Continental forces in the South during the American Revolution." This led me to look up both Menendez and Grant and to read about Menendez capturing Fort Caroline and Grant founding a Masonic Lodge in St. Augustine. I was very disappointed that the Zodiac Motel didn't have an Internet connection because I was eager to search for any information about a Mission of San Hortano, a Congregation Beth Mekor-Hayim, and a Teatro Ponce de León. It occurred to me to drive back to St. Augustine as soon as possible to do research in an Internet café. But then the obvious dawned on me: "Why? Why would I go to any effort to find evidence that either Mr. De Leon is or isn't a five-hundred-forty-year-old Spanish conquistador? Of course he isn't. Nothing needs proving." I reminded myself that, even if Mr. De Leon really believed that he was actually composing a truthful autobiography, I was merely writing a novel. I had no need for facts.

I decided that, instead of going ahead with chapter eight, I should go back and try to work on the long-overdue chapter one. In order to come up with the book's beginning, I relied on portions of the letter that Mr. De Leon had written to me in June: *Incredible as it may seem, I am, in fact, none other than Juan Ponce de León, the Spanish explorer who, at the age of forty-eight, on an Easter Sunday in 1513, discovered the land I christened Pascua de Florida. While duly acknowledging that achievement, historical accounts have ridiculed me for a credulity which, they imagine, encouraged a vain quest for the legendary Fountain of Youth. The fact is, however, that I did, much to my own astonishment, actually unearth a very real artesian wellspring, the miraculous waters of which did indeed, until very recently, have the power to render living beings essentially immune to illness and resistant to the process of aging.*

I jumped from there straight to his early childhood in Spain: *I was born on the twenty-second of July in 1465, in the town of Lebrija, the ancient Roman city of Nebrissa. The place was always notorious for the amorousness of its natives. Perhaps it was the wild mushrooms that grew in the woods around it, the pomegranates that flourished there, or maybe it was the waters of its mountain springs. In Roman times, the people of Nebrissa drank joyously. They danced and sang in wild celebration of the orgies of Bacchus. Nimble Satyrs and Maenads, scantily draped in animals skins, pranced around Hortanes, who was none other than the god Priapus. And Lebrija remained an orgiastic town in my day, when Priapus had been canonized as San Hortano, the patron saint of actors, jugglers, and mountebanks.*

I felt that I had the last words of the chapter. Mr. De Leon would certainly approve of them since he himself had suggested them: *As I boarded the caravel that would take me west, to islands across the Ocean Mar, I believed that, because my journey was being undertaken for the sake of love, any suffering I might experience in the Indies would be ennobling. At that time, in my youth, I imagined that love itself was the Fountain of Life.*

I had worked on it for an hour or so without being able to come up with either original metaphors for Queen Ysabel's breasts or satisfactory English equivalents for *cardar* or *gilipollasqueroxo.* I thought I was done for the night. After taking a shower, I got into bed and read a few pages of *Gone with the Wind,* the Genesis story of Tamar, and then John's Gospel account of the Samaritan woman in the Gideon Bible. That made me tired enough to turn out the light and give the sound of the rain against my window the opportunity to soothe me into sleep. But I couldn't help thinking about all I had to do to catch up with Mr. De Leon. So much work, and so little time. "If only we had more time." I tossed and turned. Anxiety over the manuscript was causing insomnia and, of course, the cocaine in the rum punch I had been drinking that day exacerbated my sleeplessness.

And so I decided to try Johanan Yarhoni's kabbalistic remedy for insomnia. I had intended to begin with A and work my way to Z, going through memories of former lovers, breathing in and out on their names as Mr. De Leon had done. But a **Q** immediately popped up—(**Q**uinn, Kathy)—a girlfriend in high school, a potential model, I reflected, for the flirtatious flower girl of Lebrija. It had taken Ponce de Leon three-hundred and fifty-seven years to make love to a **Q**, and, I gloated, I had done it in only seventeen.

Kathy was, I realized, distracting me from remembering an A. I worked on it, but no one, not a single woman or girl, came to mind. B was easy (Blalock, Elizabeth), and there were a couple of obvious C's. But A? A? No one. Try as I did, I couldn't recollect ever having loved, had sex with, or even just had a little crush on, a single A. I sat up, turned the light on, and worked on it, convinced that, in my sixty years of being alive, there had to be at least one beloved whose name began with A. Compromising the rules, I decided that it didn't have to be a last name, that it could be a first name, a nickname, or even a middle name. Still nothing. I got out of bed, poured a glass of rum, and downed it. Still no A. I lit a Ponce de León Maduro and drank more rum. Nothing. I paced the room, wide awake, frantically rummaging memory for the letter A. She was nowhere to be found. Ponce de Leon's cure for sleepless lovers kept me awake all night.

NINE

1821–1865

WHEREIN PONCE DE LEÓN BECOMES AN
AMERICAN CITIZEN, OPENS A YELLOW FEVER
SANATORIUM, AND, SUBSEQUENTLY, AN
INFIRMARY FOR CONFEDERATE SOLDIERS
WOUNDED IN THE CIVIL WAR

JUAN BACO. What's troubling, Juana, is not so much death itself, but the lethargy that foreshadows that inevitable oblivion. As I get older, I become perpetually more easily fatigued. I'm tired, dear Juana, so very tired. I suppose we ought to surrender to the lassitude. Yes, we should take our time, not try to accomplish anything, but rather allow ourselves to appreciate everything. Such passivity would be noble, I suppose, even wise. On the other hand, it occurs to me that I might dare to refuse to accept the torpor of age, and struggle to do more than I have ever done, to act as though I still have the old vitality of youth, and to embark on new adventures. Such endeavors might be foolish, but would they not be heroic as well? Either effort, the wisely passive or the heroically foolish, is at least better than merely being sad about aging. I know that, and yet a demonic sadness, an inexorable acedia, grips me, mocks me, and will not allow me to be either a hero or a wise man. What's wrong with me?

JUANA ESPINOSA. Cheer up, Juan Baco. Stop taking old age and death so personally! Sad old men are a nuisance.

SETHO PONCE DE LEÓN, *La brevedad desagradable de la vida*
(The Annoying Brevity of Life)

Ariana Quigley was not beautiful, but men seldom realized it when caught by her charm. It was an arresting face, pointed of chin, and square of jaw. Her eyes were pale green without a touch of hazel, starred with bristly black lashes and slightly tilted at the ends. Above them, her thick black brows slanted upward, cutting a startling oblique line in her magnolia-white skin—that skin so prized by Southern women, and so carefully guarded with bonnets, veils, and mittens against the hot Florida sun. But for all the modesty of her spreading skirts, the demureness of hair netted smoothly into a chignon, and the quietness of small white hands folded in her lap, her true self was poorly concealed. The green eyes in the carefully sweet face were turbulent, willful, lusty with life, distinctly at variance with her decorous demeanor.

That's what I had for the opening of this chapter, my rendition of the story Mr. De Leon had told me on Saturday, July 16, 2005, in the Americana Room of his Museum of Florida History. He read those one hundred and forty-two words on the next day. "Yes," Mr. De Leon commented with evident appreciation, looking even more tired and frail than the day before, and coughing more too. "Yes, Ariana's eyes were green, pale green and beguilingly turbulent. How did you know, Mr. Siegel? Did I tell you that?"

Under pressure to come up with a seductive opening for each of the chapters of the tall tale of Juan Ponce de León, I had, I confess, resorted to plagiarizing the passage from the first page of the copy of *Gone with the Wind* in my room at the Zodiac. After emending "Scarlett O'Hara" to "Ariana Quigley" and "Georgia" to "Florida," I had inserted serial commas to make the prose stylistically consistent with the rest of the manuscript. It seemed appropriate to steal the beginning of a story set in the antebellum and Civil War South from *Gone with the Wind*. I had rightly guessed that Mr. De Leon would not be familiar with the novel.

"Yes, it's promising indeed," Mr. De Leon continued, "that you intuitively knew that her eyes were pale green and turbulent. The hazel that was, as you've written, missing in her eyes was, you might mention as you continue to compose the chapter, flagrant in her nipples. They'd stare at me, following me around the room like the eyes of a predator tracking its prey. And, just as the gaze of certain wild carnivores has the power to fascinate and petrify certain prey, so Ariana's hazel nipples captivated and transfixed me. They were, by the way, like hazelnuts not only in color, but in size and hardness as well. Those nipples, no less than her eyes, were willful and lusty with life, and distinctly in contrast to the pallor and softness of her opulent breasts. Picture two shimmering mounds of *crema Susona*, a lusciously creamy vanilla custard, each garnished with a hazelnut."

Although I hardly considered a comparison of nipples to hazelnuts, let alone breasts to mounds of pudding, felicitous, I made a note of it, reminding myself, as I had to do so often during my meetings with Mr. De Leon, that I was writing only to satisfy the old man. It didn't really matter what anyone else might think. I'd given up on writing the story for the *New Yorker*, *Vanity Fair*, or *Modern Maturity*.

In recounting his adventures during the period in American history from the time when Florida became a U.S. territory through the Civil War, Mr. De Leon had focused on Ponce de León's love affair with the green-eyed, custard-breasted, hazelnut-nippled, Ariana Quigley. "I wanted her the instant she introduced herself: 'Hello, I'm Nurse Quigley, Ariana Quigley.' I needed a woman whose surname began with *Q* for my list, to help me through bouts of insomnia. As unbelievable as it may seem, Ariana is the only woman I have ever loved, in more than five hundred years of falling in love, whose last name began with a *Q*. I did meet a rather attractive schoolteacher, Drusilla Quimberger, here at the park in 1918 who interested me. But nothing came of it because she was obsessed with young boys. That's why she had become a schoolteacher."

Before telling me the story for this chapter, Mr. De Leon had naturally expected to read the previous one, the account of Ponce de León's endeavors as a theater manager and actor, that I was supposed to have written the night before. Once again, I'd had to apologize. "I didn't have time to work on that story because I felt I ought to go back to chapter one. I got a lot of it written and should be able to have it finished for you by tomorrow." And once again my employer had been disappointed. An uncomfortably long silence had insinuated discouragement.

On the day he told me about Ariana Quigley, De León's costume had, except for the ever present dark glasses, changed dramatically. He was wearing a white linen shirt with a black silk cravat in which a pearl was pinned, and, despite the heat and humidity, he sported a black woolen waistcoat with a matching long jacket and gray pleated trousers. Seeing him for the first time without a helmet or hat, I noticed that his curly hair was no more gray or thin than my own. Each time he lit a cigar or poured a glass of rum punch, his hands trembled, more than usual.

"These are the sort of clothes I wore when I was Mr. Lionel Johnson, Esq., a patriotic American land speculator from New York. The annexation of Florida had caused many residents of the Spanish colony to leave for Mexico, the Spanish Caribbean, or South America. And newcomers were immigrating from up north. That facilitated my necessary change of identity. As Lionel Johnson I purchased this estate from my former self, the

Spanish actor who had been named after the discoverer of Florida. Señor Juan Ponce de León had been constrained to close his theater after a party of renegade Indians raided his estate and made off with most of his costumes and props. Some years later, during the Second Seminole War, at the battle of Gihon River, U.S. troops were, to say the least, astonished to see Chief Coacoochee, a warrior who boasted of having killed more than three hundred white men, dressed as Hamlet. And Otulke Thlocco, a medicine man who was called 'Prophet' because of his alleged occult and mystical powers, was wearing Ophelia's blonde wig and Marian blue satin gown. Among the other Indians with whom federal forces were engaged in battle, one was wearing the crimson costume, complete with horns and tail, of the devil in my *El viejo y el demonio*, and another, one of the first to be slain on the field of battle, had on the clown's coxcomb and bells from *Los milagros chistosos de sexo*. Others were wearing conquistador helmets, ladies' undergarments, and ecclesiastical vestments. Among those captured was one warrior with Christ's halo from *La puta de Samaria* on his head, and another was wearing the not-very-authentic costume of the Seminole Indian that had been worn by Governor Zespedes in the *El robo de Sabina*."

The Americana Room was, like the others in the museum, illuminated solely by the sunlight coming in through its expansive windows. It occurred to me that, curiously, I had seen no sign of electricity in the building.

Pointing out the bronze eagle on display, Mr. De Leon noted that it had replaced the statue of the Queen Ysabel on the Fountain when Spain ceded Florida to the United States. Also in that room, there were, among the memorabilia from early nineteenth-century Florida, an American flag, a Confederate flag, and a decree, signed by President James Monroe, granting "Lionel Johnson and his heirs in perpetuity exclusive rights to the eighteen acres of lands, its waters, fields, facilities, buildings, and furnishings, formerly belonging to a subject and agent of the Spanish colonial government, and registered with United States of America Government Land Office as 'Eden Estates.' This being decreed in recognition and commendation of Mr. Johnson's philanthropic and humanitarian services to the United States Territory of Florida."

In further acknowledgment of his altruistic services, military governor of Florida Andrew Jackson had given Lionel Johnson a verge pocket watch in a gold, full hunter case engraved with a florid letter *J*. Removing the antique timepiece from its bell jar display, Mr. De Leon opened the front cover to show me the face: the numerals on the white enamel were Roman for the hours and Arabic for the minutes. Mr. De Leon snapped open the back of the timepiece to reveal a hidden automaton which, when he wound the watch with a key to activate the repeat mechanism, sprang to life: the naked pelvis of a polychrome enamel man rocked to and fro in such a way that his bright crimson penis, in time with time, once per second, moved in an out of a black-rimmed aperture between the open pink legs of a polychrome enamel woman.

"The automaton's all wrong," Mr. De Leon remarked. "It should be the woman's pelvis, and not the man's, that counts the seconds. The penis is, in my experience, a poor judge of time. The female sexual apparatus has a much more precise sense of it. Mary Jack, when she was working at the brothel, always knew exactly when an hour was over—exactly, to the minute—if an hour was what you had paid for. And likewise Bonita Burbuja, during our most intimate times together, always knew, without a watch or clock, exactly when her husband, the Commandante, would be arriving home. So too Esther Kitzler: 'Hurry up, finish as quickly as you can,' she'd whisper in my ear. 'I must get up and dress. Herr Kitzler will be leaving his office in exactly half an hour.' And then, a few minutes later, as she tied the bow string on her bonnet, she'd kiss me good-bye and utter those words which express a feeling common to everyone in love: 'If only we had more time.'

"Before I had this watch," Mr. De Leon continued wistfully, "the hours had been comfortably vague. But with it, time suddenly became empirical, unpleasantly real, personal, and precise. After having watched this little man's large phallus thrusting in and out of this little woman's pudendal aperture once per second, time and again, I began to think of him when I was doing what he, hidden inside my watch, was always doing so long as I kept him wound. It was not a pleasant thought. Before I had this watch, *cardar*ring had been a refuge from time. Now I was made more acutely aware of the fact that the woman whose legs were wrapped around me was getting older by the second, second after second, closer and closer to death. Chronos devours his children.

"Before I had this watch," Mr. De Leon repeated, "I would, on the occasions of having arranged a rendezvous with a woman for a certain time, often glance at the brass sundial I had brought from Borinquen. You might have noticed it in the Caribbean Room. Since many such amorous trysts were scheduled for the night, I eventually acquired a water clock. It's in the Mission Room. Do you remember it, Mr. Siegel?"

I did recall a primitive chronometer consisting of two glass containers, each decorated with clouds and cherubs, the upper one with a gold sun, the lower with a silver moon. It was constructed so that, as water dripped from the higher container, a float in the receiving vessel would slowly rise, forcing a notched stick to turn a gear that moved a golden hand around a porcelain face ornamented with a medieval *mappa mundi.*

"It wasn't very precise," Mr. De Leon explained, "but close enough to cause me to pace to and fro while waiting for my lover. Have you ever noticed how often lovers are late, how much being in love requires waiting, and how great, because of love, the anguished impatience of waiting is, until, after so many drops of water, so many pelvic thrusts, so many ticks and tocks, finally she arrives?

"Before I had this watch, my lover could insist that she wasn't really late. Neither the sundial nor the water clock was reliable enough to prove her tardiness. But once I had this watch, its hands moving across its face as the penis inside ticked away the time, I could, whether hurt or angry (usually a mix of both), say with menacing certitude, 'Yes, you are. Look at my watch.' 'Only eight minutes,' Ariana Quigley would answer, smiling as she began to unbutton her military nurse's robe. 'But those minutes seemed like hours,' I'd protest. 'Only eight minutes,' she would repeat. 'Look at your watch.' She would then open lips, arms, legs, heart, and the subsequent hours would seem like minutes. Chronos is a liar."

As he returned the watch, now ticking and covertly thrusting, to the bell jar, Mr. León muttered, "Yes, time's a liar. And yet, at the same time, I suppose, ultimately time is truth. The broken heart of the monarch butterfly in springtime is forgotten by the gypsy moth in winter.

"Oh, and by the way, it came back to me last night. I was in bed, almost asleep, and I suddenly remembered the name of the girl who loved clean sheets. It was Serena. Serena Sabana. Be sure to include it in the book."

Retrieving a barely smoked maduro from the ashtray to relight it, coughing, and directing me to be seated, he explained why he had been given both the land grant and the gold watch. Under the terms of the Adams-Onis Treaty, the United States authorities would accept the validity of Lionel Johnson's purchase of the Spanish title only after review by a congressional commissioner and validation by the receiver of the Territorial Land Office. "To guarantee continued possession of my property, I thought it politic to turn the theater that had been a church, a synagogue, and a cigar factory, into a hospice. There was another yellow fever epidemic, even worse than the one that had taken the lives of so many of the Indians in the Mission of San Hortano. A place to quarantine the victims was sorely needed. Because I had the waters of the Fountain of Life to protect me, I was not, of course, afraid of Yellow Jack myself. Not only did my supposedly philanthropic and humanitarian services render the Garden of Eden still mine, they also inspired Ariana Quigley to love me."

Ariana Quigley, I was told, was one of only three women to whom Ponce de León had ever revealed the secret of the Fountain of Life. "After the disastrous results of telling the truth to Justa Respalona, I had sworn that I would never do it again. But, once again love, as it is so wont to do, got the better of me. After less than a year of intimacy with Ariana, hoping to marry her and live happily ever after, I divulged to her the fact that I was Juan Ponce de León and that I had discovered not only Florida, but the Garden of Eden as well, and within it the Fountain of Life. And then I asked for her hand in marriage. You can, I hope for the sake of conveying it to my readers, imagine my disappointment: not only did she not believe that I was Ponce de León, she also declined my marriage proposal. She did so, however, with the explanation that, although she truly loved me, she was already married. 'Not happily,' she added, 'but legally. And the law has little regard for love.' Her husband was none other than Senator Matthias Quigley of Rhode Island. I am inclined to believe that if he had granted her a divorce, Ariana would have eventually believed what I had told her, kept the secret of the Fountain, and would still, now, a century and a half later, be here—alive and young, beautiful and faithful in every way. While the waters of the Fountain would have had the power to safeguard her from disease and aging, they could not, of course, protect her from the wrath of a jealous husband."

According to Mr. De Leon's melodramatic love story, Mrs. Quigley had, once the yellow fever epidemic subsided, gone home to Rhode Island to ask her husband for a divorce. When he refused to grant it, she, supposing that it would change his mind, professed her love for Lionel Johnson. Immediately after strangling his wife to death with his bare hands, Senator Quigley turned himself in to the police, was tried for murder in a courtroom presided over by his brother-in-law, the Right Honorable Rufus Benedict, and was acquitted on the grounds of temporary insanity and justifiable cause. Subsequent to his return to the Senate, Quigley assumed the leadership of a congressional committee working in opposition to granting statehood to Florida.

I thought the story had potential. Yes, I thought to myself, a tragic love story, heavily spiked with sex and violence, a gripping tale of passion, loss, and redemption set in the antebellum South. If only the story could be told by an omniscient narrator, the bodiless spirit who had narrated both *Gone with the Wind* and *The Old Man and the Sea*, I would describe the brawny fingers of a lustily panting Senator Quigley as they tightened mercilessly around the delicate neck of the angelic woman: *The clean manicure of the nails on those fingers belied the beastliness of the jealous husband. Ariana's pale green eyes slowly closed as her mouth opened and her scream was silenced.* The cocaine in the rum punch must have been getting to me.

As a nurse in the medical corps of the United States Army, Ariana Quigley had been sent to Florida to train Negro slaves to attend to those suffering from yellow fever. Mr. De Leon showed me an article in an 1824 edition of the *St. Augustine Daily Sunshine* in which a certain Dr. John Thompson, director of Territorial East Florida's Department of Health, Water, and Sanitation, had proclaimed that "Negroes have been scientifically proven to be less susceptible to the disease than are folks of the fairer race." In the same article, Dr. Thompson had blamed the epidemic on the Spanish presence in Florida, Spaniards being, according the physician, "a filthy people whose insalubrious mores and wanton habits foster all manner of infectious diseases and blights, especially those illnesses and vermin which are dietarily or venereally generated or disseminated." I was shown a later piece in the same newspaper, in which Thompson had focused specifically on "the venereal generation of yellow fever." The physician proudly announced the ratification, by both the civil and military governing bodies of the U.S. territory of Florida, of his proposed provisionary statute to have arrested and imprisoned any prostitute in Florida who "would be found to be so grievously negligent of public welfare as to continue to engage in her wanton trade with the knowledge that she has, on some previous occasion, had intimate commerce with a Spaniard."

Dr. Thompson, I thought, would make a good bad guy in this chapter (particularly if the character Mary Jack were to be arrested). Another candidate for villain, another morally righteous individual zealously bent on stamping out prostitution in Florida, another potential butt of social satire, it seemed to me, would be the Reverend Robert Jones of the Eagle Springs First Baptist Church. In his weekly sermons, the preacher had, according to Mr. De Leon, attributed the responsibility for the epidemic not to the Spanish, but to God himself: "What sins, we as faithful Christians must ask, have those who have been stricken by Yellow Jack committed to deserve such punishment as meted out by a just and all merciful Lord?"

"Other than applying cold compresses to counteract the high fevers," Mr. De Leon recounted, "there was little anyone could do for the patients who were suffering with the violent vomiting and explosive diarrhea. They either recovered or they died. Survival seemed but a matter of good luck or bad. Regardless of prognosis, kind Ariana's mission was to comfort with words whispered softly into burning ears and with gentle hands on trembling limbs, to assure them with touch, no less than with words, that they would recover. She knew exactly when to look consolingly sad with sympathy, and when to smile with hope.

"On her first day in the sanatorium, I had watched her at the bedside of a woman on the verge of death. With her hand in Ariana's hands, the dying woman recounted in detail stories of all the lovers she had enjoyed—Americans, Englishmen, Spaniards, Dutchmen, Frenchmen, Greeks, a Chinaman or two, a Minorcan, and Siamese twins joined at the hip ('just one of them, I'm sorry to say'). The inclusion of those conjoined twins made me suspect that she might not be telling the truth, that she was fabricating a life she wished she had lived, and that she was, perhaps, by the grace of her delirium, actually enjoying that life before having to leave it behind. 'I was more fortunate than most women,' she declared, 'because my husband—bless his soul—died of sunstroke early on in our marriage. I was free. As a widow with a comfortable inheritance, I was free to travel to oh so many places, and to have lovers, oh so many lovers, all of them wonderful, well, all of them except that damn Minorcan, as cruel as he was handsome. Each and every one of them but he gave me something—all kinds of pleasures and thrills, meals, money, and jewelry, everything a girl could ever want. That Siamese twin gave me a diamond earring. I did my best to get my hands on the matching one, but his brother refused to part with it.'

"I hope to be like her," Mr. De Leon said Ariana had said. Lying in his arms later that night, after the dead woman had been wrapped in a clean white cere cloth, Ariana had whispered, "Yes, I hope to be like her, and enjoy the redemption of thinking of love, only love, as I lay dying."

In telling me about the Eden Sanatorium, Mr. De Leon asked me not to mention it in his book that, just as he had used slave labor to pick and process tobacco and to roll cigars for the Gaviota Tobacco Plantation and Cigar Manufactury, so too he had owned the Negroes who were being trained in nursing by Ariana Quigley. "Many modern readers, I understand, object to slavery. At the time, I can assure you, it seemed like a perfectly reasonable social system that was not particularly inhumane so long as both owners and slaves behaved appropriately." Without writing that he was a slave owner, Mr. De Leon, however, did want me to somehow include as a character in this chapter a Negro named "Methuselah—Methuselah Jackson. The rascal claimed to be one hundred and forty-eight years old. No one believed him but me. Well, no one except me and his wife, a rather pretty mulatta who couldn't have been much more than twenty years old. The reason I supposed it to be true was that, on the day I bought him at the market in

St. Augustine, the moment he saw me, he exclaimed, 'I can hardly believe my eyes! You look just like my old boss, old Master Juan Gaviota, the tobacco man, the ladies' man!' If he had been in his twenties at the time he had worked on my tobacco plantation, I calculated, he would have been in his hundred and forties when I bought him. Who knows how long Methuselah might have lived if he hadn't come down with the fever?"

There were other things Mr. De Leon did not want written: although he suspected it might be the truth, he did not wish to suggest in writing that Ariana Quigley had fallen in love with him only because she imagined that he truly was a philanthropist. By opening the hospice, she thought he had risked catching the fever himself so that he might benevolently serve its sundry victims. "She was unaware that I had been motivated by self-interest alone, that I had created the sanatorium only to insure that, under the new government, I'd be able to safeguard my Fountain. She considered me a self-sacrificial Samaritan, as compassionate and courageous as she. Compassion and courage are, however, as I am sure you must realize by now, Mr. Siegel, not my most salient virtues, nor are they qualities I have particularly striven to cultivate. This is not to say that I do not admire them in others: compassion makes for good priests, courage for good soldiers. But neither good priests nor good soldiers make for good lovers. While the compassionate and the heroic may care about humanity, the good lover would consider letting humanity perish and suffer in hell if doing otherwise impeded just one kiss from the lips of his beloved. Although Ariana did probably only love me for what she imagined to be my courage and my compassion, I'd prefer readers to believe that it was because I was, given hundreds of years of experience, a truly good lover. Do try to give them that impression, Mr. Siegel."

I pointed out an inconsistency: "But what about Ariana? Shouldn't she be portrayed as benevolent, self-sacrificial, compassionate, and courageous? Did those qualities make her a bad lover?"

After taking a moment to consider my question, pour both himself and me another glass of cocainized rum punch, take a morphine tablet, cough, and light a fresh cigar, Mr. De Leon answered: "Well, it's different with women. I suppose it has something to do with having breasts. Yes, something to do with the maternal nurturing instinct. Ariana's breasts, as I've told you, were beautiful. Her qualities as both a beloved and lover were enhanced by her virtues. After long hours of ministering to the infirm, often staying up all night at the bedsides of the sufferers, applying cold compresses to burning cheeks, holding up buckets into which they could vomit, and covering their faces when they died, nothing soothed Ariana more than to come from their bedsides to mine. Summon up all of your rhetorical skills, Mr. Siegel, to evoke the embraces of Ariana Quigley. Describe the scent of a lover's moist skin, the zest of sweat and feel of disheveled hair, the pulsing of vessels and tremors of love-ravenous hands, the flicker of tongues in open mouths, the taste of intimate flow, the tumid swell and twitch of sex, the suck and blow, fingers clenching, toes curling, bellies rubbing, desperate breathing, loins gaping, hearts heaving, the rolling and clutching, the whispers, murmurs, the fleshy groan and gush, the voluptuous release, the outburst and eruption of love, its rhythmic echoes, and then the relaxation and the closing of four eyes." The cocaine in the rum punch, it seemed, was stimulating Mr. De Leon more than it was me.

He gasped to catch his breath, cough, and swallow another tablet with a swig of punch. I asked if I might refill my own glass. After pouring it for me with a shaking hand, he continued. "Try to write this scene in such a way, Mr. Siegel, as to so arouse my readers, to make them so sexually enkindled that they will have to put my book down and do anything they can do—anything!—to find someone—anyone!—as soon as possible!—with whom they might reenact the scene, relieving the unbearable excitation that the reading has inspired. Make them feel that they urgently need to experience the same convulsive pleasures and explosive ecstasies of love that Ariana and I have just enjoyed on the page they've been reading. And if they cannot find anyone with whom to have that experience, they should, because of what you have written, be compelled to imagine a lover as vividly as possible and proceed accordingly. After they have recovered their composure, they should immediately be eager to return to my book and pick up from where they, disarmed by desire, had been forced to leave off. There, after an orgasm of their own, they should read that Ariana would often fall deeply into a peaceful sleep in which sweet dreams provided refuge from the infernal miseries of the wards."

Mr. De Leon explained that because Ariana Quigley was the most virtuous woman he had ever known, it had been somewhat surprising to him when, on the occasion of his proposal of marriage, she had announced that she was already married. "Perhaps adultery allowed her some respite from the burden of her enormous virtue. Or perhaps it was simply that her notion of virtue was not based on legality or duty. The fact is, Mr. Siegel, that I loved Ariana Quigley more than any woman ever."

I couldn't resist reminding Mr. De Leon that he had said the same thing about Queen Ysabel, about Maria Taino-Pinzon, Liqizhotqi, Maria Fuentes,

Shulamit Morteira, and probably a few others I couldn't remember at that moment. "We can't write," I argued, "'I loved her more than any other woman ever' in every chapter."

"Why not? It is, after all, true. I loved each and every one of them more than any woman ever."

"Do you mean to say that, each time Ponce de León was in love, *at that time* he would feel *as if* he were more in love than ever? Or do you mean that he actually loved Ariana Quigley more than he loved Shulamit Morteira, whom he loved more than Maria Fuentes, and so on? Or perhaps you mean that Lionel Johnson loved Ariana Quigley more than any woman in his life, while Samson ben Aryeh loved Shulamit Morteira more than any woman in his, that Sor Maria Fuentes was the greatest love in the life of Fray Juan Arquero, and that Tatuzh-utat loved Liqizhotqi more than any woman in chapter four?"

"Whether you understand it or not, Mr. Siegel," Mr. De Leon answered impatiently, "is of no importance to me. Perhaps your experiences in love are limited. I can assure you that every real lover who reads my book will know exactly what I'm talking about. Each of them, man and woman alike, will understand in what way I loved Ariana Quigley and each of those other women more than any other woman ever."

I wanted to defend myself, to tell him some of my ideas about love, to describe some of my feelings, to reveal some of the history of my own experiences with women. "When I've been in love . . . ," I began. But it was hopeless. Playing deaf to me, he raised his voice to talk over my words, continuing to tell me about Ariana Quigley. "Because I loved her more than any woman ever, I certainly didn't want to lose her. And so I told her about the waters of the Fountain to protect her from the cruel embrace of Yellow Jack. 'As incredible as it may seem to you,' I said to her, 'I am none other than Juan Ponce de León. While it is well known that I discovered Florida over three hundred years ago, I have found it necessary to conceal the fact that I am still alive because I did actually discover the Fountain of Life, the miraculous waters of which do indeed, as ancient legends attest, render sentient beings immune to disease and resistant to the process of aging.' I told Ariana about Rabbi Solomon and how Queen Ysabel dispatched me to the New World. I described my life among the Zhotee-eloq, and told her about my mission and my synagogue, and about my careers as both a tobacco merchant and theater manager. The truth—although she did not believe it—pleased her as a story. She listened with rapt attention, just as I hope my readers will do. When I would insist that the story was not fiction, she'd put her arms around my neck and smile. 'If only it could be true, my darling, if only we could stop the epidemic, if only we could cure the people to whom you have so generously given refuge. Oh, if only you really were Ponce de León, my dear Lionel, and there were magic waters to redeem people from suffering untimely death. Lie down next to me. Hold me in your arms. Let me close my eyes and imagine it is so.'

"As proof that I had been telling the truth about myself and the Fountain, I had shown her many of same things you've seen in my museum—the old manuscripts and maps, the weapons, armor, and clothing from long ago, the sundry artifacts, objets d'art, and bric-a-brac from previous centuries. What more evidence of the truth could anyone ask for? But still, she didn't believe me."

Mr. De Leon explained that, even though Ariana Quigley never did accept the fact that Lionel Johnson was Ponce de León or that the waters from his Fountain had the power to immunize her against yellow fever, she did nevertheless, at his insistence, drink the waters from the Fountain of Life with him each day. "She indulged me by playing along with what I imagine she imagined to be the product of my imagination. I suppose all true lovers do such things for one another. And I played along with her playing along with me, pretending that I believed she believed me. I was confident that, in time—after twenty, thirty, or forty years at the most—realizing that she had not aged at all since beginning to drink the water, she would finally believe me. If only she had not gone to Providence, she would have come to know the truth."

Mr. De Leon asked me which, as a writer, was the more difficult for me to describe—"joy or grief?" He wanted them to be vivid, both the joy of holding Mrs. Quigley in his arms and the grief of losing of her. "But, in my book, grief should be described only to make the evocations of joy all the more joyful."

After lunch I learned that by the time the Civil War started, Lionel Johnson had become his son, John Johnson, who loved a woman named Florence Basolon—*the* Florence Basolon—the woman with the indescribably beautiful buttocks. And Eden Sanatorium had been turned into the Ponce de León Memorial Hospital for soldiers wounded in battle. "I must confess to you that the latter was done, like the establishment of my sanatorium years before, self-servingly, more out of expedience than compassion. I was worried that if the South were to win the war, the Confederate government might not acknowledge my United States Federal land title. I hoped my clinic would be a testimony to my loyalty to the Southern cause. I still had all the beds, blankets, and bedpans left over from the yellow fever epidemic, and nurses were easy to come by. With so few able-bodied men remaining in the county, local brothels were short on customers. And so it was easy to recruit prostitutes to work for me. Whores make good nurses no less than they make good actresses. They know how to soothe a man and have a knack for dispensing intimacy to strangers. They're adept at making a man feel cared for without his imagining that they are as indifferent as they really are. And all of them were at least passably pretty, some so lovely that it was not uncommon for recruits to shoot themselves, usually in the foot or leg or hand, so that instead of fighting battles against Union soldiers in Virginia, Tennessee, or the Carolinas, they could rest comfortably in a bed in the Ponce de León Memorial Hospital right here in northeastern Florida, tended to by women who were not averse to letting them have at least a little peek at what most women tend to keep private. Sometimes it was a lot more than a peek. I gave Nurse Naomi Tooms a bonus for the long hours she was spending in the wards at the bedsides of the wounded, trying to make sure that every single patient had the opportunity to prove to himself that, despite his wounds, he was still a man, and a potent one at that. 'I ain't no doctor, Mr. Johnson,' Naomi told me, 'but I know a few things 'bout what makes a man feel good and healthy, and lots 'bout what makes this life worth livin'.'

"Naomi loved her job, and doted particularly on a young sergeant, Socrates Bell of the Santa Almeja First Infantry Division, who had lost one of his legs at the Battle of Olustee. 'I've always taken a special fancy to fellahs with a missin' limb,' she avowed. 'They're the best lovers of all.' Sergeant Bell and Miss Tooms married right after the war. I was the best man at the wedding and they named the first son John after me. The boy grew up to become the Right Honorable John Bell, father, in turn, of none other than Santa Almeja County librarian Lilian Bell, to whom you owe the privilege of having been chosen to ghostwrite my autobiography."

Mr. De Leon spent the rest of the afternoon talking about Florence Basolon, and most particularly about her buttocks. With the outbreak of the Civil War all the men in the area between the ages of seventeen and forty-six, unless they were unfit, either enlisted or had been conscripted. This afforded John Johnson ample opportunity for intimacies with the scores of lonely women left at home. Mrs. Basolon, a schoolteacher and soprano soloist in the Eagle Springs First Baptist Church choir, was one of them. "Because she loved her husband so very much, her loneliness was all the more acute. Abraham Basolon, being the heroic type, had been one of the first men in Eagle Springs to enlist in the Confederate army. She loved to talk about him. I had to listen to endless stories about Abe's accomplishments as a hunter, a fisherman, and a shoe and boot salesman. Because I loved Florence, I feigned interest as she told me how tall he was, how thick his hair was, not to mention how thoughtful, generous, and honest he was.

"Have you ever noticed, Mr. Siegel," Mr. De Leon asked in what seemed a digression, "how much the position most preferred by a woman for sexual intercourse serves to reveal about her? There's a great difference between a woman who relishes being on the bottom, flat on her back and receptive, and those who, like Geronima Acabara and Lizabeta Vincilagnia, always insist on being vigorously on top. From hundreds of years of experience, I can tell you that women who prefer being taken from behind tend to distinguish between sexual pleasure and the pleasure of love, thinking of them as distinct from one another, but not necessarily as mutually exclusive. That was, I believe, the case with Florence Basolon. I suspect she always wanted me to mount from behind so that, without having to look at me, she could pretend that I was her husband. I'm not complaining, mind you. On the contrary, this afforded me the opportunity, as I *cardar*red her, to behold the beautiful buttocks I told you about yesterday. No sooner had I seen them, than I fell in love with Florence Basolon. Yes, it was love at first sight. So lusciously plump and firm to the grip, they were as pink to the eye and soft to the touch as the cheeks of cherubs, and, as I've already mentioned, they were adorned with seven freckles that always reminded me of the Pleiades. Alicia Olisbo's buttocks were splendid, perhaps even as marvelous as Florence's, but I only had the briefest glimpse of them, and never the honor of holding them.

"It broke my heart when, just before the end of the war, a highly decorated, but severely wounded, Private First Class Abraham Basolon, returned to Eagle Springs. Nurse Naomi Tooms told me that the injury to our new patient's groin had deprived him of what she called 'that stuff that makes a man a man.' Despite her husband's physical condition Florence insisted on breaking off her relations with me so that she could resume her life with, and fidelity to, her spouse. I admired her for upholding such noble matrimonial virtues."

Mr. De Leon ended our workday by suggesting that I might conclude this chapter with Socrates Bell and Naomi Tooms. "Unlike Lionel Johnson and Ariana Quigley, or John Johnson and Florence Basolon, but rather like characters in a novel or a play. Yes, like Juan Baco and Juana Espinosa in *La brevedad desagradable de la vida,* that comedy I starred in at the Teatro Ponce de León, they, the one-legged soldier and the prostitute, did, in real life, live happily ever after. Yes, try to end this chapter on a cheerful note. End it with something like that sweet last line that everyone likes to read, especially if they allow themselves to believe that it could be true, something like,

'They lived happily ever after.' But not that line, of course—it's been used too many times. I'm counting on you to come up with something good, Mr. Siegel, something original, something catchy. Think about it."

"I'll think about that tomorrow," I said to myself. "After all, tomorrow is another day."

1865–1915

WHEREIN PONCE DE LEÓN BECOMES HIMSELF
AT CELEBRATIONS OF FLORIDA DISCOVERY DAY,
AND AT THE OPENINGS OF THE HOTEL PONCE
DE LEON, THE PONCE DE LEON LIGHTHOUSE,
AND THE GRACE METHODIST FOUNTAIN OF
YOUTH RESIDENCE FOR THE AGED

Eighteen score and sixteen years ago, Juan Ponce de León stepped forth
from his skiff onto this great continent, discovering a land he christened
Pascua de Florida. It would be altogether fitting and proper that we should
dedicate a portion of the Sunshine State as the final resting place for one
who gave his life that this land might live. We cannot dedicate, we cannot
consecrate, we cannot hallow this ground, however, without the body of
the brave explorer who struggled here and died in Cuba. And so today,
I vow to do everything in my power as President of the United States of
America, to support a patriotic fellow American, Mr. Henry Morrison
Flagler, in his noble enterprise to have the body of Ponce de León exhumed
from its present place of interment in Puerto Rico, that it may be befit-
tingly buried here, on the Elysian grounds of the Hotel Ponce de Leon, for
the gala opening of which we are gathered here today. The world will little
note, nor long remember what we say here, but it can never forget what
Juan Ponce de León did here. It is for us the living to be dedicated to the
unfinished work which he began here, and we here highly resolve that Juan
Ponce de León shall not have died in vain. Mr. Flagler, himself a dreamer
and visionary in the spirit of Ponce de León, has offered a grand sum of
money to the Spanish Crown for the bodily remains of the discoverer of

Florida. Should that noble request be denied, I shall commit the Armed Forces of the United States of America to martial support of the independence movements brewing in both Cuba where Ponce de León died and in Puerto Rico where he is unrightfully buried. If the discoverer of Florida is not delivered to us forthwith, let the Crown of Spain be warned that it risks engagement in no less than a Spanish American war.

GROVER CLEVELAND, "St. Augustine Address"

Escorting me to the Sunshine Room of the Museum of Florida History, Isabel, delicately perfumed with hints of citrus and musk, explained that I would have to wait for my employer. "He's not feeling well today. He will, nevertheless, be here shortly, as he is very anxious to finish his work with you."

Hanging prominently on the walnut-paneled wall, opposite the window facing out onto the patio, there was a large oil painting, ornately framed with gold-leafed floral carving, and signed, "Adele Carter '89." I recognized both the signature and style of painting from the portraits I had seen of Fray Juan Arquero and Don Juan Gaviota. Aglow in the center of an otherwise shadowy canvas, the conquistador looked as much like Mr. De Leon as had the priest and the tobacco magnate. And he was dressed in the same high-collared padded plum houppelande with funneled sleeves and scalloped cuffs that Mr. De Leon had been wearing both on the first day I met him and on the previous Friday when he had told me about the Teatro Ponce de León. Kneeling by a stream in a lush grove, with azure ocean visible through dark green foliage, the Spanish explorer was drinking from a brightly shining golden goblet. On the wall to the right of the painting were three framed posters, each of them announcing a Florida Discovery Day celebration—one for 1875, another for 1882, and one more for 1889. To the left of the portrait there hung framed, autographed photographs. A man, wearing the conquistador outfit that was represented in the painting, was in the photograph of Grover Cleveland, shaking the president's hand.

I was looking at a display that contained an antique black hard rubber fountain pen with a gold filigree band on its cap, together with blotters, bottles of ink, an eyedropper, and a brush, when Isabel returned with my drink. "He invented the fountain pen—did he tell you that? Perhaps not—he can be very modest, considering his accomplishments. He came up with the name as well, letting Waterman take the credit because he didn't want to attract public attention. He has always worried that interest in him might lead to discoveries about his real identity, and that could jeopardize his control of the Fountain. The same thing with Coca-Cola—he let a man named Pemberton, a pharmacist from Atlanta who had tasted it on a visit to the park, take the credit. He's invented so many things."

"Yes," I said, "I know—rum, cigars, popcorn, even seedless oranges. Anything else? The light bulb? The telephone? Phonograph? Movies? I don't want to leave anything out when I write the book. We want the world to know the whole truth about Ponce de León."

Realizing that I was joking, and obviously hurt by that, Isabel left the room.

I regretted what I had said, was sorry to have offended her, but it was difficult for me to imagine why this lovely young woman, who seemed to be living on the estate, was bothering, behind Mr. De Leon's back no less, to play along with the charade. And it annoyed me for some reason that she took the character so seriously.

I was re-counting the words in the opening paragraph of chapter nine when Mr. De Leon appeared in a blue and white striped silk bathrobe over pale purple pajamas. There was a navy blue scarf around his neck, silver embroidered slippers on his feet, and he was still wearing those annoying dark glasses.

Without so much as a greeting, my employer asked what I had for him to read. Although he had been pleased with Ariana Quigley's pale green, turbulent, willful, and lusty eyes, he was, of course, very, very disappointed that I had not written much, much more. "One hundred and forty-one words," I was ashamed to announce, "but I also have the opening and ending to chapter one, another two hundred and eighty-nine words."

Coughing even more than ever, but smoking just as much, washing down more than the usual number of morphine tablets with great gulps of the punch that was, because of his tremor, occasionally spilled on his robe, Mr. De Leon was testy. "I'm not inclined to give you any more money. Not another dollar until the manuscript, or at least a very decent draft of it, is done. You are too slow a writer, Mr. Siegel. Time is running out. And I'm very unhappy about it."

Insisting that I was doing my best, devoting all my energy and every waking hour to his book, and hardly sleeping, I asked if I might have a little time off to catch up with him.

"Time off!" Mr. De Leon shouted angrily, slapping his hand down hard on the table. In a frantic attempt to appease him, I blurted out a rash promise: "If you will give me just two days, I will have the entire manuscript for you, everything up to the end. And if I do not, I will, I swear, return all the money you have given me." Immediately realizing what I had so impulsively and foolishly vowed, I emended it: "Yes, all of the money you have paid me since my arrival here ten days ago."

Without responding to me, Mr. De Leon rose and stormed out of the room. While I could hear him talking with Isabel down the hall, I could not make out what they were saying.

After a few minutes, he returned to the Sunshine Room, and gruffly reiterated his disappointment in me. Somewhat calmed, but still obviously exasperated and disgruntled, Mr. De Leon agreed ("only because I have no other options") to give me until Wednesday to write chapters one, three, six, eight, nine, and ten, "the story I'm going to tell you today. Shall we begin, Mr. Siegel?"

He paused to compose himself and cleared his throat. "Yes, let's begin."

Pointing to the painting of the conquistador who had discovered Florida, he explained that it had hung for a century in the lobby of the Hotel Ponce de Leon. Mr. De Leon had acquired it at auction when the hotel was converted into Flagler College. "I want you to understand the symbolism. The cup I'm holding in the painting is rendered as a Eucharistic chalice in order to identify the wine of Holy Communion, the blood of Christ, with the water from the Fountain of Life, delivering us from illness, old age, and death. The imagery further equates me with St. John the Evangelist—*Juan* Ponce with San *Juan*—as emphasized by the presence all around me of these shrubs with their clusters of little yellow flowers—St. *John's* wort. The palm trees, typical as they are of Florida, become in this context symbolic of a triumph over illness and aging, coordinating, as they do, Christ's entry into old Jerusalem on Palm Sunday with my own arrival in Florida, a new Jerusalem, during the Paschal season. Notice the eagle in the upper right-hand corner, and the serpent in the lower left. Not only did eagles, until very recently, drink here from the Fountain of Life, but also, as I was informed by the artist, the eagle, common in representations of San Juan, suggests the highest aspiration of mankind—the longing for eternal life. The eagle is, of course, also symbolic of the United States of America, this land that I, *not* Colon, discovered. The serpent, down here, is at once a reference to the tempter in Eden and also to the story of Emperor Domitian ordering San Juan to drink a cup of poisoned wine; when the apostle took up the cup to drink, the poison went out from it in the form of a snake. You will notice, Mr. Siegel, that behind me, here in this clearing, watching me drink, are eleven conquistadors, each representing one of the other apostles. The fact is, as you must certainly recall, that I came ashore with only four conquistadors and a priest, all of whom were slain by the Zhotee-eloq guardians of Haveelaq before I ever had the opportunity to drink from the Fountain of Life. But art, according to this artist, was not something to be restricted in any way by facts or literal truths. She believed that art owes allegiance to a higher truth which is beauty. The seven Indians kneeling around the apostolic conquistadors represent the seven churches that San Juan founded in heathen Asia Minor and, simultaneously, seven of the tribes of indigenous people that Juan Ponce encountered in Florida: the Taino, Calusa, Tequesta, Carib, Freshwater Timucua, Saltwater Timucua, and the Zhotee-eloq. You can see my ship in the distance, its mast a cross, at once Noah's ark, the ark of the covenant, and the New Ark—the Madonna and the Church. All that in one painting! The symbolism is so effective. I want lots of symbolism in my book, Mr. Siegel."

He stood back from the painting, gazing at it in apparent admiration. "The painting evokes the essence of who I really am and what I have accomplished. It was because of that, because the artist had so perfectly captured me, that I fell in love with her. Perhaps her portrait of me should be used for the cover of my book. Yes, that would be very appropriate. See what you can do about that, Mr. Siegel."

The artist, Adele Carter, I learned, had pronounced her name "Car*tay*"—an affectation she had picked up as an art student in Paris in the eighteen-seventies—that, and smoking cigars and drinking Mariani vin de coca ("pleasures I shared with her"), wearing men's clothes, and having occasional intimate relations with women ("other pleasures we had in common"), and "using the verb *honorer* in very much the same way I use *cardar*." I was further informed that the same artist was responsible for the statue of Ponce de León that currently ornamented the Fountain of Life. In 1891 it had replaced the bronze eagle I had seen in the Americana Room.

By the grace of the influence in Washington of her father, Josiah A. Carter, Georgia railway magnate and generous supporter of the Democratic Party, Miss Carter had, on returning to the United States from her studies at the École Nationale des Beaux Arts in Paris, been commissioned to paint a portrait of Grover Cleveland. The president, so the story went, had been amply satisfied with her rendering of him, and especially pleased that she had been able to make his gross obesity come across as a robust sturdiness. When Henry Morrison Flagler, who, as a partner of John D. Rockefeller, had made a fortune in Standard Oil, saw the painting at Cleveland's wedding reception in the White House, he was so impressed by it that he hired Miss Carter to paint a portrait of himself and his wife, Alice. Satisfied as he was with the family portrait, Flagler subsequently commissioned her to paint Juan Ponce de León for the lobby of the Hotel Ponce de Leon. Bringing her from Washington to St. Augustine, he had provided a studio for her on the corner of Grant and Menendez streets.

Mr. De Leon explained that he, in the guise of John Johnson's son, Jackson P. Johnson, had been an obvious choice as a model for Miss Carter's portrait of the discoverer of Florida. He had well established himself as the best Ponce de León in eastern Florida by his yearly appearances as that historical character at St. Augustine's annual Florida Discovery Day celebrations. "I wanted to play the part for the sake of the enjoyment of being hailed for who I really am, Don Juan Ponce de León. It was easy for me to get the job, as I had, after all, all the right makeup, costumes, props, a very good Spanish accent, and a thorough knowledge of Florida history. I had also, as you know, Mr. Siegel, played myself on the stage a hundred years earlier, not to mention the fact that I had had the opportunity of actually being myself from 1465 until 1513. I was Ponce de León on the first Sunday in April each and every year until 1898 when, by declaring war on Spain, the president of the United States made the idea of celebrating a Spanish soldier's landing on the east coast of Florida an unappealing one."

The state holiday had been the brainchild of St. Augustine mayor Benedict Turnbull Jr., whose autographed photograph was among those on the wall near the painting. Buildings were festooned with red, white, and blue bunting for the occasion, and bright flags and banners were strung along the streets. The high point of the festivities was the welcoming party for Juan Ponce de León and his band of singing conquistadors as they landed at the St. Augustine seawall and then marched triumphantly and merrily to the fort. Juan Ponce de León led an exuberant parade of the marching state militia, police on horseback, firemen on their fire engines, and carriages full of schoolchildren and representatives of St. Augustine's churches, ladies clubs, and charity organizations. Huge crowds cheered exuberantly. In the evening, there was food, drink, and orchestral music for outdoor dancing. And then, after a grandiloquent bay-front speech by Mayor Turnbull on Florida's promising economic future, there were choral performances by Ponce de León's Crooning Conquistadors and the ladies choir of the Grace Methodist Church. A Baptist Negro dance troop did cakewalks, and a group of Indian prisoners from Fort St. Augustine consented, in return for reduced sentences, to sing and dance in jubilation over the European discovery of their land. With their women chanting "hi-yo, hoy-yo, hi-yo, hoy-yo," and beating on tom-toms, the men, faces streaked with war paint, pranced about with feathered bonnets on their heads and balsa-wood tomahawks in their hands.

"At the end of the evening, I would stand in full armor at attention by Mrs. Turnbull, who, wearing a glittering tiara, sang a song she herself had composed for the occasion," Mr. De Leon explained as showed me a copy of the April 4, 1875, edition of the *St. Augustine Daily Sunshine* in which the words of the song were annually published so that celebrants of Discovery Day could sing along.

> Long ago did a man named Ponce discover our land,
> Fair Florida, fine fashioned by our Lord's gentle hand;
> Some say Ponce was searching for the Fountain of Youth,
> And all who have come here know it's the truth
> That in our sunny Florida, he found his great treasure
> A wellspring of freedom, prosperity, and pleasure.

"There were fireworks at midnight and then, after so many hours of drinking and dancing, there was always sure to be a woman or two who, not wanting the party to end, felt an impulse to indulge the fantasy of having intimate relations with the star of the show, the dashing Spanish explorer who had discovered Florida—Don Juan Ponce de León."

Mr. De Leon regretted that there would not be more time to go into the details of his sundry liaisons with these Ponce de León groupies. "It would, I'm certain, amuse you, Mr. Siegel, to hear about Catherine Alexander, president of St. Augustine's Ladies' Association of Grace Methodist Church, and wife of that church's minister, Reverend Alexander A. Alexander. It's a funny story and, at the same time, it has something serious to say about the curious nature of women, and the mysterious nature of love as well. But we just don't have time for digressions. I want to tell you more about the painting and its painter."

Mr. De Leon went on to explain that, after a winter visit to St. Augustine, Henry Flagler had become convinced of the town's economic potential as a sunny winter resort for rich tourists from the frosty North. He built railways and bridges to connect St. Augustine to the railways of the North, making the town directly accessible from New York and Washington. His

Hotel Ponce de Leon was magnificently constructed in the neo-Iberian style with neo-Moorish embellishments. "The open balconies and court-yards with their orange trees, palms, and bougainvillea," Mr. De Leon re-marked with a certain wistfulness, "brought back memories of the Anda-lucia of my youth." The luxurious hotel had a casino, grand ballroom, and therapeutic mineral baths advertised as having the salubrious properties legendarily attributed to the Fountain of Youth.

Adele Carter's painting of Henry and Alice Flagler had hung, I was told, across from her portrait of Ponce de León in the hotel lobby. The can-vases were illuminated by crystal chandeliers at night, and during the day by light filtered through Tiffany stained-glass windows. There were also engravings in the lobby of such significant figures in the area's history as Pedro Menendez de Avila, James Grant, Don Vizente Manuel de Zespedes, and Andrew Jackson. The Italian dome, inlaid with ivory and silver filigree, was supported by oak caryatids carved by French artisans. In its coverage of the hotel's gala opening, the *St. Augustine Daily Sunshine* declared it "the most beautiful hotel on earth." Taking a copy of the paper out of one of the display cases in the room, Mr. De Leon asked me to read the front-page article:

> Renowned guests included poet laureate of Florida and descendant of long-ago Governor James Grant, Wilfred Makepeace Grant, industrialist John D. Rockefeller, Mayor Benedict "Big Ben" Grant Jr., the Reverend Al-exander A. Alexander, and, most impressive of all, no less a dignitary than President of the United States, Grover Cleveland. Juan Ponce de Leon, the discoverer of our State was, much to the amusement and delight of every-one, including this reporter, also in attendance! President Cleveland gave a rousing address announcing Federal support for a statewide movement to bring the body of Ponce de Leon from Puerto Rico to here in Florida where it should rightfully be buried. This was followed by Mr. Grant's reading of his elegiac poem, "The Death of Ponce de Leon," which brought a tear or two to many an eye in the house, including those of our President, this reporter, and Ponce de Leon himself!

"So, Mr. Siegel, back to my point," Mr. De Leon continued as he took a letter from the same display case. "Flagler had been so impressed by my ap-pearance as Ponce de León at the Discovery Day celebration of 1881 that, a few years later, he had hired me both to pose for Adele Carter's portrait and to greet his guests at the opening." Mr. De Leon handed me the letter that had been scribbled on what appeared to be White House stationary:

Dear Mr. Johnson (or should I call you Ponce?),

It was a pleasure to meet you at the hotel opening. But I'll be damned if I can figure out how you won that eighteen bucks off me in cards! Keep up the good work, and remember to vote Democrat this year.

Sincerely,
Your President and friend,

Uncle Jumbo

P.S. What do you think of that pretty little artiste who painted both our pictures? I'd be curious to know, just between the two of us, man to man, if you've had any luck with her.

A few months after the opening of the hotel, the character of Ponce de León had been, I was told, recruited to make an appearance at the dedication and first lighting of the beacon of the Ponce de Leon Lighthouse. "I was embarrassed to recite the idiotic lines that Mayor Benedict Turnbull Jr., had written for me: 'If, back in 1513, we would have had a lighthouse like this, with its custom-made first-order fixed French Fresnel lens that allows its light to be seen twenty miles out to sea, it would have been one heck of a lot easier for me to discover Florida.' The puerility of that speech was matched, a few years later, by the inane drivel, written by none other than Catherine Alexander, that I had to deliver at the opening of the Grace Methodist Fountain of Youth Residence for the Aged. Facing a crowd of wrinkled, withered, and wizened human antiquities, suffering, if not enjoying, various degrees of senility, I had to say, 'Take it from Ponce de León—you're only as old as you feel.'"

Mr. De Leon explained that during this boom period in the history of Florida, complete strangers, "men who knew nothing about me, but had the nerve to pretend to be me," had been hired as Ponce de Leóns for such events as fund-raisers for the Ponce de León Home for Wayward Negro Girls and the Ponce de Leon Hospital for the Mentally Disturbed, as well as for the opening of the Ponce de Leon Alligator Ranch. Although Mr. De Leon had not seen those particular impersonations, he had watched, "with mixed feelings of amusement and resentment," the portrayals of the Spanish explorer by his chief competitor, a Jewish actor from Charleston named Leopold Roth, at the opening of the Ponce de León Funeral Home and at a ceremony in which the former Watering Hole brothel was refurbished, renamed, and rededicated as the Ponce de León Spanish Family Restaurant. Mr. Roth was subsequently hired as the maitre d' at that establishment. He'd be there every night, dressed in full conquistador regalia. "Roth's so-called Spanish accent," Mr. De Leon declared, "was as bad as the restaurant's so-called Spanish food. Speaking of which, it's time for lunch."

Despite Isabel's encouragement that he at least drink some of the *sopa de ajo* for the sake of his health, Mr. De Leon ate nothing. That neither of them spoke to me during the meal suggested that they were both still angry with me. I apologized several times, not for anything specific that I might have done, but just an "I'm sorry" for things in general.

Once we had returned to the Sunshine Room, Mr. De Leon became talkative once more. "And now," he began, "I will tell you about Adele."

I had been waiting for it all morning—the inevitable love story, lots of *cardar*ring in yet another spirited tale about one of Ponce de León's passionate conquests, yet another woman Mr. De Leon would claim to have loved more than any woman ever.

"Flagler laid rails for a tramway that connected Eagle Springs to St. Augustine. So it was convenient for me to spend more time in town. Until I fell in love with Adele, I'd often wile away my afternoons there, politely courting a demure young society girl named Miss Mary Lily Kenan, who professed to enjoy the company of older men because she thought they were less wanton in their ways than younger ones. My evenings were often spent at the Alcazar, a brothel managed by an old French woman who called herself Madame Heloise and had quite a different opinion about the differences between older and younger men. She claimed to have formerly been a mistress of Napoleon III. The girls who worked for her were costumed as famous women from history. That afforded me the opportunity to dally, in rooms appropriately furnished and decorated, with Cleopatra, Mary Magdalene, Joan of Arc, Queen Elizabeth, and Betsy Ross."

"No Queen Ysabel?" I asked. "It might be interesting to have one of the prostitutes impersonate her so that Ponce de León could, in this chapter of the book, *cardar* his first love again. In the Alcazar no less!"

"That might be interesting to you, Mr. Siegel, but it wouldn't be true," Mr. De Leon said with marked annoyance. "And yet," he paused, reflecting on his story it seemed, "while there was no Ysabel at the Alcazar, there will be a reference to her in this chapter. Flagler's red-haired wife Alice had, since moving to St. Augustine, begun to lose touch with reality. Emerging from deep depressions during which she did not speak at all, she'd suddenly imagine, in animated fits of delusion, that she was none other than Her Majesty Queen Ysabel of Spain. Supposing that the neo-Iberian architecture and decor of the Hotel Ponce de Leon was encouraging those fantasies, Mr. Flagler moved his wife out of that residence and into the neoclassical George Washington Hotel. When the delusions persisted, Flagler turned to me for help, asking that I visit his wife in my Ponce de León costume. 'I would like you to introduce yourself as the Spanish conquistador. And then you should inform her that you are absolutely certain that she is not the queen of Spain.' Flagler's therapeutic plan did not work. 'He's an impostor,' the insane woman shrieked. 'He's no more Ponce de León than I am!' Flagler tried to calm her down by telling her that if she really were the queen of Spain she'd be able to speak Spanish. 'I do speak Spanish,' she insisted. '*Yo bono yo yo señoro eskar nono buna el moro folto mia si si.*' That I didn't understand a word she was saying was further proof to her that I could not possibly be Ponce de León.

"After committing his wife to an insane asylum—none other than St. Augustine's Ponce de Leon Hospital for the Mentally Disturbed—Flagler divorced her (so, he assured her, that she could be with King Ferdinand), and then married young Mary Lily Kenan. He commissioned Adele Carter to paint his new wife's face over Alice's, to change the color of her hair from red to blonde, and to enlarge her breasts a bit."

Then redirecting my attention to the painting of Ponce de León, Mr. De Leon knelt down to assume the same posture as that of the conquistador. With a trembling hand, he held up his glass of rum punch in the same manner in which the discoverer of Florida was holding a golden goblet. "It captures my spirit, don't you think so, Mr. Siegel? Not just my features, but the awe and wonder that I naturally experienced almost five hundred years ago when I realized I was actually drinking the waters of the Fountain of Life in the Garden of Eden and that I would cease to grow any older. Adele came here to my estate on several occasions to make sketches in the Garden that she would use for the painting. Until only very recently, the Garden foliage was as lush as it is in the painting."

Rising with some difficulty from the kneeling position, seating himself across from me, and then pushing the humidor, pitcher of punch, and bowl of popcorn toward me, Mr. De Leon compared the eyes of Adele Carter, so bright blue, to the eyes of Ariana Quigley, so pale green. "Aquamarine," he said. "The color of the sea from which Venus Aphrodite was born. Use that image, Mr. Siegel. Use the metaphor to insinuate that I could see the goddess of love in those eyes, as they gazed intently at me, inspecting me as she painted. Aquamarine and shimmering. But don't use 'shimmering'—it's a trite adjective for eyes. And there was nothing trite or common about Adele."

And then Mr. De Leon actually said it, said exactly what I had been expecting him to say. With a straight face, he declared that he had loved Adele

Carter "more than any woman ever," adding that this was so even though he "rarely understood what she was talking about. Maybe that's why I loved her. She'd speak as she painted, not so much to me as to the world through me, recounting wildly enigmatic ideas that she had picked up in Paris, French philosophical reflections that made little sense to me, complicated elucidations of subtle and esoteric complicities between art and love, art and sex, art and religion, art and death, art and time, art and desire, art and fear, art and you-name-it. Art was all that mattered to her. 'It is only through art,' she professed, 'that we are redeemed from the passage of time. It is art, not religion, that makes eternity possible. Long after you are gone, Mr. Johnson, Ponce de León will continue to live on in this painting. He shall not age at all. Through the power and grace of art, he shall have found his Fountain.' She'd use lots of English words—like 'hypostasy,' 'eudemonist,' 'apotheosis,' 'oracular,' 'apparitional'—that I hardly understood, not to mention all the French bons mots and phrases which she maintained could not be translated without being stripped of their profundity. The cocaine in the Mariani vin de coca that she so enjoyed energized her philosophical side. Whenever I, likewise stimulated by that wine, attempted to say anything, or ask something, to interrupt either her speech or silent concentration, she'd sternly order me to 'be quiet and hold still.'"

J. P. Johnson had posed for Adele Carter's portrait of Ponce de León every day for ten days. "In the same amount of time that we have spent together, Mr. Siegel, Adele was able to finish this large and handsome painting of me. Let that be an inspiration to you. Of course Adele assumed that I was merely J. P. Johnson and no more than fifty-or-so years old. But, not ever imagining that it might be true, she liked to pretend that I really was the historical figure whose portrait she was painting."

I had been waiting for the sex scene. I was ready to hear about ecstatic carnal transports, every inevitable detail of Ponce de León's explorations of the aquamarine-eyed Adele Carter's body. Surely Adele Carter would pretend that he was Ponce de León not only while he was posing for her, but also when he was *cardar*ring her. I would have been willing to put bets on that one. So far that day there hadn't been much sex other than the mention in passing of dalliances with prostitutes pretending to be Cleopatra, Mary Magdalene, Joan of Arc, Queen Elizabeth, and Betsy Ross. That and the insinuation of sex with the president of the St. Augustine's Ladies' Association of Grace Methodist Church and other unidentified women carried away by the festivities celebrating Ponce de León's discovery of Florida. I was prepared for steamy descriptions of Adele Carter's lips, breasts, and thighs, of the positions in which she surrendered her body and revealed her soul to Ponce de León posing as J. P. Johnson posing as Ponce de León. That it had been noted that Miss Carter wore men's clothes and had "occasional intimate relations with women" had me expecting a lurid description of at least one ménage à trois or two. But in fact, and much to my surprise, there was no scene of Mr. De Leon with two women. And when I asked about "those occasional intimate relations with women," he confided that, although Adele Carter had indeed "indulged in tribadistic acts with various women, it had been for artistic purposes only. Their names were told to me in strict confidence, Mr. Siegel, and thus they should not be repeated in my book."

There were, furthermore, beyond the aquamarine and shimmering eyes, no descriptions of Adele's body. And I was also surprised to be told that he had only ever "*honorer*ed" her four times. *Honorer* was one of those French words that Adele had insisted could not be translated without loss of meaning, suggestion, and resonance.

One of the various profound ideas about art that Miss Carter had picked up in Paris was a notion that, in order to capture the true nature and essence of someone whose portrait she was painting, it was helpful to have sex with that person. I knew it. I would have my bet. On the third day of work on the commissioned portrait of Juan Ponce de León, Miss Carter, suddenly, just as I had imagined she would, threw aside her palette and brushes, and began to unbutton her paint-spattered smock. "I'm sorry, Don Juan Ponce," she had exclaimed, "but if I am to truly know you, so that I can justly render you, *il faut honorer ma couche*."

Adele had asked her model to please remove his puffed breeches and whatever garment he might be wearing under them, but to leave on his houppelande, morion helmet, leather boots, gloves, and the belt from which his Iberian short sword hung in its silver filigreed sheath. "Show me your lust and your affection," she had demanded. "Let me feel Don Juan Ponce de León's desire and his fear as well. Let me smell and taste the conquistador's sweat, and hear the explorer's moans and the discoverer's whimpers. *Honorez-moi, Don Juan! Explorez les regions du sud de mon corps, O Explorateur, et vous découvrirez ma Floride. Et puis, plongez-vous là-bas dans la Fontaine de ma Jouissance. C'est votre Fontaine de Jouvence. Honorez-moi!*"

"'*Soy Don Juan Ponce de León,*' I whispered in her ear, '*y te quiero, mi amante artistica.*' As I did what she had asked of me, I couldn't help but wonder if she might have used this same method of capturing the essence of her subjects for her portraits of President Grover Cleveland and the Flagler family."

Mr. De Leon bemoaned the fact that when, on the next day, before putting on his conquistador costume to pose for her, he had tried to kiss the artist, she had turned her face aside and stepped back from him. "I have no interest in you personally, Mr. Johnson. What we did yesterday had nothing to do with you. It was for Ponce de León. It was for the sake of art."

"I, Jackson Pontius Johnson, was, as absurd as it may seem to you, Mr. Siegel, jealous of Juan Ponce de León, yes, jealous because he had *cardar*red and *honore*red Adele Carter, and she cared only about him, not me, and that made me jealous even though he was me.

"Jealousy, as you may have observed—and as should be made apparent to readers of my book—has not been a significant emotion in the history of my affairs. You may recall my reactions to the infidelities of two of my wives—Justa Respalona and Shulamit Morteira. But thoughts of the other men, or women for that matter, who had been intimate with Adele tormented me, even though the liaisons in question had transpired before I knew her and had, according to her, also been merely for the sake of art. I was jealous of everyone whose soul she had ever captured. By dint of Adele's imagination, in the service of her art, and by her own proud account, she had been intimate not only with Ponce de León, but also with Orpheus, Prometheus, King David, Saint Sebastian, and, of course, Christ—Christ quite a few times, given his popularity in art."

Mr. De Leon explained that Adele Carter had been taught the particular method by which she might come to truly know the subjects of her paintings by her teacher at the École des Beaux Arts, none other than the Symbolist painter, Gustave Moreau. She had been working without much success on a painting of St. Sebastian, when Professor Moreau, after giving her a glass of Vin Mariani, had suggested that Adele kiss the flesh of the saint—the lips, the neck, the nipples, the belly, the knees, the feet, and then the five holy wounds. While doing so, she was encouraged to imagine that the man she was kissing was not the young son of a baker (an illiterate but impressively virile bumpkin from Picardy named Lionel who worked as a model at the art academy), but that he truly was a soldier in the army of Diocletian, condemned to death by the emperor because of his love for God. As a result of this lesson, Adele Carter believed that her portrait of the saint had perfectly captured his beatitude, the mixed feelings of misery and bliss, surrender and triumph. "Reality," Professor Moreau had taught the young American student, "is no more or less than what we imagine it to be."

"Adele boasted that she had been deeply honored by an invitation to pose with Lionel for Moreau's masterpiece, *Jason and Medea*. I was jealous and very upset as, kneeling in full Spanish armor and commanded to hold still, I had to listen to the account of how Moreau had captured the souls of both the Argonaut and his Colchicine sorceress. I yearned to know and capture Adele in life as perfectly as Moreau had in art.

"I feared that once Adele had finished her portrait of Ponce de León for Flagler's hotel, she would have no reason to see me again. That probably would have been the case if she had not been working on a series of paintings which were intended to illustrate the progressive ages of man. She showed me her sketches of a naked young athlete, lissomely muscular, his hair long, and his genitals unabashedly prominent. 'That's Lionel,' Adele noted. 'His portrait will come after one of an adolescent that will follow that of a baby boy. Then, after Lionel, there will be a painting of an older man, then another, older still, seven men in all, delineating, and I hope capturing, the changes, from flourishing through degeneration, of man's flesh from his infancy until he is very old, decrepit, and finally dies. I've found an old Spaniard, a Señor Julio Olisbo, who has just celebrated his one hundredth birthday at the Grace Methodist Fountain of Youth Residence for the Aged. Most graciously, and despite the puritanical protests of his daughter, he has begun to pose for me.' Adele showed me preliminary sketches of the centenarian whose beautiful wife I remembered well and still invoked on sleepless nights. The old man's genitals were no less vividly rendered than Lionel's. Would she, I wondered, be attempting to have him *honorer* her for the sake of the series? And what would she do with the adolescent boy? Would the baby suck her breast? Even that thought made me jealous. This jealousy was, however, at least somewhat assuaged by Adele's proposal that I pose naked for her as one of the men in the series between Lionel and Julio. No one since Lady Grant, a hundred years earlier, had expressed any interest in rendering, and thereby immortalizing, me or my penis. And so, once more, for the sake of her art, in order the capture the essence of man in what she assumed was his late fifties, Adele felt obliged to invite me, her model, to *honorer* her. Just as when she had imagined that I was Juan Ponce de León, I, J. P. Johnson, had been jealous of him, so too when she imagined that I was J. P. Johnson, I, Ponce de León, became jealous of him. And just as she would allow Ponce de León only one opportunity to *honorer* her, so too, as J. P. Johnson, I was permitted to do the same but once. I hope this makes sense to you, Mr. Siegel.

"I so strongly yearned to be known, captured, and rendered by her again, that, sparing no expense, I went so far as to commission Adele to paint portraits of the various esteemed gentlemen who had, in centuries past, lived on the very property that was currently my home. I posed for the painting of Fray Juan Arquero, the saintly Catholic missionary and founder of the Church of San Hortano, as well as for the one of the visionary tobacco magnate, Don Juan Gaviota. I tried not to be jealous when they were asked to *honorer* the artist. I was, I realized, becoming as crazy as she was. Love always makes one at least a little bit crazy.

"No sooner had Adele finished the portrait of the seventeenth-century tobacco merchant, than I, desperately wanting to continue spending my days modeling for her and eager for yet another opportunity to *honorer* her, commissioned her to produce another painting, a portrait of my dear grandfather, Lionel Johnson, the great American patriot, humanitarian, and philanthropist. Before she could begin work on it, however, Adele received news from Paris that Moreau was gravely ill. She left for France and never returned to the United States. 'The only way you can know a man more completely and more intimately than during *l'honoration amoreuse*,' she once told me, seeming to believe it herself, 'is to be at his deathbed, to hear the last sigh, feel the final beat of the heart, and to look into his eyes as this world is left behind and a new one is imagined.'"

After a long, and for me uncomfortable, pause during which he did not light a cigar, take a drink of rum punch, or swallow any morphine tables, Mr. De Leon spoke softly: "I suppose I believe that too. I want Isabel at my side when this story's over."

ELEVEN

1915–2005

RABBI SOLOMON. You must swear never to reveal the truth about this to anyone.

JUAN PONCE. Don't worry, old man. Even if I were ever so foolhardy as to tell this story, no one would believe it.

JUAN PONCE DE LEÓN, *Algunas hazañas estupendas de las muchas de Don Juan Ponce de León*
(Some of the Many Stupendous Exploits of Don Juan Ponce de León)

It was raining, I remember, on that Sunday when I left the Garden of Eden and drove to St. Augustine. The sudden storm promised relief from the humidity that had made my stay in Florida unpleasant at times.

Turning off Grant Street onto Menendez, I wondered which of the four corner buildings was meant to be the one in which Adele Carter had once had a studio. I could picture her paint-spattered smock, a palette in one hand, a brush in the other, and aquamarine eyes glancing from canvas to model and back again. "Hold still," she would order, "and be quiet."

I wanted a drink, but was hesitant to return to Ponce's Place for fear of running into the girl with Florence Basolon's buttocks again. The encounter had been disconcerting, making me feel oddly disconnected from myself—a young man trapped in an old man's body, or an old man with young eyes, the same eyes that had looked longingly at young women years ago. In those days, the young women looked back.

The sign for another bar, Ye Olde Watering Hole, announced that it was "The Oldest Drinking Saloon in America." I couldn't resist.

The bartender was dressed in what, I assumed, was supposed to be Renaissance garb. The generous décolletage of the cotton blouse exposed enough of her pale bosom to give it an appealing, if not entirely authentic, wenchy touch. "And what grog will ye be drinkin' tonight, matey?" she asked.

Serving a rum and coke to me in a dented and tarnished pewter mug, she persisted, "And, pray tell, what adventures bring ye to fair St. Augustine?"

"Excuse me for asking," I had to say, "but do you have to talk like that?"

"Yeah. Don't you get it? This is supposed to be a four-hundred-year-old bar. That's how people talked back then. The cool thing about Ye Olde Watering Hole is that while you sit here drinking, you can imagine what it was like to be alive hundreds of years ago."

"And what," I had to ask, "do you think it was like to be alive hundred of years ago?"

"Well, people dressed differently and talked differently, of course. But basically it was probably a lot like now. I bet this place was just as much fun in the olden days as it is now. Yeah, I'm sure it was pretty cool living back then, unless, of course, you needed to go to a dentist, or check your e-mail, or wanted to see a movie."

She could, I thought to myself, have taken a few lessons from Mr. De Leon. "Fare thee well, matey," she called out as I left the oldest drinking saloon in America.

Mr. Wiseman was waiting for me, eager to inform me that, because he had grown so fond of me, he had lowered the price of Hemingway's sock to "a measly two hundred and fifty bucks." By the next evening, he would have come down to two hundred, his "last offer." "Take it or leave it. The autographed copy of *The Old Man and the Sea* alone is worth ten times that."

I woke up early the next morning with plans to work all day, to go over my notes, expand them, outline the chapters still to be written, and then to do a rough draft of the whole that could be revised, edited, and polished the next day and presented to Mr. De Leon on Wednesday. The manuscript didn't have to be publishable, I reminded myself once again. It just had to satisfy my employer. After writing all day on Monday, I hadn't made nearly as much progress as I had hoped and I was feeling that I might never catch up. I was in bed that night, and almost asleep, when it suddenly came to me, striking me like the light that blinded Saul on the road to Damascus. It was an epiphany.

I sat up and turned on the lamp. It was all very clear. I'd begin the book with Mr. De Leon's letter: *Dear Mr. Siegel: I introduce myself here with no expectation that you will believe me, but with some hope that you might be inclined to trust in my sincerity.*

And then I'd write about my reaction: *This is, I swear and have ample documentation to substantiate it, absolutely true. I really did receive the above outlandish letter, handwritten in a barely legible small scrawl and ornately signed.*

And then I'd describe our first meeting: *The man who claimed to have unearthed the legendary Fountain of Youth was waiting for me in front of the main gate to his Garden of Eden ludicrously dressed for the occasion in a conquistador costume.*

That would be the introduction. Chapter one would open: *We began work on this book at nine o'clock in the morning on July 7, 2005. Mr. De Leon greeted me in a room in his Museum of Florida History that was dedicated to objects, books, and documents supposedly from medieval Spain.*

I would write a true story about a man in Florida claiming that he was Ponce de León and that he had discovered the Fountain of Youth in 1513. An account of my trip to Florida and my relationship with Mr. De Leon would provide a nonfiction frame for his tales about the five-hundred-and-forty-year life of the Spanish conquistador. I might even include Mr. Wiseman trying to sell me Ernest Hemingway's sock.

I had gotten out of bed, made a rum and coke for myself, and was seated at the desk making notes: "A book about the nature of belief, in fiction and in life." I mused that, just as the cynical Saul, much to his own astonishment, suddenly believed that the carpenter of Nazareth really was the Messiah, so I should, at the end of the book, finally believe that Mr. De Leon really was Juan Ponce de León. I might write about the joy that arises from allowing oneself to believe absurd and impossible things.

In this state of inspired excitement, one idea led to another. I began to see the movie based on the book, a film about love and time, but also, and more profoundly, about the nature of belief and reality in the movies and in life. I'd have to adapt it, of course. Instead of a writer, Lee Siegel would be a filmmaker. Having seen a biographical documentary about Ponce de León that Siegel has made for the History Channel, Mr. De Leon would telephone him, inviting him to come to Florida to film "the true story of Ponce de León, the real story of the Fountain of Youth." So that audiences would know that there really was a Mr. De Leon, the frame story of Lee Siegel's relationship with him would be done as a documentary with me playing Lee Siegel and him playing Mr. De Leon. Each of his stories within that real frame would be a short movie with beautiful costumes and sets. Penelope Cruz, I reckoned, would, as long as she was willing to do the nude scenes, be an excellent Queen Ysabel, unless, of course, she'd prefer to play Señora Menendez. We'd sweep the Oscars: *Love and the Incredibly Old Man* for Best Motion Picture, Lee Siegel for Best Screenplay, Penelope Cruz for Best Actress, and Steven Spielberg for Best Director.

I was eager to see Mr. De Leon. I wanted to know how to end the book as well as the movie.

Greeting me rather frostily at the entrance to the museum, Isabel asked me to follow her to the Fountain, where she told me to wait for Mr. De Leon. I could sense that she was still annoyed with me. "He's feeling worse today," she said without looking at me. "He's really very, very ill, you know. I urged him to receive you in his bedroom, but he insists on meeting you here. It's his last day with you. This book has taken so much out of him. I do hope you've caught up with him, that you have the first ten chapters done. He's counting on you to have the whole thing done before you leave on Friday."

While waiting for my employer, I rehearsed what I had planned to tell him: "I must be completely honest with you, Mr. De Leon . . ."

When he finally arrived, dressed once again as a conquistador, Mr. De Leon, as Isabel had warned, did not look well. His hands were trembling more than ever, and perspiration was visible on his sallow brow. He wasted no time in asking to read what I had written.

"I must be completely honest with you Mr. De Leon," the pitch began.

"As I have been with you, Mr. Siegel," he interjected.

"Yes," I said, assuring him that I appreciated that. "I know how much it means to you that your book gets published. And that's why I want to tell you, quite frankly, that I do not believe that our book, as you have conceived it, will have any chance of getting published. I may be skeptical, but it's hard for me to imagine that any editor, at any respectable publishing house, will be willing to accept the claim, true or not, that our manuscript, no matter how well written, is actually the autobiography of a five-hundred-and-forty-year-old Juan Ponce de León. And I don't think it really works as a novel either. I know that may be my fault, and, if it is, I'm truly sorry. But, for the sake of getting the book published, I've come up with a really good idea. It's more of a change in form than in content."

Except for his quivering lips and trembling hands, Mr. De Leon sat ominously still and, still more ominously, did not say a word.

"I'm going to write the true story of how you contacted me, and how I came here to work with you. I'll tell all the stories that you have told me, just as you told them. It's going to be a truthful book about truth and lies, about history and fiction, about the nature and meaning of belief in matters of love, literature, and religion too. And because it deals with love and aging, I'm going to call it *Love and the Incredibly Old Man*. And not only that, I've begun to work on a treatment for the film."

Suddenly standing and drawing his Iberian short sword from its scabbard, Mr. De Leon shrieked, "My book! My book! My autobiography! Why have you done this to me? How could you? Betrayer! Assassin! *Gilipollasqueroxo*! This book has absolutely nothing to do with *you*. You Judas, you Brutus! It is *my* book. *My* story. *My TRUTH*!"

It was, I suppose in retrospect, to resist the impulse to stab me in the heart with his sword that a gasping and horrified Mr. De Leon turned and hobbled hurriedly toward the museum, leaving me alone by the Fountain of Life.

Not knowing what to do with myself, I waited awhile, hoping he would return. Finally giving up on that possibility, I went back to the entrance of the museum and rang the bell. Isabel opened the door only to ask me to leave. She said that Mr. De Leon would not see me. "Come back tomorrow. I will try, for his sake, to convince him to talk to you then."

I realized my idea hadn't been a good one after all, that I should never have proposed it, and that it really didn't even matter that the book he had hired me to ghostwrite would never be published. I should have just told him what he wanted to hear. I should have assured him that I was confident that, not only would his autobiography be published, but that it was also likely to become a critically acclaimed best seller. "Thousands of men who read it will wish that they had been you," I should have told him. "And even better, the countless women who read it will wish they could have known you, known you really well, and been *cardar*red by you." He would surely have believed that.

I spent the next twenty-four hours composing and rehearsing various apologies. I was prepared to go so far as to make good on my rash and regretted offer to return the money he had given me since my arrival in Florida if he would consider telling me the end of his story. I would solemnly swear to finish the book once I was back home: "I'll have it to you by the end of the month." Maybe I'd just say that he didn't have to pay me for the last two chapters.

Half opening the door to the museum, Isabel informed me that Mr. De Leon was still refusing to talk to me. "He says he never wants to see you again. He's adamant about it. He says that you are even more despicable than Cristobal Colon, Torquemada the Grand Inquisitor, and Diego Pinzon de Carajo."

I insisted that I had come to apologize, and that, because I still hoped to finish writing the book for him, I would be very grateful if he would, to that end, reconsider and consent to tell me the rest of his story. I would write whatever he wanted me to write however he wanted me to write it.

Isabel stared at me intently as if trying to assess my sincerity from the expression on my face. "I'll try to talk to him about it, Mr. Siegel. For his sake, of course, not for yours. Go back to the Fountain. Wait there."

It seemed a very long time before Isabel came to announce that, no, Mr. León still would not talk to me. "He says that he never wants to see you again, not so long as he lives," she said. "I can't blame him. But still, I'd like to believe that you might be able to finish his book for him. That would make him very happy. And I want nothing more than his happiness." And to that end she offered to tell me what she knew about the last ninety years of Ponce de León's life.

Seating herself on the edge of the Fountain's empty basin, she took a cigarillo from the pocket of her white cotton skirt, lit it, and inhaled. "Juan wants me to cut down now that the Fountain's dry."

Isabel began the story by explaining that Ponce de León had opened the Garden of Eden and the Museum of Florida History to the public in 1915. She said that every fifteen or twenty years, he'd publish an advertisement in *St. Augustine Daily Sunshine* announcing that one Ponce de León had retired, moved on, or died, and that another one had been hired to take over management of the facilities.

"You see, by revealing the truth, he concealed it," Isabel said as she stood to recite. "'Ladies and gentleman, boys and girls, believe it or not, I am none other than Juan Ponce de León,' he'd announce to welcome his visitors. I must have heard the speech a thousand times. It hardly changed over the years. He would bring the visitors here, right here to the Fountain. 'Contrary to what's written in your history books, folks,' the speech continued, 'I did discover the legendary Fountain of Youth. Yes, and here it is, right before your eyes. And if you were to take a sip of it today, I can guarantee you that you would not get sick nor grow any older.' And then, to get a laugh, he'd add, 'at least not for the next twenty-four hours.'

"Then he'd lead the tour into the museum, taking them room by room through the story of his life, from his early years in the Spanish Room, up through the centuries to the Sunshine Room, telling them many of the same stories he told you, but leaving out, of course, the intimate accounts of his various love affairs. He told you many stories about women that he had never told me. I understand that he thought they were important for his book, because he wanted the book to be about love. Of course, I had heard about Queen Ysabel, and his first four wives, as well as a little bit about the Taino girl and Zhotee-eloq woman, and a few things about the nurse who worked here during the second yellow fever epidemic. But he hasn't told me very much about the women he loved during the twentieth century, so I don't know what he would have told you. Perhaps he imagines that I'd be jealous. I do know there was a suffragette named May Mann in the very early years of the century, and I suspect that, during the Second World War, he had some sort of intimacy with Lilian Bell, the county librarian. But at least I can tell you something about his last love affair. I can do that because the story is about me. I am, you see, his wife. Yes, Mr. Siegel, I am Mrs. Isabel Ponce de León."

I was startled by the statement and not sure whether or not to believe it. Why, I wondered would a demure, charming, and beautiful young woman like her, marry an eccentric, crazy, crotchety, and old man like Mr. De Leon?

After pausing to light a fresh cigarillo with the butt of the one she had smoked almost to the end, Isabel said something far more unbelievable still: "Yes, we were married, right here by the Fountain, in 1965. Forty years this September. It's hard for me to believe. The time has gone by so quickly."

Although it seemed all too obvious, if not sarcastic, to say it, I couldn't resist: "But you look so young."

"Yes," she said quite matter-of-factly, "Of course, that's because I was only twenty when I began drinking from the Fountain. I must look a little older now. The waters don't stop you from aging, they merely slow down the process. You become older at about the same rate as a redwood tree does."

I suppose it was too much to have hoped that the young woman was going to tell me anything true. I should have been satisfied that Isabel was, rather, going to tell me a story that she thought Mr. De Leon would want written in his book. It was, after all, the book, and not the truth, that mattered.

"I must get back to him now, Mr. Siegel," she announced. "You can see yourself out. I hope I've given you some of the information you might need to write a conclusion to his book."

How, I wondered as I drove back to the Zodiac, would Mr. De Leon have told the story about opening the Garden of Eden, Fountain of Youth, and Museum of Florida History to the public? What would he have said about Mary Mann and Lilian Bell? Of course they would have been indescribably beautiful and there would have been lots of *cardar*ring. Would he have told me that he was married to Isabel and that she was sixty years old? Or was that her idea, something she had made up? If it was his idea, there was no doubt in my mind that he would have *loved her more than any woman ever.*

I still wanted to finish the book, but wasn't sure how to do it. I had nothing better to open the last chapter with than "It was raining, I remember, on that Sunday when I left the Garden of Eden and drove to St. Augustine."

Coda

2005–2006

WHEREIN THE AUTHOR ENDS THE STORY
OF JUAN PONCE DE LEÓN

In this book I have done my very best to tell the true story of Ponce de León. There were many times, while writing it, that I wished he really had discovered the Fountain of Youth, so that, being still alive, he could help me get the facts right. If that were the case, I'm sure there would be some big surprises.

LEO GAVIOTA, *The True Story of Juan Ponce de León and the Fountain of Youth*

On the morning of my sixtieth birthday, before driving to Jacksonville to catch my plane back to Hawaii, I stopped at the Garden of Eden, still hoping Mr. De Leon might agree to see me one last time. Feeling bad about how things had gone the last few days, I wanted to return the dollar-per-word he had paid me for what I had written while working with him: $10,836 for chapter two; $6,532 for chapter four; $9,099 for chapter five; and $7,777 for chapter seven. That amounted to $34,256 minus the $100 I finally gave Mr. Wiseman for Ernest Hemingway's argyle sock.

Since I had, at that time, every intention of completing the manuscript, I considered it fair and reasonable to keep my $10,000 advance. And, upon submitting the final manuscript to him, I would ask him to pay me whatever, in addition to that retainer, he felt I deserved.

The gate to the Garden of Eden was locked. I honked the horn of my car again and again until finally Isabel arrived, asking me through the bars of the gate what I wanted.

"I want to see Mr. León. I still want to finish the book."

"He won't see you," she insisted. "He has given up all hope for his book."

Handing the package containing her husband's money through the gate to her, I promised that the manuscript would be sent in the next few weeks.

Without comment, she turned and walked back toward the museum. Despite the recent rain, the vegetation on the other side of the gate looked, I thought, even more withered, deteriorated, and sparse than it had a few weeks earlier. Or maybe I was just imagining that.

When I stopped at the Santa Almeja County Public Library to return the books I had borrowed, Miss Bell asked if the story of Juan Ponce de León was finished. "Almost," I assured her, and that seemed to please her. Again I wondered if Mr. De Leon would have told me that he had had a love affair with her during World War II. I would have liked to have heard about it. I tried to imagine this old woman as a young girl, naked, frisky, and giggling with delight, in the arms of the discoverer of Florida.

Once back home in Hawaii, I got down to work. Sometimes, for inspiration, I'd try to allow myself the pleasure of believing the unbelievable story I had been told could be true, that Mr. De Leon might actually be the Spanish conquistador who discovered not only Florida and the Fountain of Youth, but also cigars, rum, popcorn, seedless oranges, Coca-Cola, and the fountain pen. I realized, however, that even if I were to believe that, I would not dare write it, because no one would ever believe that I believed it.

Although I still didn't have an English equivalent for *cardar,* I was at least able to come up with decent drafts of chapters one, three, and six in the first month. But then there were distractions (my classes at the university, faculty committee meetings, a book review for an academic journal I was obliged to write, some health problems, a new romantic involvement, and other such things of no relevance to this story). The point is that I didn't have the time to finish Mr. De Leon's book. Still, I swore to myself, I'd get it done over Christmas break, and I wrote to Mr. De Leon to inform him of that in October.

I was disappointed, but not so surprised, that I did not hear back from him. But then, in early December, Isabel, without so much as a cover letter, sent me the following clipping from the November 24 issue of the *St. Augustine Daily Sunshine:*

Mr. John P. Deleon died last Sunday in Eagle Springs at an undisclosed age. For many years Mr. Deleon managed the Garden of Eden Recreational Park where visitors of all ages were treated to thrilling stories about the discovery and history of our beautiful Sunshine State. A special treat for one and all was a visit to the site of "The Fountain of Youth." By its gushing waters, Mr. Deleon, garbed in authentic conquistador attire, played the part of Juan Ponce de León, the famous discoverer of Florida, and regaled park visitors with fabulous legends about the Fountain of Youth and fascinating stories about our history. That history was also brought to life by a tour of Mr. Deleon's Museum of Florida History. Mr. Deleon was dedicated to entertaining and educating locals and tourists alike with tales of the past. And for that may he be remembered forever. He is survived by his wife Isabel.